THE APOCALYPSE SERIES

BOOK ONE

THE LAST

PLAGUE

GLEN E. PAGE, MD

Synergy Books

THE LAST PLAGUE: THE APOCALYPSE SERIES, BOOK ONE
Published by Synergy Books
P.O. Box 80107
Austin, Texas 78758

For more information about our books, please write to us, call 512.478.2028, or visit our website at www.synergybooks.net.

Printed and bound in the United States of America. All rights reserved. No part of this book may be reproduced in any form or by any electronic or mechanical means including information storage and retrieval systems without permission in writing from the copyright holder, except by a reviewer, who may quote brief passages in review.

Copyright© 2008 by Glen E. Page, MD

Publisher's Cataloging-in-Publication

Page, Glen E., 1949-
    The apocalypse series. Book one, The last plague /
Glen E. Page.
    p. cm.
    LCCN 2007937359
    ISBN-13: 978-1-933538-96-9
    ISBN-10: 1-933538-96-1

    1. Plague--Fiction. 2. End of the world--Fiction.
3. Science fiction. I. Title. II. Title: Last plague.

PS3616.A3375A6 2008   813'.6
                       QBI07-600271

This is a work of fiction. All of the characters and events portrayed in this book are fictional, and any resemblance to real people or incidents is purely coincidental.

10 9 8 7 6 5 4 3 2 1

I dedicate this book to my wife Jane, our nine children, and our beautiful grandchildren for their love, kindness, and support

CHAPTER ONE

THE BLACK OVARY

Stanley, Idaho, July 6, 1986

Fear shone in the girl's eyes as the cart slammed through the broad, off-white double doors leading to the unknown. The overhead fluorescent lights reflected off the tears rolling down her bloodstained face. Her trembling hand weakly reached up to touch another, searching for answers among the masked strangers racing about in their sterile greens. Now the aseptic odor was stronger, elevating her fear of what was to come. She tried to raise herself, but gasped and fell back when she saw blood-soaked bandages filling the gaping wound in her abdomen. Her attention turned to a burning sensation in her arm where the IV was located. Then a blanket of sleep overcame her, temporarily ending her hellish ordeal.

———⟫•⟪———

Nurse Edith Crockett threw the last sterile surgical drape over the girl. "We're ready, Hunter," she said gruffly. She pulled the surgical instrument tray closer to her. "Just don't figure," she murmured.

Dr. Doug Hunter finished drying his hands and tossed the towel in the nearby hamper. "What's that?"

She handed him his surgical gloves. "What's a black girl doing up there on the Yankee Fork?"

Doug pulled on his second surgical glove and shook his head. "I don't understand it either. Did she say anything?"

Edith adjusted the overhead lights to focus on the surgical field. "Mumbled something about a beautiful lady and her tigers."

"Lady and tigers—that doesn't make sense." Doug looked at the nurse anesthetist. "Are we ready?"

"Yes, Doctor."

Doug extended his arm. Edith placed the scalpel into his waiting hand. He didn't waste any time. The blade cut deep, making a long incision extending from her breastbone to her pubis. Already sweat beads appeared on his forehead as blood gushed through the incision. Edith pulled hard on the retractor to give more exposure. Pad after pad soaked up the pools of blood as he narrowed down the source of the bleeding. "It's coming from her pelvis," he finally exclaimed.

Something at the edge of the wound caught Edith's eye. She reached down and removed what looked like a hair. She then looked throughout the open abdomen. "Doctor, she has pieces of hair everywhere."

Doug stared at the end of Edith's finger. "Looks more like animal fur than hair."

"You think this may be an animal bite?" Edith asked.

Doug shook his head. "No, the wound edges are too smooth for a bite." Suddenly he darted to the left side. "Whoa," he exclaimed as the blood spurted high into the air toward him. "The bleeding is from her ovarian artery." Doug quickly clamped it and the bleeding stopped. He stepped back and turned to the circulating nurse. "See if you can get Dr. Jordan on the phone. I would like to transfer her to Boise tonight."

The circulating nurse nodded and left the room.

—————⟫•◦•⟪—————

Their eyes reflected the beaming car lights as it passed. Micah partially stood and looked both ways. He turned to the woman kneeling next to him. "It is clear, my lady."

The woman in black stepped from the bushes. The two wolves followed. She looked across the street to the hospital entrance. "I'll find out if she is there." She looked back at the two wolves. "Stay." Immediately the wolves sat down in the tall grass.

"Tess, maybe I should go with you," Micah said.

"No, stay with the wolves. I won't be long."

"But what of the rumor?"

She could sense Micah's impatience. She placed her hand on his bare shoulder. "Be patient. We have time." She again turned back to the hospital. "After I check the girl's status, we'll go to Sun Valley and find out."

Micah reluctantly agreed. He knelt next to the wolves. The three of them watched as Tess hurried across the street and entered the hospital.

—⇒◆⇐—

Doug noticed Edith nervously tapping the surgical tray. "Why, Aunt Edith, you seem in a hurry. You have some plans tonight?"

Edith slapped the needle driver extra hard into Doug's hand. "No plans, I'm just late for chores."

Although Edith lived with Doug at the Heavenly Ranch, she was his aunt only by marriage. She sounded a mean bark, cussed like a storm, and chewed tobacco with the best of them. But everyone knew her heart was gold and that Doug loved to tease her.

"Chores? Where're Jim and Indian?"

"Sun Valley."

"Sun Valley?"

"Yeah, big dance tonight. They said they were working. After they begged and bellyached for an hour, I said I'd do chores for them."

Doug took the silk suture from her and quickly tied off the bleeder. "What work is that?"

"Some potential divorce case they've been working on."

Now he remembered. "Oh, that's right. Pepe mentioned something about a cheating wife case."

"Yes, that's the one. Anyway, they said they needed the work."

Here was the opening he'd been waiting for. "Well, with all the talk I'm hearing, I just assumed you had a date."

Edith grabbed the suture scissors from the tray. "What talk's that?" she asked suspiciously.

He quickly glanced at Edith. "Oh, haven't you heard? You and Pepe."

"Pepe," Edith moaned. "People are talking about me and Pepe?"

"All over town."

She shook her head. "Damn, what's that sheep's dropping been saying about me now?"

"Well, that you two are hot items."

Edith cut the suture ends. "Hot items my butt. I'm old enough to be his mother."

"Well, that isn't what he's saying." Although her anger was building, the sense that something was missing brought Doug's focus back to the girl. "Where is it?" he asked himself.

"Ah, that Pepe would date one of my goats," Edith continued. "When I see that lying Mexican capon, I'm going to—"

"Hold it, Edith. Something's not right here."

Edith immediately turned her attention back to the girl's pelvis. "What is it?"

Doug did not answer. Quiet filled the room as everyone watched him study the same pelvic structures over and over again. Finally he looked up. "It's not here."

"What's not here?"

"This girl's left ovary is missing."

"Was she was born without one or something?" Edith asked.

"No, not like a birth defect. It's been recently cut out." Without asking, Doug grasped a tissue forceps from the surgical tray. With them he lifted up a black dangling pelvic mass for Edith to see. "And look at this."

Edith gasped. "Oh dear, this girl has cancer, doesn't she?"

Doug shook his head. "No, this isn't cancer. This black thing is the girl's other ovary."

The confusion was clear in her voice. "But ovaries aren't black, they're white."

"Well not this one. This girl has a black ovary." He rubbed the stony hard texture of the ovary between his fingers. "I haven't ever seen anything like this before." He extended his hand toward the surgical tray. "Scissors," he said. "Let's biopsy this thing." Quietly he took multiple biopsies of the ovary and handed them to Edith. "Save two samples for me and send the rest to the Boise Pathology Group."

"Yes, Doctor."

A subdued, eerie quiet filled the operating room as they proceeded to close the girl's abdomen. Shortly the circulating nurse entered the room. "Dr. Jordan is on the phone," she said. "Do you want to speak with him now or call him back?"

Doug looked at Edith. "Could you staple the skin closed?"

"Sure, Doctor."

He turned. "I'll speak with him now." He removed his surgical gown and gloves and hurried down the hall. The phone was already ringing when he entered the doctor's lounge. He didn't notice the door to the next room close.

He grabbed the phone receiver. "Hello, Harrison?"

"Hi, Doug. Is it a full moon or what?"

Doug reached for the nearby simmering coffeepot and an empty coffee cup. "You must have heard?"

"Yes, it was on the evening news. Apparently the Ada County sheriff's department has been called in to help investigate. They said the girl was stabbed and found alone in the mountains?"

"Yes, she can't be more than nine or ten years old. Campers found her staggering on the old Yankee Fork road." Doug poured the coffee and sat on the sofa. "I wanted to transfer before surgery, but there wasn't time."

"They say she's black."

"Yes, she is."

"Doug, what's a black girl doing that high up on the Salmon River?"

Doug chuckled. "Those were Edith's exact words." He took a sip of coffee. "See? You and Julie aren't the only black people who live in Idaho."

Harrison smiled. "How's she doing?"

"Well, she had a lacerated ovarian artery. We had to give her two units of blood, but her vital signs appear to be stable. I'd like to transfer her tonight."

"Sure, I'll contact life flight and make all the arrangements."

Harrison noticed his wife, Julie, enter the living room. She stopped and placed her hands on her hips. "You don't even have your tie on," she exclaimed. Harrison motioned with his hands that he knew this.

"Ah, Harrison, there's something else," Doug continued.

Harrison noticed Doug's hesitation. He once again turned his attention to the phone call. "What's that?"

"After tying off the ovarian artery, I found her left ovary was missing."

"Well, Doug, we have removed incarcerated ovaries in little ones in the past—"

"No, you don't understand. I think her ovary was removed recently."

"Recently?"

Julie sat down next to her husband on the couch. She reached up and grabbed his tie. "Here, let me tie it," she whispered.

Doug took a deep breath. "Harrison, I think her ovary was cut out earlier today."

Julie finished tying his tie and stood. She pointed to her watch. "We're going to be late," she whispered. Harrison nodded his head that he knew. He watched as she left the room for the kitchen.

"But that doesn't make sense. No hospital would release her on the same day of that type of surgery."

"That's just it—I don't think her ovary was removed in a hospital."

Now Harrison was disturbed. "What are you saying?"

"Well there were no sutures or cautery marks. I think this knife wound is actually some kind of skin incision—used to remove her ovary."

The other end of the phone was silent for the longest time. "Have you informed Sheriff Bates?"

"Not yet."

"If you're right, then we may be dealing with some kind of psychopath."

"I thought the same, but I haven't told you the most unusual part yet."

"What's that?"

"Her other ovary—it was black and hard like a lump of coal. Something I've never seen." Doug waited for a few seconds for Dr. Jordan's response. There wasn't one. "I'm not sure why, but I think this girl's right ovary has been severely damaged and turned black. Have you ever heard of such a thing?" Again there was only silence on the other end of the line. "Harrison, are you still there?"

"Las hijas del diablo," Harrison finally murmured.

Doug noticed a tremble in Harrison's voice. "What was that?"

"Ah, nothing," Harrison answered abruptly. "Did you take any biopsies?"

"Multiple."

"Good, maybe the pathologist can give us some answers. Anyway, I'll make arrangements for her transfer tonight."

"That would be great," Doug exclaimed. *Harrison fears something,* he thought. *I can tell by his voice. But what?*

"Oh, by the way," Harrison continued. Doug noticed how subtly he changed the subject. "Julie and I will be happy to watch Jason until you return. You're still coming to dinner before your flight?"

"We planned on it."

"Good, Julie is looking forward to it."

Now Doug became suspicious. "She's not going to try to line me up again with someone, is she?"

"You know I can't guarantee that."

"Harrison, that last one was really different."

Harrison chuckled. "You never use to be that picky."

"I'm older now. I'm not saying her tastes are poor, but I'd rather pick my own dates."

"All right, I'll see what I can do."

"Listen, Harrison—Jim, Indian, and Pepe are flying with me to LA for a friend's funeral. Do you think Julie would mind if they also came to dinner?"

"Nah, we'd love to have them."

"Great, we will see you then." Doug hung up the phone. He sat for a brief moment. He was puzzled by his former partner's peculiar behavior regarding the black ovary. He stood and returned down the hall. "Las hijas del diablo," he said aloud. "Spanish for the daughters of the devil, but what does that mean?" He disappeared around the corner back toward the surgical suite.

The dressing room door slowly opened. The woman in black peered into the empty doctor's lounge. *Again I understand why Nicole was so attracted to this handsome Dr. Hunter*, she thought. She reached for the phone and placed a call on the outside line.

"Hello."

"Matthias, it's me."

"Tess, what did you find out?"

"She's still alive."

Tess could sense the frustration in his voice. "I was afraid of that. Micah is such a fool, bringing those girls to the states. Why didn't he stay in Africa?"

"Because he heard rumors that Indian is here in this area."

"I want him to find Indian, too, but not at this expense. Can you contain this?"

"I think so, but not here. They are transferring her to Boise tonight. It will be easier there."

"Good, the sooner the better."

Tess took a deep breath. "Matthias, there is more."

"What's that?"

"They know of the black ovary." Tess waited for a comment. The phone remained silent. "Did you hear me? They know of the—"

"I heard," he interrupted. "This could get messy. You must contain this at all costs, do you understand?"

"Yes, I understand."

"I will wait for you report." The phone went silent.

Tess hung up the receiver. She slipped out of the doctor's lounge and hospital unnoticed. Soon she was at Micah's side.

"Well?" he asked.

"She's still alive."

Micah pulled the knife from his sheath. "Then I will end it now." He started to move toward the hospital when Tess reached out her arm and stopped him.

"No, not here. It will be easier for us in Boise. Remember, we have some unfinished business in Sun Valley. Let's find out if this Indian is the one we've been seeking." Micah sheathed his knife and nodded his head. This was what he wanted to hear. Tess immediately bent space and they were gone.

CHAPTER TWO

THE LADY IN BLACK

Jim Crockett grabbed the bottle from Pepe's hand. Pepe reached to get it back but was too slow. "But I'm thirsty."

Jim placed the bottle on the table behind him. "No Pepe—we're working."

Pepe looked across the table. Indian put up his hands. "Don't look at me for sympathy."

Pepe turned back. "Come on, Jimmy, just one beer. I've danced nearly every dance."

Jim leaned forward across the table. "That's just it. You have danced nearly every dance, and with the same woman."

Pepe didn't understand. "So what's wrong with that? I'm having fun, and I think she really likes me."

Indian handed Pepe a fresh soda bottle. "She's also married," Indian reminded.

Pepe unscrewed the cap and took a drink. "I don't know what the big deal is. All we were doing was dancing."

Jim shook his head and began to explain. "The big deal is that we're being paid to watch this woman, not to dance with her."

Now Pepe's voice began to carry to nearby tables. "Well, what was I suppose to do? She asked me."

Indian put his hand on Pepe's arm. "Calm down." He nodded his head toward the other end of the building. "See that big guy sitting alone in the corner?"

Pepe looked. "Yes, I see him."

"Well, that's Mr. Williams, and he's been watching you all evening."

"You mean—"

"Yes, her husband," Jim interrupted, "and right now he thinks you're the guy that's been messing around with his wife."

"Me?"

"Yes, you."

Indian could see he needed to smooth things between his two friends. "Look, if Mrs. Williams asks you to dance again, just turn her down, okay?"

Pepe was unhappy but agreed. "Oh, all right."

Indian turned his attention back to Crockett. "Now what were you saying earlier about David?"

"The lady on the answering machine called him Solomon."

"Are you sure she said Solomon?" Indian asked.

"Her exact words were, 'This is a Solomon. I need Chief and Alamo.' Mom thinks it was Elaine."

Indian nodded his head. "It had to be. Did she anything more?"

"Only that David's funeral was Monday."

Pepe was confused. "Wait a minute, what's all this talk about Solomon, David, and Chief? And what's the Alamo got to do with it?"

Indian started to explain but was interrupted. "Excuse me, gentlemen." Jim and Indian looked up into Mrs. Williams's face. "May I borrow my Mexican stud muffin? I saved the last dance for him."

Without turning around, Pepe stared at the mirror on the wall behind his companions. Mrs. Williams's tight cowboy shirt and blue jeans fit her well. He looked down into Jim and Indian's disapproving faces. Both were squinting their eyes and ever so subtly shaking their heads no. He looked over at the big man at the far corner booth. A broad smile came over his face. He stood, leaned over, and whispered, "Jimmy, I can take him." Then he turned on his heels and escorted his partner back to the dance floor.

Indian and Jim watched the two line up with the rest of the couples. "Ah, damn," Jim muttered under his breath.

"He'll be all right," Indian said. "Anyway, about Elaine—have you seen her lately?"

"No, not since before the wedding."

Indian noticed his soda bottle was empty. He stood. "I need another soda, do you want one?"

"No, I'm fine." Jim watched as Indian walked away. *I wonder if Elaine will even talk to me again,* Jim thought. *The last time I saw her, I was pretty cruel.* He remembered her determined look as she entered that bar several years ago.

"Jimmy, we need to talk." Jim ignored her and continued nursing his beer. "Didn't you hear me, we need to—"

"Okay," he interrupted. "I heard you, so talk."

Elaine paused and brushed the hair out of her eyes. She began slowly. "There needs to be some changes. I can't live this way anymore."

Jim shook his head in disgust. "Ah, not this crap again. So what if I have a beer once in a while."

"A beer once a while is fine, but you're drunk every single night."

"Oh, come on, you're exaggerating."

"It's no exaggeration. You have a problem."

Now he turned to face her. "You're right, Elaine, I do have a problem. It's you. You and your damn nagging."

"I know it has been hard since they kicked you out of army intelligence, but—"

"Look," he interrupted, "if I wanted your sympathy, I would have asked for it."

She was quiet for a moment before she spoke. "After all we have been through, why are you so cruel to me?" He didn't answer. "I need to tell you that David has asked me to marry him."

"Well, then marry him," Jim suggested sarcastically. "I hope you two will be happy."

"You don't mean that."

"Yes, I do. At least I won't have you nagging at me anymore." Again Elaine was quiet. Jim looked over at her and saw her head was down. *Why did I say that?* he thought. He knew he had hurt her feelings.

Elaine stood. "Good-bye, Jim." She turned and walked away.

"Does Solomon still work for the company?"

The voice interrupted Jim's train of thought. He looked up. "I'm sorry, what was that?"

Indian could tell he was in deep thought. "You were thinking about Elaine, weren't you?"

Jim nodded his head. "Just remembering. You know, the last time I saw her, I wasn't very kind."

Indian sat down across from him. "Well, you have to admit, you were hitting the alcohol pretty hard back then."

"Yes, I was. You know, she may never speak to me again."

Indian thought for a moment and shook his head. "No, I think she is more forgiving than you think."

"I hope so. Anyway, what did you say earlier?"

"I just wondered if Solomon still worked for the company."

"No. Elaine told mom that Solomon had a nervous breakdown and was placed in a mental institution."

Indian sat in thought. "Maybe we ought to go to his funeral. He was one of our best friends."

Jim agreed. "I thought the same. That's why I made us plane reservations to Los Angeles late Sunday night."

"Good. Is Pepe going?"

"Yes, I have a special job just for him."

They sat quietly as they watched the dancers. Indian finally chuckled. "Look at him."

"What?"

"A pink silk shirt, light blue suit, and Italian shoes. I think he's the only one out there without cowboy boots and jeans."

Jim smiled. "Not what a person usually wears for line dancing. I'm sure a few rednecks out there would like him to step out of line."

Suddenly Indian sat straight up in his chair. "What the—" He abruptly interrupted himself. "Jimmy, tell me I didn't see what I just saw."

"Pepe's an idiot," Jim exclaimed. "I hope no one else noticed." He looked over to the now-vacant far corner table where Mr. Williams had been sitting.

"Oh no—Jim," Indian warned.

"What?"

Indian nodded toward Mr. Williams, now heading toward the dance floor. "Do you think he noticed?"

A loud voice yelled from the corner of the dance floor. "Hey, spic, did you just touch my wife's breasts?"

Jim shook his head in disbelief. "Dammit, he noticed."

Mr. Williams stormed across the dancing floor toward the couple. "I'll teach you to mess around with my wife."

Indian and Jim watched Pepe push Mrs. Williams between him and her husband. Pepe waved to them to come and help. "Jim, do you think we ought to go over?"

Jim looked at Indian. "Didn't Pepe just get through telling us he could take Mr. Williams?"

"I know, but Mr. Williams is a pretty big guy."

Mr. Williams pushed his wife aside and grabbed Pepe by the coat lapels. "I'm going to rip off your cojones and cook them for breakfast."

Jim reluctantly shook his head. "Ah, hell, maybe we better go over."

They pushed away their chairs and headed toward the dance floor. Pepe ducked the first fist, which sent an innocent bystander reeling to the floor. That was all it took to start an all out brawl on the dance room floor.

Indian looked at Jim. "Now what?" Jim shrugged his shoulder. "Let's get the stud muffin and get the hell out of here." Indian nodded. Jim attempted to dodge in and out between the brawlers only to catch a chair that smashed him to the floor. Indian ducked one punch after another as he attempted to located Pepe, but he was no where to be seen. Jim staggered to his feet. Broken chairs, tables, and bodies littered the dance floor. Indian ducked one punch only for another to catch him unprepared in the face.

"Where is that Mexican?" Mr. Williams yelled as he searched the fighting crowd. Jim too searched the dance floor.

Jim blocked another blow and sent his assailant to the floor. Jim and Indian bumped and turned toward each other with ready fists. Both relaxed. "Did you find him?" Indian asked.

"No. Knowing Pepe, he's hiding and sneaking off somewhere."

"There you are, spic!" Mr. Williams yelled. Jim and Indian looked just in time to see Mr. Williams pull Pepe from hiding behind the bar. Mr. Williams raised his fist only to have his wife jump high on his back.

"Ethan, leave him be!" she yelled as her fists rapidly struck him in the back. The noise was so loud that no one heard the approaching police sirens. Glass shattered everywhere as Mr. Williams threw Pepe headfirst out the back picture window.

"Ay, caramba," he yelled, as he landed squarely on his back. Jim pulled Mrs. Williams off her husband's back while Indian's quick blows sent her husband hard onto the ground, out cold. Hurriedly Jim and Indian each leapt through the broken window. They helped Pepe to his feet and quickly made their way through the pine trees toward the highway.

Jim pointed toward the law entering from the front. "Quiet, the sheriff and his deputies are already here."

They reached the Bronco parked along the side of the highway. "How did the sheriff get here so fast?" Indian asked.

No one answered. Pepe crawled into the driver's seat and started the engine. "Sun Valley, Ketchum," he murmured disgustedly.

Jim got in through the passenger's side while Indian climbed into the back. "Quit your bitching, and get us out of here before the sheriff sees us."

Pepe turned and headed the vehicle down the dark, two-lane highway toward Stanley. Indian reached into the cooler behind the seat and grabbed two cold cans of beer. Pepe shook his head. "Why do I even come with you guys."

Jim looked toward Pepe. "Listen, you invited yourself, remember?" He took one beer can from Indian and applied it to his swelling eye, while Indian applied the other to his swollen lip.

"Well, I'm never going with you guys again."

Indian chuckled. "Ah, Pepe, you're just mad because you can't dance."

"You call that dancing? You don't even get to touch the woman."

"Well that sure as hell didn't stop you, did it? Where do you get off doing that to her anyway?"

"Yeah, Pepe," Indian added, "that's poor taste even for you."

There was a moment of silence. "Do you think Mr. Williams is still going to pay us?" Pepe asked.

Indian again chuckled. "After you fondled his wife? What do you think?"

Pepe shook his head in disgust. "Okay, I admit it. I messed up. I'm not sure what came over me."

The full moon was just starting to come up over the eastern mountains, illuminating the pine trees along the road. Few cars were seen as the three rode in silence.

"Crockett!" the CB radio blared. "Bates here. You got your ears on?"

"Don't answer," Pepe yelled. "Maybe he doesn't know we are here."

"Come on, Crockett," the radio blared again. "I know it was you here at the Roundup tonight, so answer the damn radio."

Jim picked up the CB receiver. "Well, Sheriff, what a surprise to hear your voice. Now, what were you saying about being somewhere tonight."

"Stop the BS. I know it was you in the brawl here tonight."

"Me? Whatever gave you that idea?"

"Come on, Crockett, how many Mexicans do we have in our county?"

"Oh, I don't know, maybe twenty to thirty."

"Well how many of them would grab Mrs. Williams's breasts?"

The radio was silent waiting for a reply. Jim frowned at Pepe. He took off his cowboy hat and slapped Pepe on the shoulder. "Ouch, knock it off," Pepe exclaimed.

"I thought so. But that's not why I'm calling. I talked with Doc Hunter earlier tonight, and he told me that you were here at the dance.

I was on my way out here to ask a favor when I received the call about the brawl."

"What kind of favor?" Jim asked.

"It's about that girl they found tonight."

"What girl?"

"Oh, didn't Doc tell you?"

"No, we haven't talked to him."

"Well campers found this black girl wandering alone up on Yankee Fork Road with a stab wound to her abdomen."

"Stab wound. Know who did it?"

"Not a clue. But Doc transferred her to Boise tonight. My problem is that I am short manned and have a meeting in Twin Falls tomorrow. I need you and Indian to go up to Yankee Fork to investigate and see what you can find out."

"Well I'm not sure where Indian is."

"Don't give me that crap. Just put Indian on the line."

Jim frowned and handed the receiver to Indian. "Hey, Sheriff."

"Hey, Indian, did you hear?"

"Yes, I heard."

"Do you think you can help?"

"Sure, we'll ride up there tomorrow."

"Good. Let me know what you find out. Now put Jim back on the line."

Indian handed the receiver back. "Hey, Sheriff, do you think the department may be able to kick out a little cash for this?"

"Don't press your luck. Oh, that reminds me—Mr. Williams told me to tell you that he is still going to pay you the money he owes."

Jim smiled. "All right."

"But there's a catch."

Jim narrowed his eyes at the radio receiver. "What's that?"

"He wants Pepe to come and collect it personally." Sheriff Bates chuckled and hung up the receiver.

Jim frowned at Pepe. "That's just great. Because of you, we just lost $500."

Indian leaned forward, resting his arms on the seat in front of him. "Seems kind of odd for a girl to be up on Yankee Fork road."

"Yes, it does, especially a black girl. Closest black families are in Boise."

"We'll be fishing with Doc and Jason in the morning. Let's ride over to Yankee Fork in the afternoon and see what we can find."

Jim nodded in agreement.

Again the three rode in silence. "How's the eye?" Pepe finally asked.

Jim knew that was Pepe's way of apologizing. "It's okay."

"I know why I did it. Pheromones. It was my pheromones."

Jim disgustingly shook his head. "Ah, don't start with this pheromone nonsense crap again. There's no such thing."

"I swear, they are real. Just look at what happened tonight."

Jim turned around. "Hey, Indian, ever hear of pheromones?"

"Nah," Indian answered, but Indian's gaze just caught sight of something else off in the distance.

"See, Pepe, there you have it."

"Get real. Indian won't know anything about this."

"Why not?"

"Because he's Native American."

"So, what's that got to do with it?"

"Well, the newspaper article said that only Mexicans and blacks have the pheromones."

"Newspaper? A Mexican newspaper?"

"No, it was an American newspaper."

"American—which one?"

"It's a newspaper científico."

"All right, which scientific newspaper?"

"*National Tattler*," he murmured.

Jim broke into laughter. "Are you're kidding?" He leaned his head back over the seat. "Hear that, Indian? It was the *National Tattler*." Indian ignored Jim's comment. Indian was now visibly disturbed by what he saw. He took his shirtsleeve and vigorously wiped the dew from his window. "Pepe, was that the issue with the baby being born with a wooden arm?"

"Go ahead and laugh, but I'm only trying to help you understand why you two can't get dates."

Jim sighed and sat back up in his seat. "Okay, let me see if I can get this straight. Women like you because of some body odor that you have?"

"Sí, they can smell my pheromones."

"And Indian and I don't have these pheromones?"

"Correcto, only Mexicans and blacks have pheromones."

"Pepe, that's a crock of BS."

"You know, Jim, you've been swearing a lot lately."

Jim looked at Pepe. "So?"

"Well you better not let mom hear you use that kind of language. You know how she feels about swearing."

"Well she ain't here, she swears more than I do, and she ain't your mom."

"I know, but it is better that I think of her as my mom too."

Jim was confused. "And why is that?"

"Well I hate to tell you this, but your mom, ah, well, I think she's been coming on to me lately."

"Coming on to you—are you crazy? Pepe, she's twice your age."

Pepe sighed. "I know, I know. It's such a burden to have these pheromones—"

"Pepe," Indian interrupted solemnly, "stop up here at that turn out."

"Good idea. I need to go too."

The vehicle slowed to a stop. The three climbed out of the vehicle into the fresh mountain air. "Pepe, why do I listen to you," Crockett continued. "First we have to fight our way out of The Roundup. Second, the sheriff is mad at us, and third, we lost $500." The three walked back behind the Bronco. "And now you blame it on your so-called pheromones."

Pepe unzipped his pants. "Jim, I couldn't help it, they just kept bouncing up and down."

Jim also unzipped his pants. "She was dancing. All women's breasts bounce up and down when they dance, but that doesn't mean you can grab them."

Neither noticed Indian continuing to walk farther down the road, peering off into the nearby meadow. Pepe finished and zipped his pants. "That's another thing. Line dancing isn't dancing."

Jim and Pepe turned to return to the Bronco. "Sure it is."

Pepe returned to the driver's side, and Jim crossed to the passenger's side. "No, it's not." He turned and realized that Indian had not followed. "Hey, Indian, let's go."

Indian did not move but stood motionless at the edge of the road.

"Indian, are you all right?" Jim called. Again, Indian did not answer. Jim and Pepe walked back toward him. As they neared, they could see Indian's gaze fixed on the nearby meadow. The moonlight reflected off his beaded headband, which held back his long, flowing black hair that waved in the summer breeze. *Must be an elk or deer*, Jim thought. He scanned the meadow but didn't see anything.

Suddenly Indian's eyes started to move as if something was running. Indian turned and pushed Pepe and Jim toward the vehicle. "Hurry, there is danger. We must leave."

"Indian, what is it?" Pepe asked, alarmed. Indian climbed into the backseat and they shut the doors.

"They know I saw them. We must hurry."

Jim now sensed Indian's fear. *Fear of what?* he thought. Pepe pulled the Bronco out onto the highway. It did not matter what Indian feared. Jim learned long ago to never doubt Indian's sixth sense.

Indian continued to gaze out the window as an eerie feeling silenced the passengers. The vehicle sped rapidly toward Stanley. Suddenly Indian's body jumped. "It's too late, they are ahead of us."

Pepe glanced back. "But no cars have passed us."

Ignoring the comment, Indian placed his hand on Pepe's shoulder. "Trust me. They are coming after me. No matter what happens or what you see, don't stop."

Jim looked into Indian's face. "Trust me." The exact same words Indian had used many years ago to a wounded and scared nineteen-year-old Idaho boy. No, Jim thought, actually his words had been "Friend, do you trust me?" How confused Jim was to see his red-blooded stepbrother and friend standing over him behind enemy lines near the borders of Cambodia.

"Hey, there's someone up ahead along the side of the road."

Jim looked forward but didn't see anything. "Pepe, what are you talking about?"

"Are you blind? It's a woman right there next to her car. She must be having car trouble."

Jim had a puzzled look on his face. "Woman? Car trouble? You're hallucinating. There's no car or woman out there."

"You mean you don't see that woman dressed in black standing there?"

"Pepe, don't stop, keep going," Indian yelled.

"Come on, we just can't leave her stranded." Pepe applied the brakes. "I'm going to stop."

"Pepe, I'm warning you, do not stop."

"Watch out," Pepe yelled, but it was too late. Something smashed into the windshield and flew over the top of the vehicle. Jim looked back behind. "We hit something. What was it?"

"Geez, it looked like a dog," Pepe answered. "We better stop."

"Pepe," Indian exclaimed, "it doesn't matter. Do not stop!"

"What do you mean, don't stop. Indian, I have to stop."

In an instant Indian's knife was at Pepe's throat. "Pepe, you either drive or we will all die. It's your choice."

CHAPTER THREE
THE COMATOSE GIRL

She cracked open the closet door just enough to see his face. *He hasn't changed much, just a little older*, she thought. Harrison abruptly moved the telephone receiver from one ear to the other. Instinctively the woman closed the door.

"Disease Control Center, Jack Barnes speaking."

"Hello, Mr. Barnes, this is Dr. Harrison Jordan, a general surgeon from Boise, Idaho. I need a database check please."

"Go ahead, Dr. Jordan."

"Any information on the topic of black ovaries?"

"Black ovaries?" Barnes asked.

"Yes."

"You know, it won't be much longer."

"What's that, Mr. Barnes?"

"Soon you'll be able to check out this information yourself from a computer in your home."

"Yeah right," Harrison chuckled, "I'll believe that when I see it."

"Okay, Doctor, hold while I check." Harrison was put on hold. He looked down at the girl who was still under the effects of the anesthesia. He again remembered what the African shaman told him years ago about black ovaries.

"Dr. Jordan?"

"Yes, Mr. Barnes, I am still here."

"There is only one reference to black ovaries on the database."

"Can you tell me about it?"

"Well it is an old article, written by two German Doctors in the late 1940s. It's called 'The Sclerotic Ovarian Syndrome.' Do you want me to send you a copy?"

"Please, I would appreciate it. You have my address on file?"

"Yes, we do."

"Good. Thanks for your time." Harrison replaced the phone receiver. He once again focused his attention on the sedated girl. Harrison took a deep breath and sighed. "Una hija del diablo here in Idaho," he spoke aloud. "How can this be?"

Harrison sat by the girl's side. *Do I tell him about the girl*, the hidden woman thought. Gently she reopened the closet door. She shook her head. *No, it's best he not know.*

———◈———

Nurse Cratch peered over the desk counter. "Julie, you are beautiful."

Julie smiled. "Thanks, Mary." She turned gracefully, showing off the full-length gown.

"Candlelight dinner and dancing. Such a marvelous evening until we ended up here."

"He didn't leave you in the car, did he?" the moderately obese woman asked disgustedly.

Julie sighed. "'I'll only be ten minutes.' How many times have I heard that line."

Nurse Cratch reached down her blouse to adjust a bra strap holding up one of the pendulous breasts that rested comfortably on her protruded abdomen. "That inconsiderate horse's butt. All men care about anyway is sex."

Julie leaned against the nurses' counter, trying hard to keep a straight face. "You think so?"

Nurse Cratch now adjusted the other bra strap. "I know so, Mrs. J. Men will not leave me alone." She signaled to Mrs. Jordan to draw nearer. "You know, I have this theory about men that would make us women a lot happier."

Julie leaned forward on the countertop. "What's that?"

"I believe that if women would band together we could castrate them all."

Julie turned her head to hide her amusement. "You know, I've had similar thoughts at times, but tonight I would just like to get home."

Nurse Cratch made her way around the counter. "Completely understand, Mrs. J. Yes, Dr. Jordan was strutting around here earlier in his tuxedo, you know, trying to get my attention. I keep reminding him that he's married and that I am unavailable. Us women got to stick together, you know."

"Right. I'm counting on you to keep him in line."

"Well, he went to see that knife wound—you know, the little girl that Dr. Hunter transferred from Stanley earlier this evening."

"Yes, he mentioned her to me."

"Fortunate for the girl that such a fine surgeon as Dr. Hunter was so close. I hear he's returning to practice with your husband again."

"At least part-time."

"They work so well together."

"It will be nice. I know Harrison has missed him since Nicole died."

"Golly, Dr. Jordan's been gone a long time. Honey, you look tired. Sit here and I'll go get him for you."

"Oh no, I can go."

"Are you sure?"

"I'm sure. Which room is it?"

The perspiration ring under Nurse Cratch's arm stood out when she pointed down the hall. "It's room 344. Turn left at the end of the hall. You can't miss it."

Julie turned in that direction. "Thanks," she called over her shoulder. She turned left at the corner. When she found the right room, it was dark and looked empty. "Now where could he have gone," she cried aloud. She turned the same way she came.

"Julie," a voice called from within the dark room.

Startled, she once again peered into the room. "Harrison, is that you?"

Harrison turned on one of the room's dim lights. "Yes, I'll bet you're tired of waiting."

Julie smiled. Her arms encircled his neck from behind. "Nah, just checking up on you."

"Checking on me?"

"You know how I worry about you when Nurse Cratch is on duty," she teased. "She told me you were hitting on her again."

Harrison chuckled. "In her dreams." He took one of her arms and guided her around him to sit on his lap. Once again he turned his attention back to the girl lying on the bed. "I'm sorry to take so long, but I keep thinking about this girl."

"Are there problems?"

"No, not medically. Doug always does a good job."

"That reminds me, did you tell Doug about dinner on Sunday?"

"Yes, I did."

"Great. I have someone else in mind for him."

"Julie, no matchmaking. He needs more time."

"It's been five years since Nicole's death. That should be more than enough time for him. Anyway it is not normal for him to live up there on that ranch with those three misfits. If it wasn't for Aunt Edith and Jason, I'm afraid Doug would wind up as loony as them."

"Ah, one other thing," Harrison interrupted sheepishly.

"What?"

"Well, the misfits—I kind of asked them to dinner also."

Julie turned her head in disgust. "Oh, how could you?"

"I couldn't help it. They are flying with Doug to Los Angeles later that night. It didn't seem right to invite Jason and Doug but not them." Harrison grasped both of her hands. "Really, they are good people."

Julie closed her eyes and shook her head. "They're perverts."

Harrison turned her face toward him. "True, but I still like them." Once again his gentle smile softened her heart.

Julie finally relented. "Okay, but if that Pepe makes any crude comments about my body, I'm going to get Nurse Cratch to perform surgery on him."

Harrison looked at his wife. "Oh, she told you her castration theory?" They both started to laugh. "Hey, Julie, Nurse Cratch and Pepe, now there's a match you can make. What do you think?"

As they laughed, the closet door again cracked open ever so slightly. Now she could see Julie. *She is beautiful*, she thought to herself. *Maybe she could help me save the girl.*

Julie regained her composure. "You are really bothered by this girl, aren't you?"

"I'm bothered more by what Doug found. He said one of her ovaries was missing."

"Was she born without it?"

"No, not a congenital thing. He thinks it was cut out earlier today."

"Did she have surgery at one of the other local hospitals?"

"No, we already called them."

"That's really odd."

Harrison now stood and walked to the foot of the bed. "There's something else."

"What's that?"

"Doug said her remaining ovary is black."

Julie approached her husband. "Black? But aren't ovaries white?"

"Yes, they are."

"And that's what's troubling you?" Harrison silently nodded. "Do you know what black ovaries means?"

"Well, as a medical doctor, I am not certain, but—" Harrison stopped short of what he was going to say.

"But what?"

"The first time I heard of black ovaries was when I was in the Congo a number of years ago." Harrison now turned and faced the girl from the foot of her bed. "There was local shaman priest who spoke of black ovaries, but I really didn't pay much attention."

"Do you remember what he said?"

"A few things. I remember once he said a black ovary was a sign of evil."

"A sign of evil?"

"Yes, he said that people with black ovaries were considered the children of Lucifer."

Julie was startled by his answer. "Children of Lucifer—you don't mean Lucifer, like the biblical devil, do you?"

"Yes, I do. You know, Lucifer, the devil, Satan, Beelzebub, or whatever you want to call him."

Julie paused a few seconds. "You're just kidding?"

"No, I'm not. Apparently these children belong to and serve Satan, and one of their characteristics is black ovaries."

Both paused for a brief moment. "You don't believe him, do you?"

"Of course not. In fact, I scoffed at him. But I do remember he believed they were of the devil."

Both were quiet for a moment. "Harrison, listen to yourself, you sound like some sort of a witch doctor."

"What do you mean?"

Julie gently caressed the girl's cheek. "Well, just look at her. Do you see evil in this face?" Harrison watched Julie's caressing hand. He knew how Julie's heart ached at not being able to have a child of her own. She looked up. "I don't know anything about black ovaries, but I know this child is not evil."

Harrison smiled. "I really do sound crazy, don't I?" He reached out and took Julie's hand. "Let's go home." Neither noticed the closet door again close ever so slightly. Harrison slipped his arm around Julie's waist. "You know, I still have some intentions for the night."

Julie smiled. She placed her arm around his waist. "Proper intentions, I hope?"

They left the girl's room and entered the hall. "Always." Harrison motioned with his head. "Hey, look, room 342 is empty."

"Those aren't proper intentions."

"It would be like old times."

"We'd get caught."

"Yeah, you're right. Ole Nurse Crotch would be down here investigating in no time."

"It's Cratch not Crotch," Julie corrected. Their voices faded turning the hall corner.

The woman slipped out of the narrow closet. She peeked down the hall just in time to see the two turn the corner. She returned to the bedside and gazed down at the child. Reaching down, she lovingly pulled the sleeping girl close to her. "Sondra, I'm so sorry," she whispered. Tears flowed as she laid the girl gently back on the bed. *I need to hurry*, she thought. *They will be waiting*. Cautiously she walked down the hall to the staircase. Hurriedly she climbed the steps to the empty surgical suites one floor above. Gently she opened the double doors leading to one of the suites.

"Were you seen?" a deep voice asked.

"No." She then closed the door. Slowly her eyes adjusted to the dark. Now she could see the two figures more clearly. "The night nurse checks the girl every two hours."

"When will that be?"

"In about fifteen minutes."

"Good. After the nurse's rounds, bring her here. I will make preparations."

The woman drew near to them. "Micah, what of the girl?" Ignoring the question, the first Sprudith placed his animal skin bag on the nearby table. The instruments he withdrew were crude but effective. She turned to the second Sprudith, who now was standing next to her. She touched his bare shoulder. Again she repeated the question. "Cerce, what of the girl?"

She saw the answer in his eyes. She again turned to the first Sprudith. "Please, Micah," she pleaded, "just the ovary. She can do no harm now."

Without warning Micah backhanded her, sending her flying across the floor. "Silence," he replied sharply. "Because of your stupidity, the wrath of Niac is upon us."

Cerce helped Cresta to her feet. Cresta wiped the blood from her mouth. "Please, Cerce," she whispered, "no one will know. I'll take her far away. Just spare her—"

Cerce firmly grasped Cresta's shoulders. "Stop," he interrupted. "It is the command, and we must obey."

How Cresta had grown to love the girls since they were babies. She had fed, bathed, and sang songs to them. But Sondra was special, for she was from her own womb. At first only the ovaries were to be harvested, but now the master had ordered their deaths. Cerce had warned her many times to bury her emotions. Now the ache in her heart told her why.

"But you can't—" Her voice faded. The glistening scalpel knife blade came into view. She backed away. Its sight seemed to sap all her energy. She remembered how she'd watched that same blade plunged deep into their small bodies.

She tried to cover her ears, but could still hear the girls' screams of pain ringing through that mountain cabin. Four of the ovaries were harvested quickly. Now it was Sondra's turn. The blade again plunged deep into her pelvis. Shortly her left ovary was harvested. "Only one ovary left," Micah exclaimed.

Cresta touched his arm. "Please, Cerce, stop him."

Cerce looked at Cresta. "I can't, it is the master's command."

Cresta picked up a wood log located near the cabin entrance. "Command or no command, I'll stop him." She rushed at Micah and smashed the back of his head. "No more," she yelled as Micah crashed to the floor. She quickly untied Sondra and told her to run and hide. Sondra fled the cabin's front door. Cerce watched with amazement. She began to untie the other two when she felt arm encircle her throat and cut off her air.

Micah unsheathed his knife and placed it to her neck. "I will enjoy spilling your blood."

Suddenly Cerce's strong arm reached over and grabbed Micah's wrist. "No, Micah. You know it is forbidden to take the life of one of our brothers or sisters."

"But she deserves to die."

"That may be, but you know the law. Only our master can order her death." Micah knew Cerce was right. He slowly removed the knife from Cresta's neck. "Come," Cerce said, "let's find the escaped girl."

Cerce was shaking her. "Cresta, Micah is talking to you." Cerce's voice brought Cresta back to the reality of the operating room.

Micah approached. "It is time, bring the girl here. We will remove the other ovary, take her life, and return her to the room. No one will know." Micah could see Cresta's disturbed state. "Cerce, accompany her," he commanded. He then motioned both of them toward the door. "Be quick."

Without word or hesitation they left the room. *I should have told Harrison*, Cresta thought to herself. *Now it's too late.* They were silent as they made their way down the single flight of stairs to the floor below. They slightly opened the stairway door just in time to see Nurse Cratch finish her timely rounds. Quickly they made their way down the hall to the girl's room and closed the door behind them. Cerce stood by the door and watched as Cresta approached and knelt before the still sedated girl.

Cerce came forward. "Hurry, Cresta, it is time."

Cresta's eyes filled with tears. She gently grasped Sondra's hand. "Cerce, just a minute more."

Cerce knew that Micah would be coming shortly if they waited too long. He gazed at Cresta's weeping. His eyes also moistened. He had come to love Cresta and the children as if they were his own. *How can I do this?* he thought. He passed Cresta and swept the girl into his arms.

"What are you doing?" Cresta asked.

"Sondra will not die like the others," he answered. Cresta followed Cerce out the door.

CHAPTER FOUR

THE HIGH MEADOW

Doug didn't notice the figure slip by him in the dark and quietly make his way down the hill toward the cabin. His thoughts were too focused on what rested before him on the ground. They were interrupted only when he heard a horse neigh off in the distance. Doug looked down at the cabin. "Who's riding this late at night?" he whispered.

Indian squinted up the hill at the lone figure outlined against the moonlit sky. He climbed down from his horse. "Great," he murmured, "I wonder how long the Doc's been up there."

"Most of the night."

Startled, he quickly turned toward the cabin porch. "Edith, is that you?"

Edith walked down the cabin steps into the full moonlight. "You know, you could have ridden up here in the morning."

"I know, but I just couldn't sleep."

Edith patted the horse's neck. "Good ole Paint is the only horse I know that could find her way up here in the dark. Jim and Pepe?"

Indian loosened the saddle cinch. "Sound asleep when I left."

"I see last night's excitement didn't affect their rest."

"Oh, you heard?"

"Yeah, Doc and I heard you talking with Sheriff Bates on the CB. By the way, did you remember the birthday cake?"

"Yes, we picked it up yesterday. Jim and Pepe are bringing it after chores."

"Good, I want this to be a special day for Jason."

Indian tied the reins to the hitching post. "I thought everyone would be sleeping."

"Jason's the only smart one here." Edith motioned toward the cabin door. "Come in. There's a fresh pot of coffee on the stove." Indian followed Edith into the cabin. "Go sit by the fire and warm yourself," Edith suggested. Indian sat on the sofa. Edith filled two coffee cups and brought one to him.

"Thanks. I understand you had some excitement too."

Edith sat in the chair across from him. "Oh, the girl. It was touch and go for a bit. Good thing Doc was here, or she would have died." Edith took a sip of her coffee. "You know, I still can't figure out what that girl was doing up on Yankee Fork Road all alone. Campers don't even travel up that high."

Indian shook his head. "It doesn't make sense to me either."

"You know there was dog fur all over her."

"Dog fur?"

"She was covered with it."

"Could it have been wolf hair?"

Edith was surprised by his question. "I doubt it. We haven't seen wolves this far south for years. Anyway the wound didn't look like an animal bite."

"I suppose you are right." He reached for and placed another log on the fire. Sensing the silence, he glanced briefly into Edith's searching eyes. *Damn, she senses it,* he thought. He quickly looked away.

Edith smiled and warmed her hands with the hot coffee cup. "Is something bothering you?"

"Bothering me? Why do you ask?"

"I've known you since you were a boy. I've always been able to sense when something's wrong." The fire crackled in the silence. Edith watched Indian fidget on the couch. "Well?" she finally asked.

Indian looked up. "Have you ever heard of the Sprudiths?"

Edith was surprised by his question. "Sure I've heard of Sprudiths. Spun many a tale about them, along with Bigfoot, Wendigo, and the Boogey man."

"Then you don't believe in them?"

"I didn't say that, but why do you ask?"

Indian hesitated. He wasn't sure he should tell her. Finally he spoke. "I thought I saw something last night."

"Not the Sprudiths?"

"I don't know. I'm just not sure."

"Is that why you couldn't sleep?"

Indian nodded his head. "I haven't even thought about Sprudiths since the war."

Edith remained quiet. She watched Indian collect his thoughts. She knew he needed to talk with someone. She watched him stare into the fire. "You know, I killed so many of them."

Edith heard his voice crack. She could see the fire glisten off his tears. Orphaned, left alone, the Crocketts were the only family he had ever known. Who would have ever dreamt that the soft-spoken, gentle little boy that she'd known and loved would become one of the country's most effective killing machines.

"I could see their faces again last night. That's why I couldn't sleep." As Indian's voice began to fade, tears also welled in Edith's eyes. Her mind wandered as she relived that day many years ago when Lone Wolf brought the small boy to this very cabin.

Joe Crockett watched the rider approach from some distance. Eventually recognizing the rider, he sunk the axe blade deep into a log that he had been cutting. He took a neckerchief from around his neck and wiped the sweat from his face. "Lone Wolf, is that you?"

Lone Wolf climbed off his horse. "It's been too long, my friend." They each grasped the other's forearm, which was the Indian way.

Joe turned toward the cabin. "Emma, Edith, children, come quick and see who is here."

They were excited to see Lone Wolf, and so enjoyed his rare visits. Living alone on the middle fork of the Salmon River could be lonely, and he always had so many stories to tell. But this particular visit, he had a surprise traveling with him.

Lone Wolf helped the small lad down off his horse. That was the first time they saw him. Jim and Nicole drew close.

Emma smiled and greeted him with a hug. "Hello, Lone Wolf. How is our most handsome and favorite visitor doing?" Emma had a way with people. She greeted everyone she met with a hug. Emma said that hugs were 'the greetings of the Gods.' She broke the embrace and looked down at the boy. "Lone Wolf, who do we have here?"

Lone Wolf knelt down on one knee and placed his hand on the boy's shoulder. "This is my friend."

Nicole spoke. "What's your name?"

"Indian," the lad replied. She remembered how surprised she was when she heard him speak English. He appeared about the same age as Jim and Nicole. In the innocent way of children, the three were off running and playing in the meadow in a manner of minutes.

"Is he a relative?" Emma asked.

"No, I actually found him cold, hungry, and alone in the high mountain country a couple of days ago."

Joe motioned for Lone Wolf to take a chair on the front porch. "High mountain country. What was he doing up there?

Lone Wolf obliged and sat down. "Well, he said he was lost."

"Has he said anything about a home or family?" Emma asked.

Lone Wolf pointed to the majestic peaks of the Sawtooth Mountains. "Only that he lives up there. We followed his tracks for two days in that direction, but the tracks were alone and disappeared in the rocks. It seems all he can remember is that he lived in the mountains and his name is Indian."

Joe rubbed his chin. "Unusual name."

"Yes, it is. I was hoping he could stay with you until I am able to find his family."

"Of course he can."

"I remember how you took in Nicole several years ago. I don't know, it just seemed natural that he should come here."

The rest was history. They never did find his family. Lone Wolf became Indian's adopted grandfather, and the Crocketts became his family.

"So what do you think?"

Indian's stare brought Edith back to reality. "I'm sorry, what was that?"

"The Sprudiths," Indian repeated.

"Oh, yes, the Sprudiths," Edith interjected, "have you talked with your grandfather?"

"No, not yet. After we check out Yankee Fork for Sheriff Bates this afternoon, I thought I would ride over to the middle fork and see him. Can you handle the ranch?"

"Oh, sure."

Jason's sleep was interrupted by the muffled voices coming from the living room. He peered out the window up the hill toward the figure mirrored against the full moonlight. "Dad is with mom," he whispered. He quietly dressed. He grabbed his long birthday box and peered out the bedroom door toward Aunt Edith and Indian sitting near the fire. *I wish I could show Indian my birthday present*, Jason thought. *It's just like his and Dad's.* Quietly he closed the door and turned. "I'll bet Auntie won't let me go." He then tucked the long birthday present box under his arm, grabbed his jacket and the fishing tackle box. He quietly mimicked her voice. "She'll say, 'Jason it's too cold,' or 'you'll catch pneumonia,' or 'you need your breakfast.'"

He slipped through the window into the brisk mountain air. Jason smiled. "Well, not this time. I'll just go this way, and she will never know." Quietly he crept under the porch window. He failed to notice another figure already crouched and hidden near the porch, watching not only him, but also Edith and Indian through the large front porch window. Jason quietly pulled the fishing float tube from the porch and down the steps. He stopped for a moment to stroke Paint's neck and mane, then took off racing up the hill. Just then he heard the cabin's front door open.

"Jason, you son of a jackass," came a woman's screaming voice from the doorway, "you get your butt back here and have some breakfast first."

Jason continued up the hill. "Later, Auntie."

Doug stood and peered down the hill toward the noise coming from the cabin. It didn't take long for him to realize who was yelling and why. He made his way down the pathway to meet his son.

"Later my butt," she screamed, "sneaking out like that. You know I'm going to tan your hide when I catch you? Now come back here!" Indian had followed Edith outside. A smile came to his face. He watched Jason scamper up the hill, completely ignoring Edith's command. "That better not be a smile on your face, Indian," Edith threatened.

She has eyes in the back of her head, Indian thought. Indian poorly smothered a grunt and a chuckle. "Oh no, Edith. You know kids these days," he added trying to appease her.

"Dammit, he's just like his mom, so independent."

"Ah, let him go. He's just excited about fishing."

Edith concurred, shaking her head in dismay. "Yeah, you're right. At least put on your jacket," she again yelled. "You'll catch pneumonia."

"Dad," Jason exclaimed as they reached each other.

Doug hugged his son. "I guess you didn't tell Aunt Edith you were coming up here, did you?"

"No, I slipped out the bedroom window. She didn't know."

"You bet she didn't know," Doug smiled. They both turned and watched Edith and Indian reenter the cabin. Doug then grabbed Jason's float tube that his son was dragging. "Better put your jacket on like she said."

Jason slipped on his jacket. "Look, Dad." He pointed to a hint of the morning light touching the eastern mountain peaks. "I was just too excited to eat breakfast."

Doug touched his son's shoulder. He could sense his son's excitement. "It's okay. Let's go down by the lake." Doug motioned his son back down the trail and to the cutoff toward the lake. "You know we are in for a scolding when she catches up with us, don't you?"

"Yeah, I know. What should we do?"

"We'll tell her it's your birthday, and maybe she'll let this one slide."

Unknowingly Doug and Jason walked by the same hidden figure, whom had followed Jason part way up the hill. Once they had passed, it gave him the opportunity to slip away into the nearby wooded area.

He moved quickly toward the thick stand of trees farther up the hill. "I must hurry. The sun will be up soon." Shortly there were two wolves that accompanied him the remainder of the distance to where Tess was waiting for him.

"Well?" she asked.

"It is him."

"Are you sure?"

"Yes, my lady, I am sure." Micah now could feel hate and anger building inside.

"Good, after all these many years we have finally found him. Come, Matthias and Niac will be pleased."

"Please, my lady, let me kill him now."

Tess pointed toward the lightening sky. "You know this is holy ground, and the sun begins to shine. The mountain people must not know we were here." Tess could tell her words did not sooth Micah's heart. She placed her hand on his shoulder. "Be patient, there will be a better time. First we dispose of the other two bodies, and then Matthias wants us to search for Cresta, Cerce, and the girl." She turned deeper into the forest while Micah and the wolves followed.

CHAPTER FIVE

THE LAKE

The sun's rays glistened off the partially snow-covered Sawtooth Mountain peaks. Doug leaned back, resting on his elbows. Jason rubbed his hand over his new fishing pole. "It's bamboo like yours and Indian's."

Doug smiled at his son's joy. "Happy birthday, Son."

"Thanks." Jason attached the reel to the pole and began threading his line through the eyelets. "I saw you up on the hill. You and mom were talking."

"Well, mostly I did the talking and she just listened."

Both were quiet for a brief moment. Jason looked at his father. "Dad, you didn't actually see mom die?"

Doug shook his head. "No, I didn't."

"Then don't you think it's possible she's still alive?"

Doug thought this nonsense had ended. "Jason, we've been through this before. Don't you remember what the psychiatrist told you?"

"Yes, I remember. He said I really don't see her but just think I do."

Doug went on to explain, "It's normal to want you mom back, even to the point you hallucinate and think you see and talk with her."

Jason looked away. "Mom said you wouldn't believe me."

Doug shook his head and thought to himself, *Maybe I should have listened to the psychiatrist and put him on medication like he suggested.*

Jason continued. "Dad, do you want to hear what she said?"

Doug humored his son. "Okay, what did she say?"

"She wants you to get her hospital stuff while you're in Los Angeles. You know, those people papers they have in hospitals."

He sat up and looked at his son. "You mean her hospital chart?"

"Yes, her hospital chart. She wants you to look at it." Jason sat up quickly and pointed toward Lake Emogine. Movement in the lake caught his attention. "Hey, look, they're starting to jump."

Doug turned. "They sure are. I guess we better get ready." Doug reached and opened his tackle box. "What fly do you suggest?"

Jason checked the gray skyline and clouds in the sky. "I think I'll try an Adam's fly."

Doug threaded his own line. "Really? I was thinking a mosquito."

Jason reached for his own fly box. "Maybe, but Indian, Jim, and I always have better luck with the Adam's this time of year."

"What about Pepe?"

Jason grinned. "Pepe has better luck catching fish at the supermarket."

They both chuckled. "Well come to think about it, your mom always used the Adam's fly here."

Jason put on his chest waders and fins. "You know, it's hard to believe that mom could fish."

"Ah, yes, your mom could fish."

Jason looked around. "Dad, there's only one float tube."

"Jim and Pepe are bringing up the others."

"Well they better hurry. This is the best time of the day."

Doug could hear the excitement in his son's voice. "Listen, you take it. I'll wait for the others."

"Are you sure?"

Doug set aside his pole. "Yes, I'm sure. The others should be along shortly."

Jason leaned over and hugged his dad. "I'll find the best places for us." Hurriedly he picked up his pole and float tube and headed toward the water edge. When he arrived at the lake, he climbed into the float tube and paddled away.

Doug pondered what Jason said. "What does he mean Nicole wants me to look at her hospital chart?" he whispered.

Doug sat so engrossed watching his son paddle out, that he did not hear footsteps come up from behind. "He does well."

Doug turned to see who was speaking. "Hey, Indian." He motioned for him to sit down on the bank next to him. "Yes, he does. You taught him well."

Indian sat down. "It wasn't me. He has the gift like his mom."

Doug smiled. "He moves his pole with such grace. It's like he's conducting a symphony." Jason noticed Indian's arrival and waved excitedly. Indian smiled and returned the greeting. Doug turned toward the cabin. "Where are the others?"

"Jim and Pepe are pumping up the float tubes. They should be along soon."

"Aunt Edith?"

"Ah, she's making the birthday preparations. She expects us back right at noon. I don't think we should be late today."

"Bad mood?"

"Oh, that's putting it mildly."

"What's upset her?"

"Ah, she's been yelling at Pepe for spreading rumors around town about the both of them. You wouldn't know anything about that, would you?"

Doug chuckled. "Maybe."

Indian smiled. He crushed a dirt clod in his hands and threw the pieces in front of him. "Doc, did you hear about last night?"

"You mean the fight? Yeah, Sheriff Bates called me."

"No, I mean did Pepe say anything to you."

"You mean about your knife at his neck?" Indian nodded his head. "Yeah, he said something about that. You know, he thinks you're crazy."

Indian crushed another dirt clod. "Maybe he's right. The war really messed me up. But being here on the ranch, I thought I was getting my life back together again until…"

"Until?"

"Until last night. I thought I saw something that reminded me of the war."

"Like a flashback or something?"

"Maybe, but it seemed so real. And last night when Pepe said he saw the woman in black with the wolves, I thought I was back in Vietnam again fighting the enemy."

"Woman? Wolves?" Doug asked. "I don't understand. I thought the Vietcong were your enemy?"

"No, not the Vietcong."

"If not the Vietcong, then who?"

Indian opened his mouth to speak but then stopped himself. "Ah, forget it, Doc. It must have been some sort of flashback. Anyway, I apologized to Pepe about the knife incident and wanted you to know."

"No harm, Indian." Indian left him with questions, but Doug knew there would be a better time to ask.

"Odd finding that girl up on Yankee Fork last night."

"Yes, it was. You know, Indian, someone cut out one of her ovaries."

"Why would someone do that?"

"Mentally ill, psychotic, I don't know."

"Doc, did she anything at all?"

"Oh, she mumbled some gibberish about a lady and her tigers, but nothing else."

"Lady and tigers, that doesn't make sense."

"No, it doesn't. We're just hoping that she can tell us more when she wakes up."

The valley quiet was only interrupted by the sound of the rushing stream emptying into the Mountain Lake. Indian watched Doug gaze at the surrounding mountains and valley. Indian began to prepare his fly rod. "It's beautiful, isn't it?"

Doug nodded his head. "Yes, it is."

Indian attached his reel and threaded his line. "Grandfather says that the high meadow here is a holy place."

"That's interesting. Nicole said the same thing."

"Once grandfather told me that the Great Spirit has designated certain places on earth where evil can't dwell, and the high meadow is one of those places."

"Holy places on earth, well I don't know about that." Doug nodded toward the mountain peaks. "But you know Nicole spoke of some people living high up in those mountains. She told me that once when she was lost, these people found her and brought her back home."

"Grandfather calls them the mountain people."

"Then you've heard of them?"

"Many times. You know Nicole and I were adopted by the Crocketts?"

"Yes, I know."

"Grandfather thinks our parents are mountain people."

"Really? I didn't know that."

"I like to think Grandfather was wrong."

"Why is that?"

"If it is true, then why wouldn't our real parents come for us?"

They both remained silent. Doug finally spoke. "Well, maybe they can't."

"I don't know. I've been all over those mountain peaks many times and haven't seen one single person."

Interrupting loud voices could now be heard coming down the trail toward the lake. "Listen, Pepe, you got to quit spreading rumors about my mom. She's madder than hell at you."

"I swear, I haven't said anything about your mom."

"That's not what she says."

"Well, I don't care, because it's the truth." Pepe came down the embankment. "Hey, boss, wait till you see my new waders." He sat down next to Doug and Indian to catch his breath. "Hey, Jason," Pepe yelled loudly. He waved both arms wildly at the boy located in the middle of the lake. A satisfied smile came to Jason's face. He waved back.

Indian put his index finger to his lips. "Quiet, Pepe, you'll scare the fish."

Jim laughed. "Scare the fish? Wait until you see Pepe's new waders." He lumbered down the embankment behind Pepe. "Hey, Doc."

"Hey, Jim," Doug answered. "Pepe, you got some new waders?"

"Did I? Boss, wait till you see these." Pepe reached in his backpack and pulled out the brightest orange waders the group had ever seen. It was too much for Doug and Indian. No matter how hard they tried, they couldn't choke back their laughter.

Jim chimed in. "See, I told you they would laugh."

Pepe slipped on the bright waders. "You three laugh all you want, but Harv at the bait shop told me that fish are attracted to fishermen who have style."

"Ole Harv saw you coming," Jim countered. "He's probably had those old waders in the back of his store for years."

"Yeah, we'll see who catches the most fish." Pepe stood and started toward the edge of the lake.

Jim followed. "Well, with those waders, you are not fishing next to me."

Indian stood to follow the others. He looked at Doug. "Are you coming?"

"No, go ahead. I want to pick some meadow flowers for Nicole's grave."

"Do you want me to go with you?"

Doug shook his head. "No, thanks. I'd like to go alone."

Indian understood. He knew how much Doug missed Nicole. "I'll tell Jason that you will be along shortly." They then split into different directions.

Doug picked the flowers as he made the uphill trek to Nicole's gravesite.

Edith shaded her eyes from the noonday sun. She grabbed her cowboy hat and started down the porch steps. "Damn it, they aren't even out of the lake yet. I'll have to go get them." She started down the trail to the lake and noticed Doug up on the grassy knoll. "Ah, hell, he's been up there all morning. I better go get him first."

Edith slowed her pace as she neared the top. "Hey, Hunter, help," she breathlessly cried. Doug turned to see her drop to her knees. He hurried down the knoll and lifted her up.

"Edith, what are you doing? You'll have a heart attack if you push yourself like that."

"Oh, I'll be all right, just let me catch my breath."

"I tell you, it's those cigarettes."

Edith waved her hand to end the matter. "Ah, I'm too old to quit now. Anyway it's not my health I'm worried about."

"What do you mean?"

"Hell, I miss Nicole too, but it's not healthy for you to sit up here for hours and pine like this."

"I know. It just bothers me I wasn't there when she needed me."

"At the end you were."

"Yes, but there was so much wasted time."

"Doug, you have to let the guilt go. It's what Nicole would have wanted." She nodded toward the lake. "Look down there. What do you see?"

"What do you mean?"

"Nicole left you a very special gift—Jason. He needs you. He needs a father."

Doug was hesitant at first to speak. "Jason says Nicole is still alive."

"Yes, I know."

"Not only does he say she's alive, but he says he sees and talks with her."

"He told me that too."

"The psychiatrist thinks he's schizophrenic."

"Then you don't believe Jason?"

"Of course not. They're delusions of motherless boy's wishful thinking.

Edith looked away for a brief moment and then turned back. "I don't know. I guess I would like to believe him."

Doug looked at her. "C'mon, Edith, you're a professional nurse. You know things like that don't happen."

"Are you sure?"

"Well, I don't know what happens after we die, but I know that the dead don't go around visiting the living."

Edith was quiet for a moment. Finally she spoke. "Let me ask you something. Do you think Jason is special?"

"Special?" Doug smiled at her and shrugged. "I suppose so. He's mine and Nicole's son."

"No, I mean more than that. Do you think Jason is a special child with special gifts that other children may not have?"

Doug chuckled. "Now you're beginning to sound like Nicole. Sometimes Nicole would start to tell me something about Jason, and then she would abruptly stop. I think she wanted to tell me more, but she never did."

Edith and Doug watched Jason and the others climb out of the lake. "Look at them all. There's Indian, who still suffers from the horrors of a war. Then Jim, my son, who battles self-humiliation and alcoholism. Even Pepe, the ex-priest, has a constant fight with God." Edith turned toward Doug. "Then you, Doc."

"Me?"

"Yes, you—a husband who can't forgive himself for his wife's death."

Doug looked at Edith. "And you?

She looked at Doug and smiled. "Yes, even me—an old maid whose every other word is a damn curse word." Doug remained silent as he listened to her. "Jason has accepted us all in spite of our faults. He has made us his family. That's what makes him special. God gave him the same gift that his mother had."

"What's that?"

"The gift of love." Edith stood, recognizing she had said enough. "Anyway, if you guys need to be in Boise tonight, we better get to Jason's cake and ice cream."

Doug held on to her arm. "Yes, we better. Indian and Jim also need to go to Yankee Fork this afternoon for Sheriff Bates." They made their way down the path toward the cabin.

"Oye, Edith." The shout echoed off the mountains. She focused her attention down toward the lake edge. "Look at this." Pepe dumped a huge live fish that was trapped in his orange waders.

She waved back at Pepe, acknowledging his catch, while muttering, "There's something wrong with that boy."

CHAPTER SIX

THE BODIES

"**A**re you sure?"

Micah handed the binoculars to Tess. "Here, see for yourself."

For the longest time she gazed at the riders winding their way down the mountain trail. "I don't know, he looks different."

"Only older." How long Micah had searched for the one called Indian, and now his archenemy was before him. Micah touched his knife handle. "I could kill him now."

Tess put out her arm and stopped him. "No, wait!" She looked through the binoculars at the other end of the valley. She could see a lone rider on a horse. "The one that followed us is returning." Tess squinted through the binoculars to get a better look. "He looks familiar to me too, but I can't place him."

Micah put out his hand. "Let me look." She handed him the binoculars, but it was too late. "Ah, I can't see him now. He's disappeared among the trees."

One of the wolves whimpered. Tess reached out and stroked his neck to calm him.

"Do you think this stranger found the bodies?" Micah whispered.

Tess grimaced. "I'm afraid so."

Micah shook his head, angry with himself. "That was so careless of me. If it hadn't been for the lady and the tigers interfering, we would have disposed of the bodies last night."

Rocks trickled down the mountain, echoing throughout the valley. Their attention returned again to the three horseback riders making their way down to the valley floor.

Indian stopped and gazed at the beautiful Yankee Fork of the Salmon River winding its way from the valley head. He smiled as he listened to the others argue. "Come on, that doesn't count."

"What do you mean it doesn't count? Jimmy, I won fair and square."

"That's not fair and square. The bet was with a fishing pole."

Pepe turned back and pointed his finger. "You didn't say that."

"Yes, I did."

"No, you didn't. You never said anything about a fishing pole."

"C'mon, Pepe, you're not going to count that."

"Why not?"

"Because the fish jumped into your waders."

"So?"

"So everyone else catches fish with fishing poles, not their waders."

"Waders or fishing poles—it doesn't matter. You're not going to squander on the bet. You owe me that dinner."

Pepe's stubbornness was quickly frustrating Jim. He looked ahead. "Indian, what do you think?"

Indian turned, not sure he wanted to become involved.

"Yeah, Indian, what do you think?" Pepe asked eagerly.

Indian smiled. "Well, Jim, I think Pepe has you this time."

Pepe clenched his fist and pumped it in the air. "Yes!"

Jim shook his head. "Ah, damn."

"See, Jimmy, didn't I tell you?

"Tell me what?"

"That my orange waders would attract fish."

"More likely blinded them."

"Listen," Indian said, "Maybe you two should have a rematch, and this time with fishing poles."

"Ah, he's too scared I'll whip his butt," Jim taunted.

"What you talking about? I'm not scared of you."

"Then it's agreed—when we get back from LA."

Indian gently nudged Paint forward on the downward trail and noticed rocks trickling down the mountainside. "Careful," he called back, "these rocks are loose and dangerous."

Slowly they made their way down the steep mountain trail. Pepe interrupted the quiet. "So this funeral in LA tomorrow, is it for David or a guy named Solomon?"

"Both." Indian answered. "They are the same person. When we worked in the intelligence service, we all had code names. David's code name was Solomon."

Pepe still didn't understand. "Why Solomon?"

"David was very smart and wise, like the ancient Israelite king. So we called him Solomon. Indian was known as Chief and my code name was Alamo."

Pepe looked at Jim. "Alamo?"

"Because Davy Crockett was my great-great-great-grandfather."

Pepe now understood. For a few minutes they rode in silence. Finally Pepe spoke again. "How is it that you two never talk about those times in the intelligence service?"

Indian grimaced. "Those times were not pleasant for us. They hold a lot of painful memories we would like to forget."

"Maybe you should talk about those times. You know, get those memories out in the open and off your chest."

Jim grunted. "Yeah, it'd be like you telling us why you're no longer a Catholic Priest. Do you want to talk about that?"

Jim is right, Pepe thought. *Sometimes it's better some things are left unsaid.* Now they neared the stream at the bottom of the hill. Pepe shook his head. "You know, guys, we are really messed up." Indian and Jim looked at each other and smiled.

"Whoa, Paint." Indian brought his horse to a stop and dismounted near the edge of the stream. He crouched and touched the ground.

Pepe and Jim pulled alongside. "What is it?" Jim asked.

"Tracks, about a day old."

"They were made this morning," a voice corrected from behind.

Startled, all three turned, but didn't see anyone. Pepe searched all around them. "Who said that?"

Jim nodded toward the other side of the clearing. "Must be coming from that bush."

A smile slowly came across Indian's face. "I hear only a voice," Indian said, leading Paint in the direction of the bush. The other two followed.

"Maybe it is the wind that speaks," the voice again spoke, but now it was coming from their left. They turned toward the voice. "Or maybe it's the voice of the earth," the same voice spoke again, but this time coming from the right."

Indian chuckled. Again they all turned in that direction. "Then maybe again, it's just the voice of an old man," the voice finally said, but this time from behind.

All turned to face him standing in the center of the clearing. Indian dropped his reins and moved toward him. "Grandfather."

Lone Wolf approached and embraced him. "Hello, Grandson."

Pepe dismounted. "Lone Wolf, you scared the crap out of me."

Jim also climbed down from his horse. He shook his head. "It's amazing how you do that with your voice."

"It's got to be some ancient ancestor power, right?" Pepe assumed.

Lone Wolf remained silent. Initially he looked at them as if he was harboring an ancient secret. Then he broke into a smile. "Nah, I learned to throw my voice years ago in Vegas. You know, from one of those ventriloquists."

"Well, I'm impressed each time you do it. But how did you know we were here?"

Lone Wolf motioned for the three to follow him. "I didn't. I was following these tracks you found, and I happened to see you coming down the mountain." Lone Wolf untied and mounted his horse. "Come, I have something to show you farther up the valley."

Indian rode up alongside his grandfather. "I was coming to see you this afternoon."

"I know. What troubles you, also troubles me."

Indian's fears were realized. "Then it's true. They are here."

Lone Wolf nodded his head. "I'm afraid so."

"Who's here?" Pepe asked.

"But why?" Indian asked.

"I don't know, but they were at the high meadow cabin last night watching you and the others."

"Who was at the high meadow?" Pepe again asked. Jim looked over at Pepe. The look on Jim's face told Pepe to be quiet and listen.

"Then they have found me, haven't they?" Lone Wolf's silence answered his question. "But I thought the high meadow was forbidden holy ground."

"It is, but they also left before daylight."

Pepe was totally confused. "Who was watching, and who forbids what?" he finally asked.

"Hush, Pepe," Jim exclaimed.

"Hush yourself. Are they speaking English or what, because I don't understand a word they are saying."

Lone Wolf smiled and pulled his horse to a stop. He turned around. "Pepe, the Sprudiths were watching."

"Sprudiths," Jim exclaimed. "They haven't been in this area for years."

Lone Wolf continued. "I followed them here this morning, but the wolves must have picked up my scent. Their tracks disappeared farther up the valley in the rocks."

Indian scoured the hillsides. "Then they may be watching us now."

Lone Wolf agreed. "I believe they are."

"Wolves," Pepe interrupted, "that's it. It wasn't a dog we hit last night, it was a wolf."

Lone Wolf turned toward Pepe. "You saw a wolf last night?"

"We hit something on the highway near Red Fish Lake," Jim informed. "Initially Pepe thought it was a German Shepherd dog, but maybe it was a wolf."

"Pepe also saw a woman in black with the wolves," Indian informed.

"And you and Jim?" Lone Wolf asked.

"No, we didn't see anything."

Lone Wolf pulled his horse to a stop near the water edge. "Our legends say the woman dressed in black is the master of all wolves that have turned evil." He dismounted from his horse. The others followed his example. He knelt near a spot on the ground. "Look, I found this pool of blood earlier today. The footprints around the blood are that of a child."

Indian reached down and touched the ground. He looked up at Jim. "I bet the blood is the girl's."

"Girl?" Lone Wolf questioned.

"Yes, a bleeding girl was found wandering up here last night," Jim explained.

Lone Wolf grew quiet for a minute and then asked. "Was she cut open?"

Surprised the three looked at each and then back at Lone Wolf. "How did you know?" Indian asked.

Lone Wolf ignored Indian's question. "Did she die?"

Jim shook his head. "No, Doc saved her life. She's at a hospital in Boise."

"This may be worse than I thought," Lone Wolf murmured. "Was she black?"

Again the three were surprised. "Yes, she was," Jim answered, "but how did you know that?"

"I will show you in a moment, but first follow the girl's blood trail."

It led them to the riverbank. "It looks like wolves and people followed the child," Indian said, "but then—" He paused. They could see the confused look on his face.

"Then what?" Pepe questioned.

"Suddenly the wolves and people sharply turned and ran away like something frightened them." Indian looked up at Lone Wolf. "What would scare the wolves and Sprudiths, but not a little child?"

Lone Wolf motioned farther downstream. "Come, I will show you." They followed him until the blood trail and tracks ended.

Jim turned himself around completely. "Her tracks suddenly stopped. Where did she go?"

Indian moved alone further down stream. "There are more tracks here," he informed.

Jim and the others moved toward Indian. "The girl's?" he asked.

"No, a woman in bare feet," Indian answered.

"Bare feet among all these rocks?" Pepe questioned.

"Not only barefoot, but she had two large cats with her."

"Mountain Lion?" Jim asked.

Indian shook his head. "Cat tracks are too big for mountain lion."

Pepe looked over Lone Wolf. "But there aren't any cats bigger than mountain lions."

"At least not on this continent," Lone Wolf answered.

Indian remembered Doc repeating the girl's murmurs about a lady and the tigers. Indian stood and moved up and down the embankment studying the soft sandy soil. "I can't find their tracks leading to or away from the river edge."

"There aren't any, Grandson. I searched earlier this morning."

"Wait a minute," Pepe interrupted. "You mean to tell me a barefoot woman and two large cats somehow flew here, landed, picked up the child, and then flew away."

Indian was confused too. "Yes, how do you explain the tracks?"

"They don't need an explanation," he answered. "These are called wind tracks or the tracks of the wind. Our legends speak of a people who have lived in these mountains for thousands of years that have learned to move like the wind."

Jim was skeptical. "Move like the wind, surely you don't believe that?"

Lone Wolf smiled. Indian suspected that his grandfather knew more than he was saying. Lone wolf motioned farther up the valley. "Come, there is more to see." Lone Wolf led them and their horses back to the mountain road where they mounted them again.

Indian caught sight of movement on his left. He urged Paint alongside Lone Wolf. "Grandfather, there is movement high on the mountain."

"I know, I saw it too."

"Should we—?"

"No, I have something more important to show you." They rode in silence until they arrived at the deserted cabin. All dismounted and followed Lone Wolf onto the cabin porch. Before entering he turned to them. "Be prepared, for what you will see is very disturbing." He then turned and opened the cabin door. A foul odor poured from the opening. They all covered their noses as they entered the cabin. It took a brief moment for their eyes to adjust to the dim light. Soon all they saw was the red color everywhere. It wasn't until Indian saw the two lifeless bodies bound to cots that he finally realized the red color was blood.

"Oh no," Jim whispered. He attempted to move toward the bodies. Lone Wolf restrained his arm. "Stay to the edge so as not to disturb anything. Sheriff Bates will want to examine this place first."

Silence filled the one-room cabin as the four of them carefully approached the two bodies lying on the blood soaked cots. Indian recognized his grandfather's jacket covering them. "They're only children," Pepe mumbled to Jim.

Lone Wolf withdrew his jacket. All could see the massive bleeding and wounds to their abdomens. "These children were slaughtered," Lone Wolf informed.

Pepe's stomach started to churn. He turned his head. "But what kind of person could do such a thing?"

Indian held up one the girl's right hand. "The end of the right fourth finger has been cut off."

"Meaning what?" Pepe asked.

"Meaning these children were killed by Sprudiths," Lone Wolf explained.

"I have seen this many times in Vietnam," Indian said. "They collect the ends of the right fourth finger from the people they kill." Indian turned to Lone Wolf. "They would not leave these bodies carelessly like this. They must still be nearby."

Lone Wolf nodded his head. "I agree. Something must have gone wrong.

Jim turned to leave. "We need to contact the sheriff.

"I already have," Lone Wolf said. "Prior to your arrival I climbed the ridge at the other end of the valley and called him on my portable radio. He and his deputies should be arriving soon. "Lone Wolf then recovered the bodies with his jacket, but purposely left their faces uncovered.

"Maybe the black girl was with these two and escaped somehow," Jim suggested.

"I believe so," Lone Wolf answered. He nodded toward them. "Look at their faces and tell me what you see.

"Well they're about nine to ten years old," Pepe stated.

"They bled to death," Jim added. "I've seen that sort of pale calm on dying faces before."

Indian was the first to notice. "Look, this girl's skin is dark, and the other girl's eyes are slanted."

Now Jim noticed what Indian was explaining. "One girl looks Spanish, the other looks

Oriental—"

Pepe interrupted. "And the third girl was black. Three different races and skin colors. It looks like some kind of racial thing."

Jim looked toward the cabin door. "I hear a vehicle. Someone is coming."

Lone Wolf moved toward the cabin door. "It must be Sheriff Bates."

Pepe followed Lone Wolf from the cabin. Jim also turned to leave, but stopped short when he saw that Indian was not following. Indian slid down the wall to the floor. Jim could sense something troubling him. "Indian, what is it?"

Indian was quiet for a brief moment, and then he spoke. "Why would they just slaughter these little girls like this?"

Jim sat down next to Indian and leaned his back against the wall. He shook his head. "I don't know." He remained quiet. He knew Indian had seen this type of slaughter time and time again. He also knew that Indian had more to say.

"The Sprudiths were relentless," Indian began. "It was my third straight year in Vietnam. The Sprudiths found my trail and chased me many miles behind enemy lines into North Vietnam."

Indian never speaks of these things, Jim thought. "Why were they after you?"

"Revenge. I had killed so many of them, they just wanted me dead." Indian paused. "I was in the jungle early one morning when I heard this child crying."

Indian pushed the vines to the side. There before him was a crying naked child with her back to him.

He spoke to the child in Vietnamese, but the child did not turn. Indian watched as she tripped and fell to the ground. *Ah, her legs are tangled in some jungle vines*, he thought. As he came closer he could see a red color smeared all over her body. "Oh no," he murmured, "that's not a vine." He gently rolled her over to her back. Her tiny abdomen was split completely open. He could see it was her intestines and not a vine wrapped around her legs. He spoke in Vietnamese. "Hold real still, and I will help you." She stopped her whimpering. Indian carefully stuffed her intestines back inside her. He then tied a long bootlace around her waist to keep them inside. "Who did this?" he asked.

"Wolfmen," she answered.

He picked her up in his arms. "Where do you live?" She pointed her finger down a small path through the jungle. It didn't take long to reach her village. Numerous moaning bodies were scattered everywhere, but none of the villagers were dead. Each had their abdomens split open with machetes left to suffer and die slow, horrible deaths. "Who did this?" he asked an old man sitting up against one of the huts.

His answer was the same. "The wolfmen."

Now Indian was quiet. Jim finally broke the silence. "What did you do?"

Indian looked at Jim and then back at the two girls lying there. "I did what I could. I cared for each one of them until the pain from their approaching deaths was too severe."

"And then?"

Indian paused and then spoke. "Then I shot each one of them in the head so they would not suffer anymore." His eyes moistened. "All seventy-two of them."

Jim put his arm around his stepbrother and helped him to his feet. "Come on, let's get out of this place."

Indian agreed. He and Jim left the cabin as Sheriff Bates and Deputy Phil pulled up in their four-wheel drive pickup.

"Jim, Indian," Sheriff Bates spoke.

"Sheriff," Jim replied. He motioned toward the cabin. "They're inside."

Indian did not answer but walked by them to the center of the clearing. He stood motionless for a brief moment and stared high up the mountain where he previously saw movement. He then unsheathed his knife and raised it high into the air. All present watched.

Pepe noticed Indian's eyes ablaze with anger. He looked at Jim. "What's he doing?"

Jim shook his head. "I don't know."

Micah looked on intently from high above. "Is this possible?" Micah murmured.

Tess watched Indian raise his knife high in the air a second time. She looked over at Micah. "What's he doing?" Micah did not answer.

Indian lowered his arm and then again raised the knife high into the air a third time. Sheriff Bates touched Lone Wolf's shoulder. "What's Indian doing?"

"Sheriff, my grandson is declaring war."

"War?" Deputy Phil asked. "With who?"

Lone Wolf pointed to the man standing up high on the side of the mountain. He too had his knife raised high in the air accepting the challenge. "With him."

CHAPTER SEVEN

GENERAL MCFARLAND

McFarland studied the papers spread out on his desk. "Fred, I like them. Send these plans off to the Pentagon."

"Yes, sir."

As the officer gathered up the papers to put back into their folder, the office door opened. A woman paused in the threshold. "Excuse me, General."

McFarland looked up. "Yes, Debbie?"

"There's a call for you from the CDC on line one."

"CDC?"

"Yes, it's a Mr. Barnes. He wouldn't leave a message. He insisted on speaking directly to you. He says it's very important."

McFarland looked across the desk at Officer Reed. "I wonder what the CDC wants." He reached for his phone. "Okay, I'll take the call now." Debbie left and closed the door behind her. "This is General McFarland."

"Hello, General, Jack Barnes from the Center for Disease Control in Atlanta."

"Yes, Mr. Barnes, how can I help you?"

"Well your name came up on our computer database."

"What do you mean?"

"Someone accessed our database about a certain topic. When they did, we received a computer message advising us to inform you directly."

Officer Reed noticed a solemn look on the general's face. "Just a minute, Mr. Barnes." McFarland placed his hand over the receiver. "Fred, would you excuse me for a moment? I need to take this phone call in private."

Officer Reed stood. "Sure, I'll wait in the outer office."

"Thanks, this shouldn't take long." McFarland waited until Officer Reed left the room. He removed his hand from the mouthpiece. "So, Mr. Barnes, what information was accessed on the database?"

"The topic of black ovaries."

McFarland shook his head and closed his eyes tight. It was what he feared. *Oh, that's just great,* he thought sarcastically.

Mr. Barnes noticed the silence on the other end of the line. "General, you did leave those instructions, didn't you?"

"Yes, I left them several years ago. Do you know who requested the information?"

"Someone up your way. Aren't you at Dugway, in Utah?"

"Yes, I am."

"This search request came from a medical doctor in Boise, Idaho, a Dr. Harrison Jordan."

McFarland changed the phone receiver to the other ear. He then picked up a nearby pen and took the name down. "Thanks, I appreciate you contacting me."

"No problem, we are happy to oblige."

"Oh, by the way, Mr. Barnes," McFarland interrupted, "did this Dr. Jordan request a copy of the article?"

"As a matter of fact he did. We sent him a copy this morning."

"Do you know the name of the article?"

"Yes, I have it here. Its title is 'The Sclerotic Ovarian Syndrome,' written by two German doctors back in the 1940s. Do you want us to send you a copy?"

"I would appreciate it."

"I'll put it in the mail today."

They both hung up, and McFarland rubbed his chin. "Damn, why has this thing surfaced?" He pushed the intercom button. "Debbie, have Captain Reed come back into my office."

"Yes, sir."

Soon the office door opened and Officer Reed entered. "Captain, I have something I would like you to do. I want you to check out a certain medical doctor in the Boise area by the name of Harrison Jordan."

"Harrison Jordan?"

"Yes, I want you to do it right away."

"Yes, sir." Reed turned to leave.

"Oh, one other thing, Captain." Reed turned back. "Check with the local law authorities in Boise and see if anything unusual has happened in that area in the past few days. Report back to me later this afternoon."

"Yes, sir." Officer Reed saluted and left the office.

General McFarland picked up the phone receiver and then replaced it. He was hesitant to place the call. He picked up the receiver again. He knew he had to. "Secure line." He then dialed the number.

"Yes," the voice answered on the other line.

"McFarland here. I need to speak with Michael."

"One moment please."

"Michael here."

"Michael, this is McFarland."

"McFarland, why are you calling me? You know the risk."

"I wouldn't if it wasn't most urgent. We need to meet."

"Meet, why?"

"The black ovary has surfaced."

"Where?"

"In the Boise, Idaho, area."

"Okay, meet me in the usual park downtown in two hours. Make sure you are not followed."

Debbie removed the small earphone from her ear and placed it back in her bra. She looked both ways to make sure she was alone. She picked up her own telephone receiver. "Secure line." She then placed the call.

"Yes?" a voice answered.

"Ben, it's me."

"Debbie, what is it?"

"McFarland and Michael are meeting at the park in two hours."

"About what?"

"I don't know."

"Okay, you be very careful."

"I will." She then hung up the phone receiver and returned to her typewriter.

McFarland's voice echoed over the intercom. "Debbie, I need a car."

"Yes, sir, I'll call the motor pool right now."

———◆———

General McFarland circled the park for the third time and then pulled to the curb. He nervously checked his rearview mirror and climbed out of the passenger side. He looked both ways down the deserted streets and then quickly disappeared among the park trees. Almost immediately a man in ragged clothes staggered toward him. McFarland could tell he was drunk. Disgusted, he brushed the wino aside.

The wino returned and reached out for McFarland's coat. "Hey you," he wino yelled.

McFarland scowled. He shoved the man to the ground a second time. "Don't touch me, you filthy louse."

A tall, slender, well-groomed bearded man stepped out from the bushes. "Why, Arthur, where's your Christian compassion?" The stranger reached down and picked up the fallen wino by the arms. He helped him to the nearby park bench. To the wino's delight, the man reached deep into his overcoat pocket and pulled out a half-empty wine bottle and handed it to him. The stranger smiled. "Drink, my friend," he advised. The wino quickly took the bottle and greedily quenched his driving thirst. The man then turned away and walked farther into the park. McFarland followed. "Now, General, see what a little kindness can do."

"That's not kindness. You're just making his problem worse."

"Drinking a problem?" Michael turned back toward the wino. "Well you never know when a person's drink might be their last. Anyway, why risk my exposure?"

McFarland shook his head at the wino. He then turned back. "I hate this part of town," he muttered. "I don't like meet—"

Michael grasped McFarland's coat lapels. He pulled him face-to-face. "General, waste not my time, for I do not care about what you like or do not like—understand?" McFarland nodded his head. Michael eased his grip. He dusted off the general's lapels. "Now, let us start again. Why do you risk my exposure?"

"Like I told you on the phone, the black ovaries may have surfaced."

Michael thought for a moment. "How do you know this?

"A Mr. Barnes from CDC called me today, about an inquiry from a doctor in Boise."

"CDC called you? What did they want?"

"Several years ago I placed a notice in their database to be contacted if anyone requested information on black ovaries. They were just responding to my request."

McFarland noticed the disturbed look on Michael's face. "Do you think the CDC is suspicious?"

McFarland shook his head. "No, they were just following my instructions."

Michael bit his lip and looked away. He then turned back to McFarland. "Why would this Boise Doctor want more information about black ovaries?"

"I don't know, but my staff is checking him out as we speak."

"Good. We need to know why this doctor is interested. Then we will know how to contain the situation."

"I am not sure something like this can be contained."

Michael chuckled. "Ah, you underestimate our power." Now a nearby public phone booth came into view. Neither saw the following wino crouch and hide in the nearby bushes. "Wait here while I speak with Matthias," Michael instructed.

"When you speak with Matthias, you tell him that I will not go down for this. This was not my screwup."

Michael turned back to the general. "What are you trying to say?"

"I'm saying my butt is sticking way out on this one. I'm not taking the blame."

"I am sure Matthias will be interested in what you said." He closed the phone booth door and dialed the number.

McFarland took a cigarette from the pack and lit it. He drew a deep breath, trying to ease as much tension as possible. He looked at Michael speaking on the phone and took another drag on his cigarette. He walked toward the hiding wino.

I better flee, the wino thought. *Any closer and he will see me.* He hesitated. *This damn leg. They may catch me if they follow.* He had no choice. He prepared to run.

"McFarland," a voice called from the phone booth. The wino relaxed as McFarland threw his cigarette in the wino's direction and turned away.

"Well, what did he say?"

"He already knew about the ovaries. He said the black ovaries have surfaced in three girls in the Boise area."

"Then this Dr. Jordan must know about these ovaries."

Michael nodded his head. "I believe so. I think that is why he contacted the CDC."

Nervously McFarland lit another cigarette. "I just don't understand. With all the precautions, how could something like this happen?"

"Matthias is looking into it. But there are some things he wants the army to do."

Now McFarland became suspicious. "Why do we need to be involved?"

The wino strained to hear Michael's instructions, but their voices were now muffled. He thought about moving closer and shook his head. "No, it is too risky," he murmured.

A loud voice caught the wino's attention. "This is insane," McFarland yelled. "Where am I going to find a Federal Judge to do that?" Again the voices became muffled. The wino watched McFarland pace back and forth. He could tell McFarland was unhappy with Michael's instructions. Angrily, McFarland stomped off in the direction of his car, while Michael left the opposite way. The wino chose to follow the general. "Those fools," McFarland murmured as he opened his car door and climbed in. "This is utter suicide for me. I will not go down for them." McFarland started his car and drove away.

The wino watched until he was gone. *I need to call headquarters*, he thought. He limped back to the public telephone both, and placed his call. Initially he spoke in Hebrew, but then changed to broken English. "They spoke of the black ovary."

"Stay close to the situation and keep me informed," the voice commanded. The wino hung up the phone and disappeared in the shadows.

———◈———

McFarland pushed the intercom button. "Yes, Debbie?"

"Captain Reed is here."

"Have him come in."

McFarland stood and met Reed at the door. He pointed to the chair in front of his desk. "Come in and sit down. Did you find out anything?"

"Yes, I did," Reed said as McFarland sat down behind his desk. "This Dr. Jordan is a general surgeon in Boise, and surprisingly he was in the news today."

"Why?"

"Apparently he is responsible for three girls found in the Sawtooth Mountains over the past twenty-four hours."

"What does that mean?"

"Well two of the young girls were found murdered in a cabin. The third one was stabbed but apparently lived. Dr. Jordan is in charge of the autopsies of the two dead girls, and he is also the doctor taking care of the third girl."

"Was there anything else mentioned?"

Reed reached into his notebook and pulled out a paper. "They do mention several other people in the news articles." He then handed him a copy of the article. McFarland took the time to read it before continuing. There were a couple names mentioned in the article that disturbed him.

McFarland looked up. "Captain Reed, we have a situation here of utmost importance."

"What is it, sir?"

"A situation of extreme national security. The mission I am assigning you is top secret. You will report only to me, understand?"

"Yes, sir."

"Good." McFarland stood and looked out his window overlooking the base. "Captain, I want you and your men to fly to Boise tonight."

"Tonight, sir?"

"Yes, tonight. I want you to go get those three girls and bring them back to the base."

"Bring them back here? But, sir, isn't this a local authority matter?"

"They will try to make it one. But no matter what, you do not leave Boise without those girls, understand?"

"Yes, sir."

"While I get one of the Federal Judges to sign the necessary legal papers, you get your men and plane ready to leave."

"Right away, sir."

Again Debbie placed her small earphone in her bra.

Unknown to Debbie, she was being watched on the security monitor. "There's our mole," Scarface said. Lenny agreed.

McFarland opened the office door. "Report to me when you get back."

"Yes, sir." Reed saluted and left the office.

McFarland again glanced over the newspaper article. *Jim Crockett and Indian*, McFarland thought. *I thought they were eliminated after their hearings.* McFarland buzzed the outer office.

"Sir?"

"Debbie, can you come in here for a moment?"

Debbie stood and entered the inner office. "Yes, General."

"I want you to pull two files for me. They are two former army intelligence operatives by the names of Jim Crockett and Indian."

"Indian—is that all?"

"No last name. I need them on my desk as soon as possible. Oh, one other thing. See if you can get Judge Simpson on the phone. I need to talk with him."

"Right away, sir."

General McFarland watched Debbie leave the office and rubbed a hand over his face.

Debbie went to her phone and placed a call. "Yes," the voice answered.

"Ben, it's me."

"What did you find out?"

"They're confiscating the bodies and taking the little girl."

"When?"

"Reed and his men are flying to Boise tonight."

"That's why McFarland was so angry in the park," Ben murmured. "Michael has ordered this. How is McFarland going to get by the local authorities?"

"I'm not sure. Maybe that why he's talking with a federal judge."

"Who?"

"His name is Simpson."

Judge Simpson, Ben thought. *Same judge involved with Indian and Crockett's convictions years ago.*

"Do you think he will get the bodies?"

"More than likely. He will just bully his way through."

"What are you going to do?"

Ben thought for a moment. "I'm flying to Boise tonight. I'll contact you when I get back. And, Debbie, good job."

Debbie smiled as they both hung up the phone.

CHAPTER EIGHT
THE DINNER

"**M**ay I be excused?"

"Sure, Jason," Julie answered. "Oh, your birthday present is in the basement on the bottom shelf."

Jason quickly turned to leave, and the others watched as he left the room. Julie looked at Doug. "I can't believe he's already ten years old."

Doug smiled. "Me neither."

Jason hurried through the kitchen to the basement door. He opened it and switched on the lights. "Let's see, the present on the bottom shelf." He started down the stairs but stopped short. "What was that?" he whispered. He took a few more steps and heard the noise again "Is someone there?" he spoke out loud. Now it was quiet. Cautiously he made his way to the back of the basement. He could see a figure crouched next to the old desk. "I see you, come out." Slowly a girl who looked about his age stood up. "What are you doing here?" Jason asked. She did not answer.

"Julie the food was excellent," Doug said. All the others agreed.

"Dr. Jordan, you are lucky to have such a beautiful woman and great cook for a wife."

"Why thank you, Indian." She turned to her husband. "Are you listening?"

Harrison reached for her hand and smiled. "Indian, I agree."

"By the way," Jim intervened, "how did you two meet?"

"Well, Jim, I met Julie over a penis."

Pepe choked on his food. Jim finally had to slap him on the back to clear his throat. "I'm sorry," Pepe gasped. "I must have misunderstood what you said."

Julie frowned at her husband. "You are so crude."

"I wasn't being crude. Penis describes an anatomical part of the body."

Pepe shook his head in disgust. "Boss does that all the time. What is it with you doctors anyway?"

"What do I do?" Doug asked.

"Come on, you always talk about body parts while I am eating. And I especially don't want to talk about that one."

Julie touched Pepe's arm. "I agree." She turned to Harrison. "I don't want you to tell that story."

Harrison put up his hands and relented. "Okay, I won't." He paused for a moment. "Instead let's have Doug tell the story of how he met Nicole."

Doug chuckled and ducked his head. "Come on," Julie objected, "that's not fair."

Harrison smiled too. "What do you mean it's not fair?"

"Because that's the exact same story."

All at the table now looked at Dr. Hunter, expecting him to say something. Doug shook his head. "I'm not saying anything unless Julie agrees."

Julie looked around the room at everyone now staring at her. She knew the others were interested. She took a deep breath and blew it out. She turned to her left side. "Pepe, what do you think?"

"Well, if it's okay with you, I would like to hear the story. I just want them to leave out the body parts."

Julie relented. "Okay, but only if Doug tells it. When my husband tells the story, he makes me sound like some kind of pervert."

Harrison shrugged his shoulders and elevated his hands as if to say, "You said it, not I."

"Okay, I promise I'll be delicate," Doug reassured.

"Thanks."

"It happened when Harrison and I were surgical residents in medical school. He volunteered me to help him teach the anatomy lab at the nursing school."

"Volunteered you? As I remember, you begged to help," Harrison corrected.

Doug smiled. "Anyway, Harrison always had his eye out for pretty ladies. It was the first day of class."

"Look at those two," Harrison whispered, elbowing Hunter in the ribs. "What do you think?"

"About what?"

"You know."

"You didn't set up that penis thing again, did you?"

Harrison smiled and winked. "I think those two would be perfect."

"Look, we're here to teach medicine, not hustle women."

"Relax, we can do both. Anyway, this should be fun."

Harrison interrupted the story. "I don't remember it happening that way."

"No, go on, Doug," Julie encouraged. "I've never heard this version before."

Doug smiled and continued. "We watched as the last of the class entered the anatomy laboratory. Harrison stood."

"Class, welcome to Anatomy Lab 201 refresher class. My name is Dr. Jordan, and this is my associate, Dr. Hunter." Doug stood and nodded to the class. His eyes caught the stare of one of the two girls Harrison pointed out previously. "We are surgical residents here at the medical school, and we will be teaching this nursing anatomy lab course." He took a few minutes to explain some of the expectations of the class. "Now before we dismiss you from orientation, we would like to introduce you to one other assistant. Would you please follow us?" Harrison and Doug led the small class of ten to the back of the room. One of the nurses grasped her nose. It caught Doug's attention. "Are you okay?"

"Oh, that formaldehyde smell always gives me a headache."

"Do you want me to get you an aspirin or something, Ms.?"

"Crockett," she answered. "Nicole Crockett."

"That was the first time I saw Nicole smile," Doug said. "You know how she could slightly curl her lip." The others could picture this in their minds. They knew that smile well.

Before them was the dissecting table. "This formaldehyde smell is closely related to the third member of our teaching team," Doug explained. He looked at Harrison. "Dr. Jordan, would you do the honors?"

Harrison approached the dissecting table. "Class, I would like to introduce you to the third member of our teaching team. We call him Joe." He stripped the overlying sheet from the naked man lying on the table. Some of the class gasped. After a moment of silence, Harrison went on to explain further. "We don't know his real name because he donated his body to the school."

"So now he's 'Joe,'" Doug added.

"Have any of you touched a dead body?" Harrison asked. No one spoke. "I know some of you may be a bit squeamish about being near a dead person, so I would like a volunteer to show the rest of the class how simple it is. He pointed his finger at Julie, the other girl he had been eyeing previously. "How about you?"

She touched her chest. "No, not me. Choose someone else."

"Go ahead, Julie," Nicole coaxed, "you'll be all right."

She was still hesitant. "Julie—is that your name?" Harrison asked.

"Murphy," Nicole answered for her. "Her name is Julie Murphy."

"Well, Nurse Murphy, in order to pass this class, all members will need to touch Joe's body many times. So come, I'll help you." Julie stepped forward. "Give me your hand." When she was reluctant, Harrison grasped it. He helped her first touch Joe's hair, then his forehead, and then down to his cheek. "See, Nurse Murphy, it's not that hard, is it?"

"No, it's not," she answered.

Harrison moved around to the backside of the table. Unnoticed by the rest of the class, he reached down behind the table and found his previously placed wire. "Now touch his arm, chest, abdomen." The class watched as she followed his instructions. Harrison looked at the remainder of the class. "See, there shouldn't be any fear among you with Joe. He looked back at Julie. "Nurse Murphy, you can skip Joe's groin region."

"Thank you," Julie exclaimed with relief.

"But go ahead and touch his thigh."

Doug paused telling the story. He looked around the room and smiled. Finally Pepe couldn't contain himself. "C'mon, boss, what happened next?"

"Well, when Julie touched Joe's thigh, Harrison started to move this hidden wire behind the table, and Joe's penis jumped up and down."

Jim, Indian, Pepe broke out in loud laughter. Even after the many times that Julie, Harrison, and Doug had heard and told the story, they themselves could not contain themselves either and joined in.

"Julie, as well as several other nurses in the class, started to scream," Harrison explained.

Doug nodded. "And then Harrison showed the class how a wire he previously threaded under the table to the base of Joe's penis caused the movement. All the class broke out in laughter."

"Except Julie," Harrison corrected.

"Yes, except Julie," Doug agreed. "I watched her clench her fists when she first saw the wire. When I saw this fire ignite in her eyes, I knew it was time for me to intervene. I said, 'Dr. Jordan, how could you embarrass Nurse Murphy like that?'"

"Intervene?" Harrison questioned. "You didn't intervene. You were on the floor laughing with me."

"Harrison, just let me finish the story. I then apologized to Julie for my colleague's disgusting behavior."

"Disgusting is right," Nurse Murphy looked at Harrison. "Dr. Jordan, you're a pervert."

"Enough of orientation," Doug said. "Class is dismissed for today. Remember to be here on Thursday at 9:00 a.m. sharp."

The two doctors sat and watched the class file out of the room.

"How did I do?" Harrison asked.

Doug shook his head. "Harrison, you are a sick puppy."

"Do you think Nurse Murphy is upset?"

"Oh yes. I'd say she's upset."

They watched as Julie and Nicole walked away. Nicole looked back at them and put her arm around Julie's shoulder. She whispered in her ear. Julie broke into laughter too.

"Doug."

"Yes?"

"I really like those two."

Doug smiled. "Yeah, me too."

Everyone was quiet. Finally Indian stood with glass in hand. "For that magnificent story, I would like to propose a toast to our hosts." All present raised their glasses. "To the beautiful Mrs. Jordan—for the good sport she is, for preparing this fine meal, and for allowing us to be in her home."

"Here, here," several present agreed as everyone gently chimed their glasses together. Jim slid away from the table. "Mrs. Jordan, why don't you sit and relax while Pepe and I do the dishes."

Pepe winced at the suggestion.

"Jim, that's kind, but it isn't necessary. You need to catch your plane soon."

"No, we have time," Indian reassured. Jason walked back into the dining room. "Jason, would you like to help clear the table?"

"Sure."

Pepe looked at Jason. "Well?"

Jason started gathering the silverware. "Well, what?"

Pepe stood and gathered some of the plates. "Where's the present?"

"Oh, I forgot to look."

Pepe followed Jason and Indian to the kitchen. "What do you mean, forgot to look? That's why you went down into the basement in the—" Pepe's voice faded behind the kitchen door.

Jim pulled out Julie's chair. He took her arm and guided her into the sitting room. Julie looked back at her husband, giving him a look that said "are you taking notes?" Harrison smiled at Doug. They followed the two into the sitting room. Jim escorted her to the soft lounge chair.

"Julie, would you like some coffee?"

"Why, yes, there's some fresh brewed in the kitchen." Jim smiled and left the room. Julie waved her hands. "Doug, they have been perfect gentlemen."

Doug winked at Harrison. "You mean the perverts?"

"Harrison, you told him what I said?"

Harrison chuckled. "Well I agree that they are behaving tonight," Doug said. "Listen, Julie, if that story embarrassed you, I apologize."

"No, I still laugh each time I hear it."

The tone in Doug's voice changed. "Julie, can I ask you something more serious?"

"Sure."

"When Nicole and I were together, was there another man in her life?"

Julie was surprised by his question. *Doug must have seen him,* she thought. "Why do you ask?"

"Well every so often I saw her speaking with this bearded long haired gentleman. I never did get close enough to see him well or meet him."

"Did you ever talk to Nicole about him?" she asked.

"Several times, but she always passed him off as an old acquaintance."

"And you didn't believe her?"

"Well I wanted to believe her, but their meetings happened so often."

Julie remained suspiciously quiet. Finally Harrison spoke. "Julie, do you know something?"

Julie shook her head. "Maybe it's better we just let this pass. You don't want to bring up things that happened years ago."

"Then there was someone?" Doug asked.

Again Julie was hesitant to explain. "Come on, Julie," Harrison coaxed, "was there another man?"

Julie relented. "Yes, there was. But not the way you think. I mean, she never was romantically involved with him."

"Then who was he?" Doug asked.

"I always called him Nicole's 'mystery man.'"

"Mystery man?"

"Yes, mystery man, because Nicole refused to talk to about him."

"Did you ever get to meet him?" Doug asked.

"Only once—handsome gentleman. His name was John."

"John who?" Harrison asked.

"She didn't say, and she never told me any more about him except for one thing. Something I didn't understand."

"What was that?" Doug asked.

Julie leaned forward and clasped her hands. "When she introduced him to me, she called him 'my friend and teacher.'"

"Teacher? Maybe he was a professor at the nursing school."

"Maybe so," Doug agreed.

"I'm sorry I don't know more."

"That's all right. You answered what I wanted to know most."

Julie smiled. "She was always faithful to you. She loved you very much." Julie wiped her moistened eyes. "I wish she was still here."

Doug winced when he saw Julie's tears. "I'm sorry I brought it up. Let's talk about something else." He turned to Harrison. "What were you saying earlier about the girl?"

"She just disappeared."

Julie shook her head. "Harrison, we just saw her a few hours ago. How could she just disappear like that?"

"I don't know. All I know is Nurse Cratch called me last night saying the girl was missing from her room, and she hadn't been able to find her."

"But she was so sedated. How could she have walked out there?"

"I don't think she did," Harrison replied. "I think someone took her."

Doug looked at them both. "I hope it isn't the same person that hurt her earlier."

"Something else happened earlier this evening," Harrison continued.

"What's that?" Doug asked.

"I received a call from a general in army intelligence at Dugway asking about this same girl."

Doug looked at Julie and Harrison. "Well that's a new twist. What did the army want to know?"

"He not only asked questions about the girl, but he wanted to know about the other two."

"Why would the army be interested in these girls?" Julie asked.

"I don't know, but when I told him the live girl was missing, he became extremely upset."

"Do you remember the general's name?"

"Yes it was a—"

"McFarland—was it General McFarland?"

Harrison looked toward the archway to see Jim enter the room. "Yes, it was this General McFarland. Do you know him?"

Jim approached with tray of coffee cups. "I knew him years ago in the intelligence community." He then allowed each of them to take a cup from the tray. "Don't cross him. He's a very dangerous man." Jim returned to the kitchen without saying more.

Doug took a sip of his coffee. "What did Sheriff Bates say?"

"I talked with him this afternoon. He said they didn't have any leads on the girl's whereabouts."

"What about the other two girls?" Julie asked.

"They're in the hospital morgue. Their autopsies are planned for the morning."

"What about the black ovaries?" Doug asked.

"Well the only article that I could find was written back in the 1940s. It was an article written by two German doctors. Apparently they reported this finding with some of the holocaust prisoners."

"Can you get me a copy?"

"Sure. CDC is sending a copy. Once I get it, I'll make you one." The three were quiet for a brief moment. Harrison took another sip of coffee. "Doug, do you think this may be some kind of racial thing?"

Doug watched Jim return through the kitchen door with the coffeepot. "It's interesting you said that, because Jim was thinking the same thing."

Jim filled Doug's cup again. "What thing is that?"

"That this may be some kind of racial hate crime."

"Why do you think that?" Julie asked.

"Well I didn't notice it until Lone Wolf pointed out that the three girls are of different races: African American, Asian, and Native American."

Pepe's muffled voice was now carrying from the kitchen. Doug whispered to Jim. "I hear some noise in the kitchen."

Jim shrugged his shoulders. "Oh, it's Pepe. I'll take care of it. Excuse me, Julie, but is there any more dishwasher soap? Pepe had an accident and spilled it."

"Yes, there's more on the middle shelf in the basement." Julie started to rise. "I'll get it for you."

Jason looked up quickly from gathering silverware from the table. "No, I'll get it," he said. He then raced toward the kitchen to drop off his load.

Pepe washed another dish and handed it to Indian. "It's women's work."

Jim placed more dirty dishes in the sink. "Pepe, washing a few dishes will not hurt us. They fed us a fine meal, and it's the least we can do."

"Yes, you're right." Pepe paused for a brief moment. "But it still doesn't make sense."

Indian placed another washed dish in the dishwater. "What's that?"

"Why do we have to wash the dishes before we put them in the dishwasher? I mean, if we are going to wash the dishes anyway, why do we need a dishwasher?"

Indian looked at Jim. "He has a good point."

"Yes, you're right. I have asked that same question myself."

Jason placed his load of dirty silverware on the countertop. "Uncle Jim, I know why. Aunt Edith told me."

Indian looked at Jason. "What did she say?"

"Well she said that when Pepe does the dishes, he doesn't get them clean."

"What do you mean I don't get them clean?"

"She says you don't get them clean because you're a lazy queer and don't wash the dishes before putting them in the dishwasher."

Indian snickered. Pepe pulled his hands from the water. "That's it. I'm not no queer, and I'm not washing these dishes."

"Jason, go downstairs and get the soap," Jim suggested, knowing that Jason was making matters worse. Jason was obedient and headed for the basement door. "Quiet down, Pepe," Jim commanded. "They can hear you out in the front room."

Indian moved around Pepe and placed his hands in the sink. "Here, I'll wash, and you put them in the dishwasher."

Pepe agreed and traded places with Indian. The room was quiet for a moment. "Indian, the three girls were about the same age, weren't they?"

"Yes, I'd say about nine or ten years old.

Pepe shook his head. "I wish I hadn't gone with you. I'll never be able to forget what we saw." The three remained quiet. Jim and Indian knew they would not forget either.

Jason again switched on the basement lights. "Girl, it's me," he whispered. He could make out her outline in the dim light. She then switched on a flashlight and Jason turned off the basement light. When he reached her, he handed her a sack. "Here, I brought you some food."

"Thanks." They both sat down on the floor next to a game board laid out with pieces set up on it. He watched her eat.

"My name is Jason."

She swallowed her first bite. "I am Sondra."

Jason nodded his head. "You know Sondra, you speak funny."

"So do you," she answered.

"I do? I speak like everyone else around here."

"Well I speak like people at my home in Africa."

"Africa, where's that?"

Sondra put down the sandwich and shrugged her shoulders. "I don't know."

"Well, are you ready?" Jason asked.

"Yes, I'm ready. I think it's your turn." They then focused their attention back to the game board.

CHAPTER NINE

CONFISCATION OF BODIES

Someone knocked at the office side door. McFarland pushed the button under his desk and the door opened. McFarland looked up to see men enter the office. "Okay, gentlemen, what's so urgent?"

"General, we have something you need to see." Lenny took the videotape from its case and placed in the nearby VCR. "We found this on one of the security monitors."

McFarland stood and circled around his desk until he stood next to them. "What is this?"

"A tape of one of your office employees," Lenny explained.

For a brief moment all three silently watched. McFarland was stunned. He looked at Scarface. "Debbie?"

Scarface grimaced. "I'm afraid so. The leak to the Jews is coming right from your very own office."

"Do you think it's the Mossad?"

"Pretty sure. We've seen her meet with one of their agents. That's when we started to monitor her activities."

McFarland turned away. "She's been with me for so many years."

Scarface removed the tape from the machine and placed it back in its case. "Those are the ones they turn." He handed the case to McFarland. "What do you want us to do?"

McFarland was slow to answer. "I think she should be eliminated," Lenny suggested.

McFarland now returned to the other side of his desk. He now sat down. "I think you're right. When do you leave for LA?"

"Tonight, but we'll be back tomorrow after the funeral."

General McFarland was quiet for a moment. Suddenly the intercom interrupted his thoughts. He reached over and pushed the intercom button. "Yes?"

"General, I have Judge Simpson on the line. Should I have him call back?"

"No, I'll take the call now." He looked up at Lenny and Scarface. "I want you to take care of her on your return."

Scarface nodded. "Yes, sir." They turned to leave.

"Oh, one other thing." Scarface turned around. "Give my love to Elaine," he added sarcastically. Scarface smiled, turned, and followed Lenny through the side door. Once the door closed McFarland picked up the telephone receiver. "Gary, it's been a while."

"Okay, McFarland, what do you want?"

"Now why do you think I want something? Maybe I called just to talk to an old friend."

"You're no friend, so just cut to the chase, and tell me what you want."

"Judge, if that is how you want it. We need a favor."

"What kind of favor?" McFarland went on to explain the need for the court order. Simpson laughed. "You got to be kidding. I'm not going to give you a federal court order. This is a local matter. You have no authority."

"Splitting hairs, Judge. When has that ever bothered you?"

"I resent that comment. I have always been a good judge."

"Right, like convicting those two innocent men."

"Look, that was years ago. You can't pin Crockett's and Indian's convictions on me."

"You were their sentencing army judge, weren't you?"

"I was only obeying orders."

"Obeying orders is right. And as thanks didn't we get you this judgeship?" Simpson did not answer. "Gary, let me make this perfectly clear. This isn't a simple request. This is an order."

"I'm not in your army anymore, and you can't order me."

McFarland smiled. "You honor me to think that this is my order. This order is from Michael."

"What? But this is sheer madness. It could cost me my judge-ship."

"Don't bother me with those trivial matters. Just tell me how long it will take to prepare the order." Judge Simpson was silent. "Judge, did you hear me? How long?"

"You can pick it up in an hour."

"Thank you, Gary." McFarland smirked. "It's always a pleasure to have you on my side." Both hung up their telephone receivers.

Pepe finally broke the silence. "Indian, about last night…what happened, you know, when I saw the woman and the wolves. Why couldn't you and Jim see them?"

"Maybe you didn't really see them."

"C'mon, then why put that knife blade to my neck." Indian did not answer but kept washing the dishes. "You know I'm right."

"Look, I think it's because they have this ability to bend space. That's why we didn't see them."

"Bend space—what's that?"

"It means that somehow they have learned to use space to not only hide themselves when they want, but to be able to move from one place to another without being seen."

Pepe took another plate from Indian and placed it in the dishwasher. "Up at the cabin Lone Wolf mentioned these Spuds or Spuders something."

"Sprudiths."

"Yeah, Sprudiths. What's a Sprudith?"

"Sprudith is actually a Native American word. It refers to a race of ancient, mystical evil people who lived here many years ago."

Jim came back into the kitchen. He handed Indian another set of dishes to place in the sink.

"Ancient, mystical people—what do you mean?" Pepe asked.

"The legends say the Sprudiths worship and serve a master known by different names in different lands and cultures. In our land we know him as Satan, or Lucifer."

"You mean the biblical devil?" Pepe asked.

Indian nodded his head. "Hey, guys," a voice called from the swinging door, "about finished?"

"Last dish, Doc," Indian explained.

"Good, we need to leave for the airport. Where's Jason?"

"He's been gone for some time." Pepe walked over and opened the basement door. He listened for a brief moment. "Jason, you down there?"

"Yes, I'm here."

"Well come on, we're leaving."

Jason scurried up the steps. Pepe was waiting at the top. "I heard voices, who were you talking to?"

"No one."

Seeing his father, Jason rushed by Pepe. "Wait a minute, where is it?" Pepe asked.

Jason stopped and turned. "Where's what?"

"The soap."

"Oh, I forgot it." Jason turned and continued toward his father.

"You forgot it?" Pepe shook his head. "First you forget your birthday present and now the dish soap. What's wrong with you?"

"There's nothing wrong with me, I just forgot."

Doug turned and motioned all to follow. "Well, we need to go."

Jason touched his father's arm. "Dad, I need to tell you something about the basement."

"Not now, Son, there isn't time." He hugged his son and said good-bye. "Now you mind Harrison and Julie. Aunt Edith will pick you up in a few days. I'll call you later tonight."

Harrison handed Doug a small case. "What's this?"

"These are tissue samples and slides from the two dead girls. Off the record, see what our doctor friends in Phoenix think."

Doug nodded and took the case. "I'll put them with the live girl's slides."

"Good. Well I guess we'll see you when you get back, and don't worry about Jason."

They all said good-bye as a group, loaded into the van, and left for the airport. When the vehicle was out of sight, Jason raced back into the house. "Where you going in such a hurry?" Julie asked.

Jason turned toward the two. "Oh, ah, I forgot the dish soap and my birthday present in the basement."

Julie nodded and watched Jason enter the kitchen. Harrison closed the front door and followed his wife into the living room. "Harrison, they were so cordial. You know, Pepe didn't say one thing about my body."

Harrison smiled and placed his arm around her waist. "Disappointed?"

"Of course not."

"I'm sure he was told to be on his best behavior." Just then the telephone rang. "Julie, would you get that, please?"

"Sure." She took off her earring and placed the receiver to her ear. "Hello." Julie paused. "Just a minute, I'll get him for you. Harrison, it's the hospital." She handed the phone to her husband.

"Hello." Harrison was silent. His emotion built as he listened to the message. "The hell they will," Harrison yelled. "Don't let them go until I get there, understand?" Harrison slammed the phone receiver down, grabbed his jacket, and raced through the front door. "Julie, I have to go to the hospital." The front door slammed before Julie could say anything.

She heard his car tires peel on the pavement road. "What's with him?" Julie whispered aloud. She turned and entered the kitchen. *It's so clean*, she thought to herself until she found one ugly dirty pan still hidden in the oven. She took the pan over to the sink. "Soap's empty," she murmured. She walked over to the basement door. "Jason, did you find the dishwasher soap?"

"There isn't any," he answered.

"Listen, will you be okay while I run and get some?"

Jason ran up the stairs. "Yes, I'll be fine.

Julie put on her jacket out of the hall closet. "I'll only be a few minutes."

Jason watched. Once she was gone, he returned to the basement.

⇒◆⇐

Harrison raced through the sliding doors of the autopsy room only to see the room filled with army personnel. "You have no rights here," Sheriff Bates yelled at the officer in charge. "This is Ada County jurisdiction. The bodies stay here until we finish the autopsies."

"Sheriff, I've heard enough. Just find that girl," the officer in charge commanded. He then turned to help his men.

"Sheriff," Harrison called from across the room. "What are they doing?"

"These federal jackasses think they can do whatever they want."

"What do you mean?" He watched four army men placing the two dead girls in body bags and pushing the carts toward the doors.

"They're taking the girls bodies, pathological slides, and anything else they can find pertaining to them."

"The hell they are," Harrison replied. He raced to the front of the body bags. "You're not taking these bodies anywhere. I'm Dr. Jordan, and I am responsible for these bodies."

The enlisted men stopped short. "Not anymore," a voice from behind the enlisted men answered. Captain Reed stepped forward with the paper. "We have a court order signed by a federal judge."

"But why?"

"National security, Doctor."

"National security, my butt. This court order is illegal." Harrison threw the court order to the floor. "Sheriff, isn't there anything you can do?"

"I'm working on it." Sheriff Bates followed the orderly, who pushed the supply cart to its usual location near the office desk. Although the orderly's limp was impressive, Sheriff Bates paid little attention. "May I use your phone?"

The orderly turned. "Sure, it's there on the desk."

Sheriff Bates picked up the receiver and dialed the number. He didn't seem to mind the orderly sitting down at the desk and listening. "Hello, Margaret, what did the attorney general say? Uh huh…yeah… you're kidding. Okay. Thanks, Margaret."

"Sheriff," Officer Reed yelled from across the room, "you get this doctor out of the way or we will."

"Don't threaten us, Son," the sheriff replied.

"Come on, Sheriff," one of his deputies exclaimed, "let me kick the crap out of this guy."

"Easy, Phil," the sheriff cautioned. "They have a signed court order and there isn't anything we can do." Bates walked over to Jordan. "Come on, Doc."

He pulled Harrison to the side. They watched the bodies pass through the double doors. "But how can they?"

"Because our attorney general has no balls. He also said it's a matter of national security."

"What do two little girls have to do with our nation's security?"

Bates put up his hands. "It doesn't make sense to me either." Bates walked over to Officer Reed. "Captain, where are you taking them?"

"Base at Dugway."

"And who's your commanding officer?"

"That would be General McFarland."

"I should have known," Harrison commented.

Bates overheard Dr. Jordan's comment. He turned to him. "What do you mean?"

"This McFarland guy called me earlier this evening. He had some questions about the girls."

Dr. Jordan, Sheriff Bates, and his officers watched as the army put the bodies in back of one of the army vehicles. Bates crossed over to the hall window. He watched the vehicles leave the hospital parking lot. "Phil, get me Crockett and Indian on the phone. Maybe they can help us find out what the hell is going on."

"What, Jim Crockett and Indian?" Harrison asked.

"Yes, you know them?"

"I do, but they're out of town."

"Do you know where they are?"

"I don't know where they are staying, but I do know they are attending a funeral in LA tomorrow."

"Do you know how I can contact them?"

"They are going to call tonight."

"Good. Have them contact me when they call you. He then turned back to the window. He watched as the last army vehicle left the parking lot. "Mark my words, Doc—the army's not going to get away with this."

The orderly picked up the phone and dialed. He looked around, but no one paid any attention to him. Someone answered. The orderly spoke in Hebrew.

"Ben, speak in English," the other voice ordered. "You know I have trouble with your Hebrew."

"Okay, Debbie, I'm sorry."

"You say they have the girls?"

"Except for the one that survived. They haven't found her."

"What will they do with them?"

"McFarland will destroy them. He can't risk further investigation."

"What do you want me to do?" Debbie asked.

"Contact headquarters and inform them what has happened."

"And then?"

"Just keep your ears open. I going to stay for a day and try to locate the missing girl."

"Okay, but be careful."

"I will." Ben hung up the phone. He stood, and quietly left the hospital unnoticed by all.

CHAPTER TEN

THE CAVE

The night was cold and clear. She could see the moonlight reflecting off the bats flying through the cave's entrance. Even though they were smaller than those from her homeland, all bats were frightening. She tried to shelter herself closer to Cerce, but the cold had already settled in her joints, making it hard to move. *It will be daylight soon,* she thought. *How fortunate we were to find this cave.* The desert here was like that of her homeland. It amazed her that a few hours earlier, there was blistering heat. Now it was so cold. They thought of building a fire earlier, but knew it was too dangerous. Tears flowed from her already swollen eyes as she again went over the previous day's events. *How could we have left her?* she thought. Quietly she began to sob. Cerce awoke.

He brushed the tears from her eyes and wrapped his arms around her. "Sondra could not have made this journey."

Cresta sought comfort in his words, but it still did not ease the heartache. It seemed like an eternity since she left Africa. Father warned her about the evil, but she was deceived. Now they were running for their lives, "What do we do now?"

Cerce was also uncertain. "Perhaps we should return to Africa where it is safe."

Cresta closed her eyes tight. She knew it would never be safe again.

"Look," Cerce nodded toward the east. "The sky turns gray. We should leave soon."

Slowly they got to their feet. They peered down into the valley below. "There are no campfires. Maybe they are not following us."

Cerce bit his lip. "No, they're following. We know too much to let us live." Cerce searched the surrounding walls. "Where should we go first?" he murmured.

"Maybe to the mountain people," Cresta suggested.

"But they are our enemies, why would they help us?"

"They saved Sondra's life," Cresta reminded.

Cerce nodded his head. "That's true. Maybe we could ask for mercy."

"But how do we find them?"

"First we get to the mountains and pray they be close by." Cerce motioned for Cresta to follow him. Slowly they crawled to the rock crevice located in front of them. Now they could see the ravine below. "Look, there is movement below in the bushes about a hundred yards down the ravine." Cresta peered through the early morning darkness. Now she could see the wolfmen and wolves following their trail. "We can't escape the way we came." Cerce again looked at the steep walls that surrounded them. "If we could scale that wall, then maybe we can circle back around them. Come." Cerce led the way as they crawled toward the canyon wall. Cerce turned. "Listen, as soon as we start to climb, they will see us. We will have only a few minutes to reach the mesa, understand?" Cresta nodded her head yes. "I will go first." He started up the wall with Cresta following.

Micah held his hand up to quiet the clan. "Listen," he whispered. Rocks trickled down the canyon wall. Micah searched the surrounding walls. "There," he exclaimed pointing to the two figures. "Get them." The wolfmen and wolves raced up the ravine and hill toward the couple.

Cerce climbed the wall rapidly. As he neared the mesa he looked back. Cresta was slower. "Hurry, Cresta, they are coming." Cresta saw the wolves and men rapidly approaching. She knew she would not make it. He climbed back down toward her.

"No, Cerce, go."

He ignored her. Shortly he arrived at her side. Now the wolves were closer. They knew there wasn't time to climb. Cerce could see the fear in her eyes, but his smile was reassuring. He took his free hand, and caressed her face. "Whether we live or die, I promise we will find each other." She smiled back. Cerce drew his knife and motioned to her. "Now stand behind me." They watched as their death approached. Suddenly someone dropped rope from above.

Cresta looked up. "There's someone on the mesa."

"Grab the rope," the figure yelled.

Cerce quickly wrapped the rope around Cresta's waist. "Hold on," Cerce commanded. The rope began to move only split seconds before the wolves arrived. Cresta turned her head. She could not watch as the pack of wolves attacked Cerce.

"To the top," she heard Micah command. "Do not let her escape."

The old man was waiting for her when she reached the mesa. She looked into his face. "Who are you?" she asked.

"No time to talk. Already the wolves come. We must hurry."

"What about Cerce?"

The old man shook his head. "I'm sorry, there's nothing we can do." Cresta could feel her legs buckle. She wanted to just kneel and cry. The old man caught her in the fall. He helped her onto the nearby horse and handed her the reins. "Follow me close," he commanded as he mounted his horse. "They will be coming." The two rode the horses like the wind. Upon reaching the first ridge, the old man pulled his horse to a halt. He peered back down into the valley. Cresta followed suit.

"There," the old man said pointing with his finger.

Cresta looked at the old man. "You can see them?"

"Yes, they are right behind us."

Cresta did not understand. "But, old man, how is that possible? No one can see them when they bend space, unless—" Cresta paused. "Are you—?"

"No," the old man interrupted. "I am not him." The old man again looked into the valley. "Come, we must reach the mountains." He once again reined his horse, and Cresta was close behind. Cerce already sacrificed his life for her, and she knew if she was to stay alive, she'd have to depend on this stranger's guidance. By this time both horses were lathered, and the old man knew they would not last much longer. As they crossed the small creek, they pulled their horses to a stop at the base of the mountain and waited.

———❖———

"Okay, Sheriff. We'll keep in contact." Indian returned the phone receiver, grabbed his jacket, and raced out the motel door."

The sky was overcast, with a light cover of rain. Indian quickly crawled into the backseat. "Indian, we're going to be late," Pepe said. "What took so long?"

"Sheriff Bates—he wouldn't stop talking."

Jim pulled the car away from the curb. "Great, we're all the way down here in Los Angeles, and he still finds us. How does he do it?"

Indian leaned his arms on the back of the front seat and studied Pepe from head to toe. "Hey, really nice threads," he teased.

Jim turned to hide his smile. Pepe frowned. "Cut it out Indian. You ought to be doing this, not me."

"I can't," Indian explained. "People may recognize me."

Jim checked the oncoming traffic. He entered the Santa Monica Freeway on-ramp. "What did Sheriff Bates want anyway?"

"He has a job for us."

Jimmy pointed to the sign. "Pepe, is this our exit?"

Pepe looked at the address slip. "No, it's farther down. Don't worry, I'll let you know when we get there."

"What's does Bates want us to do now?" Jim asked.

"You're not going to believe this, but the two girls we found yesterday in the cabin, well last night the army confiscated their bodies."

Jim was surprised by the news. "What for?"

"That's what Bates wants to know."

"But the army can't do that, can they?" Pepe asked.

"I guess they can," Indian replied. "To quote Bates's words, 'if you have a bigger army, you can.' He also said they had a federal court order from our old friend, Judge Simpson."

"Judge Simpson. I might have known," Jim murmured. "

"Who's this Judge Simpson?" Pepe asked.

"He was the army judge who had us removed from army intelligence," Jim explained. Jim looked at Indian. "Why would the army want those girls' bodies?"

Indian shook his head. "I don't know. Bates tried to get the state's Attorney General's office involved, but they wouldn't stop them either. Something to do with national security."

"National security, my butt," Jim responded. "They always say that crap when they're hiding something."

"Well, that's our job. Bates wants us to find out why the army took those girls' bodies."

Pepe pointed at the freeway sign. "Oh, here's the turnoff." Jim immediately moved to the right and onto the freeway exit. "Up here take a left." Jim stopped the vehicle at the stop sign and turned left.

"Did he know where they took the bodies?" Jim asked.

"Dugway," Indian answered.

"Oh great, I think McFarland's the general there."

"Are you sure?"

"Last night Dr. Jordan told me he just talked to a General McFarland at Dugway. The Doc said he had a lot of questions about the dead girls."

"Here's the place," Pepe said.

Jim pulled the car to the curb. He and Pepe climbed out of the car. Indian rolled down the window. "Jim, the funeral is going to start shortly."

"The cemetery is not far. I won't be long."

"Hey, Pepe, you're looking real sharp."

Pepe scowled at Indian. Indian chuckled and rolled up the window. He watched Pepe and Jim cross the street and walk through the entrance leading into the grounds. Pepe read aloud "The Whispering Pines Mental Hospital." He stared at the tall, stone wall fence completely surrounding the grounds. "Jimmy, I don't know about this. I don't think this is going to work."

"Sure it will." He then grabbed his arm and led him through the iron-rod gate down the one-lane road leading to the main building.

Pepe followed reluctantly. "I don't know why Indian couldn't be the crazy one."

"Like we told you before, someone might recognize him."

Pepe demonstrated himself with his hands. "But look at these clothes."

Jim gazed at what Pepe was wearing. "I picked them out myself. What's wrong with them?"

"Brown bell-bottom checkered pants, green corduroy sports jacket, and cowboy boots. I look like a Mexican cowboy hippie."

"Look, we need to make you look convincing."

Pepe again gestured to his clothes. "But not this convincing. Even real crazies wouldn't wear these clothes."

Jim stopped at the entrance double door. He turned Pepe toward him. "Listen, you wanted to be a private eye, didn't you?"

"Well yes, but—"

"But what?" Jim interrupted. Jim brushed off Pepe's sports coat with his hand. "They may recognize Indian or me. It has to be you. We think someone killed David, and we need to know who and why."

"Only one day, right?"

"Only one day. They'll run a few tests, interview you, and I'll pick you up tomorrow."

Pepe took a deep breath and blew it out. He reluctantly agreed. "Okay, let's do it." Jim held the door for Pepe and they both entered the main lobby.

"If you can't get his file, then at least talk to the staff and other patients. Find out as much as you can."

Pepe nodded his head. "I will. Now how do I convince them I'm crazy?"

"Don't worry about that, just act yourself."

"Oh, that's real funny."

The two approached the information desk. "Excuse me, ma'am, we have an appointment with Dr. Damion at 10:00 a.m."

The receptionist pointed to their left. "Have a seat over there in the waiting room, and I'll inform him you are here."

Jim and Pepe took seats. Jim immediately noticed a man dressed in a long flowing robe sitting across from them. Jim smiled and nodded. The man smiled and nodded back. Jim then turned to Pepe. "Oh, do you have the cemetery's address."

Pepe reached in his pocket and pulled out a folded sheet of paper and handed it to Jim. "Here's the address."

"Thanks. What's this other address, here near the bottom?"

"Indian wrote it down. It's Elaine's, in case you two miss her at the funeral." Jim looked up at Pepe, but did not say anything. "Jimmy, what's the deal with this Elaine?"

"Well, several years ago Elaine and I were engaged."

"Engaged? You never told me that. What happened?"

Jim smiled. "There isn't time. Someone's coming."

A lovely nurse approached. "Are you Mr. Crockett, who called earlier this morning?"

"Yes, I am."

"So this must be Pepe Santana."

Pepe was speechless. He couldn't take his eyes off of her. Jim smiled and answered for Pepe. "Yes, it is."

She took Pepe by the hand and led him down the hall. "Oh, nice clothes, Mr. Santana. Please, come with me. We've been expecting you."

"Do you need me?" Jim asked.

The nurse turned back. "That won't be necessary, Mr. Crockett. He'll be fine."

Jim turned toward the entrance. He failed to notice the man in the long flowing robe observing him and Pepe from a distance. Once Jim left, the man followed the nurse and Pepe down the hall.

⇒•◇•⇐

The old man and Cresta could sense their presence. "They are already ahead of us, aren't they?" she asked. The old man looked at Cresta and nodded his head. Just like magic, the wolves and wolfmen appeared before them.

Cresta attempted to turn her horse away, but the old man grabbed her reins. "There isn't time. We can't outrun them."

They watched wolves and men approach. Finally their leader lifted his arm for them to halt. He left the group and approached alone. He looked at Cresta. "Where's the girl?" Cresta did not answer. "Cerce, my best man, is dead because of you." Cresta bowed her head at the news. "No need to mourn, for soon you will join him."

"Hello, Micah," the old man interrupted.

Cresta looked up at him in surprise. How did he know Micah?

Micah turned to the old man. Slowly he smiled. "Lone Wolf, it's been so long I didn't recognize you."

Cresta looked at the old man. "You are Lone Wolf, the legend?"

Lone Wolf did not answer, but turned back to the Sprudiths. "Micah, you and your men block our way."

Micah chuckled. "You harbor one of our own. Give her to us freely, and your death will be quick."

"It appears she no longer desires to be with you."

"It's not her choice. Give her to us freely, and I promise you a speedy death."

Lone Wolf motioned to the land area around him. "You and your men need to leave. This ground is holy, and you trespass."

Micah laughed at the suggestion. "I should have killed you and your grandson long ago." He raised his hand to instruct the wolves and men to attack.

"Do you not feel it?" Lone Wolf interrupted. Micah stopped. He now looked around him. "Can you not see them? Do you not hear their roar?" Micah lowered his hand. The wolves behind him began to growl.

"Micah fears," Cresta whispered, "but what?"

"The mountain people," Lone Wolf answered.

"But, I do not see them."

"Neither does Micah, but he feels their presence."

Suddenly the woman appeared, barefoot and dressed in brilliant white.

"Is she an angel?" Cresta whispered.

"Almost," Lone Wolf answered. "She's one of the mountain people."

She signaled with her hands and two large white tigers appeared at her side.

Micah, the wolves, and wolfmen began their retreat. "You have only managed to extend your lives a little longer," Micah yelled to them. "There'll be another place and time." Just as quick as they came, Micah and his clan bent space and were gone.

Lone Wolf approached the tigers and their lady. He bowed his head. "My lady."

"Hello, Lone Wolf." She nodded her head toward Cresta. "Who is she?"

"She's a Sprudith seeking asylum with the mountain people."

The lady studied Cresta from a distance for a brief moment. "I see her heart still has goodness."

"I agree, my lady."

"She is welcome to reside with us, but speak with her first, for she may harbor information you need. I will be back for her this evening."

"Yes, my lady."

She reached and touched his cheek. "How is the battle?"

"We will win, my lady, for we have mighty warriors with great faith."

"I know. And my husband and son?"

"They are the mightiest of all," Lone Wolf answered. "They just don't know it yet."

She embraced Lone Wolf, drew back, and smiled. "Take good care of them."

Lone Wolf nodded. "I will."

In an instant the woman and the white tigers were gone.

Lone Wolf turned to Cresta. "The lady?" Cresta asked.

"She is my friend."

"But she did not take me with her. Have the mountain people rejected my asylum?"

"She sees good in your heart. Whatever evil you have done in the past is forgotten. We will water and rest the horses now. She will be back for you this evening."

"What if Micah comes back?"

"As long as we stay on holy ground, he will not bother us." Lone Wolf loosened the saddle cinches and led the horses to the creek to drink. Lone Wolf removed a sack of trail mix from his saddlebag. "Sit and rest. I know you have not eaten for two days."

"How do you know this?"

Lone Wolf handed her the bag. "Because I have been following you."

Following me? she thought. Cresta looked up into Lone Wolf's eyes. *Does he know about Sondra?*

"Micah called you Cresta?"

"Yes, that is my name."

"And the young man that was with you?"

"Cerce," she said sadly. "His name is Cerce."

"Was he your husband?"

"No, but he was a very dear friend."

"I'm sorry I could not save him." Cresta did not answer. "But what he did was noble."

"Noble?"

"To give your life for a friend is a most noble act. I honor this man you call Cerce."

"Thank you."

"You have a heavy accent. Where are you from?"

"Central Africa."

"Africa. I've always wanted to visit. I'll bet it's beautiful." Lone Wolf paused and smiled. "This is so different for me."

"What do you mean?"

"Well I've never socialized with a Sprudith."

"Sprudith? What's a Sprudith?"

"Well you are."

Cresta had a puzzled look on her face. "I'm afraid I don't know this term. What does this mean?"

"In our language the followers of Tess, Micah, Matthias, and Niac are called Sprudiths."

"Oh, now I understand," Cresta said. "In Africa Sprudiths are called Testantes."

"I'm curious. We have not seen Sprudiths in this land for many years. Why are you here, now?"

"I do not know. Initially we thought it was to harvest ovaries, but Tess and Micah speak in riddles that we do not understand."

"Riddles?"

"Yes, they use phrases like 'the chosen one,' 'the Levite,' 'the heir.' We do not know what they mean."

"Why do they want the ovaries?"

"I'm not sure. All I know is that they inject girls with something when they are babies. Then later as the girls grow, they remove their ovaries."

"Have they done this before?"

"Many times, especially in Africa. I think they study them or something, except this time it was different. This time not only did they take their ovaries, but they also killed the children."

Lone Wolf looked down at Cresta's feet. She was wearing moccasins. It was her tracks he found near the cabin. "You are the one who freed the girl, aren't you?"

Cresta marveled. "How do you know of these things?"

"I was the one who found the other two girls in the cabin. I watched you carry the third girl from the hospital to the Jordans."

"Her name is Sondra."

"Okay, Sondra—but why the Jordans?" Cresta did not speak. Lone Wolf had other questions for her, but knew there would be another time. He nodded toward the horses. "They appear to be rested. I think it's time we leave."

They gathered the horses' reins and tightened their cinches. "Lone Wolf, how is it you can see them?"

"See them?"

"You know, when they bend space?"

"It is a gift."

"Then are you the loved one?"

"No, but the loved one is my friend. Many years ago, he gave me the gift to see." They climbed on their horses. "Come, the Mountain People will be waiting."

CHAPTER ELEVEN

THE FUNERAL

"Only four people attending the funeral," she whispered. "Where are all of David's friends?" She looked across the top of the casket at Scarface and Lenny staring at her. *What are they doing here?* Scarface smiled, and she immediately looked away. *They are probably the ones who killed him.*

"Amen." The Minister closed the bible. No sooner had the funeral started than it was over. The Minister expressed his condolences to Elaine, turned, and left. Scarface approached and spoke. "I'm sorry about David."

"Yeah, right," Elaine replied sarcastically.

Scarface looked around the cemetery. "Where are David's friends?" Elaine did not answer. Scarface grimaced and shook his head. "Pity—didn't leave much of a legacy, did he?" Scarface's words hurt, for she had thought the same. "After all that David did for his country, this is all the thanks he gets. A real tragedy. What a waste of life."

Elaine could not remain silent. "You're not welcome here. Why don't you just leave?"

Scarface smiled. "Oh, we will, just as soon as you tell us what we want to know."

"Like I told you before, I don't know anything."

"Mrs. Smith," a voice from behind said, "will there be anything else?" Elaine turned. "Reverend, can you stay with me until these two men leave?"

"That won't be necessary," Scarface said. "We were just leaving."

Elaine and the minister watched Scarface and his partner walk to their car and drive away. They failed to notice the same car stop a short distance away. "Mrs. Smith, is there anything else I can do for you?"

"No, Reverend, that will be all. Thank you." He shook her hand, dismissed himself, and left.

Elaine could hear the waves pounding against the ocean cliffs. She walked the distance toward the sound. "It must be high tide," she murmured. She took no thought to protect herself from the light drizzle that began. She peered over the edge of the cliffs at the waves pounding against the cliffs. *What if I jumped*, she thought. She looked around to see if anyone was watching. *No one would miss me.* Closer she crept to the edge. *It would be so easy to slip, and all my pain and sorrow would be over.* There she stood silhouetted against the overcast sky.

———⊰◈⊱———

Tess stopped short as the bedroom door opened. Mira stepped into the hall only to have Matthias grab her once again and pull her back into his embrace. Their kiss was long and passionate. Finally Mira broke the embrace. "You were marvelous," Matthias whispered.

Mira tried to break free. "Please, master, Lady Tess will be here soon."

"She will not care."

"But I care." She now pulled away. Tess watched as she walked down the hall in the opposite direction and disappeared around the corner.

Tess knocked on the bedroom door. The door swung open. "Mira, I knew you couldn't keep away—" Matthias interrupted himself. Tess chuckled. "Oh, it's you," Matthias exclaimed. He turned and walked back into his elegant master bedroom.

Tess closed the door behind her. "Sorry to disappoint you. Apparently you were expecting someone else. Mira perhaps?"

Matthias chuckled. He approached the wet bar and poured two drinks. "Then you saw her leave?"

"Yes, I did. How long has this been going on?"

He handed one of the drinks to Tess. "Since she came."

"But she is so young."

"Yes, I know. That's what makes it so great." Now Matthias could see a hint of disapproval on Tess's face. "Come on, Tess, over the years you have been with many young men, so don't give me any of this morality crap. We agreed long ago we could be with others, remember?"

"Yes, I remember, but that's not why I'm here."

Matthias smiled and put his drink on the table. He put his arms around Tess and started kissing her neck. "I know why you are here."

She lifted his arms from her neck. Tess smiled. "There isn't time."

"What do you mean? What's wrong?"

"The third girl—she escaped."

Matthias grasped his glass tight. "How could this have happened?"

"We were betrayed. Someone took her from the hospital."

"Who was it?" he demanded. Tess was hesitant to answer.

Matthias noticed her silence. "Tell me, who would be so stupid and bold to betray us?"

"It was Cresta."

Puzzled, he looked at Tess. "Cresta…are you sure?"

"Yes, love. Micah is absolutely positive."

Matthias walked the distance of the bedroom in silence. He turned. "Has she been eliminated?"

"No, I wanted to ask you first. I know how you feel about her."

Matthias grimaced, "We need to make her an example for the others."

"You mean kill her?"

"No, it needs to be more than that. Find and bring her to me."

Tess nodded. She quickly left the room.

———✦———

The driver pulled his revolver from his holster. "Okay, she's alone now."

Scarface leaned over and placed his hand on the gun. "We won't need guns."

"What do you mean?" Lenny asked.

"Well, just suppose she fell off the cliffs into the ocean."

"You mean, look like a suicide."

"Yes, the mourning widow who took her life."

Lenny replaced the gun in his shoulder holster. "But don't you think she knows something?"

"I doubt it. David was too smart. He wouldn't put her life in danger by telling her anything important."

"But how can you be so sure?"

He looked at Lenny and smiled. "Because I know both of them so well."

Lenny opened his door. "Well, let's do it."

"Wait," Scarface interrupted. He nodded his head toward the gravesite. "Someone's coming."

Lenny noticed the car approaching and closed the car door. The car came to a stop. Jim and Indian climbed out of the car.

"Well, look who's here," Scarface snickered. "I can hardly believe my eyes."

"Do you know them?"

Scarface smiled. "Oh, yes." He rubbed the reminding scar on his face. "Old acquaintances of mine."

"This is a waste of our time," Lenny said. He reached to start the car.

"No, wait. This may work out better than expected." They both slumped down in their seats and watched.

Indian shut his car door. "So Pepe's not happy?"

Jim shut his door too. "Not at all."

"Don't worry, Jim, I'll be in there with him tonight."

"We need to find out what happened to Solomon, quickly. You two should not stay more than one day, or someone may become suspicious."

"I'll bet his file is gone. They would be sloppy if it was still there."

"Probably so, but I hope someone in the hospital may know something."

"If that's the case, we'll find out." Even though the rain had nearly stopped, Indian handed Jim the extra umbrella. "I don't see anyone."

Jim looked in all directions. "I don't either. Do you think we missed it altogether?"

Indian looked at his watch. "We're not that late. Maybe the funeral was a different time."

Jim pointed to the right. "There's a casket over here."

They walked through the tombstone maze to the freshly dug grave. Although the black sedan was some distance away and partially hidden, it did not escape Indian's cautious eye. Both gazed silently at the casket. Jim ran his hand over the carvings. "Hello, Solomon," he whispered. Silently they stared. For so many years the four had been inseparable, facing death many times. Now one of their intelligence team was gone. Only the distant sound of ocean waves pounding the rocks interrupted the silence.

Indian gazed out at the ocean vastness. "I think Solomon would like this place."

Jim smiled. "Elaine picked it out."

"Think so?"

Jim nodded. "Yes, she really loves the ocean."

"I didn't know that."

"She even wrote about it."

"Elaine wrote?"

"Mostly poetry."

Indian once again glanced at the distant sedan. " I didn't know that."

"She was really self conscious about it and never told anyone."

"She told you."

Jim looked up and smiled. "Yes, she did." They were both silent for a few seconds. "There was this one ocean poem that was my favorite." Jim closed his eyes and raised his head trying to remember. "What was that one particular line?" Slowly the words came to his memory. "Where water and land do collide—"

"Bury my love and I side by side," a voice spoke from behind. Jim and Indian turned. For a brief moment the three stood silently gazing at each other. Without a word Indian came forward and took her in her arms. Elaine clung tight. "Indian, I really missed you."

Finally Indian broke the embrace. "I missed you too." He gently kissed her forehead. "I'm so sorry about David." She again clung to him, resting her head on his chest. She eventually opened her eyes and looked at Jim. Jim could see the eye mascara smeared down her cheeks. She faintly smiled at him, but tears again swelled her eyes, forcing her to close them even tighter. Indian broke the embrace and clasped each of her arms. "Elaine, we didn't know."

"I know." She smiled and then extended her hands to Jim. "You still remember the poem."

Jim smiled and took her hands in his. "It was my favorite."

Elaine wrapped her arms around Jim and drew close to him. "Who would have ever thought a hippie cowboy from Idaho would be the only person to understand my poetry."

"It wasn't your poetry that I understood. It was your heart."

All three were quiet as the embrace lasted a brief moment. Eventually she pulled away and smiled at them. "I'm so glad you came." She wiped the tears from her eyes and intertwined her arms with theirs.

Indian carefully studied the distant dark sedan. He could make out two figures in the front seat. He didn't know who they were but suspected they were watching them. He pulled Elaine's arm from his. "Will you excuse me? I need to check out something."

"Sure," Elaine replied. Jim nodded in agreement.

Indian turned and made his way back toward the car. He watched closely out of the corner of his eye. When he was out of the sight of the sedan, he slipped into the nearby bushes.

Jim could see that Elaine shivering. He took off his corduroy sports coat and placed it on her damp shoulders. She gazed at his clothing attire. "I see you still have the same taste in clothes."

Jim chuckled. "A man of old habits."

She smiled. "They remind me of happier times." Elaine motioned toward the cliffs. "I was standing over there when you came."

"By the cliffs, in the rain?"

She nodded her head. "I was thinking about killing myself."

"Killing yourself—really?"

Elaine nodded again. "You remember when you overdosed and tried to kill yourself?"

Jim nodded. "It was not a happy time."

"I remember sitting next to your hospital bed when you were in that coma. I kept thinking to myself, how could anyone ever consider killing themselves?"

"And now?"

She wrapped both her arms around his one arm. "These are not happy times."

"Except for David's death, I think they're better," Jim encouraged.

"Are they really?"

"Yes, really. Being on the ranch is not perfect, but it's better."

Elaine smiled at his comment. "I was so happy to see you get out of the car."

"I can't believe we were late. Was it a short service?"

"Very short. No one came."

"No one? I don't understand."

"When David was declared insane, everyone avoided us."

"Solomon insane?" Jim shook his head. "I don't understand. Solomon was the most sane of us all."

Elaine smiled. "Solomon—I haven't heard David called that for years. I had forgotten how close we were during the early years."

"Elaine, what happened?"

Elaine took Jim's hand. "Come walk with me."

Jim turned to signal Indian, but could not see him. *I guess he'll find us*, he thought. They walked deeper into the cemetery toward the ocean cliffs. Neither noticed the two men in dark suits leave their car and follow from a distance.

"Shortly after we were married, David was transferred to Dugway, Utah. Because of his medical background, he was on loan to the army to work on some kind of secret project."

"Do you know what it was?"

"No, he never discussed the project, but—" Elaine purposefully paused.

"But what?"

"Shortly after he started the project, he began to change."

"Change, how?"

"He began to express some fears."

"Really? After all the things in Nam, the cold war, and what we saw throughout the world, it's hard to believe he feared anything."

"Those were the exact things that he feared most. The people he killed, the many women he deceived, the lying, stealing, and all that he hurt in the name of honor, freedom, and country."

"Then he was afraid of dying?"

"No, not of dying. David was afraid of God."

Jim was surprised by Elaine's answer. "That's odd. I don't remember David ever speaking of God."

"That's just it, he never did."

"Then why the change?"

"I don't know. Psychiatrists said he was a paranoid schizophrenic and had him placed in a mental institution."

They were nearing the cliffs. "Do you believe David was insane?"

"I don't know." She paused. "Once he told me people on this earth would cease to exist, and that he and Joe were responsible."

"Joe who?"

"He never said."

"Did he say any more?"

"Only the night he died. He said he finally found peace. The next day they found him dead and said it was a suicide."

"Do you believe it was a suicide?"

"No, I don't."

They were unaware of the two gentlemen approaching from behind. Scarface searched the cemetery, looking for Indian.

"Perfect opportunity," Lenny whispered. "It'll look like a double suicide."

Scarface studied the couple. "Something's wrong. It isn't the right time."

"What do you mean it isn't the right time? It's perfect. I'm going to do it."

Scarface grabbed him and pulled him back behind some bushes. "Listen, I can't find Indian. Believe me, it isn't the right time."

"Right time for what?" a voice asked from behind. Jim and Elaine turned, for they also heard the voice. Scarface realized who it was, but was unable to warn his partner. Lenny turned, pistol pointed, into Indian's waiting arms. There was the sickening "snap" of breaking bones. The pistol fell uselessly to the ground. A quick punch to the face sent Lenny sprawling after.

Scarface raised his hands and slowly turned. "Indian."

"Scarface, it's been a long time." He nodded toward Lenny lying on the ground. "Sorry about your partner." Jim and Elaine approached the other three.

"You'll have to excuse him." Scarface smirked. "He can be a bit overzealous."

Lenny's screams started when he saw the bleeding and fractured bones piercing through his flesh. "You bastard, you broke my arm."

Jim pushed Lenny back to his knees. "Sneaking up on us like that, you're lucky to be alive. What were trying to do, kill us?"

Lenny did not answer. Elaine looked at Scarface. "You were, weren't you? You were actually going to kill us."

"C'mon, Elaine, we weren't going to kill anybody."

Jim tore a sleeve from Lenny's jacket. Elaine reached down and held Lenny's arm in place. Jim used the coat sleeve as a tourniquet and brace for the arm. Jim glanced up. "Scarface, what are you doing here anyway?"

He did not answer. "They were watching us," Indian answered for him. "I noticed their car when we arrived."

All watched as Jim tightened the tourniquet. Slowly Scarface eased his hand into his jacket. Indian noticed the movement. He quickly grabbed both arms and locked them behind his back. With the other hand he reached inside his coat and removed a gun. "Look what we have here."

Again Jim asked Scarface, "Why are you here?"

Scarface did not answer. Indian pushed both arms up. Scarface winced with pain. "You heard his question." Indian was impatient waiting for an answer. "Maybe I'll just dislocate your shoulders." He shoved his arms higher.

Scarface screamed out with pain. "All right," he yelled, unable to break Indian's hold. "Just chill out. We just came to pay our respects to David."

"With guns in hand?" Elaine asked.

"Like I said, Elaine, my partner is somewhat anxious."

Elaine approached Scarface. "Was it you? Was it you who killed David?"

Scarface smiled. "Why, Elaine, after all we have meant to each other, how could you think such a thing?"

"You did kill him, didn't you," she said with conviction.

"You're talking nonsense. The company doesn't do those things anymore. I thought I might be able to give you some comfort in your time of time of need," he paused, "like old times." He then smiled at Jim. "But I see that someone has already beaten me to it." Indian demonstrated his disapproval by tightening his grip on Scarface. "Okay, Indian, ease off." He looked at Elaine. "We want to know what David told you."

"So you're the ones who trashed my home," Elaine accused.

"Listen, Elaine, just tell us what David told you, and we'll be out of your life."

"Like I told you before, he told me nothing."

"But—"

"But nothing," Jim interrupted. "Didn't you hear her? She said she doesn't know anything. Now get your partner and get out of here."

Indian eased his grip. Scarface helped his partner to his feet. He put out his hand toward Indian. "Our guns?"

Indian turned and tossed them over the cliff edge. "Go get them."

Scarface smiled. "Indian, we'll meet again."

"I sure hope so."

Scarface took Lenny by the arm to walk away but paused and turned toward them. "Oh, one other thing—let David's death pass."

"Is that a threat?" Jim asked.

Again Scarface smiled. "Absolutely. Things are different now. You have no idea what you're up against. For old times' sake, I'm warning you to let his death pass." Scarface turned and helped his partner back toward the car.

CHAPTER TWELVE
NICOLE'S HOSPITAL RECORD

"**M**icah and the wolves chased me to the stream. I thought they were going to catch me."

Jason held the pressure dressing tight against her abdomen. "What happened?"

"Suddenly there was this bright light in front of me, kind of like the sun."

"What did this Micah and the wolves do?"

"That was the weird thing. They turned and left like they were scared."

"Scared of what?"

"I think the tigers," Sondra answered.

Jason was surprised by her answer. "Tigers?"

"In the light there were these two white tigers and a woman. I remember the woman took my hand and led me away. That was the last thing I remembered until I awoke in the hospital." Jason pulled the dressing away again. The blood continued to seep from the incision wound. "Well?" she asked.

Jason replaced the dressing. "It still hasn't stopped." He looked at Sondra. "How do you feel?"

"I feel a little dizzy."

Jason shook his head. "That's it. I'm going to get Dr. Jordan."

Sondra pulled on his arm. "No, please."

"But you keep bleeding."

"Try pushing on it just a little longer."

Jason disagreed but relented to her wishes. He reapplied the pressure. "Look at the blood on your blouse. It's ruined."

Sondra looked down. "Yes, and it's the only one I have."

"We can go to the mall and get another."

Sondra was confused. "Go where?"

"The mall."

"What's that?"

Jason stared at her. "You mean you've never been to a mall?"

Sondra shook her head. "I don't think so. What is it?"

"It's a place where a whole bunch of stores are inside one big building."

Sondra laughed. "You're teasing me, aren't you."

"No, I'm serious."

"Come on, how can you put a bunch of stores in one big building?"

"You really don't believe me, do you?"

Sondra smiled. "No, I don't."

"Well we'll get your bleeding stopped, and then I'll show you." Jason removed the dressing again. The undersurface was still soaked with blood. "It still hasn't stopped." Jason stood. "I'm going to get some help." He turned to leave and ran directly into him. Jason was knocked to the floor. Strong hands reach down and helped him up.

"Are you all right?" the stranger asked.

Surprised, Jason looked up. The man's hair was down to his shoulders. He wore a long robe with sash. "Who are you?"

"My name is John. I'm a friend of your mom's."

"My mom?" Jason asked.

"She asked me to come. She said you may need some help."

Jason turned to Sondra. "Not me, but Sondra keeps bleeding."

John knelt down next to Sondra. "Let's take a look." He removed the dressing, reached down, and touched her abdomen. "Does that hurt?"

"A little."

"Well, let's see if I can help." He placed his hands on her abdomen and closed his eyes.

Jason watched with interest. Shortly John raised his head and removed his hands. He then touched Sondra's face with his hand and stood. "There, that should do it."

Jason stepped around and knelt next to Sondra. "That should do what?" he asked. He removed the dressing from the wound site. Jason was shocked by what he saw.

Sondra raised her head. "Has the bleeding stopped?"

Jason ran his hand over her bare abdomen. "More than that," he murmured. He turned back. "Mr. John, what did you—?" Jason interrupted himself. He stood and looked around the basement and then back at Sondra. "The man's gone."

Sondra sat up and looked. "Where did he go?"

Jason shrugged his shoulders. "I don't know." He again knelt next to Sondra and took her hand. "Here, feel this." He ran her hand over her lower abdomen. Now Sondra moved her hand herself.

"The cut is gone. How is that possible?"

Jason shrugged his shoulders. "I guess that John guy healed you."

———※◆◇———

Doug held open the hospital door. "What was his name again?"

"Scarface," Jim answered. "We worked with him off and on when we were in army intelligence. He's a real nasty guy."

"And he pulled a gun on you and Elaine?"

"Actually it was Lenny, his partner. If it hadn't been for Indian, I think Elaine and I would not be here."

"You think they would have shot you?"

"More likely forced us off the ocean cliffs. You know, make it look like suicide."

Doug scanned the posted hospital directory with his finger. "There, it's in the basement." The elevator doors opened and they entered. Doug pushed the down button and shook his head. "I don't understand why they wanted to kill you."

"Oh, they think David told Elaine something secret before he died."

"Did he?"

The elevator slowed down to a stop. "That's the point. She says she doesn't know anything except…"

"Except what?" Doug asked.

"Well she has some pictures of some of David's writings on his room wall just before he died."

"What kind of writings?"

"It looks like some kind of foreign language. Indian and I didn't recognize any of the words. Would you mind looking at them?"

"Sure, I'll take a look when we get back."

The elevator doors opened and the two stepped out. The wall signs now led them down the hallway. "You're flying to Phoenix tomorrow afternoon?" Jim asked.

"Yes, my plane leaves at five. Mom wants me over there early to help prepare for the party."

"Would you do me a favor? Would you take Elaine with you? I'd feel more comfortable with her out of LA."

"Sure, be happy too. I'll arrange for a ticket when we get back."

"That would be great. The rest of us will fly over just as soon as we get Pepe out of the hospital."

Doug chuckled. "None too soon for Pepe, I bet." Doug opened the door to the medical record's room. "I'll bet he was real excited about his assignment."

Jim smiled and entered. "You have no idea."

An older woman looked up from behind the counter. "May I help you?"

Dr. Hunter glanced at her name tag. "Hello, Mrs. Walburg, do you remember me?"

Mrs. Walburg adjusted her bifocals and studied his face. There was some hesitation in her voice. "No, I don't think so."

"I'm Dr. Hunter. I used to work here in the hospital several years ago. I came down here all the time."

Mrs. Walburg nodded her head slowly. "Oh, yes, Dr. Hunter, I believe I do remember you, now."

"Well, it's sure good to see you again. You look better than ever."

Mrs. Walburg straightened her wrinkled dress. "Why thank you. It's always nice to have gentlemen down here in the records room." Her hand brushed her hair back out of her face. "How can I help you?"

"We want to look at my wife's hospital record. She passed away several years ago."

"I'm sorry to hear that. Was it unexpected?"

"Lingering illness."

"Well I see no problem with the request. I just need to see your ID."

"Sure." Doug pulled out his wallet and handed her his driver's license.

Mrs. Walburg studied the license for a brief moment. She then handed the license back. "It seems to be in order." She picked up a nearby pen and paper. "What is your wife's full name?"

"Her file is either under Nicole Hunter or her maiden name Nicole Crockett."

Mrs. Walburg wrote both names down on a sheet of paper. "Wait a few moments while I look."

"Thank you, we appreciate it."

They watched her turn and walk toward the back. "Doc, you really don't know her, do you?"

"Not from the man in the moon."

Jim smiled. "That's pretty good. If you ever need a job…"

"Forget it. I have enough troubles." Doug chuckled. "So who do Scarface and Lenny work for now?"

"Previously they did all the dirty work for Captain McFarland."

"Captain McFarland?"

"Well, now he's a general. He works for army intelligence. After talking with Sheriff Bates this morning, I think this McFarland was responsible for removing the two dead girls from Boise."

Doug shook his head. "I still can't believe the army confiscated those bodies."

"Me either. That's why Sheriff Bates wants Indian and me to go to Dugway to see if we can find out why."

"If you find out anything, would you let me know too?"

"Sure." He paused for a brief moment. "Again, Doc, why are we looking at Nicole's chart?"

"Because of Jason." Doug could tell Jim was confused. He took a deep breath. "I know this will sound crazy, but Jason said it was his mom's suggestion that we look at her hospital chart."

Jim looked at Doug as if to say "really." Doug nodded his head. "And Jason told you that?"

Now Jim noticed how uncomfortable Doug was. "Yes, he did."

Jim wiped his face with both hands. He looked at Doug. "Let me see if I have this straight. Are you saying that Nicole told Jason to tell you to check out her medical record while we are here in Los Angeles?"

Doug sheepishly smiled. "Sounds kind of crazy, doesn't it?" Doug could tell that Jim was stunned. Suddenly Jim burst out in laughter. Doug couldn't help but smile. "What?"

"Look at us. We have to be the craziest family in the west." Jim then nudged Doc's chest and motioned with his head. Mrs. Walburg was returning.

Suddenly she stopped short in her tracks. She noticed the red tag on the front of the file. *Why is this chart flagged?* she thought. She looked up to see Dr. Hunter and Jim Crockett waiting at the front desk. Quickly she turned to retreat back into the medical record's room.

Doug watched her turn. "Mrs. Walburg, is that her hospital chart?" he called.

She stopped and turned around. "Ah, yes it is."

"May we look at it?"

"I'm sorry, but the chart is flagged."

"What does that mean?"

"Well it means I can't let anyone see this chart without permission."

Jim looked at Doug. "Permission from who?" Jim continued.

"Mr. Brown, the hospital administrator."

"Look, Mrs. Walburg, as her husband and doctor, I have a right to see her chart."

"I'm sorry, Dr. Hunter, but if I let you look at this chart without his permission, it could mean my job."

"Then let's call your administrator and get his permission," Jim advised.

"Now?"

"Yes, now," Jim answered emphatically. "It's very important."

"But he'll be asleep in bed."

Now Jim was getting irritated. "Look, you wake that administrator now, get permission for us to look at this chart, or I want his butt down here now explaining to us why we can't see it. Do you understand?"

Doug could see some hesitation in Mrs. Walburg's body movement and eyes. "Listen, if you don't want to talk with him, let me. That way you won't get in trouble."

Mrs. Walburg nodded her head. "Okay, I'll call him." She approached her desk and picked up the phone. Jim whispered to Doug. "Are flagged charts common?"

Hunter shook his head. "I've never heard of such a thing. Sounds like someone's hiding something." They watched Mrs. Walburg finish dialing the phone.

"Hello, Mr. Brown?"

"Yes."

"This is Mrs. Walburg in medical records."

"My gosh, Mrs. Walburg, it's two in the morning."

"I am sorry to call at this hour, but there's a man here who wants to review his wife's medical chart."

"Is his identification in order?"

"Well, yes—"

"Then why are you bothering me? You know the proper procedure."

"But the chart's flagged."

"Flagged?"

"Yes, sir, it's your own personal flag."

Mr. Brown now sat up in his bed. "Is the patient's name Crockett?"

"Yes, a Nicole Crockett."

"But that chart was in the vault."

"Yes, I know, sir. "I opened the vault and—"

"You did what?"

"But her husband's identification papers are in order."

"Is Dr. Hunter still there?"

"Yes, he still here at the counter."

"Mrs. Walburg, you did the right thing. Do not give them the chart. I'll be down there in fifteen minutes to handle this myself." Mr. Brown hastily hung up the phone, half dressed, and ran out his front door.

"Horse's butt," Mrs. Walburg murmured as she hung up the phone. She looked up the two men, when the elevator chimed and a man stepped into the room. "Sir, may I help you?" she asked as he approached.

Jim turned and was shocked to see Indian walking toward them. "What is this?" Jim whispered to Doug.

Indian smiled at Mrs. Walburg. "No, thanks, I can find it." Doug and Jim caught Indian's wink as he passed by them, and proceeded down one of the long medical record aisles.

Mrs. Walburg placed Nicole's file on her desk and started after him. "Find what, sir?" Indian ignored her question. "Sir, you can't come back here." Quickly she caught and passed him. She then turned and faced him. "Listen, you aren't allowed back here. This is a restricted area."

It was then that Indian signaled Hunter and Crockett. They quickly passed around the counter to Mrs. Walburg's desk. "There," Jim pointed to Nicole's chart sitting on the desk. "Hurry." Hunter quickly opened the chart and began to read.

"Restroom!" Mrs. Wilbur exclaimed, "The public restroom is on the first floor by the elevators."

"Look, ma'am," Indian explained and then his voice faded.

"Jim," Doug whispered, "most of her chart is missing."

"Missing?"

"Yes, except this lab report and—" Doug paused as he looked at the remainder of the chart.

"And what?"

"An autopsy report." Doug looked up at Jim. "How can this be?"

"Quick, Doc, let's go." Doug removed the information from the chart and stuffed it in his jacket. They returned to the other side of the counter.

"I don't care if it is plugged. You can't use the one back here." She then grabbed him by the arm and escorted him back the way they came.

Doug and Jim each took one of Indian's arms. "Let us help you. We'll take him to the restroom upstairs."

"Thank you, gentlemen." She watched them guide Indian toward the elevators. No sooner had one set of elevator doors closed than the other opened, revealing Mr. Brown. He peered around the room. "Mrs. Walburg, where is he?"

"He left."

"And Ms. Crockett's medical record?"

"On my desk." She picked it up and handed it to him.

He opened the folder. "It's empty, where's the record?"

Mrs. Walburg paled. "I swear, Mr. Brown, her chart was like that when I got it from the vault."

Mr. Brown hugged the chart to his chest. He stumbled his way to Mrs. Walburg's desk.

She helped him sit down in her chair behind her desk. "Are you all right, sir?"

"Leave me."

"But, Mr. Brown—"

"Didn't you hear me, woman? Get out!" Without another word Mrs. Walburg picked up her purse and jacket and left.

The three sat in the far corner of the empty cafeteria. Jim returned with three cups of coffee and placed them in front of the others. "Doc, wasn't there anything at all in her chart?" Indian asked.

"Only this lab slip, but this date can't be right."

"Why is that?"

"This date would only make her three months pregnant when she had the baby."

"It has to be the wrong date," Jim concluded. "Do the lab results tell you anything else?"

"Actually they do. It tells us that Nicole was not anemic after Jason's birth."

"But I thought she hemorrhaged with the birth and that's why she received the blood transfusion," Indian added.

"Me too, but according to this test, she didn't hemorrhage."

"Then why did she have the transfusion?" Jim questioned.

Doug took a sip of his coffee and put the cup back on the table. He shook his head. "That's a good question."

Indian motioned to the other paper. "What about the other sheet?"

Doug picked up the paper and looked at it again. "This one doesn't make sense either. It's an order for an autopsy."

"Autopsy?" On who?"

"On a baby. Nicole's baby."

Jim and Indian looked at Doug. Both had puzzled looks on their faces. "That doesn't make any sense. Jason didn't die."

All were quiet for a brief moment. Indian finally spoke. "An autopsy order on a baby that didn't die, and a blood transfusion for someone that didn't need it. What's going on here?"

"Are we saying Nicole contracted AIDS from a blood transfusion that she never needed?" Jim asked. No one answered. Everyone feared that Jim's conclusion might be true.

"There has to be more to it," Doug concluded.

Indian put out his hand. "Doc, let me see the lab slip." Doug handed it to him. Immediately Indian noticed the name at the bottom of the slip. "There's another name on this lab slip." Doug leaned over his arm to look. "The name looks like Tina something, like Mitchell, Metchoy, Mit—"

"Michaels," Doug interrupted. "Tina Michaels."

"Do you know her?" Jim asked.

Doug nodded his head yes. "Yes, I do."

"Then that's who we need to talk to. Do you where she is?" Indian asked.

Doug thought for a moment. "No, but I think I know where to look."

"Well, I'm afraid you are on your own," Indian said. "I need to get to the mental hospital tonight. Pepe may need my help."

"And I need to pick him up in the morning," Jim added.

"That's okay. It's best I do this alone." The three stood and quickly left the hospital.

Brown finally looked up and realized he was alone. He leaned forward and picked up the phone and placed the call.

"Hello," the voice answered. Brown hesitated and the voice commanded, "Speak!"

"Gabriel, this is Brown."

"Brown, you know it is forbidden to call me."

Brown ignored his warning. "Gabriel, Hunter was here."

"Dr. Hunter, there? Why?"

"He was seeking Crockett's chart."

"You mean he saw the chart?"

"No, he didn't see it. It has been locked in the vault for years."

"Good job, but why call me?"

"Sir, for some reason her chart is empty."

"How can that be?"

"I don't know."

The phone was silent for a brief moment. "Israeli Intelligence," Gabriel murmured. "Brown, you have failed. You know what you must do."

Brown heard the click on the other end. "Yes, sir," he whispered to himself. He took Nicole's empty chart and walked the long roll of medical charts until he reached the vault. He entered the vault and replaced her chart. Brown then slid down the wall to the marble floor. He stared forward for the longest time. Finally he reached into his coat pocket and pulled out a revolver. Without hesitation he placed the barrel in his mouth and pulled the trigger.

CHAPTER THIRTEEN

THE OLD GIRLFRIEND

"Hello, this is Warden Parks."

"Has Tina had a visitor?"

Parks immediately recognized Gabriel's voice. His hand covered the phone end. "That will be all, Ms. Jones." She picked up her notes and left his office. He removed his hand. "No one has visited her."

"Good. There may be a Dr. Doug Hunter who might try to contact my wife. Last night he attempted to obtain Nicole Crockett's old medical records."

Parks was confused. "I don't understand. How could Crockett's medical records be tied to your wife?"

"Tina was her nurse when their baby was born. It is possible Tina's name may have been mentioned in her hospital files. I know it is a long shot, but I thought I better warn you."

"So what if this Dr. Hunter shows up?"

"The same as before—Tina is to have no visitors, understand?"

"Yes, sir."

"Good." The phone line clicked silent.

Parks placed another call. "Visitor's desk," the voice answered.

"Hello, this is Warden Parks."

"Yes, Mr. Parks."

"I'm inquiring about prisoner three-forty-four. Has she had anyone try to visit her?"

"No sir. Tina Michaels is not allowed any visitors."

"Good." Parks replaced the telephone receiver and checked his watch. "Damn, I'm late for my noon meeting." Quickly he picked up his briefcase and rushed from his office.

The prison guard opened the kitchen door. "Tina, you have a visitor."

Tina laughed. "Yes, right. First one in three years."

"No, I'm serious. It's even a man," Ms. Stewart whispered loudly.

Tina stopped placing the can goods in the kitchen cabinet and turned toward the door. "Who is it?" The guard only smiled and opened the door wider. Tina gasped as she watched him walk into the room. How many times had she dreamed of this moment? Now that he was here, all she could do was shamefully turn away and continue placing the cans on the shelf.

The man approached her from behind. He gently placed his hands on her shoulders. "Hello, Tina."

Tina stopped. She looked down at the ground. After a few seconds of silence, she reached up and placed her hands on his. "How did you find me?"

"Your mom."

Tina rolled her head. "I should have known. She could never keep a secret."

The man chuckled. "Well, I had to coax her some."

"How did you even get in here?"

"That was harder. I told them I was your doctor."

"And they let you in?"

"Believe it or not, they did."

Slowly he turned her toward him. When they faced each other, he reached out his hands to grasp hers. Tina passed by his hands into a full-body embrace. "Oh, Doug, how I missed you," she whispered in his ear. He could feel her body mold to his. She held him tight. *It's been so long since I felt a woman's body like this*, he thought, *not since Nicole.*

Finally she broke the embrace and looked into his face. "Why are you here?"

Doug shrugged his shoulders. "I just wanted to see you."

Tina broke away and walked toward a kitchen counter. She attempted to smooth her prison uniform wrinkles. "I must look a mess."

"No, you look great."

Tina turned to face him. "Really?"

"Yes, really. You look as beautiful as ever."

She put a hand to her limp, long black hair. "You aren't just saying that?"

"You know I wouldn't do that."

Doug noticed the corners of Tina's eyes moisten. "That's nice." She reached up and wiped her tears. "I don't see much kindness in here."

She turned toward the counter. "Me and my manners—would you like a cup of coffee?"

"That sounds good." Doug took a seat at a nearby table. He watched her fill two coffee cups.

"Just black, right?"

"Right."

She sat down straight across from him and handed him a cup. Doug waited for her to speak first, but she just sipped her coffee and stared. She studied his every feature to the point that it started to make Doug uncomfortable. Eventually a smile came to her face. "What?" Doug finally asked.

"Puerto Vallarta." Doug smiled back but did not speak. "Remember our night in that abandoned beach hut? We were wild and reckless back then, weren't we?"

"Yes, we were."

"You know, when you wrapped your arms around me, I thought we would be together forever." Doug turned his gaze downward. "Do you remember when you told me that you loved me?"

"Yes, I remember."

"Tell me the truth, were you just saying that?"

Now his gaze met hers. "No, Tina, I really meant it."

Tina smiled. "I bet you wonder why I'm in here. I really messed up." Tina noticed a guard looking through the door window. "Would you like to take a walk in the yard?"

"Can we do that?"

"Sure." They left their coffee cups on the table. She took his hand in hers and led him through the double doors into the prison yard. Although the sky was overcast, there was a warm southwest breeze. Initially there were lewd remarks made about Doug by some of the other women prisoners in the yard, but shortly it was accepted that Doug was with Tina. It was then she began.

"When we broke up, it really hurt."

"Tina, I'm sorry—" Doug tried to explain.

"No, don't apologize. It's okay. That's when I moved from Phoenix to LA and found a job as an obstetrics nurse at a county hospital."

"You always liked obstetrics."

"Not this time. That's when my troubles began. Did you know I got married?"

"No, when did that happen?"

"About eight years ago. I married my obstetrician."

Doug chuckled. "Married your obstetrician—that's so you."

She also laughed. "Yes, I know."

"Any children?"

"We had two, a boy and a girl."

Doug placed arm around her shoulder and pulled her close to him. "That is so neat." He noticed Tina's face sadden. "Do you get to see them often?"

"Not often. Actually not since the sentencing."

"The sentencing?"

Tina's voice cracked as she tried to explain. "At the sentencing three years ago, I was declared an unfit mother. My husband left with the children." Now Doug could see the tears flowing down her cheeks.

"And you haven't seen them since?" Tina shook her head. "But that's so cruel. Why would your husband do that to you?"

"I'm not sure he ever loved me."

"Why do you say that?"

"We were both guilty, but I was the only one arrested."

"Arrested for what?"

"Selling babies. My husband Gabriel had been doing it long before we met. First we would look for single mothers. At the county hospital there were plenty. If mothers wanted to give up their babies, we would fix the appropriate records to simulate their deaths or adoptions. Then Gabriel would sell the babies. It was very lucrative. But for some reason Gabriel fixed it so that I would be found out and take the fall."

"But why would he do that?"

"I don't know."

"Is there anything I can do to help you?"

"I have left numerous messages with my attorney, but he hasn't returned any of my calls."

"Maybe I can contact him for you. There ought to be something we can do."

"It's more than that, Doug." She turned and walked deeper into the yard.

Warden Parks pulled back his chair and stood. "Continue," he commanded as he listened to one of the prison committee's reports. He turned away from the table and looked out the large picture window to the prison yard below. "Wait," he interrupted the report. "Ms. Stewart, come here."

Ms. Stewart stood and walked up next to him. "What is it, Warden?"

"The people walking there, who are they?"

"That's Tina Michaels and her doctor."

"Doctor? Who authorized her to have a doctor?"

"Well she's been sick, you know, and they just thought—"

"Stupidity," Parks interrupted. He turned to the nearby phone and called down to the visitor's desk.

"Visitor's desk?"

"Parks here. I thought I told you no visitors for prisoner three-forty-four."

"Sir, I assure you she hasn't had any visitors, except well—" he paused. "Well except her doctor."

"What's his name?

"Dr. Doug Hunter."

"Dammit," Parks exclaimed. He pointed to two prison guards. "You and you come with me. The rest stay here until I return." The three left the room.

Tina stopped. "One of the reasons that Gabriel put me in here is because of you and Nicole."

"Me and Nicole? I don't understand."

"He knows I know too much. That's why I was surprised to see you here."

"You know too much about what?"

"Well it all started when I was Nicole's OB nurse, when your baby was born. Initially I thought I would hate Nicole, because she took you away from me. But after the first few hours of her labor, I realized there was something special about her. We developed a very special bond. Doug, I am so sorry about what happened."

"I appreciate that. It's been five years now."

Tina frowned. "What do you mean, five years?"

"Five years since Nicole's death."

Horror encompassed Tina's face. "Nicole died?"

"I thought you knew."

"No, I didn't know." Tina turned and faced Doug. She was pleading when she asked, "Did she die of AIDS?"

Doug paused for a brief moment. "How did you know?"

Tina now turned away. "Oh no, they know," she moaned.

Doug grabbed Tina's shoulders and turned her toward him. "Who knows? I don't understand."

Tina looked into his eyes. "I'm so sorry to tell you this, but they killed Nicole."

"What are you talking about?"

Tina did not answer. She could see Warden Parks and two prison guards coming toward them. "There isn't time to speak more." She motioned toward the three approaching. "I wasn't speaking of Nicole's death earlier."

"Then whose death were you referring too?"

"Not only did they kill Nicole, but they also killed your son."

That explains the autopsy report in the chart, Doug thought. He looked at her. "Tina, you need to know that our son is alive."

Mr. Parks and the guards were closer now.

"No, that can't be," Tina contradicted. "I tried to stop Gabriel, but I couldn't. I watched my husband smother your son just after his birth."

"You must be mistaken. Our son Jason is alive and living with me in Idaho."

Tina was confused. As she watched Warden Parks draw near, she knew she hadn't much time. "Doug, if this Jason is truly yours and Nicole's son, then his life is in danger."

"Why?"

"Because your son is a Levite."

There's that term again, Doug thought. *What does that mean?*

"Well, Tina," Warden Parks interrupted, "I see you have a visitor." Tina bowed her head and did not respond. He extended his hand to Doug. "I'm Warden Parks."

He shook hands with Warden Parks. "Doug Hunter, a friend of Tina's."

"Well, Mr. Hunter, I'm sorry to cut this visit short, but Tina's not well."

Doug turned to Tina. "Not well, what's wrong?" Tina did not answer.

"In fact her own doctor is waiting for her right now." He turned to his guards. "Why don't you escort Tina to the infirmary, and I'll walk this gentleman out."

"Yes, sir," one answered.

Tina approached Doug and hugged him. She then pulled away, took off a locket from around her neck and placed it around his. "I want you to have this. It will help you find the truth."

"Don't worry, Tina, I'll be back to see you."

She only smiled, turned, and walked away with the two guards.

Doug watched for a brief moment. "Shall we go?" Warden Parks asked. Doug turned to follow. "Come, I'll show you the way out."

"Warden Parks, when is Tina up for parole?"

"Parole is not possible."

Doug was confused by his answer. "What do you mean not possible? Isn't she up for parole sometime in the future?"

Warden Parks opened the door leading out of the yard and demonstrated the way to the entrance. "Well, yes, she is up for parole in two years, but I'm afraid it will not happen."

"Why?"

"Didn't she tell you?"

"Tell me what?"

"Mr. Hunter, I'm sorry to be the one to tell you this, but Tina is dying."

"Dying?"

"Tina has AIDS."

Doug was stunned. Warden Parks turned to leave. "Wait! I would like to come visit her. You know I'm a doctor. Maybe I could help."

"I'm afraid that's not possible. We have our own doctors." He motioned down the long hall. "That's the way to the entrance." Doug turned to leave but knew Parks was hiding something.

Parks watched Doug walk the long hall toward the entrance and disappear around the corner. Once Dr. Hunter was out of sight, Parks entered an empty office and picked up the telephone receiver. "Outside line." He then dialed a number and waited.

"Hello," the voice answered.

"Gabriel, it's me."

"Parks, you know you're not to call me."

"But I had to. It's your wife. Without my knowledge she had a visitor."

"Who?"

"That Dr. Hunter."

"You fool. I even warned you ahead of time."

"I know, sir. He disguised himself as her doctor. The guards all know she is sick, and they let him in."

"I will need to speak with Matthias about this."

"Gabriel, Matthias doesn't need to know. I can take care of this Dr. Hunter."

"No, you leave Hunter to us."

"And Tina?"

"Find out what she told him and let me know."

"Yes, sir." Parks hung up the phone and quickly returned to his office. He touched the intercom. "Ms. Jones, would you come in here, please."

Shortly Ms. Jones entered his office. "You wanted me, sir."

"Yes, I would like to talk with the two prisoners, Ellen and Large Marge."

"Yes, sir." She turned and left the office. Parks sat at his desk contemplating what had just taken place, and his potential demise.

CHAPTER FOURTEEN
WHISPERING PINES

Indian read the sign. "The Whispering Pine Hospital," he whispered. He quickly leaped the stone wall, landing on the other side, and ducked down. He looked both ways. "I hate these places," he murmured. It reminded him of his own commitment a number of years ago to a similar facility. Countless times he was beaten and suffered months of isolation and electroshock therapy. Now sweat ran down his face. He could feel himself breathe more rapidly. "I don't know if I can do this." He reflected back to the military tribunal.

"Indian, do you have anything to say before I sentence you," Judge Simpson asked. Indian remained immobile and did not speak. "I take that as a no. Indian, it is the finding of this military tribunal court that you are innocent by reason of insanity. You are sentenced to the army's psychiatric facility indefinitely until the doctors there declare you fit to function once again in society." Simpson motioned to the nearby soldiers. "Guards, you may remove the prisoner." Two guards took each arm and escorted him out of the courtroom and back to his nearby temporary cell. They locked his door.

Suddenly they heard a voice from behind. "Leave us!" the voice commanded.

"Yes, Captain," one of the guards answered. They both left the room.

The man smiled as he approached the bars. Indian looked up. "All you had to do was fall in line with the rest of us, and you could have had riches beyond your wildest dreams." Indian glared at him, but still did not speak. "Now look at you, behind bars for the rest of your life."

"McFarland, you're a disgrace."

"Maybe so, but look who's in prison and who isn't."

"Not for long. When I get out, you better watch your back."

McFarland chuckled. He lit a cigarette and took a long drag. "You just don't get it. In prison, they give you a specific time to serve, but in a psychiatric unit, the time is indefinite." He then turned and walked toward the outer door. McFarland turned back. "Indian, I'll see you never get out of here."

The barking dog brought Indian's thoughts back to the reality of the hospital compound. He noticed a guard with a dog circulating the perimeter. He again looked at his watch. *Two minutes*, he thought. *That's plenty of time.* Slowly he made his way through the bushes until he was at the perimeter. Indian was unaware of someone watching his every movement from an upstairs window.

Crockett settled in one of the hospital lounge sofas. "Well, how's the food?"

Pepe nervously paced back and forth. "How's the food!" Pepe exclaimed. "I'm stuck in this loony bin, and all you can say is 'how's the food'?"

Jim looked around the recreation room. "It doesn't look that bad. Ping pong, pool, and three square meals. It looks to me you're all set."

"Don't tease around like that, Jimmy, this is serious." He sat down across from his friend. "The people in here are a lot crazier than we are."

Jim nodded at the nurse who walked by. "And the nurses are pretty too."

"All lesbos," Pepe whispered under his breath.

Jim didn't hear well and leaned forward. "Les what?"

Pepe also leaned forward and whispered again. "Lesbos. You know, lesbians."

"Oh, come on, not all of them."

"Yes, all of them. You got to get me out of here."

Jim watched as Pepe rubbed his perspiring hands together. "Ah, now I get it, Pepe, you couldn't get anywhere with the women, so now you want out of here. What's wrong, your pheromones not working anymore?"

"That's crap."

"Then how do you know they are lesbians?"

"My roommate, Disciple, told me."

"See, you've only been in here one day, and you already have a new friend."

"This Disciple guy's not a friend. He's some kind of religious freak." Pepe stood and began pacing again. "Come on, you promised you'd get me out of here."

"Okay, calm down." He motioned Pepe to sit once again. "I talked with Dr. Damion this morning, and well, he is concerned about you leaving."

"How can he be concerned about my leaving? I only spoke with him once."

"Well apparently that was enough. He thinks you have several things that need to be worked out."

"Like what?"

"Well one thing he mentioned is your clothes."

"My clothes?"

"Yes, you know, brown checkered bellbottom pants, paisley shirt, cowboy hat and boots," Jim demonstrated with his hands. "Don't get me wrong, I think you look real good. But he thinks you are living in the past like some kind of cowboy hippie."

Pepe threw up his arms. "That's just great. It was your idea to wear those clothes in the first place."

"And was I not right?" Jim retorted. "Is he not convinced?"

"Sí, you were right. Only crazies would ever wear the same clothes as you."

"Listen," Jim snapped.

Pepe ignored him. "I will be in here forever," he cried loudly.

Jim grabbed Pepe's arms and sat him down next to him. "Pepe, look at me." Pepe looked up. Now Jim could see the discouragement in his eyes. Jim smiled. "You did good."

"I did what?"

Jim placed his hand on his friend's shoulder. "I'm proud of you. You did real good. Don't you see you convinced them?"

Pepe thought for a minute. A smile crossed his face. He grinned sheepishly. "I did convince them, didn't I."

"You sure did. In fact Dr. Damion thinks you are one of the most mentally ill people he knows."

"He does?"

"Yes, he does. Now, don't you feel better?"

Pepe smiled and nodded his head. "But I may have caused some suspicions when I asked around about David."

"I was afraid of that. We may not have much time."

"I couldn't find David's file."

"I'm not surprised. If this place is a front for the company, then most likely the file isn't here anyway. Have you seen Indian?"

"No, I haven't."

"He's supposed to be in here somewhere. How about the staff, did you get any information from them?"

"Well not from the staff, but there is one of the patients that may know something."

"Who?"

"Me," answered a male voice from behind Crockett's left shoulder. Jim and Pepe stood and turned in the man's direction. Jim noticed the long flowing hair draping over the man's shoulders.

Pepe extended his arm. "Jim, ah, this is my roommate. You know, the friend I told you about."

"Yes, I remember." Jim extended his hand to shake his. "Nice to meet you." Jim stared at the man's flowing robe, sash, and sandals. "Ah, Jesus, right?"

"Oh no," the man said with a modest smile. He took Jim's extended hand in his. "But I am one of his apostles. That's why they call me Disciple."

Pepe motioned with his hand to the couch. "Disciple, would you like to join us?"

"Thank you." He pulled up a nearby chair.

"I loved your sermon this morning in group therapy," Pepe began.

"I'm flattered you remember." Disciple slipped off his sandals.

"Jim, you should have been there. Telling the counselor to repent of his adulterous acts was magnifico."

"So you're a judge too?" Jim asked sarcastically.

"No," the robed man replied, not offended by the question. "I just felt the counselor was casting too many stones."

"You know," Pepe tried to explain, "he who is without sin—"

"I know, let him cast the first stone."

"Oh, you know the story of Jesus and the adulterous woman?" Disciple asked.

"Sí, our mom told us bible stories nearly every day."

"So you two are brothers then," Disciple concluded.

"No, we're not brothers," Jim corrected.

"All men are brothers," Disciple pointed out.

"Yeah, Jimmy," Pepe agreed, "all men are brothers."

"Well, in that sense we're brothers, but we don't have the same— ah, never mind." Jim shook his head in frustration. He tried to again focus on their reason for being there. "Listen, Mr. Disciple," he began, not sure how he should proceed. "Ah…" he paused.

"You're here about David, aren't you?"

"Yes, we are." He relaxed, knowing the conversation was again refocused. Just then Disciple's eyes looked up and caught the glance of a woman dressed in black watching them from the doorway. "We want to know what happened to him. Can you help us?"

"Come." The Disciple motioned them toward the terrace doors. "Walk with me through the garden."

Pepe is right, Jim thought, *this guy's wacko.* He followed Disciple and Pepe through the double doors leading into the courtyard garden.

Disciple touched several of the flowers along the walkway. "Flowers are one of my favorites."

"Favorites?"

"Of God's creations."

"Ah, yes," Jim patronized. "Listen, Disciple—"

"I know. You want to know about David."

"He was my friend, and we just want to know what happened to him. Will you help us?"

Disciple gazed into Jim's eyes. "I see David was a dear friend, but the love in your heart betrays you."

Love betrays him, Pepe thought, *what does that mean?*

Jim said nothing, but knew immediately that this odd stranger referred to his love for Elaine.

"Jim, the answers you seek are already found within you."

Pepe was confused. "That doesn't make sense. Jimmy hasn't even asked you any questions yet."

Jim agreed. "Listen, Pepe's right. We don't have time for these riddles. David's wife thinks her husband was killed."

Disciple looked at the hospital doors. "Time does not permit further discussion."

"Why?"

Disciple picked a flower and placed it in his long flowing hair. "Right now they come for Pepe and me." He motioned toward the approaching Dr. Damion and his two accompanying orderlies. "Jim, you must leave. You may be in danger. I will help Pepe get the answers that you want." He extended his hand once again to Jim. "It's good to meet you."

"What of you and Pepe?"

He placed his arm around Pepe's shoulders. "Don't worry. We will be safe, for what truths can come from the mouths of the insane? Now go and wait to hear from us." Disciple motioned toward the side gate of the garden. "The gate will lead you back to the main entrance." Jim

made his way through the side gate with the two large orderlies following close behind. When he saw the orderlies coming closer, he picked
up his pace. Suddenly a man appeared from behind a bush. With a
mop handle he smashed each orderly dropping them to the ground,
allowing Jim to escape.

The man looked at the broken mop and sighed. Then he turned
toward the garden, leaving the orderlies lying on the sidewalk.

Dr. Damion approached. "Pepe and Disciple, it is time for your
session." Pepe nodded in agreement. "Disciple, I didn't know you knew
Mr. Crockett?" He motioned Disciple and Pepe to follow him back
into the main building.

"Yes, Pepe introduced me to him."

They reached the double doors. "What did you talk about?"

"Tell him nothing," Pepe whispered.

"He had questions about David Smith," Disciple answered to
Pepe's dismay. "Don't worry, Pepe, I told him nothing that he didn't
already know."

Dr. Damion agreed. "You're absolutely right. By the way, Disciple,
you have a visitor." The doctor nodded his head toward the woman
dressed in black.

The woman ignored the doctor and Pepe and walked up to Disciple. "Hello, Disciple." She smiled and placed her arms around his
neck. She kissed him on the cheek and then stepped back to look into
his face and then at his attire. "You need new clothes."

Disciple did not respond. The janitor with the broken mop watched
from a distance. Pepe felt like he knew the woman but couldn't think
from where.

"Insane asylums are some of your favorite places, aren't they?" Her hand
gently brushed the long hair out of his face. He still did not respond.

"Don't I know you?" Pepe interrupted.

The woman quickly turned. She looked at Pepe more intently. "I
doubt it," she said after a moment. Disciple could see she was caught
off guard by the question. She again looked back and smiled. "It's was
nice to see you again, but I really must go." She turned and left through
the same gate Jim and the orderlies had passed through earlier.

Disciple and Pepe reentered the building and followed Dr. Damion
down the hall to the group therapy session room. "That woman, who
is she?"

"An old acquaintance," Disciple answered. He held the door open
for Pepe. "You act like you know her too?" Disciple's attention focused
on the new janitor with the broken mop handle.

"I thought I did, but I can't remember from where."

Disciple watched the janitor moving the mop bucket toward the end of the hall. "Pepe, you go ahead. I'll be along shortly."

Indian too recognized the woman, but, just like Pepe, couldn't think from where. Slowly he pushed the water bucket and broken mop closer toward the basement door. Even Jim and Pepe hadn't recognized him in his disguise. He opened the door that led to the basement. He did not notice that he was being followed. He tried several doors, acting like he was looking for a new mop handle. What he was actually looking for was the medical records room. Like a dart the thought entered his mind. "North Vietnam," he spoke aloud. "She's the woman on the veranda who watched." Indian sat down in the nearby chair where he reflected back to that time several years ago.

"There's Micah on the veranda," Indian whispered. "I don't recognize the woman who is with him." He refocused his nighttime vision scope on the commotion now in the prison compound. Indian didn't understand what was happening. "Why are the prisoners out of their cells this time of night?" How many prisoner of war camps had he visited over the past several months since he heard that Jim Crockett had been taken prisoner? Again Indian hoped that this camp would be the one. As the prisoners lined up, Indian studied each prisoner's face carefully. His attention focused on the fourth one. "Could it be?" he whispered. He adjusted the knobs on his scope for a better image. The face was gaunt and dirty. He was much thinner, but Indian knew. "It's him." Now the guards placed bags over their prisoner's heads and forced them to kneel on the ground in a row. Suddenly one of the guards pulled his pistol and placed it to the back of the first prisoner's head. He then looked up where Micah and the woman were sitting. Both appeared to be enjoying the spectacle below them. Suddenly the woman signaled with her hand, and the shot was fired into the back of the prisoner's head. Indian refocused his scope just in time to see the man fall forward. Indian gritted his teeth. "Dammit, they're executing these guys," he whispered. The guard quickly approached the second prisoner and a second shot was fired. Indian watched the second prisoner fall forward. Indian quickly surveyed the number of guards in the tower and on the grounds. *I'll have to be quick*, he thought. He readied himself as the third shot sounded, and again the third prisoner fell forward. *Crockett is next. I need to stop this.* The guard moved to the fourth prisoner and placed his pistol to the back of the man's head. Suddenly a rifle shot rang was heard. Most of the executioner's chest tore away as he toppled to the ground. Quickly other shots rang forth killing several Vietcong in the tower and others on the ground. Indian watched at their surprise and mass confusion. He breathed a sigh of relief when the remaining prisoners were once again taken back inside the prison cell compound. Again he looked at the veranda. Unbelievingly, he watched Micah and woman completely disappear in thin air right before his eyes. Quickly he picked up his things and moved deeper into the jungle. Indian knew the Vietcong would be looking for him shortly.

"They're locked."

Indian thoughts returned to the present. He looked up at Disciple standing before him. "What?" he asked.

"All the doors are locked." Disciple nodded to the door next to them. "That door leads to the medical records room."

Indian noticed the man's hair was long and how it flowed like his own. He couldn't help but noticed that his robe was that of ancient Jewish attire. "You're looking for a medical record aren't you?"

How does he know? Indian thought. *I need to continue the deception.* He showed Disciple his broken mop handle. "No, I broke my mop handle. I thought there might be another down here in the basement."

"You must be Indian," Disciple continued. "Pepe told me you would come looking for David Smith's chart."

Indian mentally cursed Pepe for his big mouth but kept a stoic face. "I'm sorry, but I don't know a Pepe."

The man introduced himself. "I'm Disciple. I watched you sneak into the hospital early this morning. You know, you're real good."

"Again, you must have me confused with someone else."

Disciple smiled. "I'm late for group." He pulled a key from his pocket and handed it to Indian. "If David's file is still here, it will be in the medical records room. Take it and leave with Pepe tonight. You're lives are in danger." He placed the key in Indian's hand. Indian was silent. "Say hello to your grandfather."

"Grandfather?" Indian asked.

"Lone Wolf is a dear friend of mine." Disciple turned and proceeded down the hall.

CHAPTER FIFTEEN

PLANE TRIP TO PHOENIX

Elaine approached the ticket counter while Jim and Doug held back and waited. Looking at his friend, Jim could see concern in Doug's face. "Doc, is something wrong?"

Doug looked up. "Does it show?"

"Well you didn't say a word all the way to the airport. Even Elaine noticed it."

"I didn't mean to be rude."

"You found this Tina Michaels, didn't you?" Doug nodded his head. "Did you see her?"

"I did. Tina is in—"

"I got it," Elaine interrupted. "Doug, they had a seat right next to you. I hope you don't mind."

"No, that's great."

"Good, should we go to the gate?" Elaine asked.

Jim looked at his watch. "We better, you will be boarding soon." Jim picked up her carry-on bag. "Doc, you were telling me you found Tina?"

"Yes, I did." Doug looked at both Elaine and Jim. "She's in prison."

"Prison?" Elaine asked. Doug nodded his head.

Doug allowed Jim and Elaine to enter the escalators first. Jim turned back to Doug. "So that's what's bothering you. She's in prison."

"Actually, it was some things she said about Nicole and Jason."

Elaine now turned back. "What did she say?"

"Tina was Nicole's nurse when Jason was—"

"Jim, look," Elaine interrupted. "Look who's over there."

"Dammit," Jim exclaimed, "it's Scarface."

"Are those the cemetery guys?" Doug asked.

Jim nodded his head yes. "They must have followed us here."

Elaine touched Jim's arm. "They won't try anything here, will they?"

"Not likely. If they were going to do something, they would have done it before we arrived at the airport." Jim looked over at the gate. "They are boarding. Why don't you two just get on the plane."

Elaine turned and gave Jim a quick hug and kiss. "Okay, you be careful."

"I will." Elaine turned and walked through the gate. Jim touched Doug's shoulder. "Thanks, Doc."

"Sure. You watch yourself."

"We'll see you in a few hours."

Jim watched Doug follow Elaine through the concourse gate. He turned and walked toward Scarface and Lenny. He stopped short, smiled, and saluted them. Scarface smiled and saluted back. They then proceeded to follow Jim down the long concourse hall from a distance.

Doug put his and Elaine's carry-on bags in the overhead compartments. He then allowed Elaine the window seat. He sat down next to her. "I sure hope Jim will be all right," Doug said.

Elaine smiled. "You don't need to worry about him. Jim is one of the smartest espionage agents this country has ever had."

"I didn't know that."

"In their day, there wasn't anyone better that Jim and Indian." She looked at Doug. "Rest assured, Scarface and Lenny should be the ones worrying."

Doug smiled. "Thanks for the reassurance. You know, Jim means a lot to me."

Elaine smiled back and realized that he really did care. She could appreciate why Nicole fell in love with him.

Elaine and Doug fastened their seat belts. "I'm sorry about your husband."

"Thanks. The four of us were real close for several years."

"You know, Indian and Jim never have talked about those years. If I am not imposing, what did you four actually do?" Elaine looked into Doug's eyes and tilted her head slightly. Her face darkened with sadness as she reflected briefly. "I'm sorry. I guess I shouldn't have asked."

Elaine reached over and grabbed his arm and smiled. "It's all right." She thought for a brief moment. "I'll tell you, because of your heart."

"My heart? I don't understand."

"How many people could learn of what the four of us did and still be our friends?" She looked into his face and smiled. "You are one of the few that could." Doug remained quiet as he listened to her words. "We were a special covert group formed after the Vietnam War. The four of us had very special talents. We made many people in our government and covert operations very rich."

"Rich? But I thought you worked for the government."

Elaine smiled. "We thought we did too. We thought our actions were for God, Honor, Freedom, and Country."

"And they weren't?"

Elaine shook her head no. "No, we were deceived. Oh sure our checks came from the federal government, but we actually worked for a secret society of powerful people who represented many governments, banks, corporations, and wealthy individuals in the world."

Oh, not more of this secret society nonsense, Doug thought.

"They existed for only one reason. To gain power, wealth, and complete domination over people." After saying the words, Elaine studied Doug's face for a reaction. She then smiled. "You don't believe me, do you?"

"Well, secret societies trying to control the world is kind of hard to swallow."

"Why do you say that?"

"Well if these secret societies exist, then why don't more people know about them?"

"They do."

"Then why aren't they speaking out about them?" he asked. Elaine looked at Doug. He looked at her. Then she smiled. "Why are you smiling?"

"Did you hear what you said?"

Doug thought for a minute. "Sure, I know what I said."

"Then now you know."

"Know what?"

"Why Jim, Indian, I and so many others do not speak about secret societies. No one believes us."

Now Doug began to understand. "I'm sorry if I offended you."

"It's okay. At least you understand."

Doug nodded his head. "But why the four of you?" he asked. "What made you four so special?"

"Because we were blessed with great talents, if you want to call them that. That's what made us so special. Not so much different than your surgical talents."

"What were your talents?"

"Well my husband David was the genius with an IQ of 180. There was very little that he did not know. We used his wisdom and knowledge in all of our assignments."

"And Jim?"

"Jim was our leader. He was able to develop our stratagem. He would listen to our suggestions and was able to put together a plan to accomplish our assignment goals. Indian was the greatest one-man killing machine this country has ever known. He and Jim were at their best undercover and in disguise."

"And you?"

She looked at Doug and paused. Finally she answered. "I was the seducer. I was the body that men used to satisfy their lusts." She again paused. "All of us together in some way destroyed the lives of many people."

Tears filled her eyes, and Doug realized she had deep regrets.

She tried to smile. "How would you like to have that on your conscience?" Doug did not answer. He handed Elaine his handkerchief and put his arm around her shoulders. She rested her head against him and closed her eyes. Shortly she was asleep. As Doug contemplated her words, he began to understand. The existence of a secret society was only an excuse for them. They hadn't spoken about that time period because remembering what they did caused too much pain and sorrow.

"Would you like something to drink," the attendant asked. Doug shook his head no. The attendant then pointed at Elaine's lap. "Sir, those pictures are about to fall from her lap."

Doug reached over and grabbed them. He looked back at the flight attendant. "Thanks."

"Sure. If you need anything let me know."

Doug nodded. He reasoned that the pictures were the ones of David's room they had mentioned earlier. He placed them in his coat pocket and promised himself to look at them later. In the meantime, he watched Elaine sleep. Resting her head on his shoulder reminded him of the last time he saw Nicole. Doug closed his eyes and reflected back to their plane trip together.

His eyes moistened as he watched Nicole sleep on his shoulder. Her physical beauty had faded with her illness, but his heart ached as he thought of a life without her. He gently touched her shoulder. "Nicole, we are here." She smiled and opened her eyes just as the plane touched the runway.

"I'm sorry I wasn't much company. I guess I slept most of the way."

"You'll be well rested for the surprise tonight."

She looked out the portal. "We're in New York City, can't you tell me now?"

Doug smiled at her. "Not yet."

The airplane pulled to a stop at the concourse. He picked up her frail body and placed her in her wheelchair. Nicole winked at the bearded long-haired gentleman who graciously waited for her wheelchair to pass. Then from a distance he followed them off the plane and through the terminal. The limo driver helped with the bags. Doug lifted Nicole into the backseat of the car. Nicole looked around inside. "A limo. We are actually riding in a limousine."

"Only the best for you," Doug answered as he sat next to her.

Nicole grabbed his arm. "This is so neat. I've never ridden in a limo before."

"Which hotel sir?" the driver asked.

"No hotel. Go straight to Central Park."

Nicole looked out the window at the setting sun. "Central Park? Doug, isn't it kind of late for a walk in the park?"

"Not for tonight, ma'am" the driver interjected. "You must be going to the—"

"Sh," Doug interrupted with mischief in his eye. "It's a surprise."

"Oh, I see, sir." The driver smiled and closed the door. As they pulled away from the curb, the gentleman from the airplane followed from a distance in a taxi.

Nicole tugged on his jacket. "Come on, what's at Central Park?" Nicole asked. Doug just smiled. "You're not going to tell me, are you?"

He couldn't remove the grin from his face. "You'll find out soon enough."

Nicole rested her head on his shoulder and took him by the hand. She knew her life was slowly slipping away. *I know John said no*, Nicole thought, *but I have to tell him*. She looked up at him. "Doug, I have some things I want to tell you."

"What things?"

"I haven't much time, and I need to tell you—"

"Please, let's not speak of those things, especially tonight."

Nicole looked at him and smiled. "Okay."

Doug bent down and kissed her on the forehead, and they rode in silence.

The driver interrupted the silence. "I can get you within one block of the park, will that do?"

"Perfect," Doug replied. The car came to a stop. When he opened the door, familiar music filled the air. He placed Nicole in the chair, tipped the driver, and told him where to leave their bags.

"Listen, I know that song."

For just a few moments the countenance in her face changed. "Doug, is this some kind of concert?"

Doug shrugged. "Maybe."

"A concert in the park, that's what it is. Whose concert is it?"

"Listen to the music, and you tell me."

He pushed the wheelchair through the crowd as they listened to the music. When they arrived at the grandstand, he showed security their backstage passes. "I recognize the music," Nicole said, "but who is doing the singing?"

"What do you mean?"

"Well, the duo that sang this song broke up over a decade ago." People parted the way backstage as Doug brought her closer to the side of the stage. Now she could see the performers. He would always remember the way Nicole's face lit up. "I can't believe it. It's really them! It's Simon and Garfunkel."

Months had passed since Doug had seen so much glow and excitement in her face. She looked over the vast audience. She then looked back at him. "There are so many people." It was as if she had been revived with a renewed energy. For the next two hours he watched and savored every word of every song that parted from her lips. When she wasn't looking, Doug shed a tear.

"This is the happiest surprise of my life," she exclaimed and then pulled him down to her level. She wrapped her weakened arms around his neck. "Thanks," she whispered, "thank you so much." She pulled back and saw his tears. She took her weak hand and gently wiped the tears away and then took his hands in hers. "It's okay," she said. "Everything will be all right."

Feeling more tears coming, Doug turned away from her to watch the singers. When she wasn't looking, he would watch her face. It reminded him of happier times when she, Jason, and he had run through the meadows, laughing, singing, and rolling in the tall grass. *I will miss that*, he thought.

Doug did not notice the long-haired, bearded man come up behind Nicole's wheelchair. Nicole looked up into his face and smiled. He nodded at her as if to say, "Nicole, it's time." She nodded.

Doug was standing at the side of her chair. Nicole tugged on his sweater. When he looked down at her, she gave him an envelope. "Can you keep this for me?"

He placed the envelope in his pocket. She then handed him an empty paper water cup. Seeing a garbage can nearby, he walked over and disposed the cup.

Nicole gazed at her husband as he walked away. "I love you, Doug," she murmured, drowned out by the surrounding music. She then turned to the man and nodded. "Okay, John." He quickly turned her chair and pushed her away.

When Doug turned back she was gone. He searched New York for days, but she left without a trace. That was the last time he saw Nicole. A few days later he remembered the letter she gave him. Over the years he had read the letter so many times that he knew it by heart.

"Dear Doug,

If you are reading this letter, then I am gone. Do not search for me, for you will not find me. I know that you have many questions, but the answers would not console your aching heart. Just remember that the time I spent with you was the happiest time of my life. I will not miss this life, but I will miss you. I have left you a gift. That gift is our son. Realize that he is the most precious gift that I can leave you. I love him with all my heart. As long as you live at the ranch, our son will be protected. There are evil people who want him. He is a Levite, which makes him a special little boy. Guide and protect him, for later in his life he has an important mission to fulfill. He will know what the mission is.

With all my love,
Nicole

How many times have I read that letter, Doug thought. *Even to this day, the questions that this letter raises still remain.*

Someone was touching Doug's shoulder. He opened his eyes to see the flight attendant standing next to him. "Sir, you and the lady can fasten your seat belts. We will be landing in Phoenix shortly."

"Thank you." He looked at Elaine who was now awake. "Well that was a short flight," she said. They both fastened their seatbelts.

CHAPTER SIXTEEN
MENTAL HOSPITAL ESCAPE

Disciple looked up from his book. Pepe quickly looked away. Disciple returned to his reading. A brief moment passed. Disciple again looked up. "Pepe, you're doing it again."

"What?"

"You keep staring at me."

"Well I'm sorry, but…" Pepe paused.

"But what?" Pepe did not answer. Disciple closed his book and set it on the nightstand. "Okay, tell me what's bothering you."

Pepe was hesitant at first. "Well, in group this morning, they laughed at you." Pepe looked down. "I even laughed at you."

Disciple was surprised by his comment. "Did that bother you?"

"Yes, it did. I kind of wanted to slap them around a bit." Disciple smiled. "You know they all think you're crazy?"

"How about you? Do you think I'm crazy?"

Pepe grimaced. "Well Jesus did live 2000 years ago. You could have chosen someone who lived more recently." Disciple chuckled. Both were quiet for a moment, and then Pepe was more serious. "When you told us the story of Jesus and the adulterous woman this morning, it was like you were really there. Did it happen that way?"

Disciple sat back on his bed and leaned against the wall. "Not exactly. There's more to the story than what the Bible tells." Pepe settled back to listen. "Her name was Sarah, and her husband's name was Joshua. They were both my friends."

"So did they really stone people to death, you know, when they committed adultery?"

"Yes, they did."

Pepe grimaced and shook his head. "But that seems so harsh."

"The Jewish law was harsh. Jesus tried to change their thinking to the higher law of forgiveness."

"They must not have listened."

"No, they didn't. In fact it was one of the local religious leaders who brought Sarah to the Master. They wanted him to condemn her to death."

"But he didn't condemn her. He forgave her, right"

"He also forgave Joshua."

"You mean Sarah's husband? I don't remember her husband being mentioned in the bible."

"He isn't. You see, Sarah and Joshua's marriage had been struggling for quite some time. Sarah found out sometime earlier that Joshua had been with another woman. She could not forgive him. In fact she chose revenge against Joshua rather than forgiveness."

Pepe now understood. "So that is why she was with another man. She was seeking revenge."

Suddenly there was a knock on the door. One of the nurses opened the door and looked in. "Excuse me, Disciple, you are wanted downstairs in the lobby."

"Thank you." Disciple stood to leave.

Pepe put up his hands in protest. "Wait, don't leave yet. Tell me what happened to Sarah and Joshua."

Disciple returned to his bed and sat down. He reflected for a moment and then began. "The crowd threw Sarah to the ground in front of Jesus and demanded her death. I remember looking up and seeing Joshua pushing his way through the crowd to Sarah's side." Disciple paused.

"Then?"

Disciple smiled. "Then Joshua did one of the most noble things I have ever seen." Pepe waited in anticipation. "He knelt down next to Sarah and lifted her up in his arms. He then looked up at Jesus and said, 'Master, my wife was with another man because of me. Do not take her life, but take mine instead.'"

"You mean he was willing to give his life for her?" Disciple nodded his head yes. "He must have really loved her."

"Yes, he did."

"Was it then that the Jesus said, 'he that is without sin, let him cast the first stone'?"

"Yes, and when the crowd dispersed, Jesus healed their broken hearts with his words and touch." Disciple now rose to his feet and walked toward the door. "Disciple," Pepe called after him, "thanks."

"For what?"

"For that beautiful story."

"Sure."

"Disciple," Pepe called a second time. Disciple turned back a second time. "I promise—" Pepe paused. "I promise I won't laugh at you anymore."

Disciple smiled at his roommate. "Want the light out?" Pepe nodded. Disciple turned off the light switch and left the room.

Pepe sat for a moment in the dark. *I wonder if I can ever be forgiven like Joshua*, he thought. Pepe then laid his head down and rolled to face the wall. *Just a couple more hours and I will be out of this place.* He closed his eyes. He tried not to remember, but the thoughts of Margarita came vividly to his mind.

"Father Pepe Santana, I need your help."

"But, Sister, I've never done this before."

"Just get me more clean towels and hot water."

"Yes, Sister." Pepe entered the other room where the husband was waiting. He grabbed the towels and more hot water. He handed them to the husband. "Here, Pedro, take these to Sister Margarita. She needs more hot water and towels."

Pedro handed them back to Pepe. "Don't give them to me."

"But you're the husband. You should be in there with your wife."

"And who made that rule?" Pedro asked.

"Hurry, Father," a voice yelled, "the baby's coming."

"Come on, Pedro, I can't stand the sight of blood. Take these towels and hot water in to Sister Margarita."

"No way, I can't stand the sight of blood either."

"Geez, you have had other children, you should be used to these things."

"Well I'm not. In fact, I've never seen any of our children born."

"Pepe, where are you," Sister Margarita screamed. "Come, I need you now."

Pepe looked back at Pedro. "Are you going in?"

"No, I'm not."

Pepe shook his head in disbelief. He then walked toward the bedroom door and turned back. "Pedro, you're just a big wimp."

"Sí, Father, I know."

Pepe shook his finger at him. "You better never come to my confessional booth."

"Pepe, get your butt in here right now."

Pepe looked at Pedro. "Father, you better go. Sister is getting pretty angry."

Pepe frowned at Pedro, and then reentered the bedroom.

Suddenly there was a noise from the hallway that interrupted Pepe's thoughts. The door opened. Pepe began to roll over to face the open doorway. "Disciple?" he asked. He attempted to focus his eyes when a blow smashed into his face. He tried to struggle free only to feel the weight of several bodies holding him down. Suddenly a mask was placed over his mouth and nose. A pungent odor filled his nostrils. He tried to hold his breath, but soon found his lungs ready to burst until he began taking huge breaths. The last thing he remembered was the burning sensation in his chest.

"He's out," one of the orderlies said.

"Good," Dr. Damion replied. "Put him on the gurney, and take him to the fifth floor."

"Fifth floor?" the other orderly asked. "Shouldn't we wait for the anesthesiologist?"

"No, I'll give the anesthesia myself. He needs the treatments tonight."

They placed Pepe on the gurney, and pushed him out of the room and toward the elevators. Shortly the doors opened and they entered the elevator. Pepe began to moan.

"Where's the mask?" Damion asked.

"We left it in the room. Shall I go get it?"

The first orderly reached into his pocket and pulled out a second mask. "Here I have another." He poured the anesthetic onto the second mask and applied it to Pepe's face. Once again Pepe settled down.

The elevator doors opened to the fifth floor. They rushed the gurney into the first treatment room. "Tie him to the bed," Dr. Damion instructed. "Attach the electrodes to his scalp, and then you can leave. I will not need you any more tonight." Both orderlies worked quietly. They had done this before. They knew that this would be Mr. Santana's demise.

Disciple searched the waiting room. It was empty. "He wondered who'd wanted him but eventually shrugged. They were gone now. He walked back down the dim hallway toward his room. Quietly he opened and closed the door so as not to disturb his roommate. He felt his way through the dark and lay down on his bed. He hadn't been there long when a strange odor filled his nostrils. "Pepe, are you awake?" There was no response to his question. He reached above his bed and turned on the lamp. "Pepe?" But Pepe's bed was empty. Puzzled, he climbed out of his bed. There lying on the floor was a surgical facemask. He picked it up and smelled.

Immediately he recognized the odor. Pepe was in trouble. He raced from the room and down the hall toward the main lobby. He opened the basement door and scampered down the stairs.

Indian was startled from his sleep when he heard the basement door open. He jumped off the cot and hid behind the file cabinet. "Indian," a voice yelled. Suddenly the stairway light turned on. "Indian, where are you?"

Indian peeked and recognized Disciple. He stood from behind the cabinet. "Here."

Disciple rushed to his side and grabbed Indian's arm. He pulled him toward the doorway. "Come quick, Pepe's in trouble."

Indian followed Disciple up the basement stairs. "Trouble, but I just talked with him about an hour ago."

"They'll kill him if we don't hurry."

"What do you mean kill him?"

They stopped at the elevator doors. Disciple handed the mask to Indian. "I found this in the room, and his bed was empty. Smell it."

Indian smelled the mask. "This is an anesthetic."

"I think they took him upstairs to the fifth floor, to the electro-shock room. That's where they killed David."

"You mean they shocked David to death?"

Disciple looked at the elevator doors. He motioned for Indian to follow. "Better not use the elevators. Let's take the stairs." Indian followed Disciple down the hallway and entered the stairwell. They climbed the stairs to the fifth floor.

Pepe opened his eyes to the dimly lit room. He found that he could not move because of the straps. He could feel pads and wires firmly attached to his head. Now Dr. Damion's face came into view. "Mr. Santana, I wanted you awake for this."

Awake for what? Pepe thought.

"We know you are here to find out what happened to David Smith." He reached down to check the electrodes securely fastened to his scalp. "Well now you'll find out firsthand. Ever heard of electro-shock therapy?"

"Electroshock therapy?"

"I guess I can tell you now. We gave Mr. Smith shock treatments over and over again until we completely fried his brain."

Pepe struggled with his restraints. "Please, you don't want to do this."

Dr. Damion chuckled. "You know, Mr. Santana, I really like you."

"Then why are you doing it?"

"Because I am obeying orders." Dr. Damion reached for the button. "Good-bye, Mr. Santana." He then flipped the switch. Immediately Pepe's body convulsed with seizures. The shaking continued until Dr. Damion turned off the switch. Only short episodes at a time, he decided. Now he would go get a cup of coffee. By the time he got back, Pepe would be awake enough for his second treatment.

Indian and Disciple watched from the stairwell as Dr. Damion entered the elevator. Quickly they entered the first treatment room and found Pepe. Indian froze as he stared at the electrodes attached to Pepe's head. Disciple looked up. "Indian, help with the leather straps."

"He's dead," Indian exclaimed.

"No, he's just unconscious. They've already shocked him."

Instinctively Indian backed away. He watched Disciple working on Pepe's straps. He too had felt similar electrodes attached to his scalp. He remembered the times when he came to his senses only to realize he had received another electroshock treatment.

"Indian, come on. Pull those electrodes from Pepe's scalp."

Indian shook himself and obeyed. He then picked up Pepe and threw him over his shoulder. "This way," Disciple instructed. Disciple led the way toward the fire escape stairs. Disciple stopped and turned. "When I break this window, it will set off the alarm. You'll only have a few minutes to climb down the stairs and make it to the stone fence, understand?"

Indian reached out and grabbed his arm. "Wait a minute, you're not coming with us?"

"No, you two go. I'll be all right."

"I'm not worried about you." He nodded toward the body on his shoulder. "I'm worried about Pepe."

"Don't worry. He's only had one shock treatment. He should come out of it—"

"No, it's not the shock treatment, it's you."

"Me?"

"All Pepe could do today was talk about you." Indian could still tell that Disciple was confused.

Indian explained. "You know Jim, the Doc, and me, we're kind of messed up in the head, but Pepe's a good person. I think someone like you can help him."

Disciple looked into Indian's eyes. He was quiet for a brief moment. "He really spoke about me?"

"Yes, he did. You know we're flying to Phoenix tonight for a big family anniversary fiesta tomorrow. Why don't you come with us?"

"Do you think anyone would mind? You know I'm kind of an oddball."

Indian chuckled. "No one will care."

Disciple smiled. "Then let's go." He nodded toward the excess weight Indian was carrying. "Do you want me to carry him?"

No, I'll carry him."

"All right, then I'll get the dogs and guards to follow me." He pointed with his hand. "Cross the fence by the tall oak tree and you'll find an old blue ford station wagon waiting. The key is under the left front fender. Drive around the hospital once. If you do not see me, then leave. Understand?" Indian nodded his head yes.

Disciple was right. No sooner did he break the glass than the alarm sounded. Disciple helped Indian as much as he could to carry Pepe quickly down the fire escape steps. They just touched the grass when they heard the dogs barking. "Hurry," Disciple yelled.

Indian watched as Disciple raced across the compound. Indian could hear the barking and voices in the compound. He turned and went the opposite way, hugging close to the stone wall. Suddenly there was the sound of gunfire. Indian turned and watched Disciple zigzag back and forth across the compound. Suddenly something smashed into Disciple and sent him sprawling to the ground. "He's hit," Indian exclaimed. "I better go get him." Then Indian watched as Disciple stood again and disappeared into the bushes on the other side. Checking all directions, Indian boosted Pepe to the top of the fence. He then climbed up and helped Pepe down. Sure enough, there was the blue station wagon. Finding the key he opened the door and laid Pepe in the backseat. He climbed into the driver's seat and started the car. A set of headlights came toward him. He pulled from the curb and dodged the oncoming vehicle. The other car made a quick U-turn and fell in behind him. Indian followed the road around the compound as Disciple instructed. He had nearly finished the circle. "Where is he?" Indian screamed.

"Who," a voice asked from the backseat. Indian glanced quickly to the backseat to see Pepe moaning and attempting to move.

"Disciple. He's supposed to be on this road." Suddenly a figure darted in front of him. Indian slowed down and opened the passenger side door. Disciple dove into the car.

"Drive!" Disciple commanded.

Indian swerved in and out of traffic, but could not shake the following car. "Someone was shooting at you," Indian yelled.

"Yes, they were. They didn't want us to leave."

Indian checked Disciple's robe, but could not see any blood. "Disciple, I saw you fall. Where did you get hit?"

Disciple put his index finger into a bullet hole. It was located exactly over his heart. "Right here," he replied.

"But that's right over your heart. Where's the blood?"

Disciple ignored his question. "Indian, turn here, this is the quickest way to the airport."

Indian followed his advice and turned. "We won't be able to get on the plane with these guys following."

"Just get us to the far side of the airport," Disciple advised. "I know a way to lose them."

———◆———

"Last call for flight five-forty-two to Phoenix. Passengers are now boarding at gate four."

Jim looked down the long corridor. "They should have been here by now."

"Are you boarding sir?" the ticket attendant asked.

"Ah, yes." Jim handed her the boarding pass and passed through the gate. Midway to the plane he hesitated and stopped. "What if they were caught?"

A stewardess touched his shoulder. "Sir, we are about to leave."

Jim turned back toward the gate. "I better go look for them," he murmured.

"Jimmy, where you going?" a voice yelled from plane's door opening. Jim turned to see Pepe calling to him. "Come on, buddy, you'll miss the plane."

Jim approached Pepe quickly. Pepe took Jim's carry-on bag. "Where have you been anyway?" Pepe asked.

"What do you mean where have I been? The question is, where have you been?"

Pepe led Jim down the plane's aisle. "We've been on the plane waiting for you."

"But I didn't see you get on."

"Ah, we boarded another way," Pepe whispered not to let the stewardess hear. "We found this real cool way to get on the plane quicker. Great seats, too. Doc bought us first class tickets."

Jim waived at Indian, who was sitting toward the back of first class. Jim breathed a sigh of relief. "Well at least we are all safe. Where's my seat?"

"Sir, your seat is in coach," the stewardess instructed. "Follow me and I will show you."

Jim put up his hands. "Wow, there must be a mistake. I should have a first class seat with my friends."

"No, she's right," Pepe corrected. "We gave your seat to Disciple."

"To who?"

Pepe pointed to the bearded man in the long flowing robe sitting next to Indian. "You know Disciple. You met him at the hospital this morning."

Disciple now noticed Jim. He stood and motioned Jim to come back to where he and Indian were sitting. Jim frowned at Pepe. "You mean the freak. What's he doing here?"

"We invited him."

"Invited him? What did you do that for?"

"Well he said he loves parties and Phoenix, so we just asked him to come along."

Disciple extended his hand. Jim took it. "It's good to see you again. Thanks for giving me your seat."

"Pepe, you offered my seat?" Jim whispered.

"Yeah, he's got this bad back. But we did you get a seat in coach."

"Follow me, sir," the stewardess instructed. Jim started to be upset until he noticed Indian's wink and smile. It was all that Jim could do to keep from smiling himself. Jim followed the stewardess past first class to coach until he found his seat. He placed his bag in the overhead compartment and then sat down. A voice from the aisle spoke to the lady next to Jim. "Excuse me, ma'am, would you consider trading seats with me. I have a nice seat in first class, but I would like to sit here by my friend."

"You are so gracious," the elderly woman answered. "Thank you."

Indian helped her gather her things and then escorted her to his first class seat. Shortly after he returned, the plane began to move. Jim glanced at Indian and shook his head in disbelief. Without a word Indian could read Jim's thoughts. Indian finally broke the silence. "We had to leave quicker than expected."

"What happened?"

"They were trying to kill Pepe with electroshock treatments. I think we were getting too close to the truth about Solomon."

"Then you got his file?"

"No, but we learned how he died. They fried his brain with shock treatments."

"So Elaine was right; he was murdered."

"Yes, he was. Now all we need to do is find out why."

CHAPTER SEVENTEEN

DAVID'S MESSAGE

Nancy Lopez entered the kitchen. "Elaine's finally resting quietly in one of the guest rooms."

Doug looked up. "Thanks, Mom, for your help."

Arturo grimaced. "It's tragic what she has been through, losing her husband like that."

Nancy put her arms around Arturo's neck. "We'll let her rest while we pick up the others at the airport."

Arturo touched his wife's arm. "Is it time to leave?"

"No, not yet, we still have a few minutes." She sat down next to her husband and across the kitchen table from Doug. "What are you doing?"

"Looking at these pictures that Elaine gave Doug this afternoon," Arturo explained.

She picked one up. "Pictures of what?"

"Her husband's room at the mental hospital," Doug answered.

"Looks like a bunch of scribbling on the walls."

"Apparently Elaine's husband made these markings on his wall," Arturo explained. "He then called Elaine to come and take these pictures."

Nancy replaced the picture on the table. "That's weird. It sounds like this Mr. Smith was in the right place."

"I don't know," Arturo countered, "look at the scribbling in this particular picture."

He gave it to his wife. Nancy put on her reading glasses. "You know, when you look closer, this scribbling looks a lot like Latin."

Arturo agreed. "We thought so too."

Nancy looked at her son. "Do you know the story behind these pictures?"

"Apparently David called her late one night and asked her to come visit him shortly before he died."

Elaine hid in the empty room as the orderly passed on his nightly rounds. Elaine knew she shouldn't be here, but there was something in David's voice, almost like a voice of despair. She opened the door and checked the long hall. It was empty. Quickly she proceeded to David's room. She tried the doorknob. It was locked. She pulled out a ring of keys and searched them until she found the right passkey. She opened the door and went inside. The room was dark. Slowly her eyes adjusted. Now she could see a figure standing in front of the barred window. "David," she whispered. The figure did not move. Elaine moved across the room until she was behind him. She wrapped her arms around his chest and pressed her chest against his back. "David, are you all right?"

He reached up and touched her hand with his. "I was just thinking."

"About what?"

"How I've really messed up a lot of people's lives."

Elaine laid her head between his shoulder blades. She knew he referred to the time they spent together in the intelligence field. "We all have done things we regret. You just have to let it go."

David reached up and grabbed Elaine's hand with his. "Do you think there really is a God?"

Elaine was surprised by his question. "I don't know, I guess I haven't thought about it much. Why are you asking?"

David turned to face his wife. "Did you bring the camera?"

"Yes, it's in my purse."

"Give it to me."

She retrieved the camera and handed it to him. "Why do you need the camera?"

"Because of this." David reached and turned on the light switch.

It took a few seconds for Elaine's eyes to adjust to the light. She was amazed at what she saw. All four walls were covered with writings. David immediately started taking pictures. Elaine looked at David. "What are all these writings?" she asked.

"This is my penitence to God," he answered.

Now Elaine was confused. "Penitence, for what?"

David turned to his wife. "Elaine, Joe and I have destroyed the world."

"Destroyed the world," Arturo interrupted, "what does that mean?"

"Sounds to me like I was right, that this David Smith needed to be in a mental institution."

"But why write all over the walls and take pictures of it?" Doug questioned. "Why not write them down on a piece of paper in the first place?"

"Maybe he wanted everyone to think he was crazy," Arturo suggested.

Doug looked at Arturo. "What do you mean?"

"Well if everyone thought he was crazy, people may not pay much attention to his scribbling. Maybe this is just a diversion from some real meaning."

Doug nodded his head. "That's a good point. I hadn't thought of that."

"Did he say anything more to Elaine?"

"Only that these scribbles were some kind message to save the world."

"And that's what it is," Arturo informed. "These writing are about the Apocalypse."

"You mean the bible Apocalypse?" Nancy asked.

"Taken directly from the Book of Revelation," he answered.

Mrs. Lopez pointed to a certain picture location. She smiled. "Well this Latin word isn't in the Book of Revelations. This Latin word is in my music books."

"Where do you see that?" Arturo asked. She showed him the word. "You're right." He handed the picture to Doug. "Take a look at this here in the left lower corner. Do you see it?"

"Yes, I believe it's the Latin word for music."

Arturo was confused. "That's sure unusual," he exclaimed. "This David writes all this stuff about the end of the world, and then as an afterthought, he writes the word music." Arturo looked up. "Why would he do that?"

Doug noticed something else. "Not only that, but look what's in front of that word." He handed the picture back to his mother and Arturo.

"Why it looks like some kind of elephant with three tusks," Arturo added.

Doug shook his head. "Apocalypse, music, elephants, it just doesn't make sense."

Nancy looked at her watch. "Hey, we better go if we're going to meet the plane on time."

Arturo stood. "Yes, we better."

Doug put up his hands. "Listen, you two don't have to go if you don't want. I can pick them up alone."

"We want to go with you," Nancy insisted.

Doug quickly left a message on the table for Elaine in case she awakened. Arturo spoke to his wife. "Nancy, why don't we take the limo?"

"But it's Charles's night off."

He opened the door for Doug and his wife. "I can drive."

Mrs. Lopez chuckled. "You, Arturo? I don't know about this."

Doug hesitated about getting into the car. "What are you saying?"

"Well I've never seen Arturo drive before. I'm not sure he knows how."

Arturo chuckled. "Well I might not be the best limo driver you've ever had, but I'm the best looking." He gave his wife a quick kiss and helped her into the car. He then climbed in the driver's seat and drove off.

For a few brief moments they rode in silence. "Okay, Son, what's bothering you?"

"Bothering me?"

"You haven't been yourself since you arrived."

"I just have a lot on my mind."

"Like what?"

Doug paused for a brief moment. He then looked at her. "Do you remember Tina Michaels, the girl I dated before Nicole?"

"Oh, yes, I remember her. Wasn't she was one of the nurses at the hospital?"

"Yes, she was. She now lives in California. In fact I went to see her this morning."

"How's she doing?"

"Not well, Mom. In fact she's in prison."

"Oh, I'm sorry to hear that. So that's what's been bothering you?"

"Only part of it. What bothers me more is what she said about Nicole and Jason."

"What did she say?"

Doug looked up. "Mother," Doug hesitated. "Tina told me that Nicole was murdered."

"You mean died, don't you?"

"No, Mom, she used the word murdered."

"But we all know that Nicole died of AIDS, how could she have been murdered?"

"I don't know, but that's not all. She also said that Jason was not our real son."

"But that doesn't make any sense at all. Why would she say something like that?"

"Apparently she was Nicole's nurse when Jason was born. She said our real baby was killed at birth and we were given another baby."

"Come on, surely you don't believe this nonsense. It sounds like Tina's just not right in the head."

Doug took a deep breath. "Yes, maybe you're right. Prison must have done something to her mind. She's not thinking straight."

Mrs. Lopez shook her head. "To imagine someone killing both Nicole and Jason, that's totally absurd."

Both were quiet for a brief moment. "There's one other thing. When I told her that Jason was alive and living with me she became very upset."

"Upset! I think she would be happy to know that Jason was alive."

"Oh, it wasn't because he was alive. She became upset because she felt Jason's life was in danger."

"But why would he be in danger?"

Doug thought for a moment. "She said he was in danger because he is a Levite."

Although Arturo was driving, he had been listening to their conversation. With the mention of the word Levite, he looked at his wife in the mirror. She looked back at him. "Did she actually say Levite?"

"Yes, she used the word Levite. You know, she's not the only one."

Nancy looked back at her son. "What do you mean?"

"Well Nicole use to call Jason a Levite too." Over the next brief moments Doug's mom became noticeably quiet. Just then Arturo pulled the limo to the airport's loading and unloading curb. "I'm sorry, Mom, I didn't mean to upset you. I guess I shouldn't have said anything."

"No, I was just taken back. All this is just a little disturbing."

"Listen, you two stay here in the car while I go find them." He opened the door and stepped out. "I'll be back in just a few minutes." Mrs. Lopez nodded in agreement. Doug closed the door and entered the airport terminal.

In the meantime Arturo left the driver's seat and came to the back to sit with his wife. "Did you hear?"

"Yes, I heard."

"Now what do we do?"

Arturo took her hand in his. "You have to tell him. You can't keep him in the dark like this anymore."

Nancy looked at her husband. "I don't want this for him."

"Neither do I, but you have always known this day would eventually come."

She bowed her head. "He will pass through sorrowful times ahead."

"He already has. Your son is strong like his father. You've got to believe and have faith in him that he can do this."

Nancy shook her head. "I wish there was another way."

"How can Doug help Jason if he doesn't know who he is?"

Mrs. Lopez took a deep breath and blew it out. "I know, but I really don't want to tell him."

"Then don't. Give him the diary and let him learn the truth on his own."

———⊜·◊·⊜———

Doug whispered to Indian. "Who's the Arab?"

"Actually he's Jewish."

Jim chuckled. "Doc, you'll really like this winner."

Doug looked over at Indian. Indian smiled. "He was Pepe's roommate."

"You mean in the mental hospital? But what's he doing here?"

"Ah, well, we just invited him along," Indian said.

"Just like that?"

"Yeah, pretty much. He just seemed to fit in well with us."

Doug looked at all his friends, and then at the Disciple. He shrugged his shoulders and shook his head. "Why not," he murmured as they passed through the sliding glass doors behind the others. He watched as his mother and stepfather hugged and welcomed Pepe, Jim, and Indian. They then both stared at Disciple while Disciple stared back. *This will be interesting*, Doug thought.

"Disciple," Mrs. Lopez finally said, "is that really you?" Doug's mouth dropped open.

Disciple smiled. "Hello, Nancy." He wrapped his arms around Doug's mom. He then freed one arm and wrapped it around Doug's stepfather. "Arturo, it's good to see you both again."

Doug looked at Jim. "Disciple, his name is Disciple?"

Jim nodded his head yes. "Yeah, he thinks he's one of Jesus's apostles."

"Nancy, Arturo, you two know Disciple?" Pepe asked.

"For many years," Arturo answered.

"That's so neat," Pepe exclaimed. "Did you know Disciple was my roommate at the hospital?"

"He was?" Mrs. Lopez asked. Their voices began to fade as they walked together back toward the limousine.

Jim looked over at Indian. "Indian, this Disciple fruitcake seems to know everyone."

Indian remembered seeing Disciple being shot in the hospital compound. Yet in the car a few minutes later, there was no wound or blood, only the bullet hole. Indian smiled. "Well, Jim, he says he's one of Jesus's disciples."

Jim looked at Indian. "Yes, and I'm the Pope." Jim then followed the others to the car.

Doug walked up behind Indian and put his arm around his shoulder. He smiled at Indian. "This could get real interesting."

CHAPTER EIGHTEEN

FATHER'S DIARY

Mrs. Lopez looked out her kitchen window. The eastern sky over the McDowell Mountains was turning gray. She slid open the sliding glass door leading to the back patio. The cool, early morning desert breeze gently blew through her hair.

"Couldn't sleep either," a voice spoke.

Mrs. Lopez turned. "Disciple, you startled me."

"I'm sorry, I didn't mean to." He handed her a cup of coffee. "I thought you might need this."

She took the cup and they sat down at the patio table. "Thanks, I didn't sleep well last night."

"Ah, me either." Disciple nodded toward the graying sky. "This is still my favorite time of day. I never tire of sunrises."

"And you have seen your share of them, haven't you?"

Disciple smiled. "I've seen a few." He nodded toward the eastern sky. "The Arizona sunrises remind me of sunrises near my home." Disciple took another sip of his coffee. "When I was a boy, my chore was to watch the goats and sheep at night."

"But I thought your father was a fisherman?"

"He was. But sometimes I would stay with Uncle Joseph herding his sheep."

Nancy smiled. "I remember some of those stories you use to tell me years ago."

"That was a while ago."

"Ever so often I think about my favorite story."

"Which one was that?"

"The one about Jesus's sisters, I loved that one." She took another sip of her coffee. "I'd like to hear it again."

Disciple smiled and settled back in his chair. "Our family lived in the city of Capernaum on the Sea of Galilee. Jesus lived with his parents in Nazareth, which was inland. I remember one summer when Jesus came to stay with us."

Zebedee and Salome entered the boy's room. "Jesus," Zebedee whispered. He did not respond. Zebedee gently shook his shoulder. "Jesus, wake up."

Jesus opened his eyes. "Uncle Zebedee, what is it?"

Zebedee put his finger to his lips. "Sh, don't wake the others." He motioned Jesus to follow them into the other room.

"You and Jesus were cousins?" Nancy interrupted.

"Yes, my mother and Mary were sisters." Disciple continued with the story. "Father did not know, but the commotion awoke my brothers James, Matthias, and me. We crept to the door, curious about what was happening."

"Jesus, sit down," our father, Zebedee, suggested. Jesus obeyed. Father was about to speak but stopped himself. He looked at our mother and shook his head. She knew Father could not tell him.

She then began. "Jesus, tonight we received a message from you mother."

"What did she say?"

Now our mother, Salome, was hesitant to speak. I remember James whispering to us. "Something bad has happened."

He was right. Our mother regained her composure. "Jesus, it isn't good news."

"Please, tell me, what is it?"

"It's your father, he's been in accident."

"Is he all right?"

Our father knelt before the boy. He placed his hands on Jesus's shoulders. "I'm afraid not. Some timbers fell upon him and he was—" He didn't finish the sentence.

The room was silent for the longest time. I looked up at my brother and whispered. "James, I don't understand. What happened?"

James turned to me. "Uncle Joseph was killed."

I remember I was stunned by the news. *Uncle Joseph is dead?* I thought.

"I must go home," Jesus said. "My mother will need me."

"We know," Mother answered, "but you must not go alone."

"No, I will be all right," he reassured. "I know the way."

"It is not that," Father countered. "There are too many bandits on the road. It will be safer if I take you home."

"But you can't," Jesus said. "This time of year is best for fishing. You need to stay here."

James entered the room. "He's right father. I will take Jesus home."

Now we stood and walked into the room. "And we will go too."

"What are you three doing up?" Mother asked.

"We could not help but overhear," James explained.

Zebedee smiled at Jesus and us. He appreciated our great courage. "I will not hear of it," Mother exclaimed. "All four of you are much too young to make that long journey by yourselves, especially in these dangerous times."

We looked at our father for support, but we were disappointed. "I'm afraid I agree with your mother. That road is much too dangerous for you."

"But not for me." We turned and watched the young man enter the house. "Peter," my mother exclaimed. "What are you doing here?"

"I just heard the news about Joseph," he answered. He turned to our father, "You stay and run the fishing boats, and I will take him Nazareth. I have been on the road many times."

"Was it really him?" Nancy interrupted.

Disciple smiled. "Yes, it was. It was Simon Peter, my father's fishing partner."

Nancy shook her head. "It's so hard to believe that you knew each other so well when you were boys. I mean, why isn't it discussed in the bible?"

"At one time it was, but somewhere along the way this and other things were lost."

"Then Peter took the four of you to Nazareth?"

"Yes, he did."

"One thing I don't understand is why didn't Jesus raise his father from the dead like he did Lazarus and others?"

"Interestingly, my brother James asked the same question."

"Then you all knew as children that, Jesus had special gifts."

Disciple thought for a moment. "I guess we did, but James did more than the rest of us. I just remember Jesus was my favorite cousin."

"So James asked him the same question?"

"Yes, it was on the road to Nazareth. I remember Jesus walked off into the darkness.

"Don't go too far," Peter warned.

"I won't."

The group watched him leave, figuring he was going to pray. Then in a few moments he returned.

James looked at Jesus. His head was down. James put out his hand and stopped Jesus. "Well?" he asked. Jesus shook his head no. "But why?" James asked.

Jesus looked at him. "God just said no."

James shook his head. "But I don't understand."

Jesus smiled. "God said he needed him."

Now Nancy was confused. "Needed him for what?"

Disciple smiled. "Do you think when we die all we do is sit on clouds, play harps, and listen to angels sing?" Nancy didn't answer. Disciple nodded toward the heavens. "Nancy, there are many universes out there, and things to do."

"Then there is purpose in life and death?"

"Absolutely. Tears of sadness were shed when Uncle Joseph died, but others shed tears of joy for he had returned back to his heavenly home." Nancy was silent for a moment. "I'm sorry, I have said too much."

"Oh no, it's just a lot to digest."

"Do you want me to stop?"

"No, tell me about the sisters."

"Well when we arrived at Jesus's home, Jesus hugged his mother and his two younger brothers."

"You're not supposed to raise him from the dead, are you?" Mary asked. Jesus did not speak but shook his head no. Mary sat down at the table. All of us took chairs and sat with her. I remember Jesus began to speak. "Mother, I know your thoughts."

Mary looked up at her son. Tears streamed down her eyes. "First the twin babies die and now my Joseph. Jesus, why so much sorrow?"

Jesus put his arm around his mother's shoulders to comfort her. "I'm sorry,"

Mary looked at her son. "Jesus, my heart is breaking."

"Mother, I may not be allowed to raise father, but even as we speak two special gifts approach our door."

Mary looked at her son. "What do you mean?" There was a knock at the door. Mary looked away at the door and then back to Jesus.

Jesus quickly arose from the stool. "I'll get it." He opened the door and invited a strange man holding two bundles into his home. "Mother, this is Enoch. He is a friend of mine."

"Mary," Enoch began, "I have two gifts for you." He placed a bundle in each arm. They moved.

Mary unwrap each blanket. Her eyes lit up. She immediately recognized them. "They're my babies," she exclaimed. She looked at the man Enoch. "I watched them die. How is this possible?"

Enoch motioned his head toward Jesus. Mary looked at her son. "You brought them back, didn't you?" Jesus did not answer, but allowed one of the babies to grasp his finger.

Nancy stopped Disciple's story. "So they were truly Jesus's sisters?"

"Little sisters."

"This Enoch, do you know where he and the twins came from?"

Disciple looked at Nancy. "Yes, I do, but I can't tell you."

"Then what happened to the twins?"

"I can't tell you that either."

"Have you told anyone else this story?"

"No, only you. Others would not believe me."

Nancy smiled. "Still can't find anyone to believe you?"

Disciple took another sip of his coffee. He smiled. "Not since you and Arturo."

Nancy placed her cup on the table. She finally found the courage to ask. "I've always wondered something."

"What's that?"

"Well actually it's about your life. Don't you ever get tired of it all?"

Disciple was confused. "Tired of it all?"

"You know, tired of the living?" Disciple looked over at Nancy and smiled. He did not answer but turned his attention back to the graying eastern skies. "You know most people of the world would give anything to have your gift."

Disciple chuckled. "Gift?"

"To live and never die, wouldn't you say that's a gift?"

"I guess so."

"You speak as if living forever has a downside."

"For thousands of years I have been watching senseless wars with millions of people dying, millions of others suffering from poverty, disease, despair, and oppression by ruthless leaders who seek only power, wealth, and control." Disciple was silent for a brief moment. "Yes, there is a downside to living so long."

"I'm sorry. I never thought of it that way."

"But you know what is even worse?"

"What's that?"

"That I don't get to go. Over the years many friends have come and gone. Some day it will be yours and Arturo's turn to pass on." He paused for a brief moment. "That's the worse part. You will leave, and I will stay."

Nancy reached over and clasped his hand. "But soon it will be over for you too, right?" Disciple looked at Nancy. He smiled and nodded his head yes.

"Look at this," a voice exclaimed from behind. "I get up to get a drink of water, and find my wife on the patio holding hands with another man."

Both Nancy and Disciple looked up and smiled. Nancy stood and put her arms around her husband. "A good looking one at that," she added. She quickly kissed her husband on the lips. "What, you can't sleep either?"

He pulled out another patio chair and sat down next to his wife. "No, because someone next to me in bed kept tossing and turning."

"Oh, come on, I wasn't that bad."

"Yes, your right. It wasn't the tossing and turning that kept me awake, it was the constant moaning."

"Moaning?"

"She's been moaning all night about this party."

"You would be concerned too, if you had to worry about the caterers, flowers, decorations, and especially if anyone would come."

"Honey, everything will be fine. You always do such a fine job. Anyway I'm going to feed the fish early today. Once that is done, I'll help you prepare for the party."

Nancy smiled as her husband stood to leave. "That would be a big help."

"I'll be back in a little while." He then looked at Disciple. "Would you like to come?"

Disciple looked at Nancy for approval. "Sure, go ahead, I'll just sit here and watch." He excused himself and followed Arturo past the pool and across the large lawn to their backyard lake.

"I was surprised to see you last night," Arturo began.

"It's funny how life paths cross. Imagine Pepe and me as roommates in a mental institution."

"That's not too hard to imagine," Arturo teased.

Disciple chuckled. "I suppose you're right."

"Doug mentioned last night what happened to you in the mental hospital. You were fortunate to escape."

"Yes, we were."

"You know they will still be looking for you, don't you?"

"I know. I don't imagine it will take them too long to find out where we are." Arturo opened the little storage shed and a fresh bag of fish food. He then filled two cans and gave one to Disciple. "You know, Doc still thinks you're a Mexican drug lord."

Arturo nodded his head. "Sí, I know."

"How come you never told him?"

Arturo took a small handful of food and threw it out into the lake. The water clattered as hundreds of fish feeding broke the water surface. "I think it's best this way. Anyway he is still real good to me. "Have you seen his real father recently?"

Disciple took fish food out of his own can and followed Arturo's example. "Not for several years. I still think it's best he not know that he's still alive."

"I agree. It could bring unneeded danger to Jason." Both were quiet for a moment. "Disciple, do you think it's time that Doug know?"

"Why do you ask?"

Arturo took the empty fish food can from Disciple and filled them again. "He keeps asking questions about Nicole and Jason. He even mentioned the Levite last night."

"Levite?"

"He said that not only Nicole referred to Jason as the Levite, but another lady he talked to in an LA ladies' prison also called Jason a Levite."

It must have been Tina Michaels, Disciple thought. He looked at Arturo. "Maybe this is the time."

"I agree, but Nancy doesn't want to tell him. She wants him to learn it from the diary."

"I think it's the only way. Doc needs to find out for himself who he is. He would never believe us if we told him." Their attention now turned toward the voices coming from the house. "It's the Doc," Disciple continued.

Arturo handed Disciple another full can of fish food. "Here, a few more cans and we will be done."

"Mom, you want a refill?" Doug asked.

Mrs. Lopez handed her son the cup. "Please."

Doug took the cup and filled it with coffee. "What is it, your thirty-second anniversary?"

"Thirty-third," she corrected. She took the full cup from him and placed in on the table. "Thank you."

Doug shook his head. "Where did I lose a year?"

"Well that's real easy to do."

Doug sat down across from her. "Tell me, are you and Arturo happy?"

"Oh, yes, very much so. He is a good and kind husband."

"But do you love him?"

"Yes, I love him." Then she paused, "but it's not the same."

"What do you mean?"

"Even though I love Arturo, he will never be or replace your father. I don't think anyone could."

Doug nodded his head. He understood how his mom felt. "I feel the same about Nicole. I don't believe anyone could take her place either."

Mrs. Lopez sighed. "You miss Nicole, and I miss your father, but there is hope."

Doug looked at his mom. "Hope?"

"Hope that your father and I will be together again." Doug chuckled at the thought. Mrs. Lopez was disturbed. "You don't have hope?"

"For me and Nicole to be together again?" His smile faded. "Hope doesn't fill a heart's emptiness." Doug looked to change the subject. "It looks like Arturo has this Disciple guy feeding the fish."

Mrs. Lopez chuckled. "That's what Disciple gets for getting up so early."

"This Disciple guy is different, isn't he?"

"You mean his long hair and flowing robe?"

"Well not only that, but professing to be one of Jesus's disciples. He's even got Pepe believing him."

"He's harmless enough. Look at your friends. Pepe, Indian, and Jim aren't the most sane people on earth. I don't know, he seems to fit in rather well."

Doug chuckled. "You're right about that." He took another sip of his coffee. "How is it that you know him?"

"You know him too, Son."

"I do?"

"He was the one that helped us escape from Germany when you were a baby."

"Then he's the one you told me about?"

"That's right."

"But he doesn't look old enough. He looks closer to my age."

"Maybe he just holds his age well?"

"He sure does." Doug paused for a moment. "Now how did he help us?"

Mrs. Lopez sat back in the chair. She began to relate to Doug how they met. "Well, Disciple and your father were good friends during the war."

"There was a soft knock at the back door. My mother opened the door and Disciple came in. He hugged my mom and then my dad. For some reason he had known my parents for years. He asked where we were hiding and told my father to bring us out of the basement, that we didn't have much time.

"Father rushed to the basement. 'Quickly, Disciple is here.' We gathered our belongings and raced up the stairs to where he was waiting. Disciple took you in one arm, leaving the other hand for the suitcase. 'The longer we wait, the greater the danger. Already the Gestapo is suspicious.'

"'Do you know where we are going?' I asked him. Disciple looked at me. 'Far away.' He then looked at my parents. 'Please, come with us. It isn't safe for you here.' My father looked at my mother. 'No, we will stay.'

"Disciple looked at my mom. She reached out and touched his hand. 'Please understand, this is our home.' Disciple nodded his head. We all hugged each other and promised to contact each other when the war was over."

Mrs. Lopez paused. Doug looked at his mother. "Mom, what's wrong?"

"My parents…I didn't realize I would never see them again."

"What happened to them?"

"The Gestapo found out what my parents did, and after the war my uncle told me that they were taken prisoner by the Gestapo and never seen again."

"I so sorry, Mom, I didn't realize."

"It's okay."

"Then that's when Disciple brought all of you to the United States?"

"Not all, just me and you. You're father didn't come."

"Why didn't he come?"

"Well he was supposed to, but that evening when we arrived at the train station to leave, they spotted your dad. He ran and led them away from us." Again Mrs. Lopez paused. "Your father sacrificed his life to save us."

"Then that's how he died?"

Should I tell him? she thought. *No, I can't. Disciple says he will not believe, unless he learns it on his own.* She looked at her son. "It was the last time I saw your father."

Doug thought for a minute. "So my father was a German doctor who worked with Dr. Mengele in the prison camps?"

"Yes."

"Well I understand why he was wanted and hated by the Jews, but being a German officer, why was he wanted by the Gestapo?"

How long Mrs. Lopez had dreaded seeing this moment come. But Disciple and Arturo were right. He had the right to know. "Doug, the Gestapo as well as the Jews wanted your father dead, because your father was a Levite."

Doug was stunned. "You got to be kidding," he exclaimed. "What is it with these Levite guys? Nicole and Tina called Jason a Levite, and now you call my father a Levite. What does this all mean?" Mrs. Lopez was silent. He stood and walked to the pool. He then turned back. "Mom, if dad was a Levite, and Jason is a Levite, then I must be a Levite too."

"Wait. I have something that will help explain. Wait here." She walked back into the house. Disciple and Arturo finished feeding the fish and approached.

"Good morning, Doug," Arturo greeted, "where did your mom go?"

"I'm right here. Here, this is for you."

Doug took the large manila envelope from her and opened it. "It's a book." He pulled it from the envelope.

"Not just a book, but your father's diary. He wanted you to have it."

Doug thumbed through the first few pages. Disciple and Arturo looked at each other.

CHAPTER NINETEEN

THE PARTY

Doug took off his sombrero. "I hate costume parties."

"Well this isn't much of a costume for me." Doug smiled at Indian's feather headdress. "Anyway, it's only for a few more hours. It's important to your mother."

Doug nodded. "Yes, you're right."

Indian rubbed his hand over one of the large, smooth pillars. "I can't believe the size of this house. You grew up here?"

"Part of the time. When mom married Arturo, I was in grade school. Sometimes we lived here and sometimes in Guadalajara, Mexico."

"What determined which?"

"My stepfather. It depended whether he was in or out of favor with the Mexican officials."

Indian was surprised by his answer. "What does you stepfather do?"

"He's into land development, real estate, commercial buildings, and drugs."

Indian stared at Doug. "Did you say drugs?"

Doug smiled. "Arturo use to be a Mexican drug lord, who's supposedly gone straight."

"You sound a bit bitter."

"I try not to be, but sometimes it's hard."

"Well this place sure is beautiful. I like how the lawn leads right down to the edge of the pond."

"Well it's not so beautiful for Pepe and me."

"Why is that?"

Doug smiled. "We used to mow it."

Indian chuckled. "And the pond is full of fish?"

"Yes, Arturo keeps it stocked."

"I bet Jason enjoys the lake."

"It's his favorite. He'd be down there fishing right now, if he were here."

All morning long Indian recognized that something was troubling Doug. "You're mind is not here today."

Doug looked at Indian. "It's that evident?"

Indian nodded. "I'm afraid so."

Doug looked away. "I found Tina Michaels. She's in prison."

"Prison. So that's what's bothering you?"

"Not exactly. It's something she told me. When I told her that Nicole died five years earlier, she became upset. She said Nicole was murdered."

"This doesn't make sense unless someone purposely gave her blood contaminated with the AIDS virus."

"I had the same thought. She also told me that our baby was killed at birth. When I told her that Jason was still alive, she warned me that his life was in danger."

"Danger from what?"

"The warden came before she had time to tell me."

Indian could tell Doug was frustrated with all the unanswered questions. "Do you think this Tina Michaels could explain more?"

"What do you mean?"

"Why don't you fly back to LA tomorrow and talk with her again."

"You think I should?"

"Absolutely. I'd go with you, but Sheriff Bates wants Jim and I to find out what happened to those two girls the army took."

"So when are you leaving?"

"In the morning." Indian could still see the concern on Doug's face. "Look, why don't you call Jason right now. We'd all feel better knowing he's all right."

Doug nodded toward the party crowd. "Will you cover for me?"

"Sure." Doug left and went back into the house. Indian approached Elaine sitting alone at one of the poolside tables. "May I join you?"

Elaine grabbed his hand and sat him down next to her. "I want you to look at these pictures."

Indian looked around. "Where's Jim?"

"He left twenty minutes ago to get me a beer."

"Do you want me to find him for you?"

"No, look at these pictures first."

She handed the pictures to him. "What are these?"

"They're pictures of David's room at the Whispering Pines Hospital."

"It looks like someone has scribbled all over the walls."

"I know. David did it. Late one night before David's death, he called me to bring a camera to the hospital. When I arrived I found this scribbling on the wall. He then took these pictures."

"Did he say anything about them?"

"No. I found them the day of his funeral."

Indian gazed at each one of them. "Well I don't know what to make of them. Just looks like scribbling to me."

"Doug thought the scribbles are in Latin."

"Really? I didn't know David knew Latin."

"I didn't either. Doug and Mr. Lopez translated the pictures last night. They said mostly David talks about the apocalypse. In fact, when Pepe read the translation, he said that David used the exact words found in the Book of Revelations."

"I don't remember David being religious."

"That's just it, he wasn't."

"Maybe he was creating some kind of smoke screen."

"Smoke screen, what do you mean?"

"Well you remember how good he was with riddles? Let me borrow them. Maybe there's a hidden message in these pictures."

"Okay, do you think—?" Elaine was interrupted by the commotion that Jim and Pepe were making.

"Pee Pee?" Pepe complained as he followed Jim around the pool to the bar. "How could you. She was laughing at me."

"I thought it was cute."

"Sí, señor," the bartender asked.

"Four beers and a coke."

"Cute? You got to be kidding. We were hitting it off real good until you said that."

Jim watched as Disciple danced in his long flowing robe. "Why can't you be like Disciple?"

"What do you mean?"

"He hasn't settled on just one woman. I bet he has danced with every lady here." The bartender handed him the drinks. "Gracias," Jim said. He carried the drinks along the edge of the pool. Pepe followed. "Listen, you should thank me, I did you a favor."

"How do you figure?"

"She's not your type." Jim placed the tray on the patio table. He handed Elaine a beer. "Here we are, my lovely lady, especially prepared for you."

"Thank you, James, and only twenty minutes late."

"Well you can thank electroshock man for that."

"Now that's not funny, Jimmy," Pepe exclaimed. "You know that treatment could have killed me."

Jim handed Indian a beer. "Pepe, it's just your imagination," Jim explained. "Electroshock therapy doesn't hang around in your body like that."

"You're wrong, Jim. Every so often I can still feel some electrical shocks zipping through my body."

Jim gave up and looked at Indian. "Where's Doc?"

"He went to call Jason," Indian said. "Hey, Pee Pee, come sit by me."

Jim and Indian chuckled as Pepe took the seat. Pepe sneered at Indian. "Oh, that's real cute."

Elaine turned to Pepe. "What's all this talk about Pee Pee?"

"Oh, you wouldn't believe what Jim did."

Jim noticed Elaine staring at him. "Believe me, it was nothing."

"Nothing? You introduced me to this hot girl as Pee Pee and ruined my chances with her."

Elaine scowled at Jim. "Did you do that?"

"Believe me, it's not a big deal, it was just a joke." Just then the band started playing.

The stern look was still on Elaine's face. "That doesn't sound like a funny joke to me." Elaine turned to Pepe. "I agree, I don't think that was funny either." She turned back toward Jim. "I think you ought to do something."

Jim scowled. "All right, I'll do something," he relented. He turned around and located the young lady on the other side of the pool. "Okay, there she is on the other side of the pool. Go over there and use your pheromones and ask her to dance."

"Get real, Jim, even with my Pheromones, she's not going to dance with a guy named 'Pee Pee.'"

"Sure she will, just watch." Jim walked over and started talking to her.

"Now what's he doing?" Pepe murmured. Jim then motioned her toward their table. "Oh, great, he's bringing her over here."

"Everyone, this is Breann Johnson. She would like to dance with Pee Pee."

Indian snickered.

"It's Pepe," Pepe corrected.

"Oh, I understand," Breann replied with a Spanish accent. "Mr. Jim here explained it to me that it is your U.S. accent."

"U.S. accent?" Pepe asked.

"He explained to me that in español, we say Pepe, but in English because of the accent, it is pronounced Pee Pee." Jim, Indian, and even Elaine were all hiding their smiles. Pepe frowned at Jim. "Anyway, Pee Pee, would you like to dance?"

The invitation surprised Pepe. "Well, yes."

"Then let's dance." She took Pepe by the hand and led him to the dance floor.

For a few brief moments they watched the couple dance. Indian shook his head. "Pepe's got to be one of the luckiest guys I know."

Jim snickered. "Oh, I don't know about that."

Elaine looked suspiciously at Jim. "What did you do?"

"Nothing much except—"

"Except what?"

"Well, Pepe don't know it yet, but Ms. Johnson is going to cost him three hundred dollars."

Elaine gasped. "You mean she's a—?" she paused.

"Right, Ms. Johnson is a call girl."

"Oh, Jim," Elaine exclaimed, "how could you?"

"Look, I told Pepe she wasn't for him, but he wouldn't believe me."

"Look at those two," a voice said from behind. All three looked up to see Mrs. Lopez shaking her head in disbelief.

Both Jim and Indian stood. "Mrs. Lopez, would you like to join us?"

"Why thank you." Indian helped her with her chair. "I saw you three laughing at something. I had to come over to see what it was."

Jim nodded at the two dancing. "Oh it's just Pepe, Mrs. Lopez. He was just dead set on dancing with that young lady."

Mrs. Lopez chuckled. "You must mean Breann."

"Yes, you know her?"

"Oh, very well, Breann is Doug's cousin."

Jim looked at Mrs. Lopez. "Doug's cousin?" Mrs. Lopez nodded her head yes.

"Then she's your niece?"

"Well, not exactly, Elaine. You see Breann is actually Brian."

Elaine, Jim, and Indian were stunned. They sat quietly for a brief moment digesting her words. Confused, Indian finally said, "You mean Breann is actually—"

"A man," Mrs. Lopez interrupted.

Jim and Indian's jaws fell open. "He's your nephew?" Jim asked.

"Yes, he is."

Indian shook his head with disbelief. "Boy, he's really good, isn't he?"

Jim nodded, looking at the dancing couple with new interest. "I should say."

Indian shook his head again. "She, I mean he, sure had me fooled."

Jim started to laugh. Indian, Elaine, and even Doug's mom followed. "Pepe is dancing with a guy," Jim finally choked out.

"Again," Mrs. Lopez said.

The laughter stopped abruptly. They again stared at Mrs. Lopez. "Again?" Elaine asked.

"Yes, he's dancing with Pepe again. You'd think he'd learn, wouldn't you."

Jim touched Mrs. Lopez's arm. "You mean Breann, I mean Brian, has danced with Pepe before?"

"Several times. A change in hair color, style, clothes, and makeup helps."

"But why?" Jim asked.

"Well now Brian says Pepe's a challenge. He really goes overboard just to fool him."

Jim looked at Mrs. Lopez. "Do you think we should tell him?"

Mrs. Lopez smiled. "No, let's just watch and see what happens. By the way, do you know where Doug is?"

"He went to call Jason," Indian said. "I think I'll go check on them." He excused himself and entered the house. He climbed the long staircase to the second floor. Now he could hear Doug's voice carrying from the study.

Doug changed the phone receiver to the other ear. "But how can the army just come and take them?"

"I don't know. Their bodies weren't in the morgue twelve hours before the army was here with a court order."

"Were you able to do any kind of autopsy?"

"Not enough time. They even took all the slides you had prepared in the pathology lab."

Good thing I have my slides, Doug thought. "Did they say anything about the other girl?"

"Only that the court order included her to go with them, also."

"But why would army intelligence be interested in those girls?"

"Sheriff Bates said 'for reasons of national security.'"

"Sounds more like some kind of government cover-up or a screw-up. I just talked with Indian, and he and Jim are going to look into it. They still have some contacts in army intelligence."

"I hope they can find out something. But as far as Jason goes, rest assured he is safe. One other thing, I wouldn't pay attention to what Tina Michaels told you. I think she's crazy. Don't you remember even when you were dating her, I thought she was weird. I bet prison has just made matters worse."

"Yeah, maybe you are right. Oh, by the way, about that article on black ovaries written by those two German Doctors, maybe you ought to try and contact them personally."

"Way ahead of you. One of the doctors I can't find, but the other is living in New York City. I'm flying out to see him tomorrow."

"Good. Harrison, do you remember Dr. Williams?"

"Jake Williams, yes I remember him from residency."

"I ran into him today and he told me he has access to an electron microscope."

"Great, now you can look at those slides."

"I'm to meet him late tonight."

"Let me know what you find out."

"You the same."

They both hung up the phones. Harrison noticed Julie walked into the den. "That was Doug on the phone."

"I know. Remember, I was the one that answered the phone."

"Oh, that's right."

"What did he say?"

"Well, I told him about the two girls. He said Indian had mentioned it earlier."

"And what did he think?"

"He just didn't know. But he told me Jim and Indian have some old contacts in army intelligence. They are going to see what they can find out."

"Good, I just don't think it is right that they can get away with that." Julie watched Harrison approach the bar and pour himself a stiff drink. He consumed it rather quickly and poured another. This time he walked over to the lounge chair and sat down. She could see concern on his face.

"Harrison, what else did he say?" Julie finally asked.

Harrison took a sip of his drink. He did not want to worry his wife. "Ah, it's nothing, I'm just tired." Harrison could see that persistent look on her face. He knew that she would not accept that answer. "All right," he said and motioned his wife to sit across from him. Without their knowledge, the basement door opened, and two figures slipped within hearing distance of Julie and Harrison's words.

"It started when Doug tried to review Nicole's medical record at LA County Hospital. Her chart was empty, except for some nursing notes. One of the nurses that recorded the notes was Tina Michaels. Do you remember her?"

"Sure. She was Doug's old girlfriend. She graduated from nursing school with me."

"Well Doug went to see her yesterday."

"Well that's great. It's time he start seeing other people again."

"Julie, it wasn't a date. Tina is in prison."

"Prison? Oh my, what happened?"

"Doug did not say, but he did mention something that bothers me."

"What's that?"

"Tina told Doug that Nicole was killed."

"Nicole killed? I don't understand. She died of AIDS."

"I know. He didn't go into the details, but he also said that Jason was in danger."

Jason and Sondra looked at each other. They then quietly retreated back to the basement door. "Jason, did you hear that?"

"Yes, they said my mother was killed."

"But you said she isn't dead. You have seen her, right?" Jason did not answer. "Mr. Jordan said you were in danger too."

"I know. Come on, let's go back down into the basement."

Doug turned to see Indian standing in the hall. "Excuse me, I didn't mean to listen in."

"That's okay."

"Is Jason all right?"

"Yes, he's fine. He's just anxious for us to come home."

Indian could still see the concern on Doug's face. "Listen, Doc, why don't I fly home tomorrow and stay with Jason."

"What about the Sheriff Bates and Dugway?"

"Elaine and Jim can do that fine."

"I would feel so much better if you were there."

"Then it is settled." Indian placed the pictures of David's room before him on the counter. "One other thing, can you look at these pictures one more time?"

Doug picked up a couple of the pictures. "Well I looked at them before, and all I found was ramblings about the end of the world."

"I know, but I also know David. He often spoke in riddles. There may be a message here, and we just can't see it."

Doug sat down at the kitchen counter with Indian next to him. "Well to tell you the truth, there were two parts in this message I didn't understand. One was a symbol for music, and the other was not Latin but a picture. Here, I'll show you." He pointed them out to Indian.

"So what you are saying is these two items do not fit with the rest of the message?"

"Right, they just seem to be out of character."

"And this Latin word means music?"

"Yes, and this picture looks like an elephant with three horns."

"Elephant with three horns," Indian murmured, "why is that so familiar?"

"It looks too small for a regular elephant and it has three tusks rather than two."

"That's it, Doc," Indian exclaimed, "a Uintathere."

"A Uinta what?"

"A Uintathere. It's an extinct animal that lived in Utah. In fact the Unita Mountains were named after it."

"Music and Uintathere," Hunter murmured, "but it still doesn't make sense."

Indian stood. "Why don't we think about it for a while. Anyway we should get back to the party. People have been asking about you."

Hunter followed Indian back outside. He bent down and kissed his mother. "Hello, Mom."

"Son." He sat down next to her. She then nodded toward the dancers. "You're missing all the fun."

Indian took his seat and handed Doug the extra beer. Doug looked at the dancers. "Oh no, not again. Mom, is that Brian?"

"I'm afraid so."

Doug shook his head. "Pepe going to be mad."

"Only when we tell him," Jim chuckled.

CHAPTER TWENTY

THE ELECTRON MICROSCOPE

Disciple touched Doug's shoulder and motioned toward Jim and Pepe. "Do you want us to come with you?"

"No, we won't be long."

They watched as Doug and Jake Williams crossed the street toward the hospital entrance. "I don't know why we can't look at these slides in the morning," Jake complained.

Doug looked at him. "Like I said, we will be leaving in the morning."

"Then why don't you leave the slides with me? I'll study them in the morning and get back with you."

Doug shook his head. "No, I can't. This may be dangerous for you. No one else is to know about these slides."

Jake stopped Doug short of the hospital doors. "Why are these slides so special?"

"That's what we're hoping you can tell us."

Jake finally relented. "Okay, let's see what we can find." Jake peeked around the corner through the double doors.

Doug was puzzled. "What are you doing?"

"Ah, dammit," Jake exclaimed.

"What's wrong?"

"Oh, I've had a few run-ins with these two squirrelly night orderlies. When they're working, they always make things difficult for me." Jake bit his lower lip. "I wonder if any of the other doors would be open this late."

"What you mean other doors?" Doug asked. "For hell sake, Jake, we're doctors. We can go into hospitals any time we want. Orderlies can't keep you out of the hospital."

Jake grimaced. "These two can. They don't think straight. Burned out their brains with drugs years ago. They think they own the hospital."

"Then what do you suggest?"

Jake thought for a moment. He then touched Doug's arm. "Come on, let's see if we can sneak by them." Doug followed Jake as he cautiously opened the lobby doors. They quickly turned left toward the basement stairs and were nearly there when—

"Hey, dudes, where do you think you're going?" Jake winced and slowly turned. They watched as the two orderlies came around the front desk and approached them.

Fred removed the radio receiver earplug. "Dr. Williams, is that you?"

"Hey, Fred." He nodded toward the other. "Jack."

"Hello, Doc," Jack answered. "What you doing here so late?"

Dr. Williams motioned toward the stairs. "Ah, I was just going to my office."

Fred shook his head. "Ah, you can't do that. You know the rules."

Jack circled Doug. "Hey, bro, who's the stiff?"

He motioned his hand toward Doug. "This is my friend, Dr. Hunter, visiting from out of town. He's leaving in the morning. We wanted to review some slides together before he has to leave."

Jack eyed him up and down. He shook his head. "Doesn't look like a doctor to me. Looks more like a spy."

Fred studied him suspiciously. "Who do you work for, St. Joseph's, Maricopa County?"

Jake shook his head. "He's not any spy from some other hospital."

Fred ignored Jake's explanation. "Maybe it's Good Samaritan?"

Doug turned to Jake. "Who are these guys?" he whispered.

"Look, guys, give us a break. We just want to use the electron microscope to look at some slides, nothing more."

"You know you can't fire up the electron microscope," Fred exclaimed.

"And why not?" Jake asked.

"Because you need permission," Jack reminded.

Doug could see the anger building in Jake's face. Jake shook his head. "Dammit, Jack, don't you jackasses understand that I'm the one that gives that permission."

"Hey, Dr. Williams," Fred exclaimed, "no need to get hostile. We're only following the rules."

Doug watched Jake clench his fists. He knew he was ready to explode. "You know those rules aren't for doctors," Jake yelled. Doug reached up and put his hand on Jake's shoulder to calm him.

Jake turned to Doug. "I don't know why I try to reason with these guys."

Suddenly the hospital double doors opened again. All turned to see three men walk into the lobby. Jack slapped Fred on the chest. "Get a load of these guys." Fred started to laugh. They walked past them down the hall toward the main elevators.

"Now those guys really look like hospital spies," Doug said.

Jack looked at Fred. "You know, I think he's right. Just look at their outfits."

Fred nodded his head. He slapped Jack on the chest. "Come on." Fred and Jack raced down the hall to catch them.

Jake was confused. "What are they doing?"

"They're creating a diversion." Doug nodded toward the stairs. "Come on."

The orderlies stepped in front of their approach. "Wait a minute there, bros," Jack exclaimed, "where do you think you three dudes are going? Visiting hours were over long ago."

"Get out of our way, maggots," Pepe commanded.

Both Fred and Jack looked at each and burst out in laughter. Jack touched Fred's chest with his finger. "You hear that, maggot? You better get out of his way." They slapped each other with high fives.

Pepe looked at them oddly. "Are you two really orderlies?"

"You know it, man. Not only are we the night orderlies, but we are the best night orderlies."

Without saying a word the three sidestepped the two orderlies, only to have them continue to walk along side of them. "Listen, why are you all dressed up? Been to some kind of costume party?"

Disciple looked at himself. "Dressed up? We're not dressed up."

Jack and Fred looked at each other. They again burst out in laughter. "You mean you dudes dress like this all the time?"

Jim could not hold it either and broke a smile. He looked at the orderlies' name tags. "Listen, Fred and Jack, we're on our way to the psychiatric floor."

Jack nodded his head. "Oh, now I get it. The way you look and dress. It all makes sense now."

"Hell the sixth floor is our favorite floor. We go up there all the time." He smiled and winked at them. "Sometimes the crazy women walk around nude, if you know what I mean."

"They do?" Pepe questioned.

"Well not for Mexicans," Fred teased.

Pepe looked at the nametag. "Fred, you're full of crap."

Jack motioned with his hand. "If you don't believe us, come and we'll show you."

Pepe shook his head. "You two get lost. We don't need your help."

They ignored Pepe's request. Jack looked closely at Jim's coonskin cap and leather clothing. "Nice outfit."

"Thanks."

"Daniel Boone?"

"Davy Crockett."

Jack nodded his head with approval. "All right, cool."

"Jack look at this guy," Fred said. "Paisley shirt, cowboy boots, bell bottom pants, cowboy hat. I think this guy's really mental."

"Yeah, he looks like one of those crazy cowboy hippies."

Pepe was becoming irritated with the two. "Would you two scum buckets beat it?"

Now Jack and Fred laughed even harder. "Scum buckets? Hear that, Jack? He called us scum buckets." Fred put his arm around Pepe. "You know, I really like this guy."

"Yeah, me too," Jack answered.

Jack looked over Disciple's clothing attire. He reached and touched his long robe and gazed at his long, flowing hair. "Are you Jesus?"

"No, just one of his disciples."

"Really, one of his disciples? But they lived two thousand years ago. Jack, how could someone live that long?"

Jack shrugged his shoulders. "I don't know. Maybe drugs."

"Hey, maybe you're right," Fred agreed. "I bet its drugs." Now the main elevator doors opened. "Maybe it's that super marijuana we've heard about. Was it that super marijuana?" Their voices faded as the elevator doors closed.

Dr. Williams turned on the lights. "Okay, bring them over to this triple-head microscope. Let's see what we have."

Doug handed the slides to Jake. "The slides and tissue samples are broken into three groups."

"Three groups?"

"The first two samples are from the two dead girls that were found in the cabin, and the last one is from the third girl that lived and disappeared."

"And you want me to study all three of them?"

"Yes, we want to know if there are any similarities among them."

"Let me have the live girl's first. Doug handed the slides to Jake, who placed them on the microscope. He began studying the slide while Doug watched through the other microscope head. "Is this her ovary?"

"Yes."

"How old is she?"

"About nine, maybe ten, why?"

"Something caused this ovary to bleed many times. It's severely damaged."

They both looked up at each other at the same time. "What would do that?"

Jake removed the slide from the microscope deck. "I don't know. Let's see if the electron microscope shows us anything."

Jake fired up the electron microscope. "At least I can tell you why the ovary is black," he continued. "Black melanin body pigment deposited in them, probably a reaction to the damage." He nodded toward the wall screen. "There, let's see what we have." Both studied the screen projection. Jake slowly moved the focus from one field to another. Finally he broke the silence. "Doug, can you see it?"

"The damage?"

"Yes. This girl is sterile. Her eggs have been completely destroyed." Jake increased the electron microscope's magnification. He pointed with his finger. "Look, there's something there." He then increased the magnification again. "In fact there are millions of these things."

"Do you know what they are?"

"Well to me they look like some kind of virus."

"Can you tell what type of virus?"

Jake increased the magnification further. He spent several minutes studying the virus. Finally he spoke. "I'm not sure which virus it is."

"Is there someway you can find out?

"Sure, but I will need to run some tests."

"How long?" Doug asked.

"It will take a couple of days."

Doug turned to leave. "Call me when you know something."

Jake reached out and grabbed Doug's arm. Doug turned to face Jake. He could see questions in Jake's face. Doug shook his head. "I don't have any answers, but I'm afraid we have stumbled onto something serious, so not a word to anyone, understand?"

"Sure, only you." Doug again turned to leave. "Wait, I'll walk you out." Both failed to see two figures duck into a darkened room down the hall. By the way, how's Nicole?"

"Nicole?"

Jake smiled. "Yeah, you never knew, but I always kind of had a thing for her."

Doug stopped and turned toward Jake. "I guess you didn't hear."

"What?" Jake asked.

"Nicole died."

Jake was horrified. "Died!"

"Yes, about five years ago."

Jake looked down and shook his head. He then again looked up into Doug's eyes. "I'm so sorry, I didn't know." They both turned together walked toward the elevators. Jake finally broke the silence. "It must have been real hard." Doug did not answer. "To lose the baby first, and then Nicole." Doug stopped in his tracks. Jake followed suit. They looked at each other. Jake could see surprise written all over Doug's face. "What," Jake questioned, "what did I say?"

"What do you mean, 'losing the baby'?"

"Well, yours and Nicole's.

Doug took Jake by the arm. "You're the second person in the last two days to tell me that." Jake had a confused look on his face. "Who told you our baby died?"

"No one."

"No one, then how do you know this?"

"Because I was there."

"Let me get this straight, you were at the hospital when our baby died?"

"I thought you knew. I was a resident on obstetrical rotation at LA County when Nicole had her baby."

"And our baby died?"

"I'm sorry, but I thought you knew all this."

Now Doug stood and began to pace the room. He turned to face Jake. "Did you deliver the baby?"

"No it wasn't me, but—" Jake hesitated.

"But what?"

"Well there was this new Obstetrician that delivered your baby. The reason I remember this is because your baby's birth was so unusual."

"What do you mean?"

"I only saw this obstetrician one time. It was when he delivered your baby, and then he completely disappeared. It was like he came only to deliver your baby and then leave."

"Did you actually see the delivery?"

"No, they didn't let any of us in the room."

"Then you didn't actually get to see the baby's body?"

"Well, no, but the nurse told me. In fact the nurse that told me was Tina Michaels, the one you used to date."

Tina Michaels, he thought. Doug looked at his watch and stood. "Jake, I got to go." Doug turned to leave.

"Okay, I'll be in touch," Jake yelled after him. Doug acknowledged Jake's remarks with wave of the hand.

The two hidden figures watched as Jake returned to the electron microscope room. "Gabriel, it appears the army didn't get all the slides," Tess whispered.

Gabriel nodded his head. "I fear you are right."

"Then this Dr. Williams may have some answers shortly. What about Parks—has your wife said anything?"

"She will not tell them anything. Even if they beat her to death, she will not speak."

"I don't know. Parks can be pretty persuasive."

"What Parks doesn't realize is that Tina wants to die."

"How about you, Gabriel, do you want Tina to die?"

"It would make things simpler."

"That wasn't what I asked. Do you want to Tina to die?"

Gabriel ducked his head. "Is it that obvious?"

"It is to a mother. I know you still love her, and I think she still loves you. I know she loves and misses the children."

"Mother, what would you suggest?"

"Go get her and take her home."

"You know the law. It is forbidden for immortals to marry and have children."

"Maybe this time the law should be broken." Tess could tell her son was in deep thought. She touched his chest. "Come on, I need to speak with Matthias about this Dr. Williams."

Gabriel nodded in agreement. They bent space and disappeared.

CHAPTER TWENTY-ONE

THE CANCER FLOOR

Doug pushed the sixth floor elevator button. The doors closed and the elevator moved. His mind was on the things that Jake said. Now he needed to find the others and leave. He paid little attention as the elevator slowed and stopped at the third floor. The door opened but no one entered. *Why did the elevator stop here?* Doug thought. He peered out the elevator door toward the nurse's station. "Oh, I remember this floor," he whispered. Slowly he walked toward the nurse's station, not noticing the elevator doors closing behind him. "The rooms are exactly as I remember them."

"Sir, may I help you?"

Doug turned toward the nurse's station. "Hello, I'm Dr. Hunter. My wife use to work on this floor years ago."

"She did. Did she happen to come with you?"

"No, she passed away a few years ago."

"Oh, I'm sorry to hear that. My name is Jeanie, the night nurse."

"Jeanie, I'm pleased to meet you. I remember this floor as the pediatric cancer floor."

"Well it still is."

"Would you mind if I looked around a bit?"

Jeanie smiled. "Not at all."

"Thanks."

"If you need anything, just let me know."

"I will." Doug sat down on the nearby sofa. He stared down the hall, remembering that one particular night years ago.

Doug quickly passed a whimpering child in one of the patient rooms. *I hate this floor,* he thought. He stopped short of the empty nurse's station and searched the area. "Where is everyone?" he murmured.

"Well, Dr. Hunter," a voice called from the back of the nurse's station. "Any more naked bodies to show us?"

Doug stretched to look in the direction of the voice, wondering who it was.

Suddenly the nurse came out of the break room holding two cups of coffee. "I saw you coming." She handed him one of the cups. "This time of night, I thought you might need this."

Doug took the cup from her. "You're right about that. Thanks, ah, Nurse Crockett, right?"

"Right, Dr. Hunter, I'm surprised you remember."

"Why do you say that?"

"Well your reputation precedes you."

"Ah, don't believe all you hear. Anyway that was Dr. Jordan's doing yesterday in anatomy lab class with the cadaver, not mine."

A bit humble, Nicole thought, *this may be harder than I thought.* Nicole led the way back to the front of the nurse's station. "Anyway, what's keeping you up so late?"

Doug covered his mouth while he yawned. "Ah, I'm still seeing patients."

"Someone on this floor?"

"Yes, the cancer doctors want me to see a little girl here. It's a—" Doug hesitated. Reaching into his jacket pocket for a slip of paper. "What was her name?"

Nicole sighed. "Megan, right?"

Doug read the name on the paper. "Yes, Megan Koyle, do you know her?" Nicole looked away and did not reply. "They said she needs a central line for more chemotherapy."

"Yes, she does. She doesn't have any more veins, and her leukemia has returned."

Doug could see that Nicole was touched by this little girl's condition. He wanted to console her in some way but didn't know how. "I hate this place," he finally murmured.

Nicole grabbed Megan's chart from the rack and handed it to Doug. "Hate this place, why?"

"I'm sorry, but to me this floor reeks of death."

Nicole studied Doug's face. *This is going to be hard*, she thought. *This doctor may actually care about people.* Finally Nicole interrupted his concentration. "As a doctor I would think this is where you would want to be."

"Why do you say that?"

"Well isn't death a doctor's common enemy?"

Doug looked up from the chart. *That's an odd question for a nurse to ask*, he thought. "For some doctors, maybe."

"But not you?"

"No, not me. Actually death is sometimes my friend." Doug closed the chart and placed it to the side of the counter. He then leaned on the counter. "Nurse Crockett, you puzzle me."

"Why is that?"

"Of all places in the hospital to work, why would you choose the children's cancer floor?"

"Why not work here?"

"What I mean is that you see these children endure so much pain and suffering, and many die. How do you handle it?" Nicole did not answer. "You see parents grasping for any glimmer of hope for their children, when many times there just isn't any. Doesn't that bother you?"

Nicole looked down. She leaned over the opposite side of the counter just to the left of Doug. Finally she replied softly. "Yes, sometimes it does."

Doug studied Nicole's demeanor. He could see her eyes moisten and heard her voice crack when she spoke. He realized she really loved these children; that was why she worked there.

"You know something, Doctor?"

"What's that?"

"Just once in awhile, I would like us to win the battle."

"In what way?"

"Sometimes I wish someone would walk down this hall, stop at each child's room, and simply heal them all."

Doug touched Nicole's arm. "Do you believe there is such a person?"

Nicole looked up at him. "Yes, I do."

He smiled. "Then, when this person comes by, I want you to give him something."

"What's that?"

Doug took his prescription pad from his pocket and wrote something on it. He then handed it to Nurse Crockett. "When that healer comes, you give him or her this."

She opened the prescription slip and read it. She smiled and looked back at him. "I will."

They both were quiet for a few seconds. Finally Doug spoke. "I'm sorry. I didn't mean to upset you." Nicole still didn't speak. "Listen, let me make it up to you."

"Make it up to me?"

Yes, have breakfast with me?"

Nicole did not answer but started waving at someone down the hall. Doug turned. He could see a small child peeking out the doorway and waving. "That's your Megan." Doug waved at her. "She wants a peanut butter cup."

"Peanut butter cup?"

"Yes, I get her one every night."

"Does her doctor know about this?"

"No, he doesn't."

"You bet he doesn't know."

"What he doesn't know will not hurt him. Anyway I've got to go."

"Go, what do you mean, go?"

Nicole began to move toward the elevator doors. "Not for long. Listen, Doctor, will you watch the floor for a few minutes while I run down to the cafeteria and get one." Doug tried to answer. "Thanks, I'll be back shortly."

Doug watched as the elevator doors closed. "What about breakfast?" he yelled.

There was another man already on the elevator. They rode in silence the first two floors. "Did you make contact with this Dr. Hunter?"

"Yes, I did."

"Good."

Nicole turned toward the man. "John, he seems like a nice person. Isn't there any other way?"

"No, we've already been through this." They continued to ride in silence until the elevator doors opened and Nicole left.

Back on the floor, Doug again picked up Megan's chart. He felt a tug on his jacket. He looked down into a girl's tearful dark eyes. "Well, hello, Megan." He then noticed her pale, gaunt facial features. He knelt down by her. "Why are you crying?"

She showed him the material on the front of her nightgown. "I threw up in my bed."

"Great," Doug murmured sarcastically to himself. Now the foul odor reached his nostrils. "Don't cry. That thing happens around here all the time. Listen, you go back to your room. Nurse Crockett will be back soon, and I'll send her to help you when she returns." Megan nodded yes. She returned back down the hall to her room. Doug tried to ignore her by engrossing himself in the hospital chart, but each time he looked up, he could see her face peeking at him. *Now I know why I dread this floor*, he thought. He returned the hospital chart to its rack and walked down the hall toward her. She disappeared back into her room. "Don't get involved," he whispered as he entered her room. "I'll just clean up the vomit and go." She had the sure tell signs of chemotherapy, with no hair and eyebrows. "Megan, my name is Doug," he said returning her smile with his own. He turned on the brighter room light. "Should we see if we can clean up this mess?"

"I'm sorry, it just came."

"It's okay. It isn't your fault. It's the medicine that does it."

"I cleaned some," she answered motioning to paper towels piled on the nightstand. "I didn't want any of the nurses to get mad."

Doug looked about the room. There was no way he was going to clean up the vomit. It was all over the room. Instead he obtained a fresh nightgown from the closet. "Ah, don't let the nurses bother you. They yell at me, too."

"They do?"

"Heck yes. Hey, do you know what I say, when they tell me I do something wrong?"

"What?"

"I tell them it was the fairies."

"The fairies?"

"Yes, I say 'Nurses, I didn't do that. It must have been the fairies.'"

"Do they believe you?"

"Nah, they tell me there aren't any fairies, but—" He leaned closer and whispered, "I think there are."

Megan smiled. "Me too."

Doug now could see the bruising from the previous IVs up and down her arms. Her pillow was covered with her dark fallen hair. "Are you a nurse?" she asked.

"You know some people call me Dr. Hunter." He sat down on the edge of the bed. "But can you keep another secret?" She nodded her head yes. "I do magic."

Megan eyes brightened. "Magic? You know magic tricks?"

"You bet I do. Now you take this nightgown into the bathroom and change. Then we are going to move you to the magic room."

"Magic room?"

"Yes, the magic room. It's where the fairies live. Children who are in this room get better and go home," he explained. *Now why did I say that*, Doug thought as he watched Megan scamper into the bathroom to change. Megan had acute myelogenous leukemia. Her chances for living were not good.

"Mommy usually stays with me, but last night daddy made her go home," Megan explained. She followed Doug down the hall to a new room. "He said she needed her rest."

"Yes, sometimes mommies need rest." They entered the empty room. Doug folded down the bed covers for Megan.

"Is this room really special? I mean, do the people really get better and go home?"

"Yes, they do."

"I know why."

Doug lifted Megan onto the fresh sheets. "Why?"

"It isn't the fairies. It's the angels."

"Angels?"

"We saw them last night."

"Last night?"

"Yes, they were with my friend Mike. He was in this room."

"Where is Mike?"

"He left. We think he went home last night."

"We?"

"The rest of my friends here. Hey, can they watch the magic tricks too?"

"You bet they can."

"Dr. Hunter," a voice called from behind, "what are you doing?" Doug turned to see Nurse Crockett's puzzled face. He did not answer. "Megan, what are you doing in this room?"

Megan reached over and touched Doug's reassuring hand. He looked into Megan's eyes and smiled. "Gee, Nurse Crockett," he attempted to explain, "we told them you would get mad, but they just didn't listen to us—did they, Megan?"

Nicole placed her hands on her hips. "You know no one can move someone to another room without permission."

"Exactly what we told them. We told them that Nurse Crockett would get mad, but you know what, they didn't even care."

"Dr. Hunter, what are you talking about?"

Doug looked down at Megan. "You want to tell her?"

"I don't want to tell her," she whispered.

"Well I don't want to tell either," Doug whispered back. "She won't believe us anyway."

"Tell me what?"

"Okay, Nurse Crockett…" Doug paused. "It was those fairies."

Nicole facial expression suddenly softened and she smiled. Now there were faces from a number of rooms peeking into the hall. "Fairies, huh?

"Not fairies," Megan corrected, "angels."

"Angels?"

"Yes. Dr. Hunter said that anyone who stays in this room will get better and can go home."

"Home," Nicole stated. She looked at Doug. "Did you really say that?" His facial expression said "guilty." She frowned. "Dr. Hunter, may I speak with you in the hall?"

"I'll get my friends," Megan whispered.

"Do that," Doug whispered back.

Doug followed Nicole into the hall. "Dr. Hunter, what have you been telling her?"

"Come on, Nurse Crockett, don't be upset. These kids need some hope."

"It's false hope. It's inevitable that some of these children are going to die, and one of them is Megan."

"You don't know that. Look at Megan's friend Mike."

"What about him?"

"Well he got better. Megan told me Mike went home last night."

Nicole ducked her head and then looked up again. "He didn't go home. Mike died last night. Megan and her friends don't know."

Doug's facial features immediately changed. "Died?"

"Please, you're doing more harm than good. Just leave."

Doug shook his head and looked away. "You know, just once I too would like us to win." Nicole's heart was touched. He looked back at Nurse Crockett. "You're right. I don't belong here." He turned and made his way toward the elevator. "Man I hate this floor," he murmured. The elevator doors opened and Doug stepped inside.

"Dr. Hunter," Nurse Crockett yelled. Doug pushed the elevator button to keep the doors open.

"What?"

She hurried up to him. "Did you promise something to Megan?"

"Promise something?"

Nicole grasped Doug's hand. "You can't leave now. Come look at this." She led him back down the hall toward the patient rooms.

Doug peered into Megan's room. Amazingly the room was filled with children. Some sitting on the bed, others on the windowsill, and even others using their pillows on the floor. "Dr. Hunter, these are my friends," Megan said. She then went through and introduced each of them. "They have come to the magic room to watch magic tricks and get better."

Doug gazed at all the children. Amazingly they were so silent. Gaunt, pale, weakened, helpless. To him, their eyes were searching for glimmers of hope. That night he was their glimmer.

Nicole saw the tears start to form in Doug's eyes. His voice cracked as he tried to speak. "Children, I don't know what to—" Nicole noticed the hesitation in his voice.

"Do you really know magic tricks," Nicole asked. Doug nodded his head yes. "Then why don't you do some magic for us. Maybe afterward we could have that breakfast together."

He smiled. He escorted Nicole to a seat and then returned to the doorway. He tied his medical lab coat arms around his neck like a magic cape and wrapped a bath towel about his head. He then bowed before the children. "My dear children, I am Doug the Magnificent." They clapped their hands in excitement. "Meet my assistants the fairies—no," he corrected himself, "the angels." The children's eyes searched the room. Some then began to smile as if they could see them. Megan laughed and clapped her hands. "Now for my first trick. Watch this closely."

"What was your wife's name?"

Doug snapped back into reality. "What?"

"I'm sorry," the Nurse Jeanie stated. "I shouldn't have disturbed your thoughts. I just asked your wife's name."

"Oh, ah, Nicole, Nicole Crockett."

"Nicole Crockett, are you kidding?"

"Why, do you know her?"

"No, she was before my day. But look at this." Jeanie reached and handed Doug a flyer to read. "Your wife started this day about ten years ago."

"My wife?"

"Yes, your wife started the 'Day of Miracles.'"

"Day of Miracles, what is that?"

"Each year we celebrate the Day of Miracles here on this floor. Your wife never mentioned this to you?"

"No, she never did."

"Well every year all twenty-seven people who were healed on this certain day ten years ago come to the hospital floor with hope and encouragement for the other children suffering from cancer, that they too can be healed."

"Jeanie, what exactly happened ten years ago?"

"The story goes that your wife was working alone here on the night shift. She said a man with long hair and a robe came to the hospital. He told her he was a healer of children. Your wife asked him if he would heal the children here. First he visited with each child. Then he healed them. All twenty-seven children."

"Healed all the children?"

"Well the doctors took credit, saying that it was their medicines that cured them."

"What do you think?"

"No offense, Dr. Hunter, but I like to think it was a miracle."

Doug smiled. "Well I have to go. Thank you."

"My pleasure," Jeanie answered. She turned and walked away.

When elevator doors opened, the elevator was filled with confusion. Doug stepped inside, but acted as if he did not know any of the elevator inhabitants.

"Look, Fred, are we not crazy?"

"Absolutely, Pepe, you three definitely need to be hospitalized."

"And, is this not a hospital?"

Jim looked over at Doug and winked as they all walked out the main floor elevator doors into the foyer. "Well yeah, but—"

"Look, Pepe," Jack interrupted, "you just can't put yourselves in the hospital when you want. You need a doctor to do that."

"So when we find a doctor, we can come back?" Jim asked.

"Right, you come back then, and we'll have a good time."

Fred then stuck out his hand and shook Disciple's hand. "Jesus."

"Disciple."

"Whatever, it's been a pleasure."

Jack placed his arm around Pepe's shoulder. "Pepe, you come back and see us real soon."

"Breed worms," Pepe exclaimed, throwing Jack's arm off his shoulder.

"Breed worms? Fred, he wants us to breed worms."

Fred laughed. They watched as the group of men left the building. Jack looked at Fred. "This has been a great night."

"Yes, it has." Jack gave Fred another high five and they returned to the front desk.

CHAPTER TWENTY-TWO
THE PRISON

You could see the disgust in Pepe's face. "She gave you what?"
"A book."

"Geez, Doc, couldn't you ask for the Corvette or something?"

"Well actually, it's not really a book. It's my real father's diary. Wouldn't you be interested if it was your father's diary?

Pepe reluctantly agreed. "Yes, I guess so. So what did it say?"

"I haven't had a chance to read it yet. Maybe tonight." Doug paused for a brief moment and smiled. "Did you get a chance to say good-bye to Breann this morning?"

Pepe frowned at Doug. "Boss, that ain't funny. You know that Indian and Jim will never let me live that down."

"And rightly so. Didn't you have any idea that Breann was Brian?"

"Not a one. I can't believe he got me again."

"What is it, the sixth or seventh time?"

"Only the fourth."

Doug grimaced. "Still, four times is nothing to brag about."

Pepe threw his hands into the air. "Yes, I know. Can we talk about something else?"

Doug could sense his frustration. "Okay, I'll drop it. Anyway, this is a women's prison, so I want you to be on your best behavior."

"Don't worry, I will."

Doug pulled the car to a stop. "At least you won't have to worry about the women in here."

Pepe undid his seatbelt. "What do you mean?"

Doug chuckled. "Because none of the women prisoners are men."

Pepe slammed his car door. "Oh, you are so funny. I thought we were going to change the subject."

Doug put his hands up. "Okay, no more."

"Good, because I'm confused about something."

They walked together toward the prison entrance. "What's that?"

"Those black ovaries, can you explain to me again why the ovaries turn black?"

"Dr. Williams said there is a germ that destroyed the ovary and turned it black."

"Well how do they get this germ?"

Doug opened one of the double doors leading inside the prison. "We don't know that yet."

"Boss, I hope men don't get this virus."

"Why?"

"Because I would hate to have my cojones turn black."

Doug chuckled. He and Pepe walked up to the barred visitor window. "Look at her," Pepe whispered, "she's beautiful."

Doug looked at Pepe. "You really do need a date. You're beginning to think all women are beautiful."

"Boy, don't I know it."

The woman turned toward the two. "Well hello, Dr. Hunter, it's good to see you again."

"Ah, Ms. Stewart, right?"

"Right. It's nice that you remembered."

"Ms. Stewart, this is a friend of mine, Pepe Santana."

She extended her hand through the opening. "Nice to meet you, Mr. Santana."

Pepe leaned on the counter. "Ms. Stewart, have we met before?"

"I don't believe so."

"But you look so familiar."

Doug could see the puzzled look on Ms. Stewart's face. "All women look familiar to Pepe," Doug explained.

She nodded. "Oh, I see."

"Listen, Ms. Stewart, can lady prisoners go on dates?"

Ms. Stewart chuckled. "Sure they can, just as soon as they get out of prison."

Pepe was disappointed. "I was afraid of that." He looked at her uniform. "How about prison guards?"

"They can too, but I already have a boyfriend." Dr. Hunter chuckled at Pepe's disappointment.

She turned back to Doug. "Anyway, how can I help you today?"

"Tina Michaels, I'd like to see her again."

A peculiar look came over her face. "Oh, I guess you haven't heard?"

"Heard what?"

Hunter could tell she was flustered. She moved the hair from her face. "Ah, wait just a moment. Let me call Warden Parks." She walked to the back of the room and lifted the phone receiver. Her phone call was brief and she returned. "The warden would like to talk to you personally."

"Can't you just tell us?" Pepe asked.

"I'd rather the warden tell you."

This can't be good, Doug thought.

She nodded through the two swinging doors. "It's this way."

"Through the prison yard?"

"Yes, they are doing some repairs in the prison corridor."

"Hey, will we get to see the women prisoners?" Pepe asked.

"Oh, yes, that you will." She pushed open the double doors leading into the large prison yard. The prison yard was divided into inner and outer courts. Pepe stepped into the inner courtyard and walked a short distance to the fence separating the two courts. His mouth fell open.

"Look, there must be hundreds."

"Actually there are several thousand woman prisoners in this facility," she said.

"I have died and gone to heaven."

Ms. Stewart and Dr. Hunter smiled. "Come, his office is this way." To Pepe's delight, the long walk toward the warden's office was amid multiple whistles and lewd remarks made by a number of the women prisoners.

Dr. Hunter turned to the guard. "Ms. Stewart, how well do you know Tina?"

"Fairly well. I have worked her block since she was placed here."

"She said she hasn't had any visitors."

"Yes, I believe you are her first visitor in three years."

"But surely someone else has tried to visit her?"

Ms. Stewart stopped and looked back at Pepe. He was straggling along the fence talking with several prisoners. She then turned to Dr. Hunter. "Look, I just do what I am told."

"I apologize for being so nosy. It's just that Tina and I were close at one time, and I want to try to help her."

She turned back to Pepe and yelled. "Mr. Santana, please come." Once again she turned back. "Listen, Doctor, Tina is not treated like the other prisoners."

"What do you mean?"

"In my opinion Tina isn't destined to ever leave this place."

"You mean Warden Parks?"

Ms. Stewart chuckled. "Greater forces than him."

Without another word she entered the administration building. Pepe caught up with Dr. Hunter. "Boss, these are my kind of women."

Doug smiled. "All women are you're kind of women."

"No, I really mean it. I can relate to these women, except that one lady over there." He then tried to point her out, but Hunter could not see her. "She motioned me over to talk with her, but boy was she ugly. She even had a beard."

Doug chuckled. "A beard?"

"Yes, a beard." Pepe sped up to the side of Ms. Stewart. "Do you know you have a bearded lady here in this prison?"

"Well I know some of the women are pretty hairy, but I don't know of any with beards."

Pepe stretched his neck. "Well now I can't see her. But I could have sworn she had a beard."

"Pepe," Ms. Stewart suggested, "would you like to stay and talk with them some more? They don't get to see many men in here."

"Boss, would that be okay?"

Doug smiled. "Sure, I should be back soon." Pepe turned and once again approached the double fence where several inmates were waiting.

Doug turned to Ms. Stewart. "Good, Warden Parks wants to speak with you alone."

"Why is that?" Doug asked. Ms. Stewart did not answer. Doug followed the guard through the double doors into the administrative building. She stopped short of the warden's office and turned toward the Doug. He could sense her hesitancy. "Ms. Stewart, what is it?"

She touched his arm. "I need to warn you. The warden's words will make you angry. Depending on how you respond to what he says, you and your friend may be in danger. As quickly as you can, you and your friend leave this place." Before Hunter could speak she opened the door to the warden's office. "This is Dr. Hunter here to see Warden Parks." She turned back to Dr. Hunter. "Good-bye," she whispered, "and remember what I told you." Then, out loud she said, "You may go in. The Warden is expecting you." She quickly turned and left.

"Thank you." Doug opened the door and entered the inner office. "Dr. Hunter." Warden Parks stood and motioned that Doug should sit across from him. "I understand you want to see Tina Michaels?"

"Yes, I was hoping to see her today."

"But you just visited with her two days ago."

"I know, but since you explained her illness, I thought maybe I could be more help."

"I see," Warden Parks replied. Parks stood and walked over to the view window. Doug could sense something was wrong.

"Warden, is there a problem?"

Warden Parks turned back. "I'm afraid so. Something tragic occurred last night."

"Tragic, what do you mean?"

"I do not know how to say this delicately, so I am just going to tell you right out." The warden paused for a brief moment. "Tina Michaels died last night."

Dr. Hunter was stunned. "Died?"

"I know this must be a shock. It was a great shock to us all."

Hunter shook his head and turned away. "But I don't understand. She looked good two days ago."

"Like I told you before, Tina had AIDS, and, well, sometimes these things just happen." Parks stood and walked around the back of his chair. "I am truly sorry."

Doug turned. "May I see her body?"

Warden Parks hesitated. "Ah, I'm afraid that's not possible. You see, we cremated her body this morning."

"Let me see if I have this straight, Tina died last night and you have already cremated her body?"

"That's correct, sir."

"Who authorized the cremation?"

"She prearranged the cremation ahead of time. We have all the signed necessary papers."

Yes, I'll bet you do, he thought.

"It was unfortunate that she passed away, but we did not see any reason to prolong things."

"Well she must have had an autopsy?"

"No, our prison doctor didn't feel that was necessary. We all knew she was dying of AIDS."

"Warden, something is not right here."

"What do you mean?"

"To have a sudden death in a prison without an autopsy doesn't sound proper."

"Look, there's nothing improper here. Simply put, the woman had AIDS, and she died."

"But surely there will be a coroner's inquest."

"Again, sir, there isn't a need."

Doug leaned forward on the front of the warden's desk. "Warden Parks, you lock up a lady who is convicted of a crime. She is sent to prison while her husband, an accomplice in the crime, is set free. She hasn't been able to contact her attorney. She has not been allowed any visitors for over three years. She becomes sick with the HIV virus and is not allowed treatment. She suddenly dies, and in less than twenty-four hours her body is cremated. Now I ask you, doesn't that sound strange?"

"Maybe a little unusual, but not unreasonable."

Doug straightened himself. "I'm going to the coroner's office with this."

Parks stepped in front of Hunter and extended his hands. "Calm down, there are no improprieties here."

"Then you won't mind if I check with their office, will you?"

Hunter turned toward the door to leave. "Doctor, I understand you and your son live on a ranch in Idaho." Hunter stopped short of the door. He turned toward the warden. "I hear it's a nice ranch, located up in the mountains. I bet your son really enjoys it. What is his name now, Jason, right?" Doug did not answer. "I bet it's a lot of fun for Jason, you know like riding horses, skiing, and things like that."

Doug clenched his fists. He could feel the hot blood flushing his face. "What are you saying, Parks," he asked in a stern voice.

"Oh, nothing, except well, you know, you got to be careful on a ranch. Accidents can happen so easily."

"Warden, is that a threat?"

Parks chuckled. He stood up and walked over to Doug. "You better believe it's a threat." He then leaned over and whispered into Doug's ear. "Just go back to your ranch and let this go. You have no idea who you are dealing with." He then walked and opened the office door for him. "Good-bye, Dr. Hunter."

Hunter turned to leave but then turned back toward the warden. He then leaned over and whispered a reply in Park's ear. "Warden, you can go to hell." He then walked out and closed the office door behind him.

Warden Parks paused for a moment. He then opened the side office door. Two of the larger women inmates walked through the door into his office. "Ladies, we have a problem here." He opened the top desk drawer, took out two knives and handed one to each of them. "He and his friend are not to leave the yard, understand?"

"Warden, how should we do it?"

Warden Parks walked over to his wide view window. He thought for a brief moment. He then turned to the two women. "I'll open the gate to the inner yard and let all the prisoners in. This will cause some confusion. While they are walking through the population, you should get your opportunity. Once done, place their bodies in the old prison." They nodded their heads and left the room. Parks sat down and waited.

Doug looked both ways but Ms. Stewart was gone. *We've got to get out of here*, Doug thought. He hurried through the double doors leading into the prison courtyard. Pepe was waiting by the fence. "Pepe, are you okay?"

"Yes, I'm fine." Pepe could see concern on Doug's face. "Boss, what's the matter?"

"Tina's dead."

"Dead? What do you mean?"

"No time to explain. We need to get out of this place."

"Where's Ms. Stewart?" Pepe asked.

"I don't know. Come on, let's go."

Pepe led the way across the inner prison courtyard toward the other set of double doors. They had moved no more than twenty feet when Doug and Pepe abruptly stopped. "Boss, the prisoners are coming toward us."

"Yes, someone opened the gates."

Pepe looked both directions. "Where are all the guards?

"I don't know. Let's go back to the administration building." They turned only to see two large woman prisoners with knives in hand approaching from the other way.

Now quite a number of prisoners had passed through the gate and were approaching. It was as if they knew something was going to happen. "Boss, what do we do now?"

"We'll need to fight."

"Fight?"

"Yes, fight. I'll take the larger woman and you take the other."

"But they have knives."

"We have to defend ourselves. I think they're going to kill us."

"Dr. Hunter," a woman's voice yelled from off to the left. "This way, come quick."

Hunter turned in the direction of the voice. He could see Ms. Stewart had opened a utility door close to them and was motioning for them to come.

One of the prisoners broke free from the group and raced toward them. "Oh no, boss, it's that ugly bearded woman."

"Come on," Doug yelled, pulling Pepe toward the open utility door. The two large women prisoners were close behind.

"No," the bearded woman yelled, "come this way." They did not hear her and quickly passed through the utility door. Ms. Stewart slammed and locked the door behind them. The bearded woman prisoner's fists hammered on the door to no avail.

"No time to explain," Ms. Stewart exclaimed, "we have to get you two out of here. Come this way." They followed her through the open door into the corridor. She looked both ways and waved to them to follow. They crossed the prison corridor into another room. Once the door was closed she turned to face them. "Warden Parks has ordered your death. They will be watching all the entrances. Even when you are out of here, you still will not be safe."

"Well, we'll worry about that then," Doug said.

"But how do we do we get out?" Pepe asked.

"She reached into the closet and pulled a small lever. A portion of the closet wall moved, revealing an opening. "This is part of the old prison. It was placed here many years ago as an escape for the guards in case of prison riots."

"Where will it take us?" Hunter asked.

"There's an escape to the beach. It was the old sewer," she explained further. "Now go. I got to get back before they miss me."

Pepe surprised Ms. Stewart by quickly giving her a hug. "Thanks." He was first to enter the opening.

Ms. Stewart waited until she and Doug were alone. She turned him toward him. He could see tears in her eyes. "Dr. Hunter, last night they beat Tina to death."

"Beat her to death, but why?"

"Because of your visit. They were afraid she told you something."

"But Tina told me nothing."

"I know."

Ms. Stewart watched as Doug's face saddened and he turned. "I did this," he whispered. He turned back. "If I hadn't come, she would still be alive."

Ms. Stewart touched Doug's shoulder. "No, she didn't die because of you. She died because of the truth."

"I don't understand."

"By you coming to see her, she knew the truth could now be told."

"What truth? I don't even know what you're talking about."

"Tina had faith you would come back, because she left you a message."

"What message?"

Ms. Stewart paused for a brief moment. "The message was the locket."

Doug touched the same locket she had placed around his neck two days before. He hadn't opened it yet. "Now go quickly," Ms. Stewart urged. "They will be looking for you."

Doug turned and followed Pepe down the hidden passageway. Reaching up she pulled the lever, and the door closed behind them. She returned to the other room and closed the closet doors. As she turned she felt the knife pierce deep into her abdomen. Again and again it plunged into her until she slipped to the floor in a pool of her own blood. The two large inmates stepped back from the still body and turned toward Warden Parks. "Get rid of the body," he instructed.

"And the other two?" one of the inmates asked.

Parks smiled. "They're not going anywhere." He turned and left the room.

CHAPTER TWENTY-THREE
THE BEATING

"McFarland, this is Michael."

"Yes, what did you find out?"

"Tess and Gabriel followed them to one of the Phoenix hospitals. They met with a Dr. Williams, who specializes with the electron microscope."

"The electron microscope? What would Hunter want with it unless—?" McFarland paused.

"Right, I think your guys didn't get all the slides."

"Dammit, this is getting way out of hand."

"I agree. I just talked with Matthias, and he is very unhappy with you."

"Look, you tell Matthias we will take care of it, understand?"

"You better. I'll be back in touch." They both hung up.

McFarland looked at the two sitting across the desk. "Did you hear?"

"Yes, we heard," Lenny answered.

Scarface looked at Lenny. "It sounds like we need to pay this Dr. Williams a visit."

"You need to get any remaining slides and other pertinent information he may have. We need to stop this now. Where are the others?"

"Crockett and Elaine flew here to Utah this morning, and Dr. Hunter and his chauffeur went back to LA."

"Where's Indian?"

"We don't know. We lost him."

"After you return from Phoenix, I want you to keep me informed of Crockett and Elaine's activities."

Scarface tapped Lenny on the chest. "Let's go." Scarface was closing the door when he stopped. He looked back. "General, what if this doctor knows?"

McFarland looked up. "Then kill him." Scarface nodded his head and closed the door.

———⟫◆⟪———

Thirteen-thirty-four, here it is, Harrison thought. He placed the piece of paper back in his pocket and rang the bell."

After a brief moment a gray haired woman opened the door. "Yes?"

"Mrs. Montgomery? I'm Dr. Jordan. I called you earlier today."

"Oh, yes, Doctor. Come in, my father is expecting you."

Harrison followed Mrs. Montgomery from the hallway into the living room where Dr. Krugar was sitting. "Father, this is Dr. Jordan, the person I told you about." Dr. Krugar slowly stood. He looked at Harrison. "Dr. Jordan, this is my father, Dr. Hans Krugar."

Harrison extended his hand, but Dr. Krugar declined and sat back down in the chair. "Well, Dr. Jordan, please have a seat. Would you like to have a cup of coffee?"

"That would be great."

"I'll be right back." She left the room for the kitchen.

"Dr. Jordan, you're a black man."

"That's right, sir. Does that bother you?"

"I guess a little. You know, the Nazi army hated the blacks."

"How about you, Dr. Krugar? Did you hate the blacks?"

Hans did not answer but instead reached for his pipe on the end table. He filled it with tobacco and lit it. Mrs. Montgomery brought back two cups of coffee and placed them on a nearby table. "Here you go."

"You know, daughter, he's a black man."

"Father, now you be nice. I'll leave you two alone to talk." She left the living room.

"No, I didn't hate the blacks, but they did scare me some."

"Why?"

"I think we fear what we don't understand."

"I agree with you, sir."

Hans drew another breath through his pipe and blew it out. "Dr. Jordan, do you remember Jesse Owens?"

"Yes, I remember him. He won a gold medal in Munich."

"Well, I was there. In fact I examined and talked with Jesse prior to the race."

"You did? You know, he's like a hero to me."

"He was a nice person. First black man I ever met. I was happy he won the race. Sure made Hitler mad, though," Hans chuckled. "After that he hated the blacks even more." He took another draw on his pipe. "So, Dr. Jordan, how can I help you?"

"Well, I am interested in an article that you and your brother wrote back in the late 1940s."

"Article?"

"About black ovaries."

"Ah, the black ovaries piece. I remember. That article was published so many years ago, why would it interest you now?"

Harrison ignored the question. He pulled a copy of the article from his briefcase and handed it to Hans. "You said in your article that you encountered a number of women in the German concentration camps with black ovaries."

"Not a number, just a few who had autopsies. There may have been others. I don't know."

"Can you explain why their ovaries were black?"

"No, not really. My brother Stephen had a few theories, but I didn't know."

"Then you don't know much more than what is said here in the article."

"No, I don't."

"So are you and your brother close?"

"Actually, I haven't seen my brother since the war."

"But the article was written after the war."

"True, but it was my brother who wrote the article and added my name for the recognition. That's all."

"Oh, I see."

"Understand something. After the war Stephen was accused of being a war criminal. The Jews said he was the right-hand man of Josef Mengele with all his treachery."

"Is that true?"

Krugar shook his head. "No, it can't be. Although we had different fathers, he was my brother. He would not have been a part of such treachery. I knew him too well."

"Do you think your brother would know more about these black ovaries?"

"Absolutely. The black ovary findings were his obsession. That's why he fell out of favor with the Nazi party. Initially he was loyal to the party. But when Stephen started working with Mengele, he changed. He criticized the Nazi party and Mengele so much, he had to go into hiding." Hans took another drag on his pipe. He looked up at Harrison. "Do you know why Stephen's plight is so sad?"

"Why is that?"

"Even though the Nazi Party and the Jews were bitter enemies, they had one thing in common. They both hated my brother."

"And you haven't had any contact with him since?"

"Nah, he wouldn't put my life in peril by contacting me. He knows the Mossad is watching me all the time."

"Do you think someone knows that I am here talking with you now?"

"For sure, and someone will watch you hereafter."

Harrison looked down and then up again. "Hans, do you have any idea where your brother may be?"

"Germany, United States, Africa, South America—your guess is as good as mine."

Harrison put his cup of coffee down. "Well, thank you for your time and the coffee."

Hans stood. "The pleasure is mine."

"One other thing, would you have a picture of your brother?"

Hans walked to the mantle over the fireplace. He picked up a small picture frame and handed it to Harrison. "This is the only one I have left of him. Here he is with his young wife and their new baby boy, taken near the end of the war."

Harrison gazed at the picture. *Why does this Stephen Krugar look familiar?* he wondered.

"He was a handsome man," Hans continued.

"And his family?" Harrison asked.

"Sadly they are missing too." Hans sadly shook his head. "Wars destroy too many lives."

Dr. Jordan silently agreed. "Would you happen to have an extra copy of this picture?"

"Take that one."

"But I can't take your only picture."

Dr. Krugar smiled. "It's okay. I don't need the picture anymore to remember their faces."

Harrison turned to leave. "Dr. Jordan," Hans called. Harrison turned back. "It would take a miracle for my brother and his family to be still alive, but—" Hans stopped.

Harrison smiled. "I know," Harrison reassured. "If I find them, I'll tell them."

Hans smiled back. Harrison turned and walked out the front door. He failed to notice the dark van parked across the street. He entered his awaiting taxi and drove away. The man in the van dialed the number. "Identification number," the voice answered.

"Two-seven-seven-eight-six-three-nine-four-four," the man answered.

"Whom do you wish to speak with?" she asked.

"Goldberg."

"One moment please." The woman forwarded the call.

Shortly another voice came on the line. "Goldberg here."

"Ben, it's me. I have something for you."

"What is it?"

"This Dr. Jordan you wanted us to follow just finished visiting Krugar."

"Did you learn anything new?"

"Nothing we didn't already know. Sir, do you want us to continue to follow him?"

"Absolutely, and keep me informed."

"Yes, sir." They both hung up the receivers. He then nodded toward the van driver, who started the engine and drove away.

<hr/>

Jake's secretary walked into the office. "Doctor, I can't locate Dr. Hunter."

"Where could he be?" Jake murmured. He took off his glasses and rubbed his tired eyes. "Okay, Emily, we'll try again tomorrow."

"But I did find out his partner's name is a Dr. Harrison Jordan. He's a general surgeon in Boise, Idaho."

"Harrison Jordan, I believe he was a resident at the same time as Doug and me."

She handed him a slip of paper. "I have his number, would you like me to call him?"

"No, I can call him. It's late. Why don't you go home."

Emily grabbed her jacket and purse. "Shall I lock up?"

"No, I'll be leaving soon."

"Then I'll see you in the morning, sir." Emily turned to leave.

"Oh, Emily," Jake interrupted. She turned back. "Would you mail this report to Dr. Hunter for me?"

"Yes, sir." She took the envelope and turned.

Jake watched his secretary leave. He removed the slides from the microscope and put them away. He then focused again on the original laboratory reports he had received earlier that day. After a few moments he leaned back in his seat. "I just can't believe these reports," he spoke out loud. "I don't understand why the CDC hasn't jumped all over this."

He dialed the number that was on the paper. "Hello," a voice answered.

"Hello, is this the Jordan residence?"

"Yes, it is".

"Is Dr. Jordan there?"

"No, he isn't here."

"Well this Dr. Jake Williams from Phoenix."

"Yes, Dr. Williams?"

"Are you Mrs. Jordan?"

"Yes, I am."

"Mrs. Williams, do you expect your husband back soon?"

"Not for a couple of days. He left late last night for New York City on business."

"Well I've been trying to get hold of Dr. Hunter and haven't been able to locate him. I have an important laboratory report to give him. They told me that your husband was his partner, so I thought I would call to talk with your husband instead. Is there any way I may be able to reach him?"

"He's supposed to call me later tonight," Julie informed. "I can have him call you."

"Would you please?" He gave her his number. "Have him call anytime day or night. This message is very important."

"Well then can I take a message?"

"Just tell him that it is about the black ovaries and a retrovirus."

"Retrovirus?" she asked again.

"Yes, retrovirus." He helped her spell it out. "Also…" Jake paused, not sure how much he wanted to say over the phone.

"Yes?" Julie asked patiently.

"Tell him the girls with the black ovaries were all HIV positive."

"Oh…" Julie whispered. "Okay, I will give him the message." They both said good-bye and hung up the receivers.

Jake failed to realize that two men had slipped into his office while he was speaking on the phone. Without a word Scarface pulled his gun, placed the silencer to the back of Jake's head, and fired. Jake slumped on his desk.

Scarface and his partner quickly gathered slides, reports, and left.

—>•<=—

The two partially nude bodies lay lifeless on the cold cement floor. Each pair of handcuffed hands was secured to the long iron pipe running overhead. Three women and two men towered over them. "Warden, they're out cold," Marge explained.

"Well wake them up again," Parks commanded. "We need to know."

"No, wait." Tess walked over and looked at the length of Doug Hunter's body. *It has been many years since a man has stirred my passions like this one*, she thought. Doug opened his eyes slightly to look at the woman, but the blood blurred his vision.

Michael approached Tess. "Don't we need to be sure?" he whispered.

Tess looked up at him. "Yes, you're right." She turned to Large Marge and Ellen. "Be sure Tina Michaels didn't tell them anything."

"And then kill them?" Parks asked.

"No," Tess countered, "keep them alive."

Michael was stunned by Tess's unusual request. "You want them alive?" he questioned.

Tess looked at Michael. She knew he was suspicious. "Michael, they're fine specimens and can be sold in the fields."

Michael was still suspicious of Tess's intentions. *Passions stir mother's heart too easily and cloud her reasoning*, he thought.

"Yes, my lady," Parks answered.

Tess looked at Ellen and Large Marge. "Wake them again," Tess instructed. She turned to leave and Warden Parks followed her out of the room.

Michael waited and watched them leave. He turned to Ellen and Large Marge. "Once you get the information we want from them, you kill them, understand?" Ellen smiled and nodded her head. Michael followed the others out.

Doug pretended to be unconscious. *They are going to kill us*, he thought. The two women filled their buckets from the nearby pool and threw the cold water on them. Pepe and Doug began to stir.

Marge pulled Pepe's face close to hers. Pepe opened his eyes. "Please don't hit me anymore," he whispered.

"Oh, I love it when you beg," Large Marge taunted. She pulled his head high and once again slapped his face, smashing Pepe's head on the cement floor. Electrical shocks surged through his body. "Inflicting pain is my pleasure, pretty boy."

Pepe tried to regain his composure. He knew they were in for another beating. *I have to do something*, he thought. *This time they may kill us.* Large Marge raised his head a second time. He watched her raise her hand. "Wait, please, don't hit me again."

Marge lowered her hand. "Are you ready to talk?"

Pepe reached up and touched her arm. "Look, Marge, you don't have to beat us. There are other ways to get the information you want."

Marge quickly raised her hand again. "I don't have time for this nonsense," she yelled.

Ellen grabbed Marge's hand. "No, wait. I want to hear him." She bent down over Pepe. "Tell me, Santana, what other ways?"

Doug looked over at Pepe, wondering what he was up to.

Pepe glanced at Doug and then back to the two women. "Being in prison, don't you sometimes get lonely and think about being with men?"

"We don't need men," Marge corrected. "We have each other, right Ellen?"

Ellen did not answer. Instead she looked at the partially naked bodies lying before her. "You know, sometimes I think about being with a man."

Large Marge was surprised. "You do? You'd choose a man over me?"

Ellen looked up at Marge and reassured her. "Oh no, a man could never take your place." Marge seemed to be satisfied with Ellen's explanation. "But don't you think that if you and I were with a man once in a while, that it would be all right?"

"Well I guess so," Marge answered.

Pepe spoke again. "You know, some men would find you two very attractive."

Ellen stood and walked over and looked down at the Doug. "How about you, Doc, do you find me attractive?" Doug did not answer.

Now he knew what Pepe was trying to do, he was trying to keep them alive.

Ellen unbuttoned the top buttons of her blouse. "You're right, Santana, there are other ways to get the information we want and have pleasure at the same time."

Marge looked at Ellen. "What are you doing?"

Ellen ignored Marge's question. She picked up both Doug and Pepe's shirts, and soaked them in the pool. She handed one to Marge and nodded toward Pepe. "Let's clean them up. She knelt down next to Doug and began bathing him.

Mary watched through the large glass sphere. Both women were washing the blood, sweat, and dirt from Pepe and Doug's bodies. She flinched again when Marge slapped Pepe across the face. A hand touched her shoulder. She turned to him. "Enoch, they will kill them."

"Perhaps," Enoch replied, "but Tess has requested Hunter's life."

"How can we allow this," Mary insisted. "Hunter is no match for Tess."

"True, but it is still Hunter's choice."

Mary ducked her head. "She only wants him for her selfish lusts. If Nicole knew, it would break her heart."

"Mary, you know it is forbidden for the mountain people to interfere."

"It is also forbidden for Lucifer and his followers to interfere, but does that stop them?" Enoch did not answer. Mary shook her head. "I cannot watch this." She turned to leave and then stopped short of the doorway. "Enoch, Nicole loves this man with all her heart."

"I know."

"Then how about a prayer," she suggested.

Enoch was confused. "A prayer?"

"Yes, a prayer from a nonbeliever. That's not breaking the rules." Mary turned and left.

Enoch watched the clear glass sphere in silence at the brutality before him. *A prayer from a nonbeliever?* he thought. He nodded his head. "Yes, that would work." Enoch closed his eyes and slowly spread both hands over the clear glass ball before him.

CHAPTER TWENTY-FOUR

THE HOTEL

Harrison paid the taxi driver and entered the hotel. "I'm afraid this was a wasted trip," he murmured.

The young black man followed him into the hotel. When Harrison looked his way, he ducked into the gift shop.

"Room ten-forty-eight," Harrison said.

The gentleman reached for Harrison's key. "You also have a phone message."

Harrison took the message. "Thank you." Harrison failed to notice the young man follow him up the elevator and pass him as Harrison entered his room.

Man, I'm tired, Harrison thought. He took off his coat and sat down on the bed. He opened the phone message. It was from Julie, wanting him to call. He reached for the phone receiver and placed a call.

"Yes, this is Harrison Jordan in room ten-forty-eight. What's the special tonight?" He paused for a moment. "Good. I'll have the special and a beer." He paused again. "That's right. Thanks." Harrison hung up and immediately again picked up the receiver. He then placed another call.

"Hello."

"Julie?"

"Harrison, I'm glad you called. Something's happened."

Harrison noticed the concern in her voice. "What's wrong?"

"Harrison, she is here. Can you believe it? She's been in our basement the whole time. She was just—"

"Hold on, you're not making sense. Slow down and start at the beginning."

Julie took a deep breath. "Okay this afternoon I went down in the basement to get something. When I turned to leave, I heard a noise in the far corner."

"What was it?"

"Well when I called out, 'who's there,' there was no answer. Then it happened. As I walked toward that corner, she stood up from her hiding place."

"Who stood up?"

"That's what I been trying to tell you—the missing girl, she's here."

"You mean the one from the hospital."

"The same."

"What's she doing in our basement?"

"Hiding. Jason said she's been there the whole time. He's known since the first day."

"Why that rascal, why didn't he say anything?"

"She was frightened, and he promised he wouldn't tell."

"We wouldn't hurt her, why would she be frightened of us?"

"She isn't frightened of us. She's scared of whoever harmed her before."

"Did she tell Jason who it was?"

"Only that his name is Micah."

"Have you contacted Sheriff Bates?"

"No, I wanted to talk to you first. Do you think I should call him?"

Harrison paused for a moment to think. "No, don't tell anyone. My plane leaves in the morning. I will be back tomorrow evening. We can then decide what to do."

"Okay. Oh, by the way, did you get to talk with that doctor?"

"Yes, I met with him this afternoon."

"Could he tell you anything?"

"He wasn't much help. I think the trip is a waste of time."

"I'm sorry you didn't learn more. There is a message from a doctor in Phoenix."

"Did he leave his name?"

"Yes, I have it written here. Just a minute." Julie looked through her purse. "Williams—that's it."

"Williams? Jake Williams?"

"Yes, that's it, a Dr. Jake Williams."

"What did he say?"

"He said he's been trying to contact Doug but can't find him. He finished studying some slides of that girl's ovaries. He was excited about something he found and wanted to talk with Doug or you."

"Did he say what it was about?"

"Apparently he identified a virus. He called it a retrovirus."

"Are you sure he said retrovirus?"

"Positive. He even helped me spell it. Do you know what that means?"

"I'm not sure. Did he say anything else?"

"One other thing, that all three girls were HIV positive."

"HIV positive?"

"Yes. He sounded like he didn't want to tell me."

"It's okay. I'll give him a call. Did he leave his number?"

"Yes, he did." She read it out loud for him.

"Oh, did you get hold of Nurse Cratch?"

"Yes, she is here with us now."

"Good, I worry when you're alone."

"I'll be all right."

"Well then, I'll see you tomorrow."

"I love you, Harrison."

"I love you too, sweetheart."

They both replaced the phone receivers. Harrison again picked up the receiver. *Retrovirus?* Harrison thought. *There must be some mistake.*

Someone answered on the line. "Radiology Department."

"Dr. Jake Williams, please."

"May I ask who is calling?"

"This is Dr. Harrison Jordan. I'm returning Dr. Williams's call."

"One moment please." Harrison sat on the phone for about thirty seconds. "What's taking him so long?"

"Sergeant Campbell speaking."

"I'm sorry, Sergeant. They must have connected me to the wrong office. I was trying to get in touch with a Dr. Jake Williams."

"May I ask what this is in regard?"

"I'm not sure. I was returning Dr. Williams's call."

"Oh, I see. Well Dr. Jordan, there is a problem here. Dr. Williams was killed earlier tonight."

"Killed?"

"Yes. We don't have many details and should know more in a day or two."

"Sergeant, when you say killed, was it like a car accident or something?"

"No. From what we have gathered so far, this looks more like a homicide."

"Homicide?" Harrison paused for a brief moment. "Okay, Sergeant, thanks."

Harrison hung up the phone and rubbed his hand over his face. "Murder…I wonder if it has to do with what he wanted to tell us."

There was a knock at the door. "Just a minute," Harrison yelled. He looked through the peephole and undid the safety latch. "Put it over there on the table."

"Yes, sir." The young man walked into the room and placed the tray on the table. He then pulled a gun out of his coat and pointed it at Harrison.

"Oh, this is just great," Harrison exclaimed sarcastically. He nodded toward the bed. "Okay, it's in my jacket."

"Your jacket?" the young man asked.

"My wallet—aren't you robbing me?"

"Dr. Jordan, I'm not a thief."

"If you're not a thief, then why do you have the gun? And how is it you know my name?"

"Because I have been following you since you left Idaho."

"Following me, why?"

"I need to talk with you."

"You got to be kidding. You think you need a gun to talk to me?"

"Well I thought you wouldn't listen."

"Hand me the gun, son, and try me."

The young man turned the gun over to Harrison. "How did you know I wouldn't shoot?"

"The cylinder's empty. Serious people put bullets in their guns."

The young man smiled. Dr. Jordan noticed him staring at the food on the table. "Are you hungry?" The young man nodded his head yes. "Good, I'm hungry myself. There seems to be plenty of food. Why don't you join me?" Harrison began to take the covers off the food. "I noticed your accent—African?"

"Yes."

"I thought so. I lived in Africa once."

"Yes, I know."

Harrison was surprised at his answer. "You do? How?"

"Dr. Jordan, don't you remember me?"

Harrison studied the young man facial features for a moment. "No, it can't be. Joseph, is that you?" Joseph smiled and nodded his head. Harrison circled the table and grabbed the young man by the shoulders. "Joseph," he again exclaimed. He placed his arms about the young man and drew him close. "I have thought of you so many times."

"I have of you too, Dr. Jordan."

Harrison broke the embrace. He looked Joseph up and down. "Just look at you. You have grown into a man." Harrison pulled the chair out for him. "Please, sit down." Joseph followed Harrison's suggestion. "So why are you here?" He leveled him with a stern look. "And why the gun?"

Joseph swallowed heavily and picked up the sandwich. "I'm here for a reason, and like I said, with the way you left Africa, I wasn't sure if you'd talk to me." Joseph took a bite of his sandwich. He looked up Harrison. "Father sent me to get you."

"Get me?"

Joseph put down the sandwich. "He wants you to come to Africa. He is dying."

Harrison didn't know what to say.

CHAPTER TWENTY-FIVE

THE SPRUDITHS

Pepe and Doug watched as Marge and Ellen left through the old prison door. The sound of scampering rats at the distant end of the room broke the silence. It was only then that Pepe began to realize what he had done. Tears came to his eyes.

"Pepe, are you all right?" There was no answer. Doug began to worry. What if he hadn't lived through the beating? Doug too was cut, bruised, and bleeding. He slowly slid his chain down the pipe to where Pepe was laying. He placed his hand on Pepe's shoulder and could feel his friend quietly sobbing. "At least you're alive," Doug said aloud.

"I'm sorry, boss."

Doug placed his arm around Pepe the best he could to comfort him. "Sorry for what?"

"They tried to rape us because of me."

"Oh no, not because of you. They thought about that long before you said anything."

"You think so?"

"I know so."

"Boss when she was hitting me—" He paused for a brief moment. "I thought she was going to kill me. That's why I said what I did. Maybe it would have been better to die."

"You did what you had to do to keep us alive."

"Only until tomorrow. You heard what Ellen said. She expects more from us tomorrow."

"Well at least we are still alive tonight."

"So what do we do now?"

Doug thought for a moment. He knew his friend needed hope in this hopeless situation. "Do you remember Diablo Creek?"

"Diablo Creek?"

"I want you to do the same for us as you did when we were at Diablo Creek."

"But, boss, we never did find Diablo Creek. Heaven knows we tried, didn't we?"

"We sure did."

"We hunted all around Lake Chapala and never did find the place. In fact, that was the time we got lost."

"Right, do you remember what you did when we were lost?"

"Pick bananas?"

Doug chuckled. "Besides that—think."

Pepe rolled up onto one of his elbows and looked at his friend. "You mean when I said a prayer that we would be found?"

"Right, and didn't a plane find us the next day?"

"But you always said it was just coincidence, that my prayers were never answered."

"No, I said only my prayers were never answered, not yours."

Pepe shrugged miserably. "God won't listen to me. I've messed up too much."

"Look at where we are now. You could at least try."

Pepe looked at Doug and smiled. Doug could see peace begin to enter his friend's heart. "Now let's get some sleep." Pepe nodded, laid his head down, and closed his eyes, attempting to remember happier times. He smiled as his thoughts reflected back again to that small Mexican village.

Pepe sat down at the kitchen table. Pedro handed him a hot cup of coffee. "Father, thanks."

"For what?"

"For helping with the birth of our new son."

Pepe scoffed. "Oh, it was nothing. Sister Margarita did all the work."

"But I am still grateful."

"You're welcome, but I still think you're a wimp."

Pedro laughed. He pointed to the empty chair at the table. "May I?"

Pepe waved his hand. "Como no."

Pedro sat down across from Pepe. "You know, I been watching the way Sister Margarita looks at you."

Pepe looked up. "What do you mean?"

"You mean you haven't noticed?"

"No, I haven't noticed anything."

"What are you, blind? She looks at you all the time."

"You mean like a nun looks at a priest?"

"More like a girlfriend looking at a boyfriend."

"Come on, you're talking nonsense. Sister Margarita is one of the sweetest, most wholesome people I know."

"Maybe so, but she still has that look. The same way my wife looks at me. I think Sister Margarita has fallen in love with you."

Sister Margarita emerged from the bedroom. "Pedro, your wife and the baby are resting and doing fine."

"Then they will be all right?"

"I'm sure of it. Father Santana and I have to leave now in order to catch the last bus back to Guadalajara."

Pedro hugged Margarita. "Thank you, Sister, thank you so much. He then handed her a warm sack.

She looked in the sack. "What is this?"

"Tamales, for your bus ride back."

"Why thank you, Pedro. That is so kind."

"It is nothing compared to what you and Father Santana have done. We have a fine, healthy son." Pedro threw his arms around Santana. "Father, thank you again." He then whispered in his ear. "Now watch for that look."

"I'll do that," he whispered back. They broke their embrace. Sister Margarita and Pepe turned to leave. Pepe turned back. "Pedro, now you promised. Church every Sunday."

Pedro smiled. "I'll remember, Father."

"Good." Both Pepe and Margarita waved and proceeded down the stone pebble road.

They were quiet. Pepe chuckled out loud. Margarita looked at Pepe. "What?"

"Sister, that was my first birth."

"As if I couldn't tell," Margarita replied sarcastically.

"You mean it was that obvious?" She smiled and gave him that look. "Okay, Sister, maybe I was a bit nervous."

"A bit nervous? Father, you nearly passed out when I cut the cord."

"Sister, I slipped on the floor."

Sister Margarita chuckled. "Yeah, right."

"But when you handed me the baby...I don't know. It was like something happened."

"What do you mean?"

"Well it was like this calm came over me, and I wasn't nervous anymore. Like I could now see past all the bloody stuff right to the baby."

Margarita smiled. "I have felt that same feeling many times."

"You have?"

"Yes. I like to think it's because a newborn baby comes directly from God, and you can feel it."

"Do you feel it every time?"

"Most of the time."

"Sister, I think I'd like to go with you again sometime."

"Really?"

"Yes, I would. Next time, I promise I won't slip."

Sister Margarita smiled. She nodded her head. Margarita looked up at the bus schedule sign. "Father, I think we missed the last bus."

"Looks like we did. Now what do we do?"

"We'll have to spend the night."

Pepe looked up and down the village main street. "I don't see a motel or boarding house."

"That's because there isn't one."

"Maybe we should go back to Pedro's house?"

Margarita thought for a moment. "No, I know this place where I have stayed before. Come, I'll show you."

She took Pepe and led him across the street, through the fence and down the dirt road. After walking for a few moments Pepe asked, "Where are we going?"

Margarita smiled. "Here we are."

Pepe looked around. "Here we are where?"

"It's right in front you."

He looked where her finger was pointed. He then looked back at her. "It's a barn."

"Sí, I know."

Now the smell of the nearby corral filled his nose. "Sister, maybe we ought to see if we can find another place to stay."

Margarita laughed as she watched Pepe grab his nose. "If baby Jesus could stand the smell, so can we." She grabbed hold of his arm. "Come on, it will be fun." Pepe followed Margarita into the barn.

A farmer watched them from a distance. *How can this be?* he thought. *Father Santana and Sister Margarita going into my barn for the night?*

Doug's nearby snoring disturbed Pepe's thoughts of Margarita. He too felt tired and closed his eyes for some needed rest.

——>◆<——

Jason tiptoed out his door. Although Mrs. Jordan's bedroom light was still on, the door was closed. Quietly he crept down the stairs to the kitchen and opened the refrigerator door. "What are you doing up?"

Jason turned. The face was green with curlers in her hair. "Ms. Cratch, is that you?"

"Of course it is. Who else do you think it could be?"

"Well, you startled me."

"For land's sake, child, what are you still doing up? You're not even in your pajamas yet."

"I know, but I was hungry."

"Hungry again? My word, boy, you eat enough food for two."

Jason stared at her for a moment. "Ms. Cratch, there's something on your face."

"What?"

"Your face is all green."

"Oh, that's just my facial beautifying cream."

"Does it work?"

"What do you mean, does it work?"

Uh oh, Jason thought, realizing he just used the wrong words. "What I mean is, ah, do you think the cream would help others?"

"Like who?"

"Like my Aunt Edith. She's always putting different creams on her face. I don't think it helps much."

"Well my secret is to mix an egg yolk with the facial cream. It makes my skin moist and soft as a baby's bottom." Ms. Cratch bent over. "Feel."

Reluctantly Jason touched the green, greasy cream. "Feels soft to me." He then wiped it on his pants when she wasn't looking. "Maybe you could tell my aunt about it. She'll be here tomorrow."

"I'll do that." Jason was quiet and waited for her answer. "Well, all right, young man. Fix yourself something to eat, and then off to bed with you, understand?"

"Yes, ma'am."

"Be sure to turn off the lights."

"I will." He watched Ms. Cratch leave the kitchen. She entered the guestroom and closed the door.

Jason filled a plate with food. He then entered the basement where Sondra was waiting. "Sondra, did you hear?" he asked.

"Yes, I did." He handed her the plate, and they walked to the back of the basement and sat on the floor. "Did Mrs. Jordan say anything to you?" Sondra asked.

"Yes, she did. She said that they would decide what to do with you when Dr. Jordan comes back from New York tomorrow night." Jason bent forward and lifted her T-shirt. "I can't believe the wound is gone."

Sondra looked down. "Me either."

Jason shook his head. "I wonder who that man was."

"Maybe he was an angel."

"Maybe." Jason handed her the plastic bag. "So try on your new blouse." Jason could see the excitement in Sondra's face as she took the bag.

She began to remove her blood stained T-shirt. "Don't look, turn around," she instructed.

Jason turned away. "How did you like the mall?"

"It was fantastic. I've never seen so many things. I could spend every day there."

"Just like my Aunt Edith. She loves to go there too."

"Okay, turn around. What do you think?"

Jason turned. He smiled. "I like it. You look real good for a girl."

"Thanks." They both sat down next to the plate of food and began to eat.

"So that guy in the mall, do you think it was this Micah guy?"

"I hope not. If it was, then I know he saw me."

"So this is the same guy that stabbed you with a knife?"

"First he tied the three of us to a bed. He stabbed Kira and Tara first." She stopped eating. "They both died."

"Did you know them very well?"

"They were like my sisters. They were my best friends."

"I'm sorry."

"That's okay, I don't cry as much now."

"And then this Micah stabbed you?"

Sondra nodded her head yes. "If it hadn't been for my mom, he would have killed me."

"I just don't understand. What kind of person could do that?"

"Micah is our clan leader. He is the one that brought us here from our home in Africa."

"By boat or airplane?"

"No. We travel in a different way."

"What do you mean?"

She took another bite of her sandwich and thought a moment. "Well it's like Micah puts this clear blanket over us. Then he says some words in a strange language, and we move."

"Kind of like magic?"

"Yes, I guess so."

"Gee, that's really cool. Can you do it?"

"No, but I wish I could."

"Just think if you could, we could travel all over the world." Sondra smiled and took a drink of milk. Jason was quiet. Every few seconds she would look up at him watching her eat. She could sense he wanted to tell her something, but was hesitant.

"What is it?" she finally asked.

"My mom can do stuff like that too."

"Like what?"

"Well she can appear and disappear. It's really neat. She comes, talks, and tells me things."

"What things does she tell you?"

"She talks about my dad, my family, and you."

"She talked about me?"

"Yes, last night."

"Wow, what did she say?"

"She said we were related."

"You mean like cousins or something?"

"She didn't say, but she did say that we would become close friends, because we have something very important to do in the future."

"What is it?"

"She didn't tell me that."

Sondra smiled and touched Jason's arm. "Something important—I wonder what it could be."

"You mean you believe me?"

"Of course I believe you."

"Well then she also told me something else."

"What's that?"

"That our lives are in danger."

"Then we need to leave here soon, don't we?"

"Yes. We can't wait until Dr. Jordan returns tomorrow night. We need to leave tomorrow with my Aunt Edith." Sondra stood. Jason could sense something was wrong. He also stood. "What's wrong?"

"I was hoping my mom would come back for me."

"Well maybe she just can't right now. Maybe it's just too dangerous for her."

"You're probably right."

"My mom said we need to get to the High Meadow Cabin at the ranch. She said that's sacred ground and we would be safe there until Indian arrived."

"Indian?"

"He is my uncle. He will protect us."

There was a loud thump upstairs.

"Did you hear that?" Sondra whispered.

"Yes, I did. You stay here, and I'll see what it was." Jason quietly crossed the basement and climbed the stairs into the kitchen.

"Who could that be this late?" Julie asked herself as she turned on the bedside table lamp. She reached over and picked up the phone receiver. "Well the phone still works."

Nurse Cratch opened Julie's bedroom door. "You stay here, Julie. I'll see who's at the door."

Julie hated being alone when Harrison was gone. She was very grateful when Mary volunteered to stay with her. She put on her robe and slippers and crossed the hall to Jason's room. "Jason, are you awake?" His room was empty. *Wonder where he could be,* Julie thought. *He's probably the one making the noise.* Mrs. Jordan approached the top of the stairs, and Jason cracked open the swinging door from the kitchen to the dining room. Both watched as Ms. Cratch peered through the front door peek hole. "Well?" Julie called from the top of the stairs.

"Julie, there's no one here."

"I'm calling the police," Julie called back. She then returned to the guestroom telephone. She hit the receiver button a couple of times. "It was working a minute ago. I don't like this." She returned to the top of the stairs. "Mary don't open the—" but it was too late. Suddenly the door smashed open, knocking Mary to the floor. Two wolves entered the house followed by six partially naked figures dressed in animal skins. Startled, Julie stepped back out of sight. Jason also stepped back. They watched as Mary attempted to lift herself up, only to have one of the figures pin her head to the floor.

I must help her, Jason thought. He began to open the kitchen door wider, when he felt a hand restraining his arm. Jason turned. "Sondra, you startled me."

"No, don't," Sondra whispered. "It is Micah and the Testantes. We must leave, now."

"Leave? But Ms. Cratch needs our help."

"Jason, they are too strong. Come on, we need to go for help."

Jason knew she was right. Sondra grabbed his hand and led him through the sliding doors into the backyard.

"What do we do now?"

Sondra thought for a minute. "Water, we need water."

"You mean the hose?"

"No, like a lake or river. It is our only safety."

Jason didn't understand but trusted her. "Come on, the Boise River is nearby." Sondra followed Jason out the backyard gate and down the alley.

Mary tried to move, but couldn't. "Please, take whatever you want, but leave us alone."

Micah pulled her hair back and looked straight into her face. "You said us. Then the girl is here?"

"Girl, what girl?" Mary asked, not understanding.

Micah pulled harder and asked again. "Where's the girl?"

"I don't understand. What girl?"

Micah backhanded her across the face. Blood began to pour from her nose. He now pulled his knife and put the blade to her neck. "This is the last time, woman," Micah spoke softly. "Where is the girl?"

"Wait," Julie yelled from the top of the stairs, "please don't hurt her." She rushed down the stairs. Another Sprudith grabbed Julie, and held her in place. Micah struck Mary's head with his knife handle, knocking her unconscious, and dropped her head to the floor.

"She's out," Micah said. He then turned to Julie. "Lady, do you want your friend to live?"

"Yes."

"Then tell me where the girl is."

"I'm afraid you have the wrong house. There isn't a girl living here."

Upset with her answer, Micah backhanded Julie, who fell and hit her head on the end table. A Sprudith knelt down and checked her. "Micah, she is out cold too."

"Then search the house," Micah commanded. The remaining Sprudiths fanned out.

Two Sprudiths returned up the stairs from the basement. "Well," Micah asked.

"She was in the basement, Master, but now she's gone."

"There are two fresh sets of children's footprints," another reported from the backyard. "They lead away from the house."

"They can't be far. Find them," Micah commanded. "Not you two," he motioned. All except two Sprudiths exited through the back door, led by the two black wolves. Micah reached for the phone and placed a call. "Yes," the woman's voice answered.

"Tess, we found the girl."

"Do you have her?"

"Not yet, but we are on her trail."

"Don't kill the girl. Bring her to me."

"And the other two women, do they die?"

"No, Matthias wants them alive."

"Yes, Tess." He hung up the phone.

Micah looked at the two remaining Sprudiths. "Bend space and take the women to Tess," he commanded. The Sprudiths placed Julie and Mary on their shoulders and disappeared. Micah then followed the other Sprudiths out the back door.

Sondra could hear the howling. "Jason, the wolves are coming, how much farther?"

"The river is just ahead."

But the wolves were quickly catching up. *We're not going to make it*, Jason thought as he put himself between the Sondra and the wolves. They were creeping toward them with their white gnashing teeth. Suddenly a man stood between the children and the wolves. The brightness of his blade flashed in the moonlight. The knife lashed forward and slit open the first wolf's throat. As the second wolf attacked the stranger, Jason took Sondra by the hand and raced across the open field to the bank of the Boise River. For a brief moment they stopped to catch their breath. *Who was it that saved us*, Jason thought.

Sondra looked at the rushing water. "Jason, jump."

"Jump?"

"Yes, jump. It is our only chance." She then leapt into the rushing water below. Jason did not understand what she meant, but followed her lead. They were swept away by the rapid current.

CHAPTER TWENTY-SIX
AFRICA

"Last call for Belgium Congo loading at gate four."

Joseph picked up both carry-on bags. He looked down the long corridor. "There he is." He breathed a sigh of relief and handed Harrison his bag. "They just announced last call. Did you get hold of her?"

"No." He shook his head. "It's not like Julie to be gone like this."

"Then should we stay?"

Harrison showed his boarding pass to the attendant. "No, I'll try again when we arrive."

Joseph followed and presented his boarding pass. They did not notice a man watching them as they entered the ramp leading to the plane. The man switched the phone receiver to the other side. "Yes, he's going to Zaire." He then paused. "Yes, Ben, I'll keep you informed." He hung up the receiver. The man followed them down the ramp to board the plane.

Joseph watched Harrison place his carry-on bag in the overhead compartment. He could see concern on Harrison's face. "Maybe she was called away. You know, like for some kind of problem."

"Yes, you're probably right." They took their seats next to each other. "So, do you still live at the same compound?"

"Yes, near Kisangani."

"That has to be the longest you have stayed in one place."

"It is."

Harrison shook his head. "I could never understand why all the moving."

"Yes, me either. Once I asked my father why. All he said was 'fear.'"

"Fear of what?" Harrison asked.

"I don't know, but I know it lessened when my mother died. It was like he didn't fear anymore."

"I'm sorry to hear about your mother. She was a choice person."

"Thanks. I know father really misses her."

"I can imagine. How's your sister?"

"I don't know. She left home just before you returned to America."

"Yes, I remember, and you haven't seen her since?"

"Well I did once. She came to see me at school, not long after she left."

"Why at school?"

"She said she didn't want father to know."

"Know what?"

"That she was pregnant. She was afraid that father would disapprove, being single and all."

"Pregnant! I didn't know."

"She wrote and told me later that she had a baby girl."

"How long ago was that?"

"About nine years ago."

"Does your father know?"

"No, I never told him." Harrison and Joseph rode in silence as the plane began to taxi toward the runway and then stopped.

"I think about your sister sometimes."

"You do?" Harrison nodded his head yes. "Funny, when I saw Cresta last, she asked about you."

"She did?"

"You know, Dr. Jordan, I always thought that eventually you and my sister would be together."

"For a while there, I did too."

The plane moved down the runway picking up speed. The plane was well into the air before Joseph spoke. "It was the Testantes, wasn't it?"

Harrison nodded. "Yes, it was. Are they still around?"

"Every once in a while I hear about them, but not as often as before."

"You know, I just couldn't understand how Cresta could have gone with him. Every time she was around that Matthias guy, it was like she was a different person."

"Yes, I know." Joseph paused. "Did you know I saw your wife?"

"When was that?"

"When I was across the street trying to get the courage to knock on your door. She followed you out of your house on the way to the airport."

"Something to drink?" the flight attendant interrupted.

Harrison shook his head. "Nothing for me."

She looked at Joseph near the window. "And you, sir?"

"Me neither, thanks." They watched as she pushed the cart farther down the aisle. "Your wife is very beautiful. How did you meet her?"

"Just after I returned from Africa. We met in school. She was in nursing school when I was a resident at the university hospital."

Joseph took a picture out of his billfold and handed it to him. Harrison looked at the picture of Cresta and her new baby. "This is Cresta and the baby."

Cresta is as pretty as ever, Harrison thought. "The baby is beautiful." He handed back the picture.

"Sometimes I wish I knew where they were," Joseph said. They both became quiet.

Finally Harrison spoke. "That's sad, to be away from her family for so many years." He chuckled and pushed back his seat. "I was just remembering the time your sister and I had this big argument, and your father had to intervene."

"What happened?"

"Oh, your sister was always treating my patients with home remedies like jungle roots and herbs."

"And that bothered you?"

"Actually what bothered me more was that the patients seemed to get better." Joseph smiled. "There was this one day when she brought the nearby village shaman to the clinic to specifically heal one of my patients. I happened to walk into the clinic. Cresta and the shaman were bent over this woman's arm wound.

"What are you doing?"

Cresta looked up at Harrison. "The shaman has kindly created this potion cream to put on this lady's burn."

"Not on my patient, he's not. Tell him to stop."

The shaman looked up and then looked at Cresta. She then told him something in his dialect. The shaman smiled and turned his attention once again to the burn.

Harrison looked at Cresta. "What did you tell him?"

"I told him that you didn't know what the hell you were doing, and you were grateful for his help."

"You told him what? Cresta, you tell him to stop putting that crap on the burn. He'll make it worse."

"Worse, you say? You know how long you have been treating this burn?"

"Not that long."

"Not long? Dr. Jordan, it's been three weeks you've been fooling around with this burn, and you aren't any closer to getting it healed than when you started."

"And, Nurse Sullivan, you think you can do a better job?"

"Absolutely. If we would have used this cream from the first, this patient would have been home days ago."

"So what's so special about this cream? Some special herb or root?"

"Actually, the shaman makes it from cow's urine."

"Did you say cow's urine?"

"Yes, cow's urine."

Harrison stepped forward and began to herd the shaman and Cresta away. "Get out," he yelled. "Just get the hell out of here."

Cresta pushed Harrison's hands off her arms. "Back off, Jordan. Who do you think you are to push us around like that?"

"I'm the doctor, and you're not, so get out of here."

"How dare you speak to us that way?" she yelled.

"Listen, Sullivan, I forbid you or any of your witch doctor friends to use any kind of herbs, roots, potions, shaman prayers, or even cow urine on any of my patients."

Cresta's eyes flared with anger. "Forbid me? You can't do that!"

"Well I just did. In fact I don't want you to have anything to do with any of my patients, understand?"

"We'll see about that," she replied. She and the shaman left.

"Sounds like my sister was really mad," Joseph interrupted.

"You have no idea. She immediately went to your father."

"Father, you have to do something," Cresta pleaded. "I can't work with this jackass doctor."

Dr. Sullivan ignored her. "Nano, how's the leg feeling today?"

"Good, Dr. Sullivan, it feels much better today."

"Let's take a look at it." Sullivan removed the dressing. "Oh, Nano, that's a real nasty bite this time."

Cresta came around the back of him and whispered. "Father, did you hear me? What are you going to do with him?"

"Croc?" Sullivan asked. Nano sheepishly nodded his head yes. "Nano, how many times have I told you to leave those crocs alone?"

"Family's got to eat, Doc."

"Yes, I know, but how can you feed your family if the croc eats you first?"

Nano chuckled, and Dr. Sullivan replaced his dressings. "Listen, if your family is hungry, you come here for food, understand?" Nano nodded his head yes. "No more crocodiles, okay?"

"Okay, Doc."

"Now you promise?"

Nano smiled. "I promise."

"Good, let's check the leg in the morning."

Dr. Sullivan moved toward the next bed, and Cresta shadowed him. "Father, you're not listening to me."

"You're right, Cresta, I'm not listening to you."

"But, Father—"

Sullivan turned toward his daughter. "Can't you two just get along?"

"Three weeks on a burn—you know that's malpractice."

"He's not so different than I was when I first came here. He just doesn't know our ways yet. You need to give him time."

"It's now only that, but this doctor is a hardheaded, egotistical, self-centered, and a know-it-all bastard."

Dr. Sullivan looked into his daughter's eyes. "Cresta, why him?"

Cresta was taken aback by the question. "What do you mean?"

"We've had other student doctors here, some much worse. Why are you so hard on him?"

"I'm not so hard on him. I just want what's best for our patients."

"I think you protest too much."

"What's that suppose to mean?"

Dr. Sullivan smiled at his daughter. "Maybe you have some feelings for this guy?"

"Feelings?" she scoffed. "I loathe this man. He's a jerk."

"Jerk?" a voice spoke from behind. Cresta and Dr. Sullivan looked to see Harrison standing behind them. "I hope that word is not describing me, Nurse Sullivan."

Cresta stood and faced Harrison. He could see anger in her eyes. "Jerk?" she echoed. "No, Dr. Jordan, jerk is too good of word to describe you."

Harrison could feel his anger begin to boil. "Okay, Nurse Sullivan, let's clear the air once and for all. What is your problem?"

"You, Dr. Jordan."

"Me? And you call yourself a nurse?"

"Yes, I do, and a good one."

"Good nurses do what the doctor tells them, and definitely don't use all this voodoo crap on patients."

"Little do you know, Dr. Jordan."

Dr. Sullivan put his hands up and separated the two. "You two, not here on the floor. Come, let's discuss this further in my office."

Harrison and Cresta followed Dr. Sullivan to the front of the building. He opened the office door and allowed the two entered. "Now I don't want either one of you coming out of this office until you work out these differences, understand?"

"But, aren't you coming in?"

"Are you kidding? You two are adults. Work it out yourselves." He then closed his office door.

"You must have worked it out," Joseph concluded.

"Not at first."

"Are you ready for your dinner trays?" the flight attendant interrupted.

"Yes, I'm starved," Joseph answered. Harrison took one tray and handed it across to Joseph. He then took the second tray for himself.

———⟫•◦•⟪———

His clothes were soaked with blood from the wolf fight. He arrived at the river's edge and looked intently up and down the bank. They could not be found. Suddenly their tracks were before him. "Good, they're in the river." He heard scream from behind. *They found the dead wolves*, he thought. *They will be coming.* He pulled his knife and prepared for their arrival.

There were three of them. He could barely make out their faces in the moonlight. "You killed two of our wolves," one of the Sprudiths said. "How is that possible?"

Micah now came upon the scene. "It is his knife," Micah explained. "It is not of this world."

"I sense your fear, Micah," the man answered.

Now Micah recognized the man's voice. He motioned for the other Sprudiths to circle him. "Well if it isn't my friend Indian," Micah chuckled. "How long I have waited for this moment."

"Why take the women and the children?" Indian asked.

"You shouldn't bother yourself with such trivial matters when your death stands before you."

Indian considered whether he should fight or run, but then realized he needed to protect the children. He sheathed his knife. "Another time, Micah." He turned and followed the children into the swift river waters. He knew that the Sprudiths would not follow.

Sondra and Jason floated the swift waters at least a mile until they reached the other side. Jason helped Sondra up the embankment. "Hurry, they may be following."

"No, they will not follow."

"Why not?"

"Testantes fear water." Sondra sat down. "Let me catch my breath."

Jason scanned the water and the embankments. He did not see anything and decided it would be safe to rest a moment. He sat down next to Sondra. "Testantes fear water?"

"Yes, it is their weakness."

"But you're a Testante. Why doesn't the water bother you?"

"I don't know why, it just never has."

Jason again looked up river. "What did they want with Mrs. Jordan and Ms. Cratch?"

"They weren't after them," Sondra corrected, "they're after me."

"Why you?"

"Because they still want my ovary."

Jason was confused. "Ovary—what's that?"

Sondra shook her head. "Something inside my body."

"So that's why Micah cut you open, to get this ovary?"

"I guess so."

"Sh, quiet," Jason whispered. "Someone's splashing in the water." He stood and took Sondra by the hand. "Come on, let's go."

Sondra and Jason made their way up the embankment. They looked both ways. Suddenly before their eyes appeared two Sprudiths. When they spotted the children, they walked toward them. Then one more appeared and did the same. "What do we do?" Sondra asked.

Jason couldn't see a way to escape except back into the water. Without warning they felt hands grab their collars and pull them back. Jason looked up. It was Indian.

Indian nodded toward the river. "Quickly, go back into the water." They both obeyed as Indian separated them from the Sprudiths. Jason and Sondra stood knee deep in water watching the three Sprudiths circle and draw close to Indian. He studied the three of them. "Where is Micah, your leader?" Indian asked. The Sprudiths did not answer but continued to come closer. "I feel his presence, but I do not see him."

Someone chuckled, and Micah appeared. "Ah, Indian, your death is such a waste. If you had only joined me years ago, we could have ruled this world."

"Micah, you sicken me."

Micah laughed a second time. "Indian, just give us the girl."

"Go to hell."

"Oh, we plan to." Micah and the Sprudiths came closer. Indian placed his hand on the handle of his knife. "You give us the girl, and you and the boy can go free."

"Why do you want the girl?"

"That's none of your affair,"

Indian shook his head. "Micah, you haven't changed a bit. Still slaughtering innocent women and children like you and your brothers did years ago."

"You leave my brothers out of this."

"They are out of it, remember?"

You could see the anger building in Micah's face. "Yes, I remember." He pulled the knife from his sheath. He nodded to the other Sprudiths to circle closer. "Revenge is sweet, Indian. Prepare to die, for the deliverer of your death stands before you."

Indian unsheathed his knife and crouched, ready for battle.

"Sprudiths, hear my words," a deep voice rang out from the river. All turned toward the voice, located behind Sondra and Jason.

Jason turned. "Do you see anyone?" Sondra asked.

"I hear the voice, but there isn't anyone there."

"Sprudiths, hear my words," the voice again said, but this time from a nearby stand of trees to the right of them. "Leave this place or forfeit your lives." This time the voice sounded from the opposite side.

Indian smiled each time the voice spoke, for he had heard this voice before. He watched as the three superstitious Sprudiths searched for the source of the voice in all directions. When they could not find it, they began to back away.

"Do not back away," Micah commanded, "this is a deceit."

"No, master," one of the Sprudiths answered, "it is our God warning us of him."

"Indian is your dreaded enemy. He has killed thousands of Sprudiths," the voice continued. This time the voice again came from the original location in the river. "If you do not leave, you also will die. The three Sprudiths looked at each other, bent space, and disappeared. During this time Indian reentered the river and stood next to the children.

"Micah, it appears your followers have left."

"I am still here. Come, Indian, leave the water now. Let's end it here and now."

"No, there will be another time."

"You have to leave the water sometime."

"Oh, we will," the voice spoke again. "See the gray skies. Dawn is nearly here."

Now Micah recognized the person as he came forward from the river center into view. "Lone Wolf, I should have known it was you."

Lone Wolf placed his hand on Indian's shoulder. "Grandson."

Indian smiled. "Hello, Grandfather, I'm sure glad to see you." Lone Wolf then put his arms around the shivering children and drew them close to him.

"Neat trick, Lone Wolf," Micah exclaimed.

"I'm glad you liked it."

"But it won't work again."

"But it worked this time."

"Another time, gentlemen," Micah said. He bent space and disappeared.

"Come," Indian instructed. Lone Wolf and the children followed Indian further down the river.

THE DINER

Tess pulled back the bed sheets. "Lay her here." The Sprudith obeyed. He looked at Tess for further instructions. "That will be all." Bowing, he left the bedroom. Tess straightened Julie's legs on the bed. She brushed the long black hair out of her eyes. She noticed the bruise on her forehead where Micah knocked her unconscious. How soft her skin was as Tess gently caressed her face and neck. She stopped short at the tops of Julie's breasts, which were partially protruding from the neckline of her nightgown.

"She is beautiful, isn't she?" a voice spoke from behind.

Tess did not turn. She recognized the voice. "Yes, she is"

"I have been attracted to her since I first saw her with Nicole. She stirs my passions like only you can do."

Tess smiled. "Matthias, she is also married."

"And so were you."

Her smile faded. "Yes, you're right."

"Anyway, when has morality ever stopped you?"

It used to, Tess thought.

Matthias approached Tess from behind. He wrapped his arms around her neck and chest and whispered in her ear, "Tess, what do you think my chances are?"

Tess again looked at Julie's beauty, and then into his face. "To seduce her? Poor."

Matthias chuckled. "Come on, poor?"

Tess smiled. "Yes, poor at best. Even as good as you are, Matthias, she will be your greatest challenge."

"Even greater than you?"

Tess then turned into his arms with a full body embrace. "Even greater than I," she whispered. She wrapped her arms around him, reached up, and passionately kissed him.

—————◦◦◦—————

"Okay," Lone Wolf said. "I believe it is safe."

"What about the Sprudiths?" Jason asked.

"We'll be all right during the daylight," Indian reassured.

The four of them climbed up the bank to the road. "I'm cold," Sondra said.

"Yeah, me too," Jason added.

Lone Wolf looked up the road to the nearby coffee shop. "We can dry off up there. I know the night waitress."

"Okay," Indian agreed. He grabbed the children's hands and led the way.

"So how do you do that?" Jason asked.

"It's what we call throwing your voice," Lone Wolf explained. "Would you like me to teach you?"

"Yes, that would be neat."

"When we get back to the ranch, I'll show you how it is done. Now you run ahead to the coffee shop and get warm, and we will be along shortly." Jason and Sondra then took off in a dead run toward the coffee shop. Indian and Lone Wolf admired their energy level. "Ah, to be young again," Lone wolf chuckled.

Unnoticed, the man and woman remained hidden in the small grove of trees. They watched Indian and Lone Wolf walk toward the coffee shop. "Your Sprudiths failed," Michael whispered.

Tess looked at Michael. "Only this time," she defended. She then looked back at Indian and Lone Wolf. "Micah underestimated them."

"What will they do now?" he asked.

"Take the children to the ranch," she answered.

Michael touched Tess's shoulder. "If they get to the ranch, we will never get the children. Maybe we should try to take them now."

"No, you saw what his knife did to the two wolves. He could do the same to us."

"Then what do we do? The ranch is on holy ground."

Tess thought for a moment. She looked at Michael. "Only for us," she said. She could tell that Michael did not understand. "But not for the army."

"You mean—"

"McFarland," Tess interrupted. "Holy ground will not bother them. Command McFarland to send his men to get the children."

"He will not like it."

Tess smiled. "Yes, I know."

Michael returned her smile. "Then shall I take my leave?"

"Yes, go now."

Michael nodded, bent space, and left. Tess turned back to watch Lone Wolf and Indian near the coffee shop. It was then she felt the presence. She turned quickly. There she was standing before her. Tess smiled. "Hello, Nicole."

Nicole walked toward here. "Tess, it's been a while."

"Quite a while, why are you here?"

Nicole stopped in front of Tess. "I want you to leave my family alone."

Tess chuckled. "You know I can't do that, but it's sweet that you care."

"Stop now, or they will destroy you."

Again Tess chuckled. She nodded toward Indian and Lone Wolf now entering the coffee shop. "You mean the likes of them?"

"And others." Nicole added.

Tess laughed. "Others, like the ex priest, the alcoholic cousin and his government whore." Tess stared at Nicole. "Is that the best army your God can muster?"

"And my husband," Nicole interrupted.

"Ah, yes, your husband, who soon will be mine." Nicole did not answer. Her aching heart told her that Tess was right. It was part of Doug's destiny. "Good-bye, Nicole," Tess taunted, "it's so good to see you again." She bent space and was gone.

Indian and Lone Wolf approached the coffee shop entrance. "When did you get back from Phoenix?"

"Last night." Indian pulled the double doors open.

Lone Wolf rubbed his hands together. "Hot cup of coffee sounds good, doesn't it?"

"It sure does. There's an empty booth over there." He led the old man toward it.

"Whoa, cowboys," a heavyset waitress yelled. "Where do you think you're going?" They stopped. They turned to see the waitress holding the hands of the two children. She had already taken off their wet clothes and wrapped them in warm dry blankets. Indian nodded toward the empty booth. "Not in those clothes, you're not," she stammered, "You're dripping all over my floor. Lone Wolf, are you responsible for these kids being soaking wet?"

"Well," Lone Wolf stammered.

"Dammit, Lone Wolf," Bertha exclaimed. "Wet and chilling in the night air, these kids will catch pneumonia."

She reached out and touched Indian's and Lone Wolf's wet hair. "What the hell happened to all of you anyway?"

"Bertha, we fell in the river."

"All four of you fell in the river?"

"Well, yes."

Bertha now looked at Indian. "Are you drunk?"

Indian shook his head. "No, we're not drunk."

"Then how in the hell could all of you fall in the river?"

"I don't know," Indian answered, "we just did."

"The whole damn Boise River is fenced off to keep kids from falling in, but does it stop you two jackasses? No. Not only do you fall in the river, you dragged these two small children in with you. Then you uninvited twits bring half the river in here, and leak it on my floor." Lone Wolf and Indian ducked their heads, trying to hide their grins. "Oh, you think that's funny, do you? I have a mind to kick both of you out of here. And if it wasn't for the children, believe me, I would."

The cook was watching from the kitchen. "Do it, Bertha, just kick their butts out of here."

"You mind your own business, you old fool. I'll take care of matters out here."

Lone Wolf approached her. "Bertha, we are sorry. We just came in out of the cold for a cup of coffee. But if you give me and my grandson a mop, we will clean up the water."

She studied both of them for a moment. "He's your grandson?"

"Yes he is."

"And the children?"

Indian nodded toward Jason. "He's my nephew."

She studied their faces for a brief moment. "All right, I'll get you some coffee," she relented. "But first let's get you out of those wet clothes."

"Oh, that's not necessary," Indian answered.

"You want the coffee don't you?"

"Well, yes."

"Then let's get your butts out of those wet clothes." Bertha first put the children in a booth. Then she led Lone Wolf and Indian to the backroom and gave them two blankets. "Put these on and leave your wet clothes on the floor. I'll put them in our dryer for you."

"Thank you, Bertha."

"If it had been anyone else but you, Lone Wolf—"

"I know," Lone Wolf interrupted, "and we appreciate it."

"Well you're welcome." She turned toward the door. Halfway there she called back. "Your coffee will be waiting on the table."

They watched her leave the back room. "Boy, did we ever come into the wrong coffee shop."

Lone Wolf chuckled. "Bertha can be nasty at times." He then slipped out of his wet clothes and wrapped the dry blanket around his naked body. Lone Wolf smiled at his grandson and handed him the other blanket. "Here, I think it's safer to do what she says." Indian agreed. He slipped off his wet clothes and wrapped the other dry blanket around himself. They both returned to the empty coffee shop and sat down at the booth. The steaming cups of coffee were already on the table. In the meantime Jason and Sondra had fallen asleep on the booth benches. Long Wolf touched their cheeks. "It's been a long night for them. Best we let them rest."

Bertha came up to them. "Two handsome naked men sitting in my coffee shop." She laughed.

"You're not going to tell anyone?" Indian asked.

"Oh, you bet I am," she chuckled. "This is the best night shift I've ever had. But to show my gratitude, how about some breakfast? It's on the house."

"Thank you," Lone Wolf said. "That would be great." Lone Wolf turned his attention to Indian. "You look like something's troubling you, Grandson."

Indian nodded his head yes. "Tonight didn't seem random. I think the Sprudiths are looking for someone."

"They are," Lone Wolf said.

"I don't understand," Indian said. "Jason? Why would they want Jason?"

"It's not Jason. It's Sondra."

"Sondra? How do you know this?"

"The girl's mother told me. You see, the girl's mother defected from Micah's clan." Lone Wolf proceeded to tell Indian about his encounter with Cresta and Cerce.

"So this Sondra is the same girl they found up on Yankee Fork?"

"Yes, she is, and her mother kidnapped her from the hospital and left her with the Jordans."

"Why the Jordans?"

"I have my suspicions, but I don't know for sure. I followed the Sprudiths to the Jordan's home, but I was too late to save Mrs. Jordan and her friend from being taken."

"Taken!" Indian said, alarmed. "Taken, where?"

"Probably to the wolf woman, otherwise Micah would have killed them immediately."

"And this Sondra's a Sprudith too?"

"Only half. Her father is not."

Indian shook his head. "So much has happened in the past few days." He then proceeded to tell his grandfather about all the events that took place in Los Angeles, from the funeral to the mental institution. "By the way, there was this mental patient there that knew you."

"Who?"

"He calls himself Disciple. Do you know him?"

Grandfather chuckled. "Ah, yes, he's an old, dear friend." Both were quiet for a brief moment. Lone Wolf took a sip of his coffee. He could sense Indian's concern. Finally Lone Wolf broke the silence. "I'm sorry, Grandson, I thought you were through with them."

Indian looked up. He knew his grandfather spoke of the Sprudiths. "Their presence brings back horrible memories that I buried long ago."

Lone Wolf pulled the blanket even tighter around his shoulders. "Remember, we are at war—a war of good and evil. We follow the footsteps of others who have come and gone before. Now we lead the way for other warriors to follow us. We stand for honor, freedom, love, courage, kindness, and all that is good."

"What does all that mean?" Indian asked.

Lone Wolf now could see Bertha bringing their breakfasts. "Our course is very simple. What it means to us is that we enjoy this breakfast. We then get dressed."

"And after?"

"We will take care of Jason and Sondra. Then we will find Mrs. Jordan and her friend."

Indian smiled at Lone Wolf's simple wisdom.

�><0><⟨

Joseph put the bags in the trunk as Dr. Jordan exited from the airport door. "Any luck?"

"No, all the lines out were tied up."

Joseph closed the trunk. "Do you want to wait a few minutes and try again?"

"No, I'll try again when we get to the compound." Harrison and Joseph entered the car with Joseph driving. "How far is it?"

"It's about a two hour drive."

Joseph pulled away from the curb. Neither noticed the car follow-ing from a distance. Harrison looked at the beautiful greenery that was on both sides of the road. "I had forgotten."

"What's that?"

"I had forgotten the beauty."

Joseph smiled. "I am fortunate to be able to grow up in this part of the world."

Harrison looked at Joseph and smiled. "Yes, you are."

"So, how long did it take, you know, for you and Cresta to work out your differences?"

Harrison chuckled. "Actually we never did work out our differ-ences. We just learned to stay out of each other's way. And then—" Harrison paused. Jacob waited patiently for Harrison to continue. Finally Harrison looked at him. "Something happened to change all that."

"What was it?"

"It was when your father was away."

Cresta rushed into Harrison's bedroom. "Dr. Jordan, Dr. Jordan wake up." She shook him hard until his eyes opened.

Harrison rubbed his eyes adjusting to the dark. He was surprised to see Cresta standing before him. "Nurse Sullivan, what is it?"

"Come quick, I need your help."

"But it's two in the morning."

"It's Nano. He's hurt real bad this time."

Harrison quickly jumped out of bed. She watched as he pulled on his T-shirt and pants. *Maybe father is right*, she thought to herself. *Maybe I have feelings for this man.*

Harrison put on his foot thongs. "Where is he?"

"In the clinic."

They both raced out of his room into the compound yard. The only light was coming from the clinic itself. Harrison was the first to arrive. "Oh no, Nano."

Nano was shaking in spite of his wife holding him and several blan-kets covering his body. Nano opened his eyes and looked up. "I'm sorry, Dr. Jordan," Nano whispered, "it's real bad this time."

"Cresta, his vital signs?"

"Doctor, his blood pressure is low, pulse is rapid and weak, and he has a fever."

Harrison pulled back the blanket. Nano's right leg had been par-tially torn from his body.

Harrison looked at Cresta. "Do we have a hematocrit?"

"It's down to eighteen."

"He needs blood and surgery."

"Do we ship him out?"

"No, there isn't time. Start another IV and run the fluids wide open. We need volunteers for blood."

Cresta grasped Harrison's arm. "But what of blood incompatibility?"

"We'll have to chance it. If we don't he will die. You start the blood, and I will prepare the surgery room."

Harrison stopped telling his story. Joseph looked at him. "What happened?"

"Cresta started the blood transfusion, and we took him to surgery." Harrison paused and looked down. "We couldn't stop the bleeding. Nano went into shock and died."

"I'm sorry," Joseph replied.

Harrison smiled. "Me too. Cresta walked out and told Nano's family. I remember hearing his wife sobbing. Shortly Cresta came back into the clinic crying."

"I had forgotten how emotional she could be."

"Then your sister did something that would touch my heart forever."

"What was that?"

"She walked up to me, and put her arms around me. 'Harrison,' she said. I remember that was the first time she called me by my first name. 'Just hold me for a moment.' And I did while she wept."

Harrison and Joseph rode in silence.

CHAPTER TWENTY-EIGHT

THE FOUR TOWERS

Julie's hands moved over the cool satin bed sheets. She opened her eyes to the unfamiliar, beautifully crafted vaulted ceilings. *Where am I,* she thought. Instinctively she touched the soreness on her head and wondered what had happened. Slowly she sat up at the edge of the bed and stayed until the dizziness passed. The adjacent bedroom door opened. A woman looked through the doorway.

"I thought I heard you stirring." Mary entered and sat down next to Julie on the bed. "Confused?"

"I sure am."

"Yes, me too. She reached up and touched Julie's forehead. "How did you get that nasty bruise?

"I don't remember."

"Here, let me find you an ice pack."

"No, that's okay." Julie again looked around at the lavishly decorated bedroom. "Mary, where are we?"

"I don't know. I woke up earlier in the bedroom next door, but I still don't know where we are. Last thing I remember was those wolves and half naked men attacking me."

"That's the last thing I remember too."

Mary stood and extended her hand to Julie. "But you've got to see this. Come!" She took Julie's hand and led her through the balcony doors to the private terrace.

Julie could not believe her eyes. As far as the eye could see, it was green. "What is this place?"

"I'm not sure, but I think it's some kind of tropical rain forest."

"But I don't remember coming here."

"That's just it, neither do I." Mary pointed down. "Look below—it has beautiful walkways, terraces, gardens, and pools. To me it looks like some type of resort hotel." Suddenly there was a knock at her door. Mary turned toward the door. "I'll get it. Maybe we'll get some answers." She returned inside the room and opened the door. Standing before her was a beautiful young woman.

"Good morning," the woman said. She then entered the room and placed a tray of fresh fruit on the table. "Breakfast should be ready in about an hour." She then looked over at Julie who also had returned from the balcony. "Good morning, my lady."

"Good morning...who are you?"

"I am Mira, your maid servant."

Mary reached for some fresh grapes. "Is this fruit for us?"

"Yes, there is fresh fruit whenever you want."

Mary had already helped herself to the fruit. "You need to try this, Julie, the fruit is excellent."

Julie ignored Mary's suggestion and approached the maidservant. "Mira, right?"

"Yes, my lady."

"What is this place?"

Mira was confused. "This place?"

"Where we are at right now, what is this place?"

"Oh, this place is called Four Towers of Eden."

Mary took a bite of the banana. "Four Towers of Eden, kind of like a resort hotel?"

"I guess so. We do have guests here sometimes."

Julie touched Mira's arm. "Now I'm really confused. I don't remember coming here."

"Yes, me either," Mary added.

"You don't remember because last night when you arrived, you were asleep." Mira opened the clothes closet. It was completely full. "I believe you will find that all the clothing in your closets is in your size. I hope they meet with your approval."

Julie shook her head. "Mira, there's been a mistake."

"Mistake, my lady? I don't think so."

"Better check your records, honey," Mary suggested. "I don't know how we got here, but you brought the wrong people."

"Yes, we need to get back home," Julie added.

Mira looked at Julie. *If you only knew, Julie Harrison*, she thought sadly. *Like me, you will never leave this place.*

"Is there someone we can talk to about this?" Julie asked.

"You can speak with Tess."

"This Tess, where can we find her?" Mary asked.

Mira opened the door to leave. "You may speak with her at breakfast." She then turned and left.

———◁◆▷———

Joseph steered the car through the gate into the compound. "Here we are, Dr. Jordan."

Harrison looked at the multiple wild birds and animals about the compound. "It's nice to be back."

He stopped the car in front of the house. An older white haired man rushed through the front door down the steps of the porch. He wrapped his arms around Joseph. "Master Joseph, you're home."

Joseph broke the embrace. He then smiled. "Motumbo, I brought someone with me." Motumbo stepped back and approached the stranger. He studied his face. "Motumbo, do you remember him?"

"Dr. Jordan, can that be you?"

Harrison smiled and extended his hand.

Motumbo took it. "It is you."

"Hello, Motumbo."

"This is such a pleasant surprise. I know that Dr. Sullivan will be so happy to see you both."

"How is my father?"

He looked at Joseph. "Not well. He worsens every day."

"May we see him?"

"Maybe later, he's resting right now."

"Nonsense, Motumbo," a voice spoke from behind.

"Father." Joseph rushed forward and hugged his dad.

Dr. Sullivan broke the embrace. "Look at you. To the United States and back by yourself. Did you have any problems?"

"No, all went well."

Dr. Sullivan smiled at him. "My son is all grown up. Please, help me to the chair there on the porch." Dr. Sullivan put his arm around his son and used him to support his weight. He then smiled at his guest.

"Father, I brought him."

"You did good."

Harrison came forward, "Here, let me help." He took Sullivan's other arm and, with Joseph's help, they placed him in the porch chair.

"There," Harrison said once Sullivan sat down. Jacob and Harrison took chairs across the table from him.

"May I bring you something?" Motumbo asked.

"Four coffees, please," Sullivan answered.

"Yes, sir." Motumbo turned and went back into the house.

"Harrison, it is especially good to see you again. Thank you for coming."

"My pleasure, sir. How's the pain?"

"It's worsening every day."

Harrison leaned forward in his chair. "Stephen, maybe we could cure this."

"Cure it? Come on, Harrison, you know better."

"Look, Father, we could take you anywhere in the world for the best medical care."

Dr. Sullivan listened to his son and smiled faintly. "Joseph, I will go with you anywhere in the world, if Dr. Jordan can answer yes to one simple question."

"What question is that?" Joseph asked.

"Harrison, do you know of anyone who has ever been cured of pancreatic cancer?"

Joseph looked at Harrison, waiting for an answer. It did not come. "No one?" he finally asked.

Harrison shook his head no. "No, I don't know anyone."

Dr. Sullivan watched his son's head drop. "Hey, you two, don't be sad. I have so much to tell you with so little time." Motumbo brought the four cups of coffee and placed them on the table. He turned to leave. "Aren't you staying?"

Motumbo turned back. "No, I have some things to do."

"But if you are not going to stay, why the fourth cup of coffee?"

He smiled. "Ask your father."

Joseph turned to his Father. "Why the fourth cup?"

"I have a surprise for you."

"What?"

"We have a visitor."

"Who?"

"Me," a voice called from the doorway.

Joseph turned. He and Harrison were speechless. Cresta was standing in the doorway.

"My lady, Mrs. Jordan questioned me about her being here."

"Don't worry, Mira," Tess said. "I knew there would be questions. We have been through this before."

"My lady, she is coming," Mira said.

Tess nodded toward Mira. "Okay, you may go." Mira bowed and left.

Julie walked up to the woman sitting on the terrace eating her breakfast. "Are you Tess, the person in charge?"

"Yes, I am. May I help you?"

"My name is Julie Harrison. I think there has been a mistake. I shouldn't be here."

"What do you mean?" Tess asked.

"Well, my friend and I awoke this morning, and do not remember coming here."

"Did you and your friend make plans to come to the Four Towers of Eden?"

"No, we didn't. We haven't even heard of this place."

"And you came here last night?"

"We must have, but we don't remember it."

Tess looked at her clipboard. "And your name again?"

"Julie, Julie Jordan."

"Julie Jordan." She scanned the board. "I don't see you name on the list." Tess took off her sunglasses. "Mira," she called out.

Mira immediately came. "Yes, my lady."

"Do you know this lady?"

"Yes, this is Mrs. Jordan. I met her this morning."

"How could this have happened? My clipboard says a Mrs. Wilson, not a Mrs. Jordan, should be in that room." Tess pulled out a chair next to her. "Please sit down, Mrs. Jordan, while we sort this out. Would you like a cup of coffee?" Julie nodded her head yes. Mira poured Julie a cup.

Julie watched as Tess thumbed through the back pages of her clipboard. She stared at Tess. *This is uncanny*, Julie thought. *Except for the dark hair, this woman looks just like Nicole.*

Finally Tess looked up. "I'm sorry, Mrs. Jordan." She then stood to leave. "There has been a mistake, and I need more time to find out what happened."

Tess turned to leave. "Oh, miss, before you go," Julie interrupted, "can you tell me what this place is?"

"It's kind of like a fancy hotel resort created for the super rich." Tess turned to Mira. "I want you to stay and attend to Mrs. Jordan's and her companion's every need."

"Yes, my lady."

Tess turned back to Julie. "Will you excuse me?" she continued. "When I learn something, I'll let you know."

"Thank you," Julie replied.

Tess left and went inside the building. She met Matthias waiting for her. "Well?"

"So far, we have deceived her, but the question is, for how long?"

Matthias smiled. "Don't worry, it won't take long." When they turned and left, neither noticed Mary standing nearby listening.

CHAPTER TWENTY-NINE
THE BARN

P epe looked up at the light coming from the small window. "Boss, it's getting late. Why haven't they come?"

Doug shook his head. "I don't know."

"Maybe they won't come today."

They'll come, Doug thought, *but I can't tell Pepe that.*

"I'm so thirsty. Boss, do you have any more water?"

"Sorry, but it's all gone."

"You're right, boss."

"What's that?"

"I guess my prayers aren't answered either."

Doug could hear the discouragement in his friend's voice. "Don't get discouraged. It's only been one day."

"I guess you're right. If I hadn't left the priesthood, then maybe—" Pepe paused.

Both were quiet for a brief moment. "Why haven't you ever told me about that?" Doug asked.

"You mean leaving the priesthood?"

"Yes, what happened?"

Pepe became quiet for a brief moment. Then he began. "You remember my first assignment was in Guadalajara."

"Yes, I remember."

"Well there was this nun there I really liked. Her name was Margarita. Boy could she play cards. When we were partners, we would beat everyone."

Doug smiled. "I'll bet the fathers liked that."

Pepe laughed. "Oh man, boss, sometimes they would get so mad, they would threaten to quit and not play with us anymore. Then Margarita would just start giggling, and before we knew it, we would all be laughing." Pepe paused.

Doug saw Pepe smile. "What?"

"When we played we would give each other signals."

"You mean you were cheating?"

"Oh no, Margarita would never cheat. We just acted like we were giving each other signals just to make the other priests mad."

Doug chuckled. "Is she still in Guadalajara?"

Pepe looked into his friend's face. Sadness began to appear. Then he turned away. "No, she's gone."

Doug knew there was more to the story. *I'll give him time*, Doug thought. *He'll tell me when he is ready.*

Pepe once again reflected back to the time when he and Margarita spent the night in the barn.

Father Santana and Sister Margarita went to sleep on different sides of the straw pile, but it must have become chilly during the night. By morning they were wrapped in each other arms. The barn doors swung open and the bright morning sunlight shone in their eyes. Even though they covered the brightness with their hands, all they could see were shadows standing in the doorway. Pepe's eyes focused first. "Father Ramirez, Father Garcia?"

Now Sister Margarita's eyes focused and she could make out the four of them. "Sister Maria, what are all of you doing here?"

Father Ramirez studied the both of them. "The question is what are you two doing?"

It was then that Margarita and Pepe then realized how close they had slept together. They separated from each other. "Father Ramirez, this is not what you think."

"Father Santana, what do you think we are thinking?"

"Well that Sister Margarita and I slept together." Pepe thought about what he said.

"And you didn't sleep together?" Father Garcia asked.

"Well, yes, Father, we slept together, but we didn't sleep together."

"Father, what are you trying to say?" Sister Maria asked.

"Well what I'm trying to say is that—" Margarita put forth her hand and touched Pepe's arm. She interrupted his remarks. Pepe remained quiet. "What are all of you doing here?" Sister Margarita asked.

Father Ramirez spoke. "Mr. Alvarez called me last night. He said the two of you were sleeping together in his barn. When you didn't return last night, we came up to investigate."

"How could you, Sister Margarita?" Sister Maria exclaimed. "Breaking vows you made with God."

"Sister Maria, your mind is in the gutter. Father Santana and I didn't do anything."

"You were wrapped in each others arms," Father Garcia said. "What are we suppose to think?"

"Father Garcia," Margarita continued. "I swear to you, Pepe and I didn't do anything."

"Pepe," Sister Maria interrupted. "You called Father Santana by his first name. Do you do that often?"

"No, Sister, that just slipped out."

"Just slipped out?""

Now Margarita's feathers were ruffled. "Look, Sister Maria, what are you insinuating?"

"I'm insinuating nothing. It's a fact that you slept all night in this barn with a man. What would you think?"

Father Ramirez saw Margarita's red face and clenched hands. "Sisters," he interrupted. He then nodded his head toward the farmer next to him. "Let's discuss this further back at the church, shall we?"

Pepe and Margarita gathered all their belonging and followed the others out of the barn.

"Pepe, do you think Tina is right?"

Doug's comments brought Pepe's thoughts of Margarita back to reality. "What was that?"

"Well I just wonder if you think Tina was right."

"About what?"

"About Jason not being our son."

"Ah, boss, Jason's your son."

"You remember, Pepe, when we were younger, I never wanted any children."

"I remember."

"Do you remember the day Nicole told me she was pregnant?"

Pepe did not answer but closed his eyes. He remembered that day all too well.

Nicole stared out the car window at the drizzling rain. The bearded man pulled the car to a stop about a block away. He turned to her. "Nicole, don't do this."

"You mean you want me to just leave?"

"Yes, it is best he doesn't know."

"What, we just grab his sperm and run?"

The bearded man looked away. They both sat in silence for a brief moment. Then Nicole turned toward him. "John, I'm sorry." In her eyes he could see her silent plea. "But isn't there another way?"

He reached for her hand. "There isn't another way."

"But he has a right to know."

John turned to her. "He'll hurt you."

Nicole's eyes began to moisten. She bowed her head. "Yes, I know."

John climbed out of the car. He opened the umbrella and proceeded to Nicole's side. He then opened her door. "Here." He tried to hand the opened umbrella. "You'll need this."

She shook her head no. "Thanks, you keep it. You know how I love the rain." Then she turned and walked away.

"Nicole." She turned around. "I'll be right here, waiting." She smiled and proceeded down the street. John watched her walk away.

Nicole climbed the stairs and rang the bell. Shortly Pepe opened the door. "Nicole, did you forget your key?" She didn't answer. He looked at her wet clothes. "You're soaking wet. Come in, and let's get you some dry clothes before you get sick."

Pepe escorted her into the bedroom. "Doc should be home soon. He just called from the hospital. In fact he was asking about you."

"He asked about me?"

"Sí, he hadn't seen you all day and was wondering where you were."

Nicole watched as Pepe helped get dry towels and hand them to her. It was then that she realized the strong bond that had developed between her and Pepe. She knew that she would miss his kindness and friendship. "Pepe."

Pepe continued to lay out some fresh clothes. He did not hear her. "Pepe," she called louder.

Now he turned toward her. "Yes?"

"Pepe, I'm pregnant."

Pepe's mouth dropped open. "What did you say?"

"I said I'm pregnant."

Pepe gasped. "Really?" Nicole nodded her head yes. "You and Doug?" Again she nodded yes. "Pregnant," he exclaimed. He whirled around and tossed her fresh clothes high into the air. "I can't believe it," he laughed. He ran to Nicole, lifted her high in the air, and twirled with her like a dancer. "A baby," he again exclaimed. "A baby."

Nicole laughed. "Pepe, put me down."

He stopped and gently let her back to the ground. "When?"

"In a few months."

"Few months," Pepe laughed again and clapped his hands together. "A baby in a few months. Does Doc know?"

Nicole broke their embrace and turned away. Suddenly the mood changed. "No, he doesn't know."

"Nicole, what's wrong?"

Nicole turned back toward him. "I'm afraid to tell him."

"Why?"

"You know he has never wanted children."

"Ah, that's just the Doc talking. Listen, you change your clothes while I get a bottle of wine to celebrate." Pepe then turned toward the door. "You watch, the Doc will be so excited." He then ran back to Nicole and gave her another hug. "That's great, a baby."

Nicole laughed as she watched Pepe turn and leave. "Oh, I wish Doug would be that excited." She reached for the dry clothes. Doubts still filled her heart.

Pepe placed the two wineglasses on the table. He lit the candles. "What's the occasion," a voice said from behind.

Pepe turned and saw Doug hanging up his coat in the entrance. "Oh, boss, Nicole's here."

"She is?"

"She's in the bedroom changing her clothes. She was caught in the rain."

Doug motioned to the setting on the table. "What is this?"

Pepe snickered. "I thought you two might like a romantic dinner tonight. Nicole has something to tell you."

"That's nice." Pepe chuckled again. "Pepe, what's got into you tonight?"

Pepe ignored Doug's question as he saw Nicole walk into the room. "Here she is." Pepe raced to her side and escorted her to the table. "This is so exciting."

"Pepe, tell me, what's so exciting?"

Pepe helped Nicole with her chair. Doug came around the table and caressed and kissed Nicole. "What's with him?"

"Boss, you'll see, but first a glass of wine for my favorite couple." He poured each a glass. He then left and entered the kitchen.

Doug looked across the table. "Something's happened?"

Nicole smiled and set the wine aside. "It's nothing."

"Come on, what is it?"

"Well, if you must know, I think I'm going to be named the director of nursing."

Doug was surprised. "Nicole, that's great." He came around the table and took her into his arms. "Imagine you as director of nursing, and I as chief surgical resident. Could we have it any better?"

"I don't know. We were talking about a family."

"There's plenty of time for that."

Pepe now reentered the room. He could see them locked arm in arm. "You told him."

"Yes, she told me."

"And?" Pepe asked.

"And, I think it is just great."

"I knew it, boss. I knew you would be excited. See, Nicole, you worried for nothing."

Doug looked at Nicole. "Why would you be worried?"

"That's exactly what I told her," Pepe interrupted.

"But, Pepe," Nicole began to explain, "I didn't get a chance—"

"See, Nicole," Pepe again interrupted, "I knew he would be excited. Now you two relax, and I will fix one of the finest meals you have ever had." Pepe stopped short of the kitchen door and turned. "Imagine a new baby in this home. I'm so excited." He turned back and went into the kitchen.

Doug turned toward Nicole. He was initially silent. "It isn't your new nursing position, is it?" Nicole pulled away and went to the window. She looked at the drizzling rain and the lone car parked down the block. "You're pregnant, aren't you?" Nicole slowly turned back. She nodded her head yes. "But, I thought you were using some kind of birth control."

"I was, but I stopped."

"Stopped—why?"

"Because I wanted a child."

"But what of your career?"

"I don't care about my career. I want a family."

"I want a family too, but of all times, why now?"

"What do you mean?"

"I'm chief surgical resident, and you could have been director of nursing if only—"

"If only I wasn't pregnant."

"Nicole, this isn't the time to have a family."

"Well, it's too late."

"No, it's not. This matter can be corrected."

"What do you mean?"

"Well I know a doctor in LA. He could—"

"You mean an abortion?"

"It's not as if we couldn't have other children sometime." Nicole put on her jacket and began to walk toward the front door. Doug touched her arm. "Where are you going?"

She reached up and kissed him on the cheek. "Good-bye, Doug."

Doug's eyes widened. "Nicole, you're leaving, aren't you?"

Tears began to appear in her eyes. She tried to smile, but it was faint. "Say good-bye to Pepe for me. He was always so kind." She then opened the door and disappeared in the pouring rain.

Now Doug's words brought Pepe thoughts back to the present. "What if she had done what I wanted, and had an abortion. I wouldn't have Jason now."

"Yes, you're right."

Suddenly the hidden door opened. Ellen and Large Marge appeared. "Hello, guys," Ellen greeted. "Ready for that roll in the hay?"

Pepe closed his eyes. "Please, God," he whispered, "help me through this."

CHAPTER THIRTY

THE ARMY BASE

Jim changed the phone receiver to the other ear. "Calm down, Mom, now what do you mean they're missing?"

"I've been in Boise all day looking for them. I'm telling you, Jason and the Jordans are missing."

Elaine walked into the room. She pointed to her watch. Jim nodded his head yes. "Maybe you should tell Sheriff Bates."

"I already have. In fact he called me this morning asking if I knew where they were."

"Maybe they've just taken a short trip somewhere."

"I thought the same until the sheriff found the house in shambles and blood on the floor. He suspects some kind of foul play."

Jim shook his head. "That's just great, as if there isn't enough going on around us already."

"I feel the same. I haven't been able to reach Doc Hunter. Have you seen him?"

"Not for two days. He and Pepe went to the women's prison in LA and we haven't heard from them since."

"Did you talk with the prison officials?"

"This morning. They said Doug and Pepe were there earlier, but left." Elaine again pointed at her watch. "I know, I know," Jim mimicked with his mouth. "Mom, have you seen Indian?"

"I thought he was with you."

"He was, but Doc sent him back to the ranch."

"For what?"

"I don't know. I'm in the dark about this too. Are you staying in Boise tonight?"

"No, I'm driving back. I need to do chores." He heard her sigh. "Well you and Elaine try to find the Doc, and I'll watch for Indian."

"Okay, Mom."

"By the way, are you coming up to the ranch?"

"If we can, but we have some things to do here first for Sheriff Bates."

"Okay, tell Elaine hello."

"I will. I'll talk to you tomorrow." They both hung up the receivers.

"Let's go, Jim. We need to be there right at the shift change."

"Okay." Jim grabbed his jacket and escorted Elaine through the motel room door out to the rental car.

Elaine noticed Jim's troubled look as he started the car. "Bad news?"

Jim steered the car into the mainstream of traffic. "Ah, my nephew Jason and the people who were taking care of him are missing. Sheriff Bates hasn't been able to find the Doc either."

"He's not the only one. Maybe they are away just for the day."

"I hope so." He then took a deep breath and blew it out. "Anyway, do you think we can get in?"

Elaine pulled out two badges from her purse and handed one to Jim. "We can with these." Jim looked at his badge. "It's mine and David's security badges."

"This may be fine for you, but mine has David's picture and name on it."

"I know, but the evening shift isn't as cautious as earlier shifts. I doubt they will even look."

"Will these badges also get us into the lab?"

"Oh no, the security is much too tight for that."

"Well I hope your friend knows something about this apocalypse file or this Joe guy."

Now the base was coming into view. "I hope so too." Jim glanced over at Elaine. "You know McFarland is the general here."

"Yes, I know."

"Are there any feelings between the two of you anymore?"

Elaine frowned at Jim. "Come on, that was a long time ago."

"Just checking." Elaine knew it was McFarland who made the false accusations against Jim and Indian, drumming them out of the army intelligence service. "Let's just try hard to avoid him, okay?"

Jim pulled the car to a stop at the main gate. "Passes please." The guard took the passes and then looked at the occupants. He then handed the passes back. "Go ahead."

The soldier watched as the car pulled away. Immediately he picked up his phone. "General McFarland, please. This is the front gate."

The general picked up the phone. "McFarland here."

"General, the two you asked about earlier just passed through the gate."

"Thank you, soldier." McFarland hung up the phone and dialed another number. "Captain Reed, this is General McFarland."

"Yes, General."

"I know you may be planning to go home, but could you come to my office instead?"

"Yes, sir, I'll be there in a few minutes."

"Good." McFarland stood and walked over to the large picture window and looked over the base. "Just like old times," McFarland murmured to himself. "Elaine, Jim, and I back together again."

"Well that was easy."

Jim scanned his rearview mirror. "Too easy."

Elaine motioned with her hand. "The officer's building is up here on the right."

Jim turned into the designated parking lot and stopped the car. Except for a few cars the lot was empty. The only sound he could hear were flies buzzing a nearby night light. He opened the door, took Elaine's hand, and led her toward the administration building. "Now where do we meet her?"

"She said in the library."

"Elaine, I'm a little concerned about seeing this lady."

"What do you mean?"

"Well, several people have already died. How do we know she can be trusted?"

"Debbie's like a sister to me. I would trust her with my life."

"Look, I'm not doubting you. I just want to be sure. What does this Debbie do anyway?"

"She's General McFarland's secretary."

Jim stopped on the steps. "McFarland's secretary?" Jim exclaimed. "What are you doing?"

Elaine turned him. "Listen, I know what you are thinking."

"And what's that?"

"That we should call this meeting off."

"You're right about that!" Jim turned to leave.

Elaine grabbed hold of Jim's arm. "Wait, listen to me first." Jim reluctantly stopped and turned toward Elaine. "It was Debbie who told me that she suspects David was murdered. That's why we need to talk with her."

"Then you trust her?"

"Absolutely."

Jim smiled and took Elaine's hand again. "All right, let's go." He opened one of the double doors and allowed Elaine to enter first. They approached the guard at the desk.

"Sir, can you tell us where the library is?" Elaine asked.

"Basement floor, ma'am."

"Thank you." She led the way down the stairway toward the empty basement. The hallway lights were dim.

Jim checked each door they passed. "Here it is." He nodded at the name on the door.

Elaine turned the doorknob. "It's locked."

"Elaine," a voice whispered from ahead.

Elaine walked in the direction of the voice. "Debbie, is that you?"

"Yes, hurry, come in here."

Elaine and Jim walked another twenty steps and entered a dark, small conference room. The occupant closed and locked the door behind her. She switched on the light. "Elaine," the heavyset woman exclaimed. She came forward and wrapped her arms around Elaine's neck. "It's so good to see you."

Elaine broke the embrace after a brief moment. "It's good to see you too." Now Elaine noticed that Debbie was looking at Jim. "Excuse my manners. I want you to meet a good friend of mine—"

"Jimmy Crockett," Debbie interrupted.

Jim and Elaine were surprised. Elaine touched Debbie's shoulder. "Do you know Jim?"

"It was a long time ago." Jim studied her face, but could not remember her. "You don't remember me, do you Mr. Crockett."

"I'm sorry, but I'm afraid I don't."

"That's okay. Please come and sit down. I brought a pot of coffee." She placed three cups on the table and poured coffee in each. "I hope you like it black."

"Black will be fine," Elaine reassured.

Debbie placed the pot on the table and sat down at the head of the conference table between the two of them. She took a sip of her coffee then set the cup down. She stared at Elaine for a moment. A faint smile came to her face. She reached over and squeezed Elaine's hand. "I'm sorry about David. We're all going to miss him." Debbie turned her attention to Jim. "He was your friend, wasn't he?"

"He was. That's why we are trying to find out what happened to him."

Debbie looked at Elaine. "Some people think David killed himself, but I don't. That's why I contacted you."

"Is there any reason why you think David was killed?" Elaine asked.

"I know he knew something," Debbie answered.

"Why do you say that?" Jim asked.

"Because what he knew worried others."

"Others," Jim said. "You mean in the intelligence field?"

Debbie nodded her head. "Them and others like my boss."

Elaine touched Debbie's arm. "Have you seen or heard anything to confirm your suspicions?"

"No, nothing has come across the general's desk, or I would have known." Debbie paused to collect her words. "I don't have any proof, but it's this feeling like intuition." She could see Jim's frustrated face. "I'm sorry, Mr. Crockett, I don't know how to explain it any better."

Jim grimaced. "We were just hoping you might have more concrete information."

Debbie could sense his disappointment. Elaine thought for a moment. "Do you know what David was working on?"

"It was germ warfare projects."

"Do you know which projects?" Jim asked.

"No, I wouldn't have access to that sort of thing."

"Debbie, have you ever hear of a project named 'The Apocalypse Project'?" Jim asked.

Debbie thought for a moment. "No…I guess I'm not helping much."

"It's okay, you're doing the best you can," Elaine reassured. "One other thing, David once mentioned a man named Joe, who worked with him on a project here."

"Joe, Joe," she repeated aloud. "The main researcher with David was a man whose first name was Ed—Edward Sorenson. You know, I remember all the people in David's lab, but I don't remember anyone named Joe."

Elaine looked at Jim. "Why would David say and write these things? He even wrote them on the wall."

Jim shook his head. "I don't know." He then turned back. "Debbie, has anyone around here ever mentioned an animal called a Uintathere?"

"I've never heard of such an animal."

"How about some secret military project named after some kind of music?" Elaine added.

Debbie thought for brief moment. "No, nothing comes to mind."

Jim turned to Elaine. He shrugged his shoulders and shook his head. "I don't know, maybe we need to just face facts."

"What's that?"

"That maybe Solomon was really crazy."

"Solomon?" Debbie questioned.

Elaine and Jim looked at Debbie. "Yes, Solomon, David's code name."

Debbie's face brightened. "Why didn't I think of that before? That's it!"

"That's what?" Jim asked.

Debbie ignored Jim's questioned. She began to thumb through her briefcase on the floor and pulled out a file. "Let me see," she spoke aloud as she thumbed through it. "Joe, Joe," she repeated. Then she saw it. She looked up. "That's it, it was Joe."

"What do you mean?" Elaine asked.

"David's partner's name was Ed Sorenson, and his code name was Joe."

"Great, now we are getting somewhere. Where can we find this Ed Sorenson?"

"You can't. Ed Sorenson was killed last year in a hunting accident. It was so tragic. He left his wife Megan with two children."

Jim looked at Elaine. Now she could see the frustration on his face. Jim and Elaine stood to leave. "Well I guess that's all the questions we have, thanks." Elaine reached over and hugged Debbie.

"I wish I knew more," Debbie explained.

"At least you answered some of our questions. That helps."

Debbie pulled away. She looked Elaine in the eyes. "Again, I'm so sorry about David."

Elaine smiled and turned to Jim. "Shall we go?"

Jim nodded his head yes and led the way to the door. He then turned back to Debbie. "I'm curious, how is it that you know me, you know, from before?"

Debbie smiled. "You saved me once."

"What do you mean?"

Debbie looked down at the floor. "It was years ago when I was young, foolish, and real drunk. I was at this party and these three men took me upstairs to an empty room. When they started tearing off my clothes, I screamed and tried to resist, but I just too weak and drunk."

Elaine was alarmed. "Debbie, you never told me this."

"Yes, I know. I was too embarrassed."

"Then these guys raped you," Elaine surmised.

"Well, they tried, but what I remember was someone pulled the first guy off of me, and there was a fight. I thought I saw this Native American beating these three guys to a pulp, but it was probably the alcohol."

Jim and Elaine looked at each other and smiled. They knew she must be speaking about Indian.

"The next thing I knew was that I was being cradled in the arms of this really handsome man. Now do you remember, Mr. Crockett? You took me home."

Jim gently smiled. "Yes, I remember."

"There is evil here on this base, and sometimes I get scared. But I feel much safer now that you and Elaine are here."

Jim nodded and walked out the door down the hallway.

Elaine touched Debbie's hand. "I'll call you soon."

"Please do!"

"Wait here until we are gone."

Debbie nodded yes. Elaine then left the room and followed Jim down the hall.

THE CHASE

McFarland looked up at Reed. "The boy and girl?"

"Nothing yet, sir, but we think they are at the ranch." Both were quiet as they watched the monitors. "General, if I may be so bold as to ask something?"

"What is it, Captain?"

"Why did we need to cremate those girls' bodies?"

"What do you mean?"

"Well it seems to me we may have some future troubles with the local authorities, and disposing their bodies so quickly could we have made matters worse."

McFarland reached for some papers on the desk behind him. "That's not your concern, Reed. Just find that man and woman."

Reed refocused on the monitors. "Yes, sir." They were quiet for several moments as Reed continued to scan the monitors. Suddenly they appeared. It caught Reed unexpectedly. He placed his hand on the monitor and drew close. *Why that's Jim and Elaine*, Reed thought himself. *I wonder what they are doing here.*

Once again McFarland was at Captain Reed's side. "Anything yet?"

Captain Reed nodded at one of the camera monitors. "Are they the two?" he asked.

McFarland moved closer. "Yes, that's them." He searched the surrounding monitors to get his bearings. "Reed, where is this monitor?"

Reed searched the monitors himself. "It's the one in the basement of this building."

McFarland thought for a brief moment. "Have some of your men follow them."

"Yes, sir." Reed turned to leave.

"And, one other thing. Talk to no one about them."

Reed nodded his head. "Yes, sir." The moment he left, two men entered the monitor room from the opposite door. "You wanted to see us, General?"

McFarland nodded at the monitor. "You recognize them?"

For a brief moment they focused on the monitor. "Why that's David Smith's widow," Lenny exclaimed.

"The other is Crockett," Scarface added.

"I was afraid of that," McFarland said. He bit his lip. "I really worry when these two are involved." The general watched Elaine and Jim leave the administration building and walk to their car. They also watched two of Reed's men follow them.

"Why, look at this," Lenny exclaimed.

McFarland turned back to the monitors. "What?"

Lenny pointed to the monitor. "There, General. Someone else is in the basement."

McFarland was stunned. "Why, it's Debbie," McFarland murmured. He turned to Scarface. "Do you think she was with Elaine and Crockett?"

Scarface grimaced. "It looks like it to me."

McFarland turned toward the door. "You two wait here, I'll be back in a couple of minutes." McFarland proceeded down the hall toward the main lobby. He was there waiting when Debbie came out of the basement.

Debbie gasped, "General, you frightened me."

"You're here late. Is everything all right?"

"Yes, I just had some extra work. Is there anything you want me to do?"

"Oh no, I was looking out the office window and thought I saw two old friends come into the building. Were you downstairs?"

"Yes, I was."

"You didn't happen to see a man and a woman down there?"

"No, I was all alone."

"Oh, well, no matter. It must have been someone else. So you're on your way out?"

"Yes, it's been a long day."

"Well goodnight, you drive safely."

"I will, goodnight."

General McFarland held the administration door open for Debbie until she left. He then quickly returned to the monitor room. "Well?" Scarface asked.

"She's hiding something. She lied about Smith and Crockett being in the basement."

"We told you before we think she's the mole," Scarface reminded.

"Yes, I know." The general looked down at the cast on Lenny's arm. "What happened to you?"

"I had a little accident. That bastard Indian caught me off guard and broke my arm."

McFarland looked at Scarface. "Was it him?"

Scarface nodded his head yes. "Yes, it was."

"That's just great. Jim, Elaine, and now Indian are all involved. Somehow we have to get back in control."

"We will, General," Scarface reassured. "You just tell us what to do."

"Well, first, take care of Debbie. No screw-ups, understand?"

"Understood," Scarface replied.

Debbie slipped back into the administration office to the phone in the lobby. "Secure line," she spoke. Quickly she dialed the number and switched the phone to the other ear. "Please be there," she whispered. She failed to see the nearby elevator doors open. Lenny put up his arm and stopped Scarface. He nodded toward Debbie.

"There she is," he whispered. They both backed into the shadows and watched.

"Hello," the phone answered.

"Ben, I think he knows. I think he's going to get me."

Ben could sense the urgency in her voice. "Calm down, and tell me who knows what."

"General McFarland caught me coming out of the library in the basement."

"So, you're responsible for the library."

"No, this time it was different. I had been talking to Elaine Smith and Jim Crockett."

"What do you mean you were talking to them?"

"Elaine called and said she wanted to meet."

"Oh, Debbie, how could you? You may have blown your cover."

"I know. It was stupid of me."

"Well we can't take any chances. Let's get you out of there now." Ben looked at his watch. "Leave the base right now and meet me at the Salt Lake airport parking lot in one half hour."

Debbie hung up the phone. She grabbed her purse and immediately left the building. Lenny and Scarface followed her from a distance.

She searched the empty parking lot and did not see anyone. Quickly she climbed in and started her car. She remembered the general's look when they came face-to-face. She had seen it before and that's what frightened her. *If was as if he knew*, she thought. She turned on the two-way road leading to the front gate. She failed to notice another vehicle lights turn on. She stopped at the front gate. Patiently she waited for the cross gate to rise. It didn't. "Come on," she murmured, "what's taking the guard so long." She looked in the rearview mirror to see another car pull up behind. Now the guard came to the doorway. She rolled down her window.

"Debbie, you're working late tonight," the guard exclaimed.

"Yes, the general has me doing some extra work. It's keeping me here pretty late."

"Slave driver."

"You're right about that."

"Well you drive carefully," the guard advised. He then pushed the button and the gate elevated. He then saluted. "Have a good evening."

"You too, Corporal." She drove through the gate and out onto the roadway. Debbie took a deep breath and blew it out. "I made it," she whispered. She made the proper turns until she was on the freeway heading east. She could see Salt Lake City lights illuminating the eastern sky. Eleven years she had been the general's secretary, and had been oh so careful. "How could I have been so stupid." she whispered.

Very few cars were on the freeway at this late hour. Debbie kept looking in her rearview mirror. She noticed a set of car lights had followed her onto the freeway. *I wonder if someone is following me*, she thought. She began to slow down to let them pass, but they slowed down too. She waved her hand for them to pass, but they didn't. Finally she pulled to the side of the road and stopped. The following car pulled up next to her and stopped. Debbie recognized it was one of the cars from the base, but couldn't make out the driver due to its tinted windows. After a brief moment the window came down. Now she could tell that two people were in the car, but she still could not see their shadowy faces. Finally the passenger spoke.

"Are you having some car trouble?" Debbie had heard the voice before but could not put a face with it.

"No, I'm fine." She waited for the car to leave but it didn't.

"Debbie, we know what you did."

"I don't know what you are talking about."

"Talking with Elaine Smith and Jim Crockett. You know, the general is not too happy about that."

Debbie realized she'd been right. The general did know. Now the passenger stuck his head through the window. Debbie could see his face well. "Scarface, what are you doing?"

Scarface smiled. "You know, Debbie, I like you," he said. "But General McFarland doesn't tolerate Mossad spies in army intelligence."

Debbie looked both ways for help, but the freeway was empty. She turned back to Scarface in time to see him point a gun at her. "I'm sorry," he said. Immediately she hit the gas. With tires screeching, she fled away onto the freeway.

"You didn't shoot?" Lenny asked.

"No, we want this to look like an accident. Just stay close. She's doing exactly what we want."

Ben read the sign. "Airport exit, two miles." Even though she volunteered for the assignment eleven years ago, Ben was against it from the first. Since Ben's wife died, Debbie was all he had. He had already been on the telephone making arrangements for her to be flown out of the country tonight. *If she can just get to the airport*, he thought. He was ready to take the airport exit when he saw two cars speeding toward him on the other side of the freeway. *Wow, they're traveling fast*, he thought. He slowed down to watch the cars pass. "That's Debbie's car," he exclaimed, as the first car passed followed by the second. "And someone's chasing her." Quickly he slowed his car further and crossed the midway between the freeways and began to follow.

"Okay, it's coming up. Pull up beside her," Scarface instructed. Lenny applied more gas. Scarface rolled down his window. Debbie looked over to see Scarface and Lenny pull up next to her. Now Debbie could see Scarface's gun again. She stepped down on the gas pedal but to no avail. Lenny was able to keep up. She again glanced at Scarface's smiling face. He pointed his gun from the open window, but not at Debbie, but rather her car.

"What's he doing?" she murmured. Suddenly the gun fired. Debbie felt the car pull to her left. Immediately she knew her front tire had been shot. She fought with the steering wheel to regain control but felt the car swerve back and forth until tire rims met with the road pavement.

Ben watched from behind. He saw the red car fly high over and over again into the air and down the road. "No!" he exclaimed as he raced closer to the scene. He pulled his car to a stop and ran toward the overturned car. He could hear Debbie's screams. Gas fumes filled the air. Suddenly the second car was backing up the freeway past the scene of the accident next to Ben. When Ben saw who it was he immediately went for his gun, but it was too late. Scarface pointed his gun.

"Ben, I wouldn't do that," Scarface exclaimed.

Ben nodded toward the overturned car. "Let me go to her. The car is going to explode."

Scarface looked at the overturned the car and nodded. "You know, I think you're right." Ben again moved toward the car. "I told you not to move."

"Go to hell," Ben exclaimed. Immediately Scarface shot Ben in his good leg. Ben went down. He immediately grabbed his leg and felt the warm blood oozing through his fingers. "Please, Scarface, help her."

"As much as you are trying to help her, she must mean a lot to you." Ben didn't say anything. "What is she, you lover, wife, daughter?" Ben immediately looked up. "Ah, I thought so. A Jew spy sacrificing his daughter's life. That's so pathetic." Scarface pointed his gun at the overturned car and fired. Immediately the car blew up.

"No!" Ben screamed as the fireball raised high into the sky. Ben stared at Scarface. "I'll get you, you bastard."

"I look forward to it." Ben watched as they swiftly drove away. Ben looked up and down the empty freeway. He knew the police would be here shortly with questions about the accident and how he was shot. Quickly he removed his belt and wrapped it around his upper leg as a tourniquet, which stopped the bleeding. Slowly he made it to his feet and stared at the burning vehicle. Sounds of police sirens in the distance caught his attention. He limped his way back to his car, climbed in, and drove away.

CHAPTER THIRTY-TWO

THE ESCAPE

H er open hand slapped Pepe hard across the face. "Kiss me." Pepe was too exhausted. Disgusted she threw him back against the hard pavement. "You're pathetic," she yelled. She again clamped his hand-cuffs to the metal pipe.

"Leave him alone, Marge," Ellen commanded. She then refastened Doug's cuffs back onto the same metal pipe. "That was nice, Doc," she snickered. "You get to live another day." She then handed him two slices of bread and small bottle of water.

"Our clothes?" Doug asked.

Ellen chuckled. "I don't think so." She then stood and walked away.

"No food or water for you, Santana," Large Marge yelled.

"Come on," Ellen contended. "Give him the food and water."

"Hell no. If he can't do better than that, then he ain't worth it."

"Well how do you expect him to respond if you starve him to death?"

Marge thought for a moment. "Yeah, I guess you're right." She then him threw him the crusts of bread and water. She reached down and pulled his face up close to hers. "You better do better tomorrow, understand?" Pepe nodded his head yes.

Ellen motioned toward the doorway. "Come on, it's almost time for lockup." They both walked over to the hidden door that led back into the main prison. Ellen turned back. "Rest up, guys. We'll be back in the morning."

"Ellen, tomorrow I get the Doc."

"The hell you do. He's mine—" Their voices faded as the door closed.

Doug turned toward Pepe. "Are you all right?"

"My nose is bleeding. I think she broke my nose."

Doug tore off a piece of rag and threw it to him. "Put pressure on the bleeding with this."

Pepe placed the rag on his nose. "Boss, I'm giving up."

"What are you talking about?"

"I can't do this anymore."

"Pepe, if you hadn't talked to Marge that first day, we both would be dead right now. Don't you realize you saved our lives?"

"I don't know. Today when she was hitting me, I was praying I would just die."

Doug could tell his friend's mental state was on the fringes. "Look, we've made it another day, and we're still alive."

We got to get out of here. I don't think I can take another day." Doug knew Pepe was right. He knew they were living on borrowed time. Pepe looked around the large room. "I have studied this place over and over. I just can't see a way out. Maybe Ms. Stewart was wrong."

"I can't see one either," Doug agreed. Hunter looked up at a small window allowing the only light illuminating the large room. "It will be dark soon."

"That's just great, another night with the rats."

"Think of it this way, if those rats can get in here, then there has to be a way out."

Pepe ate the bread and drank the small amount of water from the bottle. "I just have to have more water." He reached to fill his bottle with water from the stagnant pool located nearby.

"No, that's seawater. It'll make you sick."

"What if I don't swallow it?" Doug still shook his head no. "But, I am so thirsty."

Doug looked at his small bottle of water. "Here, drink mine." He then tossed his bottle to him.

Pepe drank the second bottle and then collapsed on the pile of rags. "Kiss me, Pepe, kiss me," Pepe yelled mimicking Marge's voice. "How can anyone kiss a four hundred pound pig lying on top of them?"

Pepe turned and looked at Doug. "I really tried." Doug slid his handcuff down the pipe until he was next to Pepe. "I really did try, but she just kept hitting me."

Doug could see Pepe's eyes start to moisten. "It's okay." He handed him his two pieces of bread. "Here, have this too."

Pepe took the pieces of bread. "Are you sure?"

"I'm sure." Doug watched his friend eat. *If I don't get him out of here, he's going to crack*, he thought.

Pepe took a bite of the bread. "Do you think anyone misses us?"

"Absolutely, I'm sure Jim and Indian are looking for us right now."

He wiped a crumb from the side of his mouth. "But how are they going to find us in here?"

Doug had thought the same and shook his head. "I don't know."

"I guess we just have to have hope," Pepe exclaimed.

Doug chuckled. "There's that word again. You sound like my mom."

Pepe had a puzzled look on his face. "What do you mean?"

"Oh, the other day mom was talking about my father and Nicole. She said the same thing—that we have to have hope."

Pepe was confused. "And you don't have any?"

"Not for what she said."

He took another bite of bread. "And what was that?" he mumbled.

"Some silly belief that she and my father would be together again someday, and—" Doug paused.

Pepe knew what he was going to say. He finished his sentence. "And hope that you and Nicole will also be together someday, right?"

Doug chuckled. "Crazy, huh?"

"You don't believe that?"

"Of course not."

"What if your mom is right?" What if somehow you and Nicole could be together again?"

"Well, it won't happen, so let's just drop it." Pepe was quiet. Doug shook his head. *I don't know why I say these things*, he thought. Doug didn't want to be, but recognized many years ago that he was a bitter realist. He knew the chances of someone finding them here were slim. This part of the prison had been closed for years. Seeing several human skeletons scattered about told him that no one ever checked this place. Doug knew that it was just a matter of time.

Pepe kicked a skeleton bone with his foot. "That will be us soon."

I need to encourage him, Doug thought, *take his mind off this predicament.* Doug sat back against the block wall. "Pepe, do you remember that cave we found when we were boys?"

Pepe was surprised by the question. He moved his chains and handcuff to where he was able to lean against the wall next to Doug. "You mean the one near our summer home on Lake Chapala?"

"Yes, that's the one."

Pepe chuckled. "Ah, yes, I remember. You would always take girls there and make out with them."

"You did too."

"But not like you. It seemed like you took every single one of them out there."

"Oh, now you're exaggerating."

"Girls, fishing, girls, baseball—boy those were great times, weren't they?"

"They sure were."

"Then off you went to medical school and became a doctor, and I went to the seminary and became—" Pepe paused. He then looked away.

"A priest," Doug finished.

Pepe looked at Doug. "Yeah, some priest."

"Well, it sounds like you kind of liked this nun Margarita."

Pepe smiled. "Yes, she was so much fun."

"We're not going anywhere, why don't you tell me some more about her."

"Like what?"

"Well, you mentioned she was card playing partner, but how did you two meet?"

Pepe reflected for a moment. He then smiled. "Well I told you my first assignment after the seminary was in Guadalajara?"

"Yes, you mentioned that earlier."

"I remember that first day when I walked into the cathedral compound."

"Excuse me, are you the new Father?"

Pepe turned around. "Yes, I'm Father Santana. I just arrived today."

The nun briskly grabbed and shook his hand. "It is so good to have you here, Father. I'm Sister Margarita, but most people call me Sisterita for short."

She is so beautiful, Pepe thought. More beautiful than any of the other nuns he had met.

"Father, I need you real bad," she whispered. "You have no idea how long I have been waiting for someone like you."

Pepe was caught off guard. "Pardon me?"

"For months I have ached for fresh young blood here at the compound. Please come with me now."

"Come with you?"

"Yes, Father."

Pepe looked at her sleek body. She fit her fashionable nun's clothing perfectly. *I can't believe it*, Pepe thought. *It's only my first day as a priest, and already the devil is tempting me.* Pepe stopped short. "Wait, Sisterita, it is my pheromones."

Sister Margarita didn't understand. "It's your what?"

"Sister, it's my body odors, they do this to people."

"Body odors? Father, what you are talking about?"

"Listen, I am honored, but I can't do this."

Margarita turned and faced Pepe. "What do you mean, you can't do this? You didn't take a vow or something against this sort of thing, did you?"

Pepe was shocked by her question. "As a matter of fact, I did."

Now Margarita was frustrated. "You did." She threw her hands into the air. "I can't believe it. Don't you know you are the first new young priest we have had come here in years? Why would you go and do a dumb thing like that?"

"Dumb thing! Sister, have you forgotten that you took that same vow?"

"I did?"

"Yes, you did, when you became a nun."

"Well I don't remember it. In fact, I'm sure I didn't. So I don't want to wait." She grabbed Pepe's hand and led him down the long narrow hall.

"You mean right now?"

"Yes, let's start right now."

"Wait, aren't you one of the brides of Jesus?"

"Yes, I am, but what's that got to with it?"

"Everything. Because you are married to Jesus, it would be adultery."

"Adultery?" She stopped and looked at him. "What do you mean, adultery?"

"You know, me going to bed with you."

"Going to bed with me?" Sister Margarita thought for a minute. She then broke into laughter.

Pepe was now confused. "What are you laughing about?"

"Father Santana, you're so funny. You think I want to go to bed with you?" Margarita smiled at Pepe, for now she understood. "I need you now as my new bridge partner," she explained, "not a bed partner."

"Bridge partner?"

"You know, bridge, cards. The older nuns and fathers are really poor bridge partners. I have been waiting for a new partner for months. That's why I was so happy to hear you were coming."

Doug's laughter interrupted the story. Pepe joined in. "I bet you were real embarrassed."

"I sure was. I tried to apologize to her, but I stammered so bad… She just smiled, reached up, and kissed my cheek. 'It's okay. Now let's get to that card game.'"

"That's a great story."

"Sí, I know." They both sat quietly reflecting. "Boss, do you remember our earlier religious discussions?"

"You mean our religious arguments, don't you?"

Pepe chuckled. "Boy they were humdingers sometimes, weren't they?"

"Yes, they were."

"You know, you've changed."

"What do you mean?"

"Oh, I don't know. It seems that since Nicole's death your feelings about God have changed some."

"Why do you say that?"

"Well didn't you ask me to pray?"

"That's true."

"And you don't bring up the evils of the world as much as you did before."

"Maybe I don't, but that doesn't mean I don't think about them."

"You still do?"

"Nearly every day. The pain, sorrow, and suffering of so many—" Doug paused. "Pepe, don't be fooled. My feelings about God's existence have not changed."

Pepe looked down. "Really, they haven't?"

Doug could tell his friend was disappointed with his answer. "Except—" Doug paused.

Pepe looked up. "Except what?"

"Except now, I sometimes find myself wishing that there is a God."

Pepe smiled. They both remained quiet for a brief moment. Suddenly Pepe's attention focused on the pool of water. Pepe pointed to the pool of water. "Hey, look, are those water ripples in the pool?"

Doug looked at where he was pointing. "Sure looks like ripples."

"What do you think—fish, maybe rats?"

"I don't know, but the ripples are getting bigger."

Suddenly to their utter shock and surprise a large burst of water broke the pool surface. Doug and Pepe jumped back in disbelief. For in that burst of water was a man. The man took a deep breath and quickly looked around the room to get his bearings. Seeing Pepe and Doug at one end of the pool, he leisurely swam toward them. He then climbed out of the pool, shook the loose water from his clothes, and pulled the long dark hair out of his eyes. "Pepe, I don't suppose you have a towel?"

Pepe squinted to get a better look at his face. "Disciple, is that you?" The man didn't answer but walked toward them with a big smile.

He chuckled. "I am so glad to find you two alive."

Pepe stood up. "It's you. I can't believe it. It's really you." He threw his arms around the disciple's neck and hugged him tight.

"Ah, Pepe, it's been a long time since I've been hugged by a man with no clothes." Pepe felt his face redden. Doug chuckled as he quickly broke his embrace. Pepe turned to Doug. "We're saved, boss. We're saved."

Doug extended his hand to Disciple. "Boy, are we gland to see you."

"Yes, well, I would have been here sooner, but it took a couple of days to escape." Disciple looked around the room. "Where are your clothes?"

Doug pointed to the two piles near the far wall. Disciple walked over and picked them up. He returned and gave them to Pepe and Doug. "Only the underpants," he instructed. They put on their underwear. Disciple stuffed the rest of their clothes in a bag he was carrying. "I tried to warn you, Pepe."

"Warn me?"

"Yes, warn you, but all you kept saying was 'get away from me you ugly bearded lady.'"

Pepe had a surprised look on his face. "That was you? You're the ugly bearded lady?"

Doug chuckled. "A woman prisoner with a beard—how did you ever get away with that?"

"Yeah, you were in that yard with all those women prisoners and the guards around. Didn't anyone suspect your beard?"

"You would think they would, wouldn't you," Disciple answered. He shook his head in disbelief. "But no one ever asked. It was like my beard was not there." Disciple now noticed the multiple bruises and cuts about their faces and the rest of their bodies. "They sure beat on you good. Did they—?" Disciple paused.

Pepe shook his head. "The raping comes tomorrow."

Disciple looked at Doug. "Really?" he asked. Doug nodded his head. Disciple looked down. "I'm sorry I didn't get here sooner."

Doug touched Disciple's shoulder. "No need for an apology, we are just glad you are here now. We had to do what we had to do to stay alive, to survive." Disciple nodded his head. He understood completely.

"So, Disciple, how did you finally escape?" Pepe asked.

"Your prayer."

Doug was confused. "Pepe's prayer, but how did you know he prayed?"

"Because I knew Pepe would be the only one that would pray. You see, I knew where you were at, but I couldn't get out my cell."

"So what happened?"

"Well for some reason last night, they put me in the extra cell. It doesn't lock automatically like the others. Anyway the guard forgot to lock it manually. Escaping from there was easy."

"See, boss, you were right. Prayers do work."

Doug smiled back at his friend. *Coincidence, mere coincidence,* Doug thought.

Disciple took a deep breath. "Whew, I need to rest a bit. That was a long swim to here." Disciple reached in his bag and pulled out a bobby pin. He then began to twist and bend it. He leaned over and picked Pepe's handcuff lock. "I should have waited for low tide, but sometimes I just get too impatient." The cuffs opened and Pepe removed them from his wrists. Disciple then moved to Doug's cuffs.

"Disciple, you think you can get us out of here?" Doug asked.

"Oh, sure. We'll leave the same way I came."

Doug's cuffs quickly fell open. "Well, great," Pepe exclaimed. "What are we waiting for? Let's go."

"Not yet," Disciple countered, "it's a safer swim at maximum low tide."

"And when is that?"

"About an hour. It will be darker and more difficult for the prison tower guards to see us."

Doug and Pepe rubbed their wrists. Both were grateful to be rid of the handcuffs. "So you have swum this before?"

"Several times, when I have helped innocent men to escape. You see this portion of the prison is well over a hundred years old. This pool here was like an open sewer for the prisoners. That's why there is a passageway that leads to the ocean."

That is not possible, Doug thought. *He was helping people escape more than a hundred years ago?*

"You didn't happen to bring any water, did you?" Pepe asked. Disciple smiled. He reached into the bag and pulled out and handed Pepe a water bottle. "Bless you," Pepe exclaimed as he took a drink from the water bottle.

"Not too much," Disciple advised. He reached back into his bag and pulled out two candy bars and handed one to each of them. "They may be a little wet."

Pepe passed the bottle to Doug and tore off the paper of one of the candy bars. It was nearly half eaten before he mumbled, "thank you." Doug was slower, but grateful for the food and water. The three leaned back on the pile of rags. They could hear the rats scampering at the other end of the room.

"Why are they trying to kill you?" Disciple asked.

Pepe shook his head. "We don't understand. We came to see Tina Michaels and wound up trapped in here."

"I'm sorry about Tina," Disciple said.

"Did you know her?" Doug asked.

"Not well. Word in the yard is that she was beaten to death."

"Why would they beat her?"

"I don't know."

"Did the other prisoners say anything else?" Doug asked.

"Only that the warden ordered the beating and was upset when she died."

"She must have known something that they wanted to know," Doug said.

"The way they acted, I don't think she told them anything, but she may have told you something."

"She actually told me very little. We talked about our dating years ago, and how she was jealous of Nicole at first. Tina was Nicole's nurse when Jason was born."

"I didn't know that," Pepe said.

Doug shrugged. "Neither did I, but she said something that bothered me."

"What was that?" Pepe asked.

"She said our newborn baby boy was killed."

·"But Jason is still alive."

"That's the puzzling part. When I told her that Jason didn't die and was living with me, she became frantic."

"About what?"

"Her last words to me prior to warden taking her away were 'hide your son, or they will kill him.' That's why I sent Indian home to watch over him." Doug reflected for a brief moment. "There was one other thing. She called Jason a Levite."

Pepe looked at Disciple and then back at Doug. "Levite? Are you sure?"

"Yes, I'm sure." Doug looked at the both of them. "You know Nicole also called Jason a Levite, and I don't even know what a Levite is."

"Levites are one of the tribes of Israel," Disciple explained.

"You mean like the Jewish people in the bible?" Pepe asked.

"Yes. The Jews descended from the tribe of Judah, and the Levites descended from the tribe of Levi. Judah and Levi were brothers. There were twelve brothers in all."

"Where are the tribes now?" Pepe asked.

"Except for the tribe of Judah," Disciple explained, "the other tribes were scattered and lost."

"But what do Levites have to do with my son?" Doug asked. Disciple wondered if he should tell them but decided against it. It would be better if they found out for themselves. Suddenly there was a noise from the secret hidden door. "Someone is coming," Doug said.

"Quickly," Disciple whispered, "let's get out of here."

Pepe and Doug stood and followed Disciple to the pool. The three quickly slipped into the water. Doug scanned the room one last time as the hidden door opened. He took one big breath and followed Disciple and Pepe into the depths of the pond toward freedom.

Mr. Parks rushed into the room. "They're gone!" he screamed.

Large Marge raced through the room. "They can't be. We just left them a few minutes ago."

"Then where are they?"

"I swear to you, sir, we left them handcuffed to this pipe."

He walked to the pool edge and looked at the wet cement surrounding the pool. "The pool, they escaped through the pool." He turned toward Ellen and Marge. "You fools, you have let them escape."

Mr. Parks turned and walked toward the hidden door. Ellen and Large Marge followed. He then pulled a gun from his coat. He pointed the gun at the two women. "Step back," he commanded.

"Warden," Ellen yelled, "what are you doing?"

Large Marge put up her hands. "Don't do this, sir, we'll find them."

Warden shook his head. "Because of your stupidity, I will die, but I will not die alone." He fired two shots and the women fell to the floor. He slipped out the door and locked it behind him. Hurriedly he raced through the second door into the main part of the prison and toward his office. He had to stop their escape.

Doug pulled Pepe to the surface, and his friend gasped for breath. "I can't make it," he exclaimed. Doug and Disciple pulled him from the water onto the rocks. The three then collapsed on the sand, attempting to catch their breath.

"Leave me," Pepe suggested. "Save yourselves."

"Okay, suit yourself. Let's go, Disciple." Both stood up and started down the beach, leaving Pepe behind. It was only then in the dark quiet that Pepe heard the waves pounding the beach. *Are those waves?* Pepe thought. Now he could hear carnival music in the distance. He opened his eyes to myriad number of stars in the sky.

"We made it. We escaped." He staggered to his feet and lumbered down the beach after the others. "You guys weren't really going to leave me, were you?" he yelled.

"Sh," Disciple whispered. He then pointed back toward the prison. "See the lights coming toward us. The guards must know you have escaped."

"It was Parks," Doug informed. "Just before I went under the water, I saw him come through the hidden door."

"Then we barely escaped with our lives," Pepe added.

"Not yet," Disciple reminded. "Come quickly. We must make it to that wharf down by the carnival."

A light reflected off of Doug's bare chest. "Your locket," Disciple exclaimed. "Hide it, it reflects light."

Doug quickly grasped the locket. "That's it. It's the locket."

"What about it?" Pepe asked.

"The last thing Tina did was give me this locket." Pepe had a puzzled look on his face. "Remember what Ms. Stewart said? She said Tina's last words for me referred to 'the locket.'"

Now they understand, Disciple thought. The message to him was Tina's locket. "Come, we must hurry. The guards will be coming soon." Pepe and Doug followed him down the beach toward the wharf.

EAST LOS ANGELES

J ulie and Mary finished walking the perimeters a second time. "Like I said, Julie, there just isn't a road."

"But there has to be. How else do people get here?"

Mary pointed to the gardener off to the right. "Look at him trying to get my attention." Julie tried not to notice the handsome gardener the first time around the compound, but couldn't help it the second time. They watched him take off his shirt. "Look at his body," Mary exclaimed. The gardener looked up and smiled at the both of them. "Julie, did you see that?"

"What?"

"The way he smiled at me."

"It looked like a polite 'hello' smile to me."

"That's not a polite 'hello' smile. That's a 'hey, I'm really horny' smile. I've seen it before." Julie smiled at Mary's comments. Mary pointed up ahead. "Hey, look, they're serving sandwiches." Mary took off at a fast pace. She turned back. "Are you coming?"

Julie motioned with her hand. "You go ahead, I'll catch up." Once again Julie's eyes returned to the gardener. *Why am I so attracted to this man?* she asked herself. She paused for a moment. *I will,* she thought. *I'm going to ask him.* She stepped off the pathway and walked across the grass to where he was kneeling. "Excuse me, sir, I wonder if you could help me."

The gardener stood. Not only was he handsome, but Julie could not but help notice his sculptured shoulder and chest muscles. "I can try."

"Well, sir—"

"Matt," he interrupted. "Call me Matt." He extended his hand.

Julie shook his hand. "Julie, I'm Julie Jordan."

Matthias smiled. "It's nice to meet you, Julie Jordan. Are you a guest here?"

"No, not exactly. I was just informed that I was brought here by mistake."

"How could that happen?"

"I'm not sure. Apparently a Mrs. Wilson was supposed to be here, but I was put on the plane instead. The funny thing is I can't remember any of this happening."

"Is that what's bothering you?"

"No, not exactly. This lady named Tess said that it will be at least a week before we can return home."

"You mean you don't like it here?"

"Oh no, this is such a beautiful place. You keep the gardens and grounds so immaculate."

"Thanks."

"But what I was wondering is why I do not see any roads leading in or out of this place."

"That's because there aren't any. Air travel is the only way in and out of here."

"And someone only flies here once a week?"

"If we're lucky. Sometimes it is even longer."

Julie was disappointed. "Sometimes more than a week?"

Matthias could see the disappointment in her face. "But maybe not this time."

They both stood looking at each other. Matt's smile began to make Julie uncomfortable.

"Julie," Mary called across the compound. Julie looked over at Mary. "Hurry before the food's all gone."

She turned back to Matt. "Well I better go. Thank you."

"Anytime, Julie Jordan."

Julie smiled and walked away.

⇒◆⇐

Doug handed Disciple a sandwich. "Now you say Judah and Levi were brothers."

"Yes. There were twelve brothers all together."

"So if Jason is a Levite, then wouldn't that make Nicole or I Levites too?"

Disciple began to answer but was interrupted by Pepe. "Boss, it must have been fate. I mean what are the odds that two Levites would find each other and have a child."

"Maybe it wasn't fate," Doug suggested.

Pepe was confused. "What do you mean?"

"Perhaps our meeting was planned." Doug turned to Disciple. "Tell me, what is it about these Levites?"

"What you mean?"

"Why is there so much interest in this Levite tribe?"

"Power," Disciple answered.

"I don't understand."

Disciple took a sip of milk and placed the cup on the table. He then cleared his throat. "God's power passed from father to son. It was first given to Levites when Moses led the twelve tribes of Israel out of Egyptian bondage. Moses and his older brother Aaron were Levites. When Moses was given the Ten Commandments on stone tablets, he had a wooden box made, to preserve and hold these tablets. This wooden box was called the Ark and it contained the Covenant."

Doug was still confused. "But what does the Ark of the Covenant have to do with the tribe of Levi?"

Disciple picked up his sandwich and took another bite. "Because the Levites were the only tribe given the power to open, transport, and take care of the Ark of the Covenant."

"But that doesn't make sense, why would anyone need special powers to care for a wooden box?"

"Boss, it's more than a wooden box. It's special because it contains the original Ten Commandments written by the finger of God."

Disciple continued. "The ark is so special that if anyone other than a Levite touched the Ark, they died."

"Like Uzza, right?" Pepe added.

"Who's Uzza?" Doug asked.

"Uzza was a man who lived many centuries later during the reign of King David. They were moving the Ark of the Covenant from one place to another when one of the oxen stumbled, and the Ark began to tilt. A man named Uzza was nearby. He reached up with his hand to steady the ark, and because he wasn't a Levite, he died instantly."

Doug was stunned. "You mean God struck him dead? Doesn't that seem a bit harsh? I mean all he was trying to do was keep the ark from tipping."

"They were harsh times, boss," Pepe answered.

"The reality was that Uzza didn't have God's authority to touch the ark," Disciple explained.

Doug thought for a brief moment. "With Jason being a Levite, do you think he may have something to do with this Ark of the Covenant?"

"I don't know, boss, maybe so," Pepe replied.

"Do we know where the Ark is?" Doug asked.

"No, it was lost centuries ago. Some say it was taken to Ethiopia or other parts of Africa. Others say it was buried years ago near Jerusalem."

Doug thought for a minute. "Disciple, suppose the Ark of the Covenant were found today..." Disciple smiled. He already knew Doug's question. "Even today would the same restrictions apply to it? Yes, even today. Only a Levite would be able touch the Ark of the Covenant without suffering the consequence of death."

Doug yawned. "That is a lot to think about."

Pepe notice Doug yawning. "Boss, why don't you lie down and rest. I think you need it."

Doug nodded. "You're right, I think I will." They both watched Doug remove his shoes and lie down on the bed.

Pepe reached for a folded newspaper and smashed a cockroach scampering across the table. He shook his head. "Disciple, this place is a rat hole. You couldn't have picked a worse place to stay."

Disciple took the folded paper from him and began to read it. "Believe me, I have stayed in worse."

"But why not a nice hotel, and why East LA?"

Disciple looked up. "People are chasing you guys. It's unlikely they will follow you here."

"You're right about that, because I wouldn't follow me here, either."

Doc opened his eyes. "Pepe, be grateful. A few hours ago we were handcuffed in a prison."

"Sí, I know, boss." Pepe stood and walked across the room. He filled a water glass, returned, and sat down across the table from Disciple.

Doug opened his eyes. "Disciple, do you think it is the prison guards who are following?"

"Probably them and others. You have some very important people worried about what you may know."

"But that's just it," Pepe said. "We don't know anything."

"That may be true, but these people don't know that." He looked over at the window. "It will be dark soon. I'll check with those out on the street and see what I can find out."

Pepe looked toward the window. "You mean you're going out there?"

"Sure."

"But, aren't you concerned about being mugged or hurt?"

Disciple smiled and put his hand on Pepe's shoulder. "It's nice that you care, but remember, I can't be killed."

"Yeah, right. You'll get killed, and we'll be stuck in this hotel room forever not knowing what to do."

Disciple chuckled. All were quiet for the next few minutes. Disciple stopped reading the paper and looked up at Pepe, who was watching him. He smiled and then went back to reading. Pepe kept staring. Disciple looked up again. "What?

"Ah, it's nothing."

"But you keep staring at me."

Pepe looked over at the bed. The Doc's eyes were closed. "Well…" Pepe paused. Disciple folded his paper and set it down. He knew that Pepe wanted to discuss something. "Can we talk before you leave?"

"Sure, what is it?"

"Well you know that I was once a priest?"

"Yes, you told me."

"And that I also left the priesthood."

"You told me that too."

Pepe again looked over at the bed. Doug's eyes still remained closed. He turned back to Disciple. Now he spoke in softer tones. "Well what I want to know is…" Disciple waited. "Well if people like me who have really messed up their lives, you know, can they still make it to heaven?"

"Then you really do think I am one of Christ's disciples?"

"Oh no, I still think you're crazy. But somehow you seem to know a lot about God."

"Well, then, let's talk. What have you done to ask such a question?" Pepe bowed his head and did not answer. His silence caught Doug's attention. He kept his eyes closed and waited for Pepe's answer. But the answer did not come. "It was Margarita, wasn't it?"

Shocked, Pepe stared at Disciple. "How did you know?"

Disciple didn't answer. "Go ahead."

"Well, over time Margarita and I fell in love. It was me that wanted to leave the priesthood and get married, but she just wasn't sure."

"Not sure that she loved you?"

"I think she loved me, but she was very committed to her vows. One day Sister Margarita and I were in an outlying village delivering a baby."

"Delivering a baby?"

"Yes, Margarita was also a midwife. The delivery took longer than usual and we missed the last bus and had to stay the night. There wasn't a motel, so we spent the night sleeping together in an empty barn." Doug listened to every word. "That night one of the villagers called our parish and told them we were in his barn spending the night. The next morning our superiors came to the village and found us together. They accused us of being immoral, and we both were dismissed from our positions with the church."

They were quiet for a brief moment. "I'm sorry you both were dismissed, but at least now if you truly loved each other, you could get married."

"That's what I thought. Even Margarita was beginning to think that it was meant to be. But when we went to see her parents, it was really bad."

"What happened?"

"We stopped in front of her parent's house."

"Here it is, Pepe," Margarita said. Pepe and Margarita stood hand in hand in the middle of the street hand staring at her parent's home. "I don't know, my parents raised me to be a nun. Maybe we should just leave and forget about this."

"They're your parents. I'm sure they will be happy for you."

Margarita wasn't so sure. She took a deep breath and blew it out. "I hope so." Together they approached the front door. Pepe knocked.

Mr. Sanchez came to the door. "Hello, Papa." He looked at Margarita and then at Pepe. Without a word, he slammed the door.

Pepe looked at Margarita. "What going on?"

"Let's leave," Margarita suggested.

"No, he's your father. He's not going to treat you that way." Pepe again knocked on the door. Again Mr. Sanchez came to the door. "Can't you get the hint? You two are not welcome here. Now leave." Again he tried to slam the door, but this time Pepe slipped his leg inside.

"Mr. Sanchez, don't do this to your daughter."

"I have no daughter."

"You're wrong. Look at her. She's standing right here."

Mr. Sanchez turned his head. "My daughter died when she betrayed Christ. Now get out." He then closed the door the second time.

"Margarita's parents really disowned her?" Disciple asked.

Pepe nodded his head. "Yes, they did."

"Is there more?" Pepe nodded his head yes. Disciple could tell he was hesitant. "Would you rather not discuss it?"

"No, I want to talk about it." Disciple waited for Pepe to continue. "That night we stayed in a nearby motel. She was in one room and I in another. The next morning I knocked on her door, and there was no answer. I obtained a pass key and opened her room…Disciple, Margarita hung herself during the night."

Doug now sat up. "She killed herself?"

Pepe looked over. "Boss, I thought you were asleep."

"I'm so sorry, but I couldn't help but overhear. Why didn't you tell me?"

"It wasn't a happy time. I guess I'm just glad it is now out in the open."

Doug was still confused. "I just don't understand. So what if you slept together. That's no reason for her to kill herself."

"He's right," Disciple agreed. "I sure there are other nuns and priests that have become involved with each other. That sort of thing may not be approved by the church, but it still happens"

"You think so?"

"I know so. You can't keep carrying this guilt. It's tearing you apart.

"You didn't kill Margarita," Doug added. "It was her decision to take her life."

Pepe looked at the two. He contemplated what Disciple and Doug told him. "Pepe, I think those things can be forgiven by God, if that's what you want to know."

Pepe nodded his head. He looked at Doug and then Disciple. *You two still don't understand*, he thought to himself, *for I'm afraid to tell you the remainder of the truth.*

⇒⋄⇐

Parks pulled the handkerchief from his pocket and wiped the sweat beads from his forehead. "Gabriel, that is what she said."

"Tina told you that the chosen one lives?"

"Yes, sir. Those were her last words."

"You must be mistaken. I killed the baby myself after his birth."

"I swear, those were her last words before she died."

Impossible, Gabriel thought. *There is no way I could have been deceived and killed the wrong baby.* "Listen, Parks, question that Dr.

Hunter. See if he knows anything about his son." Parks nervously placed the phone receiver to the other ear. He then took his handkerchief and again wiped the sweat from his forehead. When Parks did not reply, Gabriel finally said, "I sense something is wrong."

"Well, sir, there is a problem."

"What kind of problem?"

"Dr. Hunter and the other escaped."

"What? How could you let them escape?"

"Sir, the city is closed off. We will have them found shortly, I promise."

"Were they not in the old prison?"

"Yes, but somehow they escaped through the pool."

"How would they even know about the pool?"

"I don't know, but somehow they found out."

Gabriel took a deep breath and blew it out. "So what have you done so far?"

"The city is shut down. They will not be able to leave without us knowing."

"But how do you know they are still in the city?"

"Hunter accessed a credit card this afternoon. We think he is in downtown LA."

"Good. When we find him, we have to know what my wife told them."

"Yes, sir."

"One more thing." Parks waited in silence. "Matthias may require your life, understand?" Parks did not answer, but hung up the phone receiver. He sank back into his high-back chair to ponder.

Immediately Gabriel dialed another number. "Hello."

"Matthias, it is Gabriel."

"What is it?"

"The chosen one, he may be alive."

"How is that possible?"

Gabriel explained the events that led up to this conclusion. "Then you suspect you may have been deceived?"

"Perhaps. The Jews may have somehow switched the babies."

"So what do you plan next?"

"To find this Dr. Hunter."

"Remember, Niac wants to see us next week. He will want a full report about this by then."

"I understand. What about Parks?"

"Did he not let them escape?" Matthias asked.

"Yes, he did."

"Parks is to sacrifice his life, understand?"

"Yes, sir." They both hung up the receivers.

Matthias pondered what Gabriel said. He then noticed some clothing lying in front of the large sliding glass doors leading to the pool. A smile crossed his face. He picked up a tiny bikini top and bottom. He looked toward poolside where she was naked. He watched as she dove into the pool. Just then one of the house servants entered the room with chilled champagne and two glasses.

"Sir," Mira interrupted, "the Mistress ordered this."

Matthias smiled. "I'll take it to her." She handed the chilled champagne and two glasses to him. "Mira, has Mrs. Jordan asked for me?"

"No, sir."

"Okay, you may go."

Mira bowed and left. The sliding glass doors opened automatically. Matthias placed the drinks on one of the poolside tables. She swam toward him. He grabbed a dry towel and carried it to the poolside. She started up the steps toward the open towel. Matthias noticed how bronze her skin was. "Tess, the years are still good to you," he said as he wrapped his arms with the towel around her body.

"You weren't expecting me to be back so soon, were you?" She placed her arms around his neck and kissed him gently on the lips.

"Well, no. How did it go?"

"All women and children were delivered to the fields as you directed."

"Good." He let her go.

She wrapped and folded the towel around her body. "I see you brought the champagne."

"I met Mira in the hallway." She took a sip from her glass and sat it down on the table. She then looked at Matthias and smiled.

"What?" he asked.

"Mrs. Jordan?"

"What about her?"

"She's harder than you thought, right?"

Matthias chuckled. "Why do you assume that I am even trying?"

"I know you. She's a challenge you would not be able to pass up."

Matthias poured more champagne. "Tell me, Tess, do you get jealous?"

"What do you mean?"

"You know, jealous about me, Mrs. Jordan, and other women."

"Do you ever get jealous about me with other men?"

"No, never. That's the genius of our master's plan. It doesn't allow for jealousy among us, and that has worked well for me."

"It has worked well for me also."

"But don't you ever regret leaving your husband?" Momentarily Tess was caught off guard by the question and did not answer. "You still think of him, don't you?"

Tess was slow to respond. "Sometimes I do."

Matthias smiled. "I thought so."

"Well technically, after all these years, we're still married," Tess explained. "But it's no different than you and your brothers."

"What do you mean?"

"What would have happened if Christ had chosen you instead of your two brothers, James and John? Don't you think our life paths may have taken a different direction?"

Matthias nodded his head. Discussion about his brothers made him uncomfortable. He wanted to change the subject. "Maybe you're right, but I have something more important to discuss with you."

Tess took a sip of her drink. "What's that?"

"Gabriel called."

"And?"

"Dr. Hunter, do you remember him?"

Tess smiled. "Ah, yes, Nicole's husband. That man gives me the chills."

"I bet he does. Well he and the other escaped the prison."

"Escaped? But, I just saw them a couple days ago."

"Yes, I know. Apparently they escaped through the pool."

"But how would they know how to escape through the pool?" Tess paused and looked at Matthias. "Unless—"

"I thought the same. Disciple must be helping them."

"Does Gabriel have any idea where they are?"

"In East LA somewhere, but it's like they have disappeared. None of our contacts can find them."

Tess thought for a brief moment. "I'm not surprised. There are several places Disciple could have taken them." Tess leaned back in the chair with both hands on her glass. She smiled at Matthias. "This will work out well for you, love."

"Why is that?"

"While I'm helping Gabriel look for them, who will be here to protect Mrs. Jordan?"

Matthias chuckled. "Don't worry, I can do that."

CHAPTER THIRTY-FOUR
THE MOUNTAIN PEOPLE

Pepe opened the empty paper bag. "Are there any sandwiches left?"

"No, they're gone," Disciple said.

Pepe checked the counter. "How about the doughnuts?"

"Gone too."

Pepe turned to Disciple and Doug. "Well, is there any food left?"

Doug looked up. "Pepe we just ate an hour ago."

"I know, but I'm still hungry."

Disciple leaned forward. "I saw a candy machine down in the lobby."

Doug reached into his pocket and removed his change. He handed it to Pepe. "Bring me a Baby Ruth."

Pepe looked over at Disciple. "Do you want anything?"

Disciple shook his head. "No thanks."

"I'll be back in a few minutes." Pepe opened and closed the door.

Disciple looked at Doug and smiled. All was quiet for the next couple of minutes. Disciple felt he was being watched. He looked up to see Doug staring at him. "Doc, is there something bothering you?"

"Well actually, it's you."

"Me? What did I do?"

"It's not what you do that bothers me, but it's what you don't do."

Disciple leaned back in his chair. He was totally confused. "I don't understand."

"Well, if I explain myself, then you'll think that I believe you are one of Jesus's apostles."

"And you don't want to believe that?"

"Not that I don't want to believe it, but I can't."

Disciple began to partially understand what Doug was trying to say. "Okay, let's pretend that I am not a disciple of Christ, then could you tell me what's bothering you?"

Doug looked up. "Just pretend?"

"Just pretend."

Doug nervously rubbed his hands together. "You remember when you said the world is really messed up?" Disciple nodded. "And when you said it really bothered you that there is so much poverty in the world?"

"Yes."

Now Doug stood and looked out the window to the streets below. "Why don't you do something?"

"I don't understand."

Doug turned sharply. "Geez, you're supposed to be an apostle for hell's sake, yet you stand here and do nothing while millions of people suffer." Doug waited for an answer, but Disciple did not speak. "You tell us our God is a loving God. But how can a loving God stand by and watch thousands of people suffer and die every day of hunger, oppression, and disease?"

"What do you want me to do?"

Doug quickly turned. Disciple could see the frustration in his eyes. "Anything, just do anything." Both were quiet for a brief moment. Doug now felt he should not have said anything. How could he expect this unique, delusional man to be able to change the world? "Look, I'm sorry. I should have never said anything."

Disciple was quiet for a brief moment and then began to speak. "Doug, would you mind if I tell you a story?" Doug sat down again across from Disciple. This was Doug's silent signal of approval. "We were traveling with Jesus near the city of Jericho when a wealthy farmer invited us to eat and spend the night with him. We finished eating when Jesus began asking the farmer questions."

"Aaron, how are your crops this year?"

"Master, they are so abundant. Come, I will show you."

Jesus and the disciples stood from the table and followed Aaron outside to his barn. He swung the barn doors open. "Look at this!" he exclaimed. The barn was completely full of wheat.

"You have been truly blessed," Peter said.

"Yes, I have. God has blessed me more than I dreamed imaginable."

"Why do you think it was God that blessed you?" Peter asked.

"Because I prayed for it. I told God that if he would bless me, I would share with the poor and needy."

James noticed more wheat piled to the side of the barn. "You have more wheat than your barn can contain."

Aaron nodded his head. "Yes, I do."

"Are you going to give the extra grain to the poor and needy?" Jesus asked.

"No, not this wheat," Aaron answered.

"But won't it spoil if you leave it out in the rain?" James asked.

"Yes, it will. That's why I'm building another barn."

"Another barn?" Jesus asked.

"Yes, one much bigger that can hold more grain."

"But what about the grain for the poor and needy?" Jesus questioned.

"Next year," Aaron answered. "With all the money I get from selling this grain, I'll be able to buy more land and grow more wheat. Then I will be able to give even more to the poor."

Disciple stopped speaking. He looked at Doug.

"So are you saying that we are responsible for the poverty of the world? That's a real cop-out."

"Not only responsible for the world's poverty, but also alleviating the world's poverty. Doc, did you know that several hundred people have more wealth than over two billion people?"

"What does that mean?"

"It means that many people are blessed by God with abundance. But instead of sharing the blessings with others, they just keep building bigger barns."

———⊰✦⊱———

Edith Crockett turned down the long winding gravel road leading to the Heavenly Ranch. She reflected on what Sheriff Bates had told her earlier. "Jason and Mrs. Jordan are missing," Sheriff Bates said.

"Missing?"

"Along with Nurse Cratch, who was staying with them. We know that Dr. Jordan is in New York, but we haven't been able to find him."

"Maybe they went with him," Edith suggested.

"Edith," Sheriff Bates said, "you are not listening. With the blood we found in the Jordan home, we think there has been foul play. That's why we are trying to find Dr. Hunter and Dr. Jordan."

"Well, Sheriff, Jim says that Hunter and Pepe have also disappeared."

Edith swerved to miss a jackrabbit that darted in front of her vehicle. "Damn rabbit," she exclaimed as she returned to reality. Now the ranch house was coming into view. "I don't remember leaving the lights on," she murmured. The driveway was empty of vehicles. She pulled to a stop and turned off the headlights. Suddenly the house lights turn off, and the curtains in the front window closed. "What in the hell is going on," she said. She reached into the jockey box and pulled out a pistol. "All I can say is that you better be someone I know." She left the car and proceeded around to the back of the house. Quietly she opened the door and entered. Slowly she entered room after room with her gun pointed forward. Suddenly someone in the dark grabbed the gun from her hand and wrestled her to the floor. "Dammit, you bastard, let me go!" she yelled.

"You'll hurt somebody with this," a voice answered. The living room light turned on.

Edith looked up. "Dammit, Indian, you scared the pee out of me."

Indian helped her to her feet. "I'm sorry, we didn't know who you were."

"We? Is Jason here?"

Indian smiled but did not answer. "Aunt Edith," a voice said from behind.

Edith turned. "Jason," she exclaimed. Jason ran forward into her waiting arms. "Thank God you're all right."

Jason broke the embrace and nodded toward Indian. "Thanks to Indian and Lone Wolf. They rescued us from the Sprudiths."

Edith turned to Indian. "Us? Then you have Julie and Ms. Cratch?"

"No, Edith." Edith turned to see who spoke. He came forward into the light holding the hand of a girl.

"Lone Wolf, I'm so glad you are here."

Indian touched Edith's arm. She turned toward him. He shook his head. "We couldn't save Mrs. Jordan and Ms. Cratch. The Sprudiths took them."

Edith slowly turned away. "Then they are dead."

"No, I believe Mrs. Jordan and Ms. Cratch are still alive," Lone Wolf corrected.

She looked at him. "Why do you say that?"

"Because they would have taken their lives immediately if they were going to kill them. They wanted them captive for something."

"For what? Unless—" she paused. She looked at Indian. "They want you to know, don't they?"

Indian nodded his head yes. "I think they are challenging us to try and get them back."

Edith then noticed the girl holding Lone Wolf's hand. She approached and knelt before her. "I know you. You're the girl they found in the mountains. My dear, where have you been?" It was then they all sat down in the living room and explained the recent events to Edith. "So why do the Sprudiths want you children?" Edith asked.

Lone Wolf shook his head. "We don't know, but we think it best we are up at the cabin on holy ground. Once we know you're safe on holy ground, we'll start looking for Julie and Ms. Cratch."

Edith nodded. "Then no more questions. Let's get ready and leave for the cabin now."

Edith snickered as she watched Sondra tangle her line in the tree again. "Jason," Sondra whined.

Jason closed his eyes. "Not again. The only tree around, and she finds it again."

"Now, you be patient with her."

Jason shook his head. "I'll try."

"I'm going to fix lunch." Edith started up the trail. She turned back. "I'll call you when it's ready."

"When do Indian and Lone Wolf get back?"

"Sometime this evening. Now go and help Sondra untangle her line."

"Yes, ma'am." Jason watched Edith turn and begin the walk back up the hill to the cabin. He approached Sondra, who was attempting to untangle her fishing line. "I thought you said you could fish."

"I can fish, but not with this stupid fishing pole. Back home we use spears."

"Spears? How do you catch fish with a spear?"

"Come, I'll show you." They broke off branches, and with Jason's pocketknife, they made sharp points. Once they were finished, they raced back to the lake.

Edith checked the children frequently. Even though Indian told her that this area was holy ground, she still worried. She watched Sondra try to teach Jason how to spear fish. She laughed when Sondra fell into the lake and pulled Jason in with her. Just then the telephone rang. "Who, the hell knows this number?" she whispered. She picked up the telephone receiver. "Hello."

"Mom?"

"Jimmy, is that you?"

"Yeah, Mom."

"How did you know I was at the cabin?"

"Well no one answered at the ranch. I just took a chance."

"I'm glad you called. Indian and Lone Wolf found Jason."

"Oh, thank goodness, is he all right?"

"Yes, he's safe with us now."

"That is such good news."

"But, the Sprudiths took Mrs. Jordan."

"Oh no, she may be dead by now."

"I thought the same, but Lone Wolf and Indian feel if they wanted her dead, they would have killed her immediately."

"Then why take her?"

"Indian feels by taking her alive, they're extending an invitation to us to come get her. If it hadn't been for Lone Wolf and Indian, Jason and the girl would be dead right now."

"What girl?"

"The girl they found up on Yankee Fork."

"You mean the girl that disappeared from the hospital?"

"Yes, that's the one. She'd been hiding in the Jordan's basement the whole time."

"And that's why the Sprudiths attacked the Jordan home?"

"Right. Somehow they found out she was there. Jimmy, they want this girl really bad."

"Are Indian and Lone Wolf there?"

"Yes. Well they were, but they left early this morning to ride up to the Twin Peaks. Has there been anything more about David's death?"

"We have had a couple of leads, but there isn't much more to tell you, other than what we told you yesterday."

"Well say hi to Elaine and be careful."

"Love you, Mom."

"Love you too, Son."

They both returned the phone receivers. Jim returned to his restaurant booth where Elaine was waiting. "They found him. He's at the ranch with Indian and mom."

"That's good news."

"Will there be anything else?" the waitress interrupted.

"Just the bill, please."

"You know it's a long shot, but Debbie said her name was Megan Sorenson."

Jim nodded toward the pay phone. "Why don't you check the phonebook while I pay the bill?"

Elaine passed the cashier and stopped at the pay phone near the entrance "How was your breakfast?" the cashier asked.

Jim looked at his nametag. "Leonard, it was superb." He handed the cashier his credit card. Jim focused on what the cashier was doing. "Tell me, Leonard, are you married?"

"Yes, I am."

"Any children?"

"Two."

"Let me ask you something. Suppose you were transferred here to work on the army base. Where in the valley would you live?"

"I'd live right here."

"Why is that?"

"It's a good family community, and closest to the base."

"Thanks." He turned and walked over to Elaine, who was searching the phonebook.

"Jim, there isn't a Megan Sorenson listed in the phonebook."

"Is there an M. Sorenson?"

Elaine scanned the page. "There's one. In fact, the address is nearby."

Jim opened the door. Elaine led the way to the car. "Let's start there." They left the restaurant and got in their car. Jim pulled onto the main road only to be followed by another car that had been parked across the street.

—⊰◈⊱—

Indian dismounted his horse. He reached into his saddlebag and pulled out his jacket. "That breeze is a little chilly."

Lone Wolf had already put on his jacket earlier. "Yes, especially up this high."

Indian stared far into the valley below. He could barely see the cabin off in the distance, and the Heavenly Ranch was further down. "This is just beautiful."

Lone Wolf dismounted his horse. "When you see this beauty, you begin to understand why the mountain people choose to live here."

"Now, this is where the mountain people are supposed to be?"

Lone Wolf looked around. "Yes this is the right location." Indian shook his head in disbelief. Lone Wolf knew something was wrong. "Something seems to be bothering you."

"Well." He then hesitated.

"What is it?"

"I know you and Jason believe in these mountain people, but I have a hard time believing."

"Even though Jason and I have seen them?"

"I'm sorry to doubt you, but I have ridden in these mountains for years, and I haven't seen anyone."

"Just because you can't see them, doesn't mean they are not here."

"I know, but it would be nice just to see one of them."

Lone Wolf chuckled, "Grandson, what about her?"

"Her? Grandfather, who are you talking about?"

"Hello, Indian," a woman's voice spoke from behind.

Startled, Indian turned toward the voice. There she stood. He could not believe his own eyes. Suddenly he felt strength leaving his legs, and he fell to his knees. She came forward, reached out, and took his hands. She raised him to his feet. "Nicole, is it really you?"

She smiled and wrapped her arms around his waist. "Yes, it's really me."

CHAPTER THIRTY-FIVE

UINTATHERE JAZZ

"**S**ondra touched her shirt. "It's nearly dry."

"Yeah, mine too. We didn't catch any fish."

Sondra giggled. "But we had fun."

Jason smiled. "Yes, we did."

"I laughed so hard when you fell in," Sondra chuckled.

"You mean pulled in."

"If you hadn't pushed me first." They both laughed and leaned back down on the small, sandy beach. Sondra looked at the sun high in the sky. "The sun feels so good."

"Yes, it does."

Sondra rolled over on her stomach. "You're really lucky."

Jason rolled to his side, now facing her. "Why is that?"

"Because you live here."

Jason looked at the surrounding mountains and the nearby lake. "Yes, I guess I am."

Now Sondra rolled to her side. "In the winter, do you get snow?"

Jason chuckled. "Do we get snow? You wouldn't believe the amount of snow we get."

"That's neat. I'd like to see it sometime."

"You mean you've never seen snow?"

"Only in pictures."

"Sometimes the snow will be as high as the rooftops."

"Oh, quit teasing."

"No, it really does."

"Wow, that would be so neat to see."

"Well if you stay with us this winter, I'll teach you how to snow ski."

"Snow ski?"

"Yes, we usually go skiing every week at Sun Valley, except when the roads are snowed in. Then we either ice skate or go on sleigh rides."

"But what if my mom comes and gets me first?"

"You could still come back to visit."

"Maybe I could. That would be so fun." They both were quiet for a brief moment. "Jason, what if my mom never comes back? What if she is dead?"

"You just have to believe that she's fine," Jason said. Both remained quiet for a brief moment. "You know, my family thinks my mom is dead."

"But you've told them she's alive."

"But they still don't believe me."

"Not even your father?"

Jason shook his head no and the stopped. "I think he wants to believe me, but he just can't."

Again they were quiet. "When you're mom visits, what does she say to you?"

"Mostly she teaches me."

"Like what?"

"About things that are going to happen."

"You mean like in the future?"

"Yes, but sometimes the things just pop into my head."

"Like what?" Jason looked at Sondra, then turned away. "Did I say something wrong?"

"No, it's like some of the things that are going to happen in the future are real bad. I don't like to think about them."

Sondra realized this was not the time to discuss this further. "I think my clothes are dry."

Jason sat up. "Mine too." They both quickly put on their outer clothes.

"Should we go back to the cabin?"

"No, not yet," Jason answered. He took Sondra's hand. "Come on, I want to show you something."

Sondra pulled back. "Wait, I want to ask you something."

Jason turned back. "What's that?"

"Really suppose my mom never comes back?"

Jason smiled. "That's easy, you can stay with us. Now come on, I want to show you something really cool." Together they raced hand in hand toward the thick underbrush.

———⟫•⟪———

"Thirteen thirty-four, thirteen thirty-six, here it is, thirteen thirty-eight." Elaine pointed to the house, and Jim pulled the car to the curb and turned off the engine. "Now, let me do the talking," she said.

Jim climbed out of the car and went around to the other side. He then helped Elaine out. "Why you?"

Elaine smiled up at him. "Because sometimes you say the wrong thing."

Jim led the way up the sidewalk to the Sorenson home. "No, I don't."

She encircled her arm in his as they walked up the sidewalk to the Sorenson home. "Yes, you do," she firmly replied. She stopped and turned him toward her. "Now promise me you will let me do the talking. Promise?"

"Okay, you can do the talking."

The car that had been following them parked down the street about a block away. Jim rang the doorbell. Soon a young child came to the door. "Yes?"

"Hello, does a Megan Sorenson live here?"

The girl turned and screamed. "Mom, there's someone at the door." She raced away, leaving Jim and Elaine standing there alone.

Soon an attractive young woman in her midthirties came to the door. "Hello, may I help you?"

"Are you Mrs. Sorenson, Megan Sorenson?" Elaine asked.

"Yes, my name is Megan Sorenson."

"The Megan Sorenson that was married to Edward Sorenson?" Elaine probed further.

Mrs. Sorenson's demeanor changed when her husband's name was mentioned. "Listen, if you are here from the base, I have told everything I—"

"No," Elaine interrupted, "we are not from the base."

"Mrs. Sorenson," Jim piped in to Elaine's dismay, "we just want to ask you a couple of questions about your husband."

"I have nothing to say." She attempted to close the door.

Jim stepped forward and placed his hand on the closing door. "Please," Elaine pleaded. "I am David's wife, your husband worked with my mine."

Mrs. Sorenson stopped pushing the door closed. She stared at Elaine. "David's wife?"

"Yes, and this is Jim Crockett, one of David's best friends." She then stared for a brief moment at Jim.

"Then it's true, David is dead." Both Elaine and Jim were quiet. Finally Jim nodded his head yes. "Please come in, I've been waiting for you." Jim and Elaine shared a glance, wondering what she meant by that. Megan showed them the way to the living room. On the way she picked up a few scattered toys in the hallway. "Forgive me for my rudeness."

"You probably have had many questions since your husband's death." Elaine could empathize.

Megan smiled and nodded her head yes. "Too many." She motioned with her hand. "Please, sit down." Elaine and Jim sat next to each other on the couch. "Would you two like a cup of coffee?"

"No, not for us," Elaine answered.

Megan sat down in the chair across from them. "I heard they put you husband in a mental hospital."

"Yes. He died about ten days ago."

"I'm so sorry. David was a nice man and a good friend to my husband."

"We were sorry to hear about your husband too. We heard it was a hunting accident."

"Hunting accident?" Megan questioned sarcastically.

Jim looked at Elaine. "Mrs. Sorenson, it sounds like you have some doubts."

"Doubts, yes, I've got doubts."

"What do you mean?" Elaine asked.

Megan looked down as she spoke. "Suppose one day your husband leaves for work as usual, and a few hours later, you get a call stating that he was found in the mountains killed in a hunting accident. Wouldn't you have doubts?"

"You mean your husband didn't tell you he was going hunting?" Jim asked.

"Oh, they found him in hunting clothes and with a deer rifle, but when he left that morning for work, he was dressed in a suit and tie, just like every other day."

Jim was confused. "Maybe he took his hunting clothes and deer rifle with him?"

"Mr. Crockett, you're not listening. Ed never hunted a day in his life. He didn't even own a rifle."

"Then someone must have—" Jim caught himself before he finished.

"Killed him," Megan finished. Jim and Elaine looked at Megan but did not speak. "It's okay. I have believed this all along."

"What did the police say when you told them?" Elaine asked.

"I didn't tell them."

"But why?"

"Someone called me one night shortly after Ed's death. He told me if I valued my children's lives, I would keep my mouth shut."

Elaine shook her head. She could understand how she was feeling. "Mrs. Sorensen, we're sorry, but we think my husband was murdered too. That's why we have come to see you."

"Well, I'll try to help if I can. What do you want to know?"

"Did you husband ever talk to you about his work?"

"He didn't say much. In fact he was quiet about those things."

"Did your husband say anything unusual about David?"

"No, he didn't speak much about your husband either."

"Do you have any idea why someone would want your husband and David killed?" Jim asked. Jim caught Elaine's frown. He knew she was not pleased with his blunt question.

Megan wiped her sweaty hands on her pants. She shook her head in dismay. "I'm sorry, but could we discuss this further some other time?"

Elaine could tell these questions were upsetting her. "Sure, we've stayed long enough. We'll come back another time."

"I'd like that."

Jim and Elaine stood and walked toward the door. "If you think of anything else, would you call me?"

"Sure."

Elaine handed her a personal card.

Jim turned back. "One other thing, Mrs. Sorenson, have you ever heard of animal named Uintathere?"

Megan laughed. "Who told you?"

Elaine and Jim looked at each other. They were stunned by her answer. "Told us?" Elaine repeated.

"Someone must have said something, right?"

Jim shook his head. "No one told us anything."

"Then how did you know?"

"The reason we asked is because my husband drew a picture of one on his wall at the mental hospital. That's where we heard the word for the first time."

"Well a Uintathere is this extinct animal," Megan explained. "It was slow and looked like a small sized elephant. They use to live here in the mountains of Utah."

Elaine nodded her head. "Yes, we learned that much, but we just didn't know why David referred to these animals."

"The Utah Jazz," Megan explained.

Elaine and Jim looked at each other. "You mean the basketball team?"

"Yes, David and Ed were their greatest fans."

The music symbol on the wall must refer to jazz, Jim thought.

Megan continued to explain. "The Uintathere Jazz was what they called the team when they played like a slow moving Uintathere. It was like a joke between my husband and yours."

"The Utah Jazz," Jim spoke. "That's what David was trying to say." Jim opened the front door and was ready to leave.

Megan grasped Elaine's arm. "Wait a minute, I have something for you." Megan disappeared to the back part of the house. She then returned a moment later with a key in her hand. "This is for you."

Elaine looked at the key. "What is this?"

"I don't know, but it is from your husband."

"What do you mean?"

"A couple of months ago I received a letter from him with this key."

"Why to you?"

"He was worried about his life, and this key was too dangerous to give to his wife. That's why he sent it to me."

"Do you know what it is to?" Jim asked.

"No, the letter did not say."

"Do you still have the letter?" Elaine asked.

"No, I burned it, like he instructed."

"Then why give it to us now?" Jim asked.

"David knew that someone would come to me. He said people would come talking about the Uintathere Jazz, and that I was to give this key to them. He then said that these people would right the wrongs, and avenge my husband's death." Megan paused for a moment. "Please, for our husbands' sakes, right the wrong."

Elaine nodded her head good-bye, and Jim shut the door.

CHAPTER THIRTY–SIX

THE CAPTURE OF THE CHILDREN

L one Wolf placed another log on the fire. It was quiet. He smiled as he watched Nicole and Indian sitting on rocks looking at each other. Now Nicole laughed softly. "You really didn't think I was dead, did you?"

"Of course I did. I watched you slowly die for months."

"And did you ever see my dead body?"

"No, but when we didn't find you, we all just assumed you were dead."

"Not all," Lone Wolf corrected.

Indian looked at Lone Wolf. "If you knew about this all along, why didn't you tell me?"

"You wouldn't have believed me."

"You're probably right. Unfortunately it took seeing with my own eyes before I would believe."

"That's a sad thing, Grandson, for great faith could accomplish so many more good things in this world."

Indian nodded his head. He then smiled at Nicole. "I am so happy to see you, again. But where have you been all this time?"

"I have been with our people, the mountain people."

"You mean I'm a—" Indian interrupted himself.

"A mountain person?" Lone Wolf finished for him. "You and Nicole were sent here to help the world."

"You mean like aliens from another planet?"

"Oh no," Nicole reassured, "we are from this world. But because of the way our people lived, many years ago God gave us special gifts."

"What kind of special gifts?"

"Well, can you see the city before you?" Lone Wolf asked, pointing to the region out in front of them.

Indian looked about him. "I don't see anything."

"That's because the gift has not been given to you," Lone Wolf explained.

Indian looked at Nicole. "Can you see a city?" She nodded her head yes. He then looked at Lone Wolf. "And you can see it too?"

Lone Wolf nodded his head yes. "You see, Grandson, that is one of God's gifts that was given to the mountain people. The gift of bending space. That's why the city looks hidden to you."

Indian looked at his grandfather. "The Sprudiths can do the same thing, can't they?"

"Yes, they can. For every gift God gives to good people, their master is allowed to do the same thing for his followers. It balances the power of good and evil here on the earth."

"Their master. You mean the rumors about their master are real?"

"Absolutely," Nicole answered. "Their master is very real."

"You don't mean like the devil or something like that?" Indian asked. "You know I've never believed in that kind of stuff."

"Oh, you will," Nicole warned. "The time will come when you will know his power in its fullness."

Indian shook his head. "This is so hard to believe."

Nicole smiled. She stood and walked over to Indian. She reached out and took his hand. "Come," she said. He stood and walked with her into the nearby meadow. She then waved her hand and space moved. Just like a stage curtain moving from one side to the other, a large beautiful city came into view. Indian gasped. "Indian, this is our home. This is where you lived when you were a little boy."

Nicole turned and took both of his hands. "My dear friend, I have to go."

"No, please stay a little longer."

Nicole closed her eyes and shook her head no. "It's not possible."

"Sure you can. Just ride down the mountain with me."

"My disease will rage on if I stay, and I will die."

"But we want you to stay. We all miss you so much."

Tears came to her eyes. "I so want to, and maybe someday I can, but not right now. Please, don't tell anyone that you saw me. Only Jason and Lone Wolf would believe you anyway. There is much that will happen in the future. Our family needs to pass through this refining period of time before they will believe and know that I still live."

"Now is your time, Grandson," Lone Wolf added.

"But it is not the time for the others," Nicole explained. "They need to wage the war first, and they will need yours and Disciple's help."

"You both speak in riddles that I don't understand," Indian complained.

"Someday you will," Lone Wolf said. "Believe me, this is the only way."

Only way, Indian thought. *What do you mean the only way?*

"Lone Wolf, we have to go."

Indian looked at Lone Wolf and then back to her. "Grandfather is going with you?"

"Yes, we need him to come with us."

"But I need him to stay. How can I fight the Sprudiths without him?"

"You no longer need him," Nicole explained. "Now go, for as we speak my son and the girl are in danger and need your help." She then reached her arms around him and held him tight. She pulled away and looked up into his eyes. Tears rolled down her cheeks. "I love you, Indian," she whispered. "Please be there to help my husband and my son. They will need your strength, for the struggle will be great." She then turned and walked away toward the gates of the city.

Indian watched in silence as she walked away. Soon she was met by two white tigers, which accompanied her. He then turned to his grandfather. Tears now flowed down his own cheeks. "Grandfather," he whispered. He put his arms around him and pulled him close. "There are so many questions. I don't know what I am to do next."

Lone Wolf broke the embrace and smiled. "Remember this, the Great Spirit has chosen our family to fight this war."

"But there are so many of them, and so few of us."

"The Great Spirit couldn't have picked mightier warriors." He then let his grandson go and turned to follow Nicole.

"Grandfather," Indian called out, as if to say he loved him.

Lone Wolf turned again. He smiled as if to say, "I know, Grandson, and I love you too." Soon the curtain of space returned. Nicole, Lone Wolf, and the city disappeared. Indian was left alone.

⟫◈⟪

Captain Reed studied the valley with his binoculars. He didn't understand why the general wanted the girl. "Sergeant, what did you find out?"

"The children weren't there, just the woman."

"What did she say?"

"Nothing. We had to tie her up."

"Why in the hell did you do that?"

"Well when she found out we were after the children, she came at us with a butcher knife."

"But she's an old woman."

"Beg your pardon, sir, but you would have to be there to understand."

"Never mind. Those children have to be around here somewhere."

"Look, Captain," the sergeant interrupted, "something spooked that herd of deer." They all watched as ten to twelve head of deer fled up and over a nearby knoll.

"Sergeant, take your men and check that area first."

"Yes, sir." He signaled his men to follow. Captain Reed continued to scour the valley below for the children.

"Sh," Jason whispered. "We just scared the herd."

"Herd?"

"A herd of deer." Jason continued crawling on his hand and knees through the thick underbrush tunnel. Now Sondra could make out something brown up ahead. Jason stopped. He did not say anything, but pointed with his finger. She crawled up next to him to see more clearly.

Sondra's eyes widened and a smile crept across her face. "Baby deer," she whispered.

"Two fawns. I found them a couple weeks ago. I think one of the does had twins. Look, they still have the spots on their backs."

"Can we pet them?"

"No, they're too wild."

Both sat for a moment watching the fawns. Suddenly they both heard a twig snap behind them.

"Jason, what was that?"

"Sh, someone's here. Maybe it's Indian and Lone Wolf. You stay here, and I'll go look."

Sondra remained still as she watched Jason crawl back toward the underbrush opening.

Paint made his own way slowly down the narrow mountain pass toward the cabin. It was good that he knew the way, for Indian's thoughts were miles away. Nicole was still alive, but why the secrecy, and why couldn't he tell anyone? When he reached the meadow base, he began to lope Paint toward the cloud of smoke curling from the cabin chimney. He pulled his horse to a stop at the hitching post and dismounted. He looked over the lake and meadow. He didn't see anyone around. "Edith," he yelled as he entered the front door. There wasn't an answer. "Edith, Jason, are you here?" He heard moaning from one of the bedrooms and rushed in. "Edith," he exclaimed. She was lying on the bed bound and gagged. He immediately removed her gag. "Edith, what happened to you?"

"The army," she exclaimed.

Indian began to untie the rope knots. "What do you mean?"

"These damn army men rushed the cabin looking for the children."

Then Nicole was right, he thought. *More than Sprudiths are looking for them.* Indian helped Edith to her feet. "Did the Army find them?"

"I don't know. The last time I saw them, they were down by the lake."

"I'm going to look for them. Will you be all right?"

"Yes, I'll be all right, just hurry."

Quickly he raced from the cabin and began searching. Army boot tracks were everywhere. Although his eyes searched the lake, valley, and mountainsides, there wasn't any sign of life. "Jason, Sondra," he finally yelled, but no answer. He began to follow the boot tracks.

Edith made her way to the cabin porch. She rubbed both wrists. "I don't know why they had to make those knots so tight." She too scoured the valley for any sign of life. "I hope these army jackasses are still around here, so I can shove my foot right up their—hey, there's Indian," she interrupted herself. She watched him crawl into the thick underbrush and disappear. "I sure hope he finds the children," she murmured. Hurriedly she rushed down the pathway to the area where Indian had disappeared. She arrived at the same time that Indian reappeared. "They're not there, are they?"

Indian shook his head no. "The tracks say the army took them."

"Oh no, what's going to happen to them?"

"I should have been here. I thought they would be safe."

"It's not your fault. The holy ground kept them safe from the Sprudiths."

"But not the Army," he countered.

"But where will the Army take them?" Edith asked.

"I think to Dugway. This looks like the work of McFarland."

"Indian, can we get them back?"

"You bet we can." He whistled, and Paint came running. He

grabbed the reins and swung upon the saddle. "I'll keep in touch." Edith watched as Paint galloped away toward the ranch house in the valley below.

———⊰◦⊱———

Tears started to form in her eyes. "What's wrong, Sondra?"

"The ropes are too tight. They are hurting my hands."

Jason looked at one of the soldiers. "Can't you loosen these ropes? They're really hurting her hands."

The soldier looked at his superior for approval. Jason looked at the officer also. "Come on, we're thousands of feet in the air. Where are we going to go?" Still the officer didn't respond. "Sir, she's crying. The ropes are too tight."

"Okay, untie both of them," Reed commanded.

Two soldiers knelt down and removed their bonds. Shortly they stood and looked around. "You two," Reed commanded, "come sit by me." They followed his command. "What are your names?"

"My name is Jason, and this is my friend Sondra."

"Sondra and Jason, I'm Captain Reed. Here, let me help you put these seat belts on. The plane ride can sometimes get rough."

Sondra rubbed her wrists to reestablish the circulation. She looked at Captain Reed. "Sir, what did we do?"

"What do you mean?"

"What did we do wrong? Aren't we being arrested?"

"No, you're not being arrested."

"Then why did you take us from our home?" Jason asked.

Reed looked at Jason and then at Sondra. "You know, that's a good question. We are just following orders."

"Aren't you just a bit curious why the Army would want us?" Jason asked.

"Now that you mention it, I have wondered why you two children have demanded so much special attention. Do either of you know why?"

Jason and Sondra shook their heads no. "Do you know where we are going?" Sondra asked.

"Dugway Army Base in Utah."

"Utah is the state next to Idaho," Jason whispered to Sondra.

"What did you say?" Reed asked.

"I said that Utah was a state next to Idaho. Sondra is from Africa and doesn't know our country very well."

Africa? Reed thought. *What is this girl doing here, and why is the general interested in her?*

"What going to happen to us when we get to this Dugway?" Jason asked.

"General McFarland wants to talk with both of you."

Jason turned to Sondra. "Is he a Sprudith?"

"I don't recognize his name."

"Sprudiths?" Reed asked.

"They are the ones trying to kill us," Jason replied. Now Reed became alarmed. He hadn't heard the term Sprudiths since Vietnam.

"My Uncle Indian will be coming after us," Jason warned.

"Did you say Indian is you uncle?"

"Yes, he will not be happy you took us."

"If he's the same Indian I know, I know he won't be happy." Reed reflected for a moment. *The Sprudiths and Indian, what's going on here,* he thought. Suddenly the plane touched down, interrupting his train of thought.

⟫◆⟪

"Yes."

"Michael, the plane just touched down," McFarland said.

"Good, you have both of them?"

"Yes, we do. I'll interrogate them within the hour."

"What for?" Michael asked.

"To see what they know."

"General, they are children. We're not interested in their knowledge, only their birthright."

"Birthright? What we are doing just doesn't make sense."

"What doesn't make sense?"

"First we want them dead, and now we want them alive for some special purpose?"

"That's correct. Things change. To us these two lives are the most important lives on earth."

"For what, Michael? What's so important about these two children?"

"McFarland, you just do what you're told. You don't need to know everything."

"Well I'm getting to the bottom of this. I'm going to have a little talk with these two children."

"That won't be necessary, and there isn't time."

"What do you mean there isn't time?"

"They both will be on a flight to Mexico with me within the hour."

"But I thought they were to travel with me tomorrow."

"Plans change."

"The hell they do. I'm going to take them with me tomorrow."

"General, this is not by my command."

"Well you can tell Matthias to shove it."

"It is not by Matthias's command either," Michael informed. "If you want to talk with Niac directly about this order, then I'll let him know right now."

"You didn't say anything about Niac." McFarland paused for a moment. "Why does Niac want the children with him?"

"That's simple. It's because he only trusts himself to watch over them." McFarland was quiet. "Now, will you have a plane ready?"

"Within the hour."

"And the children?"

"On the plane."

"Good. I'll see you at the meeting in Cancun. Michael hung up the phone, leaving the general in deep thought.

McFarland hurried up the steps of the plane. He rushed into the seating area to see the two children sitting by themselves under guard. He stared at them. "My name is General McFarland. I'm the one that brought you here."

"General, why are we here?" Jason asked. "We didn't do anything wrong."

Before he could answer, a voice called "General" from behind. He turned to see Captain Reed. Reed motioned the general closer.

He turned and approached. "What is it?"

"I thought you might want to know. The children told me that the Sprudiths have been chasing them."

"But why would the Sprudiths want them?"

"I don't know. The only thing they said was that the girl was a Sprudith, and that they wanted her back."

McFarland shook his head. "Some things just don't make sense."

"There's one other thing, General."

"What's that?"

"The boy."

"What about him?"

"He has an uncle named Indian."

"Indian. Do you think it is the same Indian?"

"I don't know. First there is Elaine and Jim, then the Sprudiths, and now Indian. It doesn't sound like coincidence to me."

That's just great, McFarland thought. *I also have to deal with Michael and Matthias, and now Indian.* McFarland turned and looked at the children sitting quietly. He then turned back to Reed. "Okay, Captain, that will be all."

"Yes, General." Reed turned and left.

McFarland knelt down to the level of the children. "Captain Reed tells me that Indian is your uncle?"

"That's right."

"Then Jim Crockett is your uncle too?"

Jason nodded yes. "You know they will be coming after us, don't you?"

"I don't doubt that one bit." McFarland looked over the young boy. *Is it possible that he is the one?* McFarland thought. "I'm curious, Jason, what was your mother's name?"

"Nicole Hunter."

He is the one, McFarland thought. *All this time we have thought he was dead.* "How is your mother?"

"She died five years ago."

"I'm sorry to hear that." McFarland stood. *Now I understand why they want him alive. He is the chosen one.*

"McFarland, what are you doing here?" a voice called from behind.

He turned to see Michael. "I was talking with the children."

"I told you that wouldn't be necessary."

"Well I wanted to make sure the plane was ready as you desired."

"And?"

"I was wondering why you are traveling by airplane instead of bending space?"

"Sometimes it nice to travel the old-fashioned way. Is everything ready?"

"As you requested."

"Good."

McFarland turned back. "Oh, Michael, where are you taking them?"

"Niac's Tower, why?"

"I was just wondering. Well, I'll see you at the conference."

Michael nodded in agreement. "Well, children," Michael said, "your plane trip is not finished."

"Where are we going?" Jason asked.

"First to Mexico, and then to the tower."

They watched as Michael placed his carry-on bag into the overhead bin and sat in the seat across from them. They both looked around. There weren't any other passengers but the three of them.

McFarland walked down the plane steps and toward the concourse. *So Niac wants the children*, McFarland thought. *If I had control of the children, then maybe I would have the power to take Niac's place.*

CHAPTER THIRTY-SEVEN

THE LOCKET

"Come on." Doug finally gave up and replaced the phone receiver.
"Still no answer?" Pepe asked.

"Where could they be? It's like everyone has disappeared." Doug stood and walked to the hotel window. "I'm calling Sheriff Bates in the morning. Maybe he knows something."

Doug stared at the street below. Pepe watched as Doug rolled the locket between his fingers. He interrupted Doug's train of thought. "The locket, doesn't anything come to mind?"

"You know I have gone over and over this in my mind and do not remember a thing."

"Let me look at it again." Doug slipped the locket off his neck and handed it to Pepe. "Are you sure Tina was trying to tell you something?"

"No, I'm not sure, but why would she give me her locket?"

"Maybe the locket reminded her of you. Maybe you gave her this same locket, you know, a long time ago.

"I thought of that too, but I'm sure I would have remembered."

Pepe opened the locket and looked at the two pictures inside. "Tina sure has cute children, doesn't she?" Pepe handed the locket back to Doug.

Doug smiled. "Yes, she does." He again looked at the street below. "Now they're motherless." They both were quiet for a brief moment. "Pepe, when we checked in here earlier, wasn't there a pawn shop next door?"

Pepe thought for a moment. "Yes, I believe there was, why?"

Doug looked at his watch. *Fifteen minutes to nine*, he thought.

GLEN E. PAGE

"Disciple won't be back for a while. I have an idea. Come on, let's go."

"Go where—out?"

"Yes, out."

"This part of town at night? Boss, you're kidding. I don't even want to leave this room."

"You're just being paranoid."

"Listen, let's just wait until morning."

Doug turned to leave. "Suit yourself, but I believe that pawn shop closes at nine."

"All right, wait. Maybe there's some food nearby." He slipped on his shoes and followed Doug into the narrow hallway. They scampered down the stairs to the front desk. "Going out tonight?" the night manager asked.

"Only next door," Doug answered.

"I'd be careful. This is a rough area at night."

"Thanks, we will."

Doug and Pepe stepped out onto the street. Pepe looked both ways carefully as he followed Doug next door to the pawnshop. The night manager looked at the photo poster under the counter. He then picked up the phone and dialed the number. "Yes, the two you seek are here." He paused for a moment. "First, there was talk of a reward." Again there was a pause. "Good, the Arms Hotel, East LA." He then hung up the phone.

Doug opened the pawn shop door and entered. "We are closing," a voice yelled. Doug ignored the voice and walked toward the back. Pepe followed. The man looked up to see the two coming toward him. He then reached under the counter and pulled out a pistol. "I guess you didn't hear me. We are closing."

Pepe looked at his nametag. "Mike, we want just a minute of your time."

Mike raised the pistol off the counter. "Hit the road, chico."

Without saying a word, Doug placed a hundred-dollar bill on the counter. Mike looked at the bill but did not say a word. Doug then placed another hundred on top of the first. "Just for a few minutes of your time."

Mike took the two bills and placed them in his pocket. "I guess we could stay open for a few more minutes. What can I do for you gentlemen?"

Doug took the locket off his neck and handed it to Mike. "Can you examine this?"

Mike opened the drawer and pulled out an eyepiece. He took the locket and studied it for a brief moment. "Five hundred is my top offer."

316

"No, it's not for sale."

"Then why am I looking at it?"

"I just want you to study it real close, and tell me if you see anything unusual."

Mike shrugged his shoulders. "It's your money."

"What are we doing?" Pepe whispered.

"Sh."

Mike turned the locket in all directions and studied it for several moments. "Gentlemen, it looks normal to me." He handed the locket back to Hunter.

Doug shook his head. "I was hoping there would be something. Well, okay, we appreciate your—"

"Wait a minute," Pepe interrupted, "can you look on the inside?"

"Sure." He took the locket again from Doug, opened it, and studied the inside.

"Anything at all?" Pepe asked.

"No, I don't see anything—oh, hold it," he interrupted himself.

"What?" Doug asked.

"Well it's not the locket, but rather one of the children's pictures. One eye is blue and the other eye is black. "Wait a minute," Mike suggested. He reached behind him and pulled down an old microscope from the shelf. He then carefully removed one of the locket pictures and placed the picture under the microscope. After careful adjusting and study, Mike looked up at Doug and Pepe. "The dark eye, I think it is microfilm."

"Microfilm. Are you sure?"

"Pretty sure."

"Can you read it?" Pepe asked.

"No, you need a microfilm reader for that."

Pepe turned to Doug. "Boss, where can we find one?"

"Probably a library."

"I have one," Mike said.

"You do—could we use it?"

"Sure, for another two hundred." Doug reached into his pocket and pulled out two more bills and handed them to him. Mike took the two bills and walked to the front of his shop. He locked the door and pulled the blinds. "Follow me." He then led them into the back room and down the stairs into the basement. "Here it is."

Pepe watched Mike dust off the machine. "Geez, Mike, this machine is pretty old. Are you sure it still works?"

Mike smiled. "Ah, yeah, it works."

After several adjustments, he was able to illuminate the film on the screen. The three tried to read the film, but were having some difficulties with adjustments. "This is some foreign language," Mike informed.

Doug peered hard at the words. "Some words seem familiar, but I still can't tell what it is saying. Can you make us a copy?"

"I can make a rough copy that you should be able to read."

"Okay, do it."

As they watched the copy being made, there was a ring of the doorbell upstairs. Initially they all ignored it. Then they heard glass break. "Dammit, someone is breaking in," Mike yelled. He pulled out his pistol and started up the stairs. "You stay here."

Doug took the finished copy, folded it, and placed it inside his pocket next to his father's diary. He removed the picture from the microfilm machine and placed it back in the locket.

Pepe neared the stairs to listen. "We are looking for two men. We think they came in here."

"Boss, someone's asking Mike about us."

"You bastards, you broke my window and door," Mike screamed.

Suddenly there was gunfire. Doug then looked at Pepe. "Let's get out of here."

Pepe looked around the basement. "There a door." He grabbed a nearby iron bar and pried off the inside locks. The door then opened easily to stairs leading to an adjacent building. Pepe scampered up the stairs. Doug heard a noise from behind and turned to watch Mike with bloody hands clinging to his chest, stagger, and then tumble down the stairs.

"Come on," Pepe yelled from the stairway. Doug quickly followed Pepe up the stairs. "Now where do we go?"

"Out of the building. We need to get to the street."

"The street?" Pepe questioned, "I rather take my chances in the building. What about going back to the hotel room?"

"No, I'm sure they are waiting for us. Someone tipped them off."

Quickly they ran down the narrow halls to the other side of the vacant building. "What about Disciple?" Pepe asked.

"He can take care of himself." They could hear others following them closely, as they entered a dimly lit alley. One end of the alley was blocked off. "Pepe, I don't like this. There's only one way out."

Suddenly bullets began to hit around them. "I can't hear the shots, but someone is shooting at us," Pepe yelled. Both Doug and Pepe dove behind the nearby garbage bin. Not only could they hear others following them, but now could see men with guns coming toward them from the other end. "Boss, we're trapped."

Doug looked in both directions. He could not see any means of escape. He then looked down into the nearby window well. "The window to the basement is missing," he whispered to Pepe.

"Through there? We can't fit through there."

"We better." Doug quickly dove headfirst into the window well and easily squeezed through the adjacent building's window opening. Pepe was different story. He too dove headfirst. Doc pulled and pulled, but Pepe was stuck.

"Breathe out completely," a woman's voice said from behind. Startled Doug looked behind him. A woman dressed in rags grabbed one of Pepe's arms while Doug grabbed the other.

"You heard her, Pepe, breathe all the way out." This time, with Doug pulling on one arm and the stranger on the other, they were able to pull him through the opening. Just in time for the shots began to ring around them again, and this time through the basement window. "Ouch," Doug whispered as he felt a burning sharp pain on the left side of his abdomen.

"Hurry," the woman instructed, "this way." Doug and Pepe followed the woman through the dark, each holding onto the one in front. There was very little light to show the way. Now they could hear sounds coming from the upstairs. "They're in the building," Pepe whispered.

"Sh, be quiet. They will hear us," she spoke.

Doug could feel something warm and wet on the side of his shirt. He reached down and touched the area. *I've been shot*, he thought as he felt his oozing warm blood. He removed his handkerchief and put pressure against the wound. He did not say anything, but followed the woman who carefully led the way. It was like a maze, first to the left and then to the right. Crawling on hands and knees through holes in walls, under stairs, and always down deeper into the underground. Finally the woman stopped. It was pitch black.

"Can you hear them?" she whispered.

Doug was silent and listened. "I can't hear them anymore."

"Me either," Pepe added.

"Good, for where I take you now, they must never find."

Pepe and Doug did not understand. She started to push on the wall, and it began to move. Soon a faint light could be seen coming from a crack. As the wall moved further, the faint light grew. Now Doug and Pepe could see part of the woman's face. She motioned with her head to the newly created opening. "Go in." Pepe entered first. Doug tried to follow but instead felt faint and fell to the floor. "You've been shot," the woman exclaimed. She reached down and lifted him up. Doug placed his arm around her shoulder and used her as a crutch. Once inside she pushed on the wall again, this time from the other side, and the opening closed.

All three turned at the same time. Pepe and Doug could not believe their eyes. "What is this place?" Pepe asked.

"This place is called Hope," the woman answered. "Come, we need to stop the bleeding." Fortunately the first tent was empty. The woman carefully laid Doug on the cot. "Your friend has been shot. He has lost a lot of blood." She sent Pepe off to get some water and find some bandages. She helped him out of his bloody shirt and then rolled him to one side. "Good, the bullet passed through. She then tore his shirt and made compression dressings to slow the bleeding.

Doug felt faint. He looked up. Now he saw her full face. "Nicole," he whispered. Fatigue overpowered him and he closed his eyes.

———◆———

"Everyone is so quiet," Motumbo said.

"Well it is either the food is so good," Dr. Sullivan suggested, "or everyone is intimidated by everyone else."

"Maybe a little of both," Motumbo added. "Master Joseph, did you tell Cresta and Dr. Jordan of your medical studies?"

"Medical studies?" Cresta asked. "Are you studying medicine?"

"Yes, I want to start my studies next year."

"Congratulations," Harrison said. "You didn't say anything."

"Well, it just didn't come up."

"So, are you going to specialize?" Harrison asked.

"In your footsteps, Harrison," his father said. He wants to become a general surgeon."

"That's great! I'll help you set up a surgical residency in the states when you are ready."

"Joseph, don't leave Africa." Cresta said. "Africa needs the doctors, not the United States. Why not just continue your studies here?"

Harrison looked at Cresta. "Isn't it obvious?"

"No, it isn't."

Dr. Sullivan sighed and shook his head. "Oh no, here we go again."

"Come on, Cresta, think of his training."

"I am, and he can be trained just as well here in Africa."

Joseph wanted to quell tempers. "Well I haven't made up my mind yet." They both ignored his comment.

"Be practical, the best medical training for Joseph is in the United States."

"That's BS. You know he'll go to the United States and never return."

"Sure he'll return, once his training is over."

Now all could see Cresta's ire come to the surface. "Like you? Like you promised?"

Dr. Sullivan leaned over and whispered. "It's like they have never been apart." Joseph smiled at his father's comment.

"That was different."

"It isn't any different. You just sold out."

"What do you mean I sold out?"

"You sold out for the riches and glamour of the United States, and you forgot your people."

"And what about you, running off with that guy Matthias? Did you not forget your people too?"

The room was quiet. Everyone looked at Cresta, waiting for an answer. Cresta looked down. She knew that he was right. Now Harrison regretted his remarks. "Cresta, I'm sorry, I was way out of line."

"No, you are right. I made a mistake."

"I guess we all have made mistakes," Harrison continued.

"Yes, we have," Dr. Sullivan answered. "Maybe it's time to let all wounds heal."

Joseph took Cresta's hand in his. She looked up at him. He smiled at her. "I'm just glad you are home." Cresta put her arms around his neck and hugged him.

"Me too," Dr. Sullivan added. "We're all grateful you've come home."

Motumbo was watching from the corner. "We all are happy you are here, Ms. Cresta, but it will be the last time that I suggest that we are too quiet at dinner." Everyone laughed.

"Well that was an excellent meal, Motumbo."

"Thank you, Dr. Jordan."

"Yes, Motumbo, you outdid yourself. Now can you get me my wheelchair? I would like to take a walk."

"Yes, sir."

Joseph and Cresta began to clear the table.

"Harrison, would you care to join me?"

Harrison helped Dr. Sullivan into the chair and pushed him down the ramp into the compound. "Sir, I had forgotten the beauty of this land."

"Yes, how fortunate I am to have lived here so long." Dr. Sullivan grabbed his lower chest.

Harrison reached and touched his shoulder. "Maybe we ought to go back in."

"No, it's just this damn pain. It will pass." Harrison pushed his wheelchair toward some patio furniture in the middle of the compound. "Please sit," Dr. Sullivan suggested. Harrison sat down across from him. He looked at Harrison. "I perceive something is bothering you."

"Dr. Sullivan, we found black ovaries."

"Where?"

"In a girl near my home."

"Is that why you were in New York?"

"Yes, I was visiting this German doctor there who wrote an article on black ovaries."

"The Sclerotic Ovarian Syndrome?"

"Yes, that's right. Are you familiar with the article?"

"Familiar? Hell I wrote it."

Harrison was stunned. "Sir, you wrote that article?"

"Yes, I did, way back in the 1940s."

"But, sir, that would make you a—"

"Nazi criminal?" Sullivan interrupted.

"No, sir. I was going to say Hans's brother."

"Ah, yes, Hans. How is he, anyway?"

"Confused."

"Confused?"

"Confused because after all these years, he still misses you."

Sullivan smiled. "I miss him too."

"Here, Stephen, he gave me this." Harrison pulled a picture out of his wallet.

Sullivan studied the picture. He then chuckled. "It's my family. It was so many years ago. He then looked up at Harrison. "My real name is Dr. Stephen Krugar."

"Dr. Krugar," a voice spoke from behind. Both turned to look at the voice. They could see a shadow of a man limping toward them. "After all this time, I have finally found you." They now could see the man's pistol pointed in their direction.

Joseph handed the clean dish to Cresta. She wiped it dry and placed it on the shelf. "I appreciate your help," Motumbo offered.

"Glad to do it," Joseph responded. Motumbo then left to return to the dining room.

Cresta caught Joseph looking at her. He was smiling. "What are you smiling about?"

"Is she close by?"

"Who?"

"Your daughter."

Cresta looked at him. "How did you know about her?"

"Don't you remember? You wrote me. You even sent me a picture."

Cresta smiled. "I had forgotten about that. Did you tell father?"

"No, I never did. So tell me, is she close by?"

"No, she's staying with some people in the states."

Cresta could tell that Joseph was disappointed. "I was hoping to see her. She's got to be around nine years old, now."

"Almost ten. Her birthday is later this month."

"What did you name her?"

Cresta smiled. She handed a dish to Joseph to dry. "Her name is Sondra."

"Sondra, I like that name." Both were quiet as they continued with the dishes. "I think you should bring her here."

"You think so?"

Joseph nodded his head yes. "We would all love to see and meet her."

"Maybe I will," she agreed. Joseph could see she wanted to say more.

"What?"

"I need to tell you about her father—"

Motumbo rushed into the kitchen. "There's a stranger in the compound. I'm getting the shotgun." He then fled the kitchen to the living room. Joseph and Cresta followed.

"Hello, Benjamin," Sullivan spoke.

"Stephen, it's been many years."

"No need for guns here, Benjamin." He then pointed to his wheelchair. "I'm not going anywhere. Benjamin lowered his gun. He limped forward toward them. "Let me introduce you to Harrison Jordan." Stephen turned toward Dr. Jordan. "Ben's people have been following you since you left New York."

Harrison looked up at him. "They have?"

Benjamin nodded his head. "Yes, we were hoping you would lead us to Stephen."

Harrison now realized what he had done. "Dr. Sullivan, I'm sorry. I didn't—"

Dr. Sullivan grabbed Harrison's arm. "It's okay, there's no need to apologize. I'm just happy to see my old friend Ben one more time before I pass on."

Ben replaced his gun in his shoulder holster. "Then the rumors are true. You are really dying?

"We are okay, Motumbo," Sullivan yelled. "You can put the gun down and return it to the house."

"Are you sure, sir?"

Ben turned to see two shotgun barrels pointed at him. "Yes, he's an old friend." Motumbo lowered the shotgun and returned with Cresta and Joseph into the house. "Ben, why don't you join us?"

"Dammit, Stephen, you know how long I've been chasing you."

"About thirty years."

"Closer to forty."

"Has it been that long?"

Ben took a chair between the two. "So, Stephen, what is it?"

"Cancer."

"How much longer?"

"Just a few more days, I reckon."

"I'm sorry. I wish it wasn't this way."

"I know."

Harrison studied Ben. "So who are you to follow me?"

"Oh, I'm sorry, Harrison, this is Benjamin Goldberg. He's an Israeli intelligence agent."

Intelligence agent, Harrison thought. *Why is Israel interested in Dr. Sullivan?*

CHAPTER THIRTY-EIGHT

THE CITY OF HOPE

Pepe peeked around the edge of the tent. With stick in hand he crawled to the backside of the next tent and peered around its edge. *Where are those two hiding,* he asked himself. Suddenly two small heads popped up from behind a rubbish pile. *There they are,* he thought, *I'll crawl around to the other side and surprise them.*

Doug slowly sat up to the side of the cot and casually watched from his tent opening. Again the two heads popped up from behind the rubbish, looking for Pepe. Still they could not find him. The two children came over to Doug's tent opening. "Mister," the girl whispered, "have you seen that guy that came with you last night?

"You mean Pepe?"

"Yeah, Pepe. Do you know where he is?"

Doug smiled and nodded his head in Pepe's direction. "Thanks," the boy said. Carrying their sticks, they quickly turned and headed in that direction.

Doug watched as the young girl and boy crept up behind Pepe's hiding place and caught him off guard.

"How did you find me?" Doug heard Pepe say. The boy and girl talked with Pepe and then pointed their fingers at Doug. "I thought so," Pepe said. He then waved good-bye to the two and came over next to Doug. "You know, you betrayed me."

Doug smiled. "For the kids, I didn't think you would mind. What was it, cowboys and Indians?"

"No, Kristin and Sam said it's a game that Disciple played when he was a boy. He calls it Israelites and Philistines."

"And you?"

"I was Goliath, the Philistine."

"See, Goliath is supposed to lose."

"I suppose you're right."

"Isn't it interesting that everyone seems to know Disciple?"

"Well they sure do down here. Anyway, how do you feel?"

"Weak."

"You should, you lost a lot of blood."

"I was shot?"

"Yes, you were. Fortunately the bullet didn't hit anything vital and passed on through. It was also fortunate the lady found us."

"Where is that lady anyway?"

"Funny thing, once she got the bleeding stopped, she just disappeared."

"Did you check around?"

"Yes, I did. This morning I walked through the whole camp. You know, if it hadn't been for her, right now we both would be dead."

"Yes, I know."

"Through all those rags for clothes, I never did get a real good look at her face, did you?"

Doug reflected for a moment. "Only once. She was beautiful. When I first saw her face, I thought it was Nicole."

"Nicole?"

Doug chuckled. "I must have been delirious." He looked around. "Anyway, what is this place?"

"Well, from what I can tell, it's an old convention center room."

"Convention center?"

"Yes, it's kind of like someone built a new hotel or something over the top of it and sealed this part off."

"And these people live here?"

"I guess so. Somehow they were able to tie into the city's water, power, and even sewer lines."

"Surely authorities must know about this place."

"Yes, they do," a voice stated from behind. Startled, Pepe and Doug turned.

"Disciple," Pepe exclaimed, "where have you been?"

"Where have I been? Where have you two been? I've been looking all over the city for you guys." Disciple looked at Doug's bandage and then back to his face. "What happened to you?"

"He was shot last night," Pepe answered for him.

"Are you all right?"

Doug stood up from the cot. "I think so, just a little weak."

Disciple shook his head in disbelief. "How in the world did you ever find this place?"

"We didn't. Some woman brought us here last night."

"What woman?"

"We don't know. Last night when someone started shooting at us, this woman found us and led us here."

"Where is she now?"

"I looked for her this morning to thank her, but I couldn't find her," Pepe said.

"How did you know we were here?" Doug asked. Disciple nodded toward the children playing nearby.

"You mean Kristin and Sam," Pepe asked.

"No, it was their father. I saw him on his way to work this morning. He told me of two new men that entered Hope last night. I just figured it was you two."

"Hope—is that what this place is called?" Doug asked.

Disciple nodded his head. "Doc, do you feel strong enough to walk around?"

"I think so."

Disciple and Pepe helped Doug to his feet. "Then come, I'll show you around." Doug and Pepe followed Disciple to the center of the arena.

"Disciple, do these people have homes or places they can go?" Pepe asked.

"Sure, their home is here."

"But if the authorities know about this place, why don't they do something about it?"

"What do you want them to do? Do you think the authorities want all these people back on the street, sleeping in the parks, on the beaches, and under the overpasses?" Doug and Pepe didn't answer.

They watched Disciple place the cart he was pushing in the arena center, and then backed away. "Why the groceries?" Pepe asked.

"A lot of these people can't take care of themselves, so when I come to visit, I usually try to bring some food."

"Does each of them own their own tent?" Doug asked.

"No, the people may come and go, but the tents stay here."

"Then all these people move from city to city," Pepe assumed.

"Some do, but most of them just stay here. Take, for example, Mrs. Lang right there." They looked to see a lady taking some cans of food from the cart and returning with them to her tent. She is the mother of Kristin and Sam. Mr. Lang has a janitorial job. When they no longer could afford rent on top, he moved his family down here."

"What of the children?" Pepe asked.

"They still go to school, just like other children."

"Then you live here too?" Doug asked.

"No, I just visit often."

"There must be other places like this?" Doug asked.

"Oh, yes, most cities have them."

"Have you seen them all?" Pepe asked.

"Some of them."

"But why visit them?" Doug asked.

"Boss, isn't it obvious? Disciple is one of God's apostles. That's what he's supposed to do."

Doug shook his head. "Surely you can't think your visits will help all the homeless people."

"You're right, Doc, I can't help them all." Disciple paused for a brief moment and then continued. "But let me introduce you to a few that I can help." Pepe and Doug followed Disciple to a nearby tent.

An older woman came through the tent opening. She smiled. "Disciple, I didn't know you were here."

"Hello, Maggie, I came down this morning."

Maggie looked at the shopping cart. "And with groceries too." Maggie then put her arms around Disciple and gave him a hug. "Thanks."

Disciple looked over at Pepe and Doug. "Maggie's my girlfriend."

Maggie broke the embrace and hit his shoulder. "Oh, you're such a charmer." She smiled. "Will you be here long?"

"Only a few days."

Maggie looked at Doug and Pepe. "I see you are not alone this time."

Disciple turned toward the others. "Maggie, these are my friends, Doug and Pepe."

"Doug and Pepe, it's nice to meet you. Welcome to Hope."

"Thank you, Maggie," Doug replied, "it's nice to meet you."

"Listen," Maggie said, "I'm making some hobo stew this evening. Why don't you all come and eat with me."

Disciple looked at Doug and Pepe. They all seemed to be in agreement. "We'd be honored," Disciple finally answered.

"Good. Is six okay?"

"We'll be there," Disciple promised.

Maggie looked at the grocery cart. "Now if I just could get over to the groceries."

"Let me help you," Pepe volunteered.

"Would you? I would appreciate it." Pepe then took her by the arm and slowly helped her to the food cart.

Doug watched her difficulty with walking and coordination. He looked at Disciple. "Maggie has syphilis, doesn't she?"

Disciple looked at Doc. "Yes, she does. She came here two years ago when she became ill. How did you know?"

"By her walk. The syphilis has severely damaged her nervous system."

"Maggie's been a prostitute all her life. She started when she was eleven years old."

Doug looked at Disciple. "Eleven?"

Disciple nodded his head. "She once told me, her father began sexually abusing her when she was about five. At age eleven he prostituted her to the miners for whiskey money." Disciple shook his head. "Maggie was a prostitute for forty-six years."

Doug looked at Disciple. "I don't understand."

"Understand what?"

"I thought Maggie's was your friend?"

"She is my friend. So what do you mean?"

"Well Maggie's a prostitute. I didn't think Jesus approved of prostitution. "Shouldn't you tell her to repent?"

Disciple looked at Doug. "You're being sarcastic, aren't you?"

Doug smiled, "Yes, maybe a little. Sometimes your God and I don't see eye to eye."

Disciple smiled back. "Jesus would always say all people are God's children."

Doug nodded his head as if he understood. Both were quiet for a brief moment. "Disciple, there wasn't anyone around to protect Maggie, was there."

"I'm afraid not. Her mother died when she was a baby."

Doug sadly shook his head. "I wonder how many other children in the world are going through the same type of trauma right now."

"Thousands, maybe even millions."

"You really think that many?"

"I'm afraid so."

Again Doug shook his head. "Dammit, Disciple, why doesn't God do something? I can understand why God wouldn't help me, because I am not the best person in the world. But what have little children done to deserve this?"

Disciple wanted to explain why God allowed these things to happen, but he knew that Doug was not ready to know. So he remained quiet. They both watched how hard it was for Maggie to walk.

"She really struggles, doesn't she?" Doug said finally. They sat quietly watching Pepe help Maggie with her groceries. "Disciple, who is going to protect Maggie now?"

"I guess I will."

Doug looked over at Disciple and smiled. "Then I will help too."

Disciple returned the smile. *This man cares,* Disciple thought. *He really does care. Now I understand why God chose him.* Disciple touched Doug's arm. "Come, Doc, I want you to meet Fred." Fred was already at the grocery cart when Disciple and Doug arrived. "Hello, Fred, you scallywag you."

Fred stopped and turned toward the voice. "Disciple, is that you?"

Disciple chuckled. "How did you know?"

"Because you're the only one that calls me scallywag." Fred reached out his hand and touched Disciple's face and cheek. He then put his arms around his neck. "It's so good to have you back." He then pulled away.

"Fred, I have a friend I want you to meet."

"A friend?"

"Yes, this is my friend, Doug."

"Doug it is nice to meet you." Doug noticed that Fred extended his hand in the wrong direction. He realized Fred was blind.

He reached over and grasped Fred's hand. "Fred, it's nice to meet you, too."

"Listen, Fred, don't cook anything for supper tonight," Disciple advised.

"Why is that?"

"We are having a party over at Maggie's."

There was excitement in Fred's voice. "A party?"

"Yes, she's cooking some of her hobo stew."

Fred face filled with a grin. "You won't forget me now, will you?"

Doug was touched by Fred's question. "Of course not. In fact, we will pick you up first," Disciple reassured.

"And I can go with you to pick up the others?"

"You bet you can."

Fred smiled again. "Thanks, Disciple. I'm so glad you are back." Disciple and Doc watched as he turned and made his way back to his tent.

"Fred has no family," Disciple explained. "He has been on his own since he was a small boy."

"When did he lose his vision?"

"Last year. He was beaten badly by a gang of boys. The beating caused him to lose his sight."

It was then another walked up to the grocery cart and took some cans. "What about him?" Doug whispered.

"You mean Jeff?"

"Are you going to introduce him also?"

"It will not do any good. Two years ago he and his wife were sleeping in the park downtown San Francisco when they were attacked by four men. The men raped and killed his wife. They beat him and left him for dead. He hasn't spoken a word since the incident. But see the woman standing next to him?"

"The one in the blue blouse?"

"Yes, that's Susan. She's unique. She hears voices and sees visions."

"Sounds like she's schizophrenic. Are they all like this?"

"What do you mean?"

"You know, sick, outcasts, mentally ill?"

"Not all, but in some ways most are pretty much society's rejects."

Disciple noticed that Doug was visibly touched. "You know, Doc, some people say these people deserve what has happened to them, you know, kind of like God's punishment."

Doug did not answer, but looked away. "I'm probably not the one to ask about that."

"Why is that?"

"Well with all the wars, disease, hunger, and other suffering on this planet, I am not one of God's favorite fans."

"Oh, I see."

Doug watched again as Maggie winced with pain and nearly fell with each step. He saw Fred struggling to find his tent opening. He watched Susan over in a far corner all alone speaking herself. He then turned and looked at Disciple. "No, Disciple, you don't see. Do you really want to know how I feel about these people?"

"Yes, I do."

"Well I think that if you were really an apostle of God like you profess to be—" Then Doug paused and shook his head. "Nah, I better not say it."

"Go on, say what you were going to say."

Doug looked at Disciple and smiled. "What I was going to say, is if I was really one of Jesus's apostles like you profess to be, then I would heal these people."

Pepe had returned from Maggie's tent and heard the conversation. "Yeah, Disciple, why don't you just heal these people?"

"Because, it takes faith."

"Yeah, right," Doug agreed sarcastically.

"Boss, he's right, you do need faith."

"Come on, Pepe, faith is the same answer they always give." Now Doug's anger began to surface. "Disciple, you're no more Jesus's disciple than I am. You're just a fake—" Doug interrupted himself. Pepe and Disciple stared at Doug. Now Doug began to regret his words. He put up his hands and slowly backed away. "Listen, I'm sorry. I just need to keep my mouth shut." Disgusted with what he had said, Doug turned and walked toward the cart. Upon arriving he helped hand out other grocery items to some of the others.

Disciple turned to Pepe. "Listen, I'm going up top to get a newspaper. I want to see if anything was printed about you and the Doc today. I'll be back late tonight."

"But, what about the hobo stew?"

"Why don't you save me some?"

Disciple turned to leave. Pepe reached out his hand and stopped him. "Listen, Disciple." Pepe paused. "I'm sorry for what Doc said. He didn't mean to hurt your feelings."

"It's okay. I have heard it all before."

Pepe continued. "It's just seems that since Nicole died, Doc has become, well, you know, real bitter."

Disciple smiled. "Pepe, you're a good man and a good friend." He turned and nodded toward Doug. "Would you like to see Doc's heart change a little bit?"

Pepe was surprised by his question. "What do you mean?"

"Come with me and watch." Disciple and Pepe walked over to Doug. "Doc, I have something for you."

Doug handed out another can of soup and then turned toward Disciple. "What is it?"

Disciple reached into his backpack and pulled out a crumpled piece of paper. "Doc, do you remember learning about something called 'The Day of Miracles' last week?"

Doug thought for a moment. "Day of Miracles? Well, yes, it's a special day of celebration at one of the Phoenix hospitals, where I use to work. How do you know about that?"

"That doesn't matter. Do you remember what they celebrate?"

"Well apparently about ten years ago there was this group of children who were all cured of their cancer in one single day."

"Cured or healed?" Disciple asked. Doug was surprised by his question. He then handed Doug the crumpled piece of paper.

"What's this?" Doug asked.

"Read it and see," Disciple replied. He turned to Pepe. "I'll be back late tonight." He then turned quickly and walked toward the entrance.

Doug undid and read the crumpled paper. He was stunned. He looked up. "Disciple, wait!" Disciple stopped and turned toward Doug. "Where did you get this?" Disciple did not answer. Instead he smiled, turned, and disappeared through the entrance.

Pepe was confused. "Boss, what's going on?"

Doug looked at Pepe. He lifted the crumpled piece of paper. "It's my prescription."

"Prescription?"

"Yes, a prescription I gave to Nicole years ago."

"What do you mean?"

Doug handed the piece of paper to Pepe. Pepe read it aloud. "Dear Healer, Please heal all twenty-seven children on this floor who have cancer. Thank you. Dr. Hunter."

"Boss, what is this? I don't understand."

Doug reflected on what happened. He and Pepe sat down. "One night ten years ago, Nicole and I were working on the children's cancer floor. She said she wished a healer would come through there, and heal all the sick children. That's when I wrote this prescription and gave it to her."

"And all the children got better?"

"Yes, Pepe, all twenty-seven of them."

"Wow, boss, that's the greatest miracle I have ever heard."

"Come on, Pepe, that wasn't a miracle."

"Why sure it was."

"No, it had to be the chemotherapy."

Pepe chuckled. "Chemotherapy—yeah, right."

"But how did Disciple get this message?"

"You told Nicole to give this message to a healer, didn't you?"

"Well yes."

"Then Nicole must have given Disciple your prescription, and simply put, he healed all the children."

"Get real. Disciple didn't heal those children."

Pepe was frustrated. "Why do you say that?"

"Because people don't heal other people."

Pepe shook his head. "You know…" He paused and then continued. "I really feel sorry for you."

"Why do you say that?"

"Didn't you ask for those children to be healed?

"Well yes, but—"

"And weren't those children healed like you asked?" Now Doug did not say anything. "Even after your request was answered, it still wasn't enough for you to believe it could really happen. That's sad. I feel sorry for you." Pepe then handed the crumpled slip of paper back to Doug and walked away.

—⟹·◆·⟸—

"Tess you can't do that." Gabriel advised. "They have to use their own free will. Anyway Matthias will never agree."

"Oh, come on, Gabriel, Matthias breaks the rules all the time."

"You may get it by Matthias, but not Niac."

"Sure I can. Niac hasn't found out that your children are still alive, has he? You know how upset he was when he found out you had two children with Tina Michaels. Imagine how he would feel if he learned you didn't kill them like he commanded."

Gabriel relented. "All right, Tess, you win. What do you want?"

"I want Dr. Hunter."

"Impossible, he will never consent to go with you."

"You don't get it. I am not seeking his consent."

"You mean against his will?"

"Well maybe initially, but eventually I know I can get him to stay."

"Mother, you would risk all you are and have for your desire and lust?"

Tess smiled. She arose from the sofa. She placed her arms around his neck. "Gabriel, you don't understand, it's not for my lust. That's just a bonus."

"Then what is it?"

"Because of Nicole."

Gabriel chuckled. He placed his arm around Tess's waist. "All right, Mother," he relented, "if that is what you want."

"Then your children and my Dr. Hunter will be our little secret, agreed?"

"Agreed. When do you want to do this?"

"Tonight. We'll wait until Disciple leaves."

"And what about the others?"

"The young men, women, and children, they will go to the fields."

"And those left?"

"Kill them."

CHAPTER THIRTY-NINE

CRESTA'S SURPRISE

"**N**ow, Cresta, you have the list?"

"Yes, it is right here."

Motumbo handed her two large shopping bags. "Are you sure you don't want me to go with you? The marketplace can be rough sometimes."

She took them from him. "No, I'll be fine."

"Now your father likes the smaller bananas."

"Motumbo, I remember." She reached up and kissed him on the cheek. "Don't worry, I have done this many times."

Motumbo smiled and shook his head. "I'm sorry. Since you're mom died, I've become like a mother hen."

"It's okay. I should be back in a couple of hours."

"Cresta," Motumbo called out. She looked back toward him. "I'm glad you're home." She smiled and left by way of the kitchen door.

The three of them watched as Cresta walked across the compound toward the main gate. "Where's your sister going?" Harrison asked.

Joseph noticed the shopping bags she was carrying. "Today's market day. Motumbo probably has a long list of things for her."

Harrison handed the garden hose to Ben. "Here, you water the flowers for Motumbo, and I'll help Cresta with the shopping."

Ben moaned as he stood on his wounded leg and took the hose from Harrison. "Okay, I guess watering is better than weeding anyway." Harrison then left to follow Cresta out of the compound.

Joseph took the hose from Ben. "You sit down and rest."

"No, I'll be all right."

"You heard my father. He said you needed to rest that leg or that bullet wound would start bleeding again."

"Oh, what does that old quack know anyway."

"Now go on," Joseph commanded. "Sit and rest, Mr. Goldberg."

"You're as bossy as your father."

Joseph smiled. "I'm really sorry about your daughter. Her name was Debbie?"

"Named after her grandmother." Ben elevated his leg on a second chair. "After her mother died, she was all I had left."

"So you are alone now?"

"Yes, Debbie was all I had."

"Soon when father is gone, all I will have is Cresta."

Ben looked up at Joseph. "What about your brother?"

"I don't have a brother," Joseph answered. "Just Cresta and me."

Apparently no one has told him, Ben thought.

"What about the other one?" Joseph asked.

Ben didn't understand. "Other one?"

"Your other leg. I heard you moaning when you stood on it also."

"Yeah, it's this bum knee. Although it actually feels better in this tropical climate."

"How did you hurt it?"

"During the war."

Joseph began raking up the pulled weeds left on the pathway. "Which war?"

"World War II. When I was a boy in Auschwitz."

Joseph placed the weeds in a nearby basket. He looked back. "Mr. Goldberg, you were in one of the concentration camps?"

"Call me Ben," he said. "I've known your father for so long, I feel like a member of your family."

"Was it the same camp where my father was stationed?"

Startled by the question, Ben looked at Joseph. "You know about your father?"

Joseph nodded his head. "They tried to hide it from me, but with the bits and pieces I've heard over the years, I kind of put it all together." Joseph picked up the basket of weeds and turned toward Ben. "Was it the same camp?"

Ben looked up. "Yes, it was."

Joseph's head dropped. "I thought so." Ben watched Joseph carry and empty the basket of weeds nearby. He looked up at Ben. "I know my father worked with Dr. Mengele and was involved in his experiments on prisoners. Is that why you are after him, you know, because he's a Nazi war criminal?"

Ben was silent for a brief moment. He stood and moved the garden hose to the next set of blooming flowers. Finally he spoke. "Would it bother you, if your father was a war criminal?"

"Then it's true, my father did do all those horrible things."

"Only on the official record," Ben corrected.

"What do you mean?"

"Sometimes things are not always as they seem." He took the basket from him and set it down. He wiped the sweat from his forehead. "You need a breather. Come and sit with me. I want to tell you what happened to my leg." Joseph followed Ben back to the chairs in the gazebo and sat down.

"Cresta, wait up."

Cresta stopped. "Harrison, what is it?" she asked impatiently. "I'm not in the mood to argue today."

"That's just it—I wanted to apologize for the way I talked to you at dinner last night."

Cresta's heart softened. "Well it's just as much my fault. I'm sorry too."

Harrison shook his head. "I just couldn't believe it."

"What's that?"

"Well it has been over ten years since we've seen each other, and immediately we get into an argument."

Cresta smiled. "It's like we were never apart."

"Exactly. Anyway I'm sorry."

Cresta paused for a moment. "Would you like to go with me to the open market?" She then showed him the two large market sacks. "Motumbo has a large order he wants filled."

"I'd like that."

"Good." Cresta handed him the market sacks. Together they walked down the road toward the marketplace.

"I was just a boy when they broke my legs," Ben explained to Joseph. "Dr. Mengele took me from my parents into the laboratory. We feared the laboratory."

"Why is that?"

"Because of the screams we heard continuously coming from it. We knew people were being tortured."

Joseph was a bit reluctant to ask. He feared that his father might have been at fault. "Ben, did my father break your legs?"

"Oh no, your father wasn't even there." Joseph breathed a sigh of relief. "It was Mengele, himself, who broke them. He had me tied to a table. He took an iron bar and shattered one leg, and then he shattered the other one."

"But how could a man be so cruel?"

Ben shook his head. "You're too sheltered, my boy."

Joseph did not understand. "What do you mean I am sheltered?"

"Do you think cruelty ended with the concentration camps? Countless people have suffered, and still suffer, from man's cruelty."

"From who?" Joseph asked.

"From cruel people like Mengele, people who delight and enjoy the suffering of others."

"The world must not hear about the cruelty," Joseph surmised.

"Oh, the world hears, but it just chooses to ignore."

"Will that ever change?"

"I don't know. I just don't know."

"So when did you meet my father?"

"A few days later. I remember his eyes. They were full of compassion. Then he began to speak."

"What happened to this boy?" Dr. Krugar asked.

"His legs were broken," the nurse replied.

"Broken, both of them?"

"Yes, Doctor."

He then examined each leg. "These legs were smashed or crushed by something," Krugar spoke aloud. He then looked at each of the leg x-rays, and shook his head. "We have to fix these, or he may not be able to walk."

"Doctor, he is in a lot of pain."

"I see that. Nurse, give him up to ten milligrams of morphine as he needs it for pain."

"I can't, it's not allowed."

"What do you mean it isn't allowed?"

"Morphine cannot be used on the prisoners."

"Who made that rule?"

"Mengele, sir."

"Listen, Nurse, you do what I say, and if anyone talks to you about it, you send them to me, understand?"

"Yes, sir."

"Now where is Mengele?"

"He's in his office."

"Thanks," Dr. Krugar replied. He then turned to the boy. "Son, what's your name?"

"Ben, Ben Goldberg."

"Well, Ben Goldberg, we're going to get you something for the leg pain, and then fix your legs, okay?"

The scared boy nodded his head yes and watched Dr. Krugar leave the room.

"Cresta, I hear you have a daughter."

Cresta felt one of the fresh melons. "How did you find that out?"

"Joseph told me. Is it true?"

She smelled the melon, set it down, and picked up another. "Yes, I do."

"Is she with the Testantes?"

"No, I am no longer with the Testantes."

"Left the Testantes. I didn't think you could do that."

"You can't."

"Then they are looking for you."

She placed the melon in one of the market bags. "I'm sure they are."

"So where is she?"

"Staying with friends in the States."

Harrison followed Cresta down the narrow marketplace aisle. She stopped at the fruit stand. "So, the guy you left with?"

"Matthias?"

"Yes, Matthias—is he her father?"

"No, he isn't. That relationship with Matthias ended years ago." Cresta picked up some fresh tomatoes and placed them in her bag. She then handed the bag to Harrison to carry. "I understand you are married," Cresta continued.

"Yes, I am. How did you know?"

"I saw you with her once when I was in Boise. You were at one of the local hospitals."

"Why didn't you talk to me?"

She picked up a fresh pineapple. "How much?" The woman answered. She then placed it into her bag and paid the clerk. "I was embarrassed to talk to you."

"Embarrassed, why?"

Should I tell him about Sondra? she thought for a brief moment. *No, maybe it is best he never knows.* She handed the second bag to Harrison. "Things in my life had not worked out the way I planned."

"You mean with the Testantes?"

"I hate to admit it, but Father was right. They are evil."

"Then why did you go?"

"Because all I could see was this handsome, rich man with all his promises of wealth and power."

Harrison thought for a brief moment. "You know, I remember this shaman saying something about the Testantes that really bothered me."

"What did he say?"

"Something about them worshiping the devil."

"Worshiping the devil?" she asked.

Harrison shook his head. "I don't know why I let that nonsense bother me."

Cresta looked up at Harrison. "Maybe it bothers you because it isn't nonsense."

"You mean what the shaman said is true?"

"Testantes believe that they are adopted sons and daughters of Lucifer.

"You mean like some kind of god?"

Cresta stopped at the meat counter. "Not like some kind of god, but rather as God."

Harrison chuckled. "Well I guess it doesn't hurt anyone to worship someone that doesn't exist."

Cresta looked at Harrison. "You don't believe in Lucifer?"

"Of course not. Lucifer is a figment of people's imaginations."

She turned back to the clerk at the meat counter. "I'll take two chickens and two pounds of ham." The clerk nodded his head.

"Horns coming out of his head, a forked tail, and hooves like a horse—who would believe that?" Cresta smiled at Harrison. "What, why are you smiling?"

"Lucifer doesn't have horns, tail, and hooves. He looks like a man—" Cresta interrupted herself. Harrison could see the alarm on her face. She then ducked her head and turned away. Harrison scanned the crowded marketplace, but didn't see anything unusual.

"Cresta, what is it?" he asked.

"It's Micah."

"Who's Micah?"

"He's the leader of our clan. He must be looking for me."

"Do you think he saw you?"

"No, I don't think so. We need to get back to the compound."

"Come, I'll cover for you." He then led Cresta away from the crowd to the back of the marketplace.

"Come in, Stephen, have a seat," Mengele requested. "Now what's the problem?"

"Sir, the boy in the infirmary, we need to reduce and pin those fractures."

"We're not going to do that," Mengele explained.

"But if we don't, he may not walk again."

"Stephen, this boy's a Jew."

"So?"

"So we don't care if he walks or not. Anyway that would ruin the study."

"What study?"

"Bone healing," Mengele answered. "We are seeing what factors promote and delay bone healing."

"But, sir, those studies have already been done."

"Only on animals. Humans are not the same."

"May I remind you, Dr. Mengele, that we are physicians. We took oaths that we agreed to follow."

"We are also Nazi Germans officers, and our orders are to be followed. Do you understand, Captain?"

Stephen stared at Mengele for a brief moment. He then turned to leave. "Captain Krugar," Mengele called out. Stephen turned back to face Mengele. "You forgot to salute me."

Stephen bit his lip. He finally saluted. "That's better, Captain. You are dismissed." Dr. Krugar turned and left the room.

"So Dr. Mengele and my father did not get along?" Joseph asked.

"Not at all. Eventually your father was able to get me and my parents out of the concentration camp."

"He did?"

"Not only us, but he helped many others until he was found out and had to flee for his life." Ben then paused. "So you see, Joseph, things are not always as they seem."

Joseph nodded yes. Now he began to understand. His thoughts were interrupted by the arrival of his sister and Harrison. Both watched Harrison look back down the road to see if anyone was following.

The two men watched the others from the porch. "I will miss my family," Dr. Sullivan stated. "Do you have to tell them?"

"Yes, they will need to know."

Dr. Sullivan sighed. "I feel sorry for them."

"Why is that?"

"Because they have no idea what will be required of them." The man behind did not answer. Sullivan looked up from his wheelchair into his face. "You and I would take their place if we could, wouldn't we?"

The man looked down at Sullivan and smiled. "Yes, we would."

"This damn cancer.

"Believe me, Stephen, this is the best way. Our time is over."

Sullivan smiled. "Over...I can't believe it. It came so quickly." Both were quiet for a brief moment. "If I only knew they would succeed," he continued.

His friend knelt down next to him. "Your children are good. They are brave and have courage. You have taught and prepared them well. Rest assured, old friend, they will win this war." Sullivan took his old friend's hand in his. He knew his friend spoke the truth. They both then turned their attention to those in the compound.

Perceiving something wrong, Joseph asked, "Cresta, what's the matter?"

"Micah—he was at the marketplace."

"Micah the Testante?" Ben asked.

"Who is Micah?" Joseph asked.

"Micah is the leader of the Testantes," Cresta replied. "Mr. Goldberg, do you know him?"

"Oh, yes, Micah and I go back many years. I wonder what he is doing here."

"He's after me," Cresta explained.

"No, Cresta," a voice called from the porch. All present turned toward the voice. They watched as the same man pushed Dr. Sullivan in his wheelchair toward them. "Micah is not following you. He is following me." Harrison and Cresta's mouths fell open.

"Lone Wolf," Harrison exclaimed. "I can't believe it. What are you doing here?"

Cresta ran and took Lone Wolf's hand. She accompanied him to the veranda. The others followed with Joseph pushing his father in the wheelchair. "I'm so happy to see you again," Cresta exclaimed, "I did not know you knew my father."

Lone Wolf smiled at Sullivan. "We have been friends for many years."

"Lone Wolf helped me escape during the war," Dr. Sullivan explained. "He saved my life."

"He saved my life too," Cresta said. "Lone Wolf helped me to return home."

"But I could not save Cerce," Lone Wolf said regretfully.

"Cerce?" Harrison asked. "Was he your husband?

"Like a husband," Cresta explained. "He was a Testante like me, and a dear friend." She then explained to the group how Cerce had given his life to help her and her daughter escape.

"Daughter?" Sullivan asked. "I have a granddaughter?"

"Yes, Father."

"She is almost ten years old," Joseph added.

Sullivan looked at his son. "You knew about this?"

"Yes, I did."

"Why didn't you tell me?"

"I'm sorry, Father," she answered. Lone Wolf caught her quick glance at Harrison and then back to her father. "I told him not to tell."

I thought so, Lone Wolf thought. *That is why Cresta left her daughter with the Jordans.*

"I meant to tell you, but when I became pregnant and did not marry, I wasn't sure how you would feel."

"That is why I am here," Lone Wolf interrupted. He looked at Cresta. "I have bad news."

Horror struck Cresta's face. "Oh no, Micah found her, didn't he?"

Lone Wolf nodded his head. "I'm afraid so."

"Then Sondra is dead," she murmured.

"Oh no, Cresta," Lone Wolf said. "Sondra and Jason saw the Sprudiths coming, and they escaped." Lone Wolf looked at Harrison. "Dr. Jordan, the Testantes attacked your home."

"My home? You mean this Jason you are talking about is Jason Hunter?" Lone Wolf nodded his head yes. Now Harrison remembered Julie speaking of the girl she found in their basement. "Cresta, the girl they found in the mountains, is she your daughter?"

"Yes, she is," Cresta replied.

"And when you took her from the hospital, you left her at our home?"

Cresta was becoming uneasy with Harrison's questions. "Sondra was in danger and hurt. I didn't know where to take her."

Alarm appeared on Harrison's face. He had not been able to contact his wife for days. Now he feared the worse. He now looked at Lone Wolf. "What of my wife? Is she…" He feared to ask more.

"No, the Testantes took her alive."

"Where?"

Lone Wolf shook his head. "We don't know."

Harrison clenched his fists and started toward Cresta. "Stupidity," he raged. "Cresta, how could you?"

Joseph and Ben placed themselves between the two. "Stupidity?" she screamed back.

"Don't you know what you did?" Harrison yelled.

"I know what I did," she yelled back, "I was saving my daughter's life."

"By leaving your daughter at our home, you put my wife and other people's lives in danger." Frustrated Harrison flung his arms into the air. "How could you do such a thing?"

Cresta did not answer. For the longest time no one spoke. Tears rolled down Cresta's cheeks. Lone Wolf finally broke the silence. "Harrison, you really don't know why Cresta left her daughter at your home?"

Harrison had now settled down some. He shook his head. "No, I don't."

"Because, Sondra is your daughter too."

Stunned, Harrison turned toward Cresta. "My daughter?" he whispered. Cresta looked away.

CHAPTER FORTY
THE CAR BOMB

"Well, Mom, I'm sorry they tied you up, but what do you want me—" Again he was interrupted. "You want me to kick the what?" He paused. With disbelief he shook his head at Elaine. The language was so horrific that Jim held the phone piece away from his ear. Elaine chuckled at the one-sided conversation. "What do you mean if I loved you, I would do something?" Again Jim paused. "All right, Mom, I got to go. I promise I will. Right, love you too. Bye, Mom." Jim then hung up the receiver. "Whew, that will teach me to call my mom."

Elaine laughed, "What was that all about?"

"Ah, she's pretty upset."

"I got that from your conversation."

"It seems that yesterday afternoon the army came to the ranch and took Jason and the girl."

"Took them?"

"Yes, the children were down at the lake fishing. She's mad because they tied her up and she couldn't stop them."

"But the Army just can't do that. First they take the two dead girls, and now Jason and the third girl. I wonder where they went."

"Indian thinks they took them to Dugway. He thinks McFarland is the bold one behind all this."

"He may be right. Then Indian was there?"

"He was up the mountains with Lone Wolf when it happened. He arrived back too late to help."

"First the Sprudiths want the children, and now army intelligence. What's with these kids?"

"I don't know, but it's something very important for army intelligence to be involved. Anyway Indian is supposed to be here in the valley somewhere. Mom wants us to keep an eye out for him."

"So, your mom contacted Sheriff Bates?"

"Yes, and Sheriff Bates contacted the army."

"And what did the army officials say?"

"Oh they denied any knowledge of such a thing happening and called my mom some type of loony bird."

"I bet she was excited about that."

"Excited is an understatement. I can't repeat what she wants to do each of them."

Elaine chuckled. "Maybe we will find out something today. Open the envelope we found in that locker at the Jazz Center."

Jim opened it and handed the top letter to Elaine. He thumbed through the sheets quickly. "Elaine, this looks like some kind of journal."

"It is. It's Dr. Ed Sorenson's journal. Listen to his introductory letter." Elaine and Jim sat down at the table. Elaine began. "'My name is Edward Sorenson. I have a doctorate degree in virology from Harvard University. I have worked in germ warfare for army intelligence since graduation. Several years ago I was assigned to work with Dr. David Smith, who also has a doctorate in virology from Harvard. We worked together on a secret project at Dugway Army Base in Utah. The name of this project was The Apocalypse. I fear the two of us have done something so horrible that it may threaten the existence of all of Earth's inhabitants. If you are reading this letter, then David and I are dead. I pray this information falls into the hands of good people, who will continue to seek truth, and use this information to ensure the continued existence of this world as we know it. This is our story.'" Elaine looked up. "Should I go on?"

Jim looked at his watch. "It's getting late. Why don't we get something to eat first?"

Elaine shook her head. "No, you go, I want to stay and read."

"Okay, what kind?"

"How about Chinese?"

"Chinese sounds good." He kissed Elaine on the forehead. "I should be back in an hour."

Once he left, Elaine opened the cover to the first page of the journal, settled back against her headboard, and began to read.

In the summer of 1976, I was summoned to Utah to meet with Captain McFarland of army intelligence.

Dr. Ed Sorenson knocked on the office door. "Come in," a voice directed. He opened the door and walked in.

"Captain McFarland?" Ed asked.

McFarland stood and walked from behind his desk. "You must be Dr. Sorenson." He reached out and shook his hand. "Please come in. We've been waiting for you." McFarland pointed to the other gentleman in the room. "Do you know each other?"

"Yes, I know Dr. Sorenson," Dr. Smith replied. He extended his hand. "Hello, Ed, welcome."

"Hello, David, it's good to see you again."

"Great, now that we are all acquainted, let's get started." He motioned Ed to take a seat next to David.

"Gentlemen, you both have worked in various aspects of the intelligence community for many years. You have seen and heard many things that are top secret. But what I am about you to tell you is more classified than any information you have received previously. From now on what I am about to say can only be discussed among the three of us, understand?"

Both nodded their head yes. "Before I proceed further, you two need to understand your very lives will be sacrificed if any of this information is divulged."

"As if that is anything new?" David whispered to Ed. Ed smiled.

McFarland paused and looked at David. He knew of David's disrespect for army officers. "Before I proceed further, Smith, you and your mouth have a right to withdraw with no questions asked."

"Excuse my outburst," David relented. "Please go on."

"Okay, the main focus of your college degrees involved viruses, correct?"

"That's correct, sir."

"Good. Let me fill you in on what we are concerned about. When we captured Berlin at the end of World War II, thirty years ago, we found German scientists working on a top-secret germ warfare weapon project named 'The Apocalypse.' It caused such great fear among the top German scientists, that at one point we toyed with the idea of destroying the project without studying it further."

"Apparently we didn't," David concluded.

"That's correct."

"Figures," David murmured.

"What's that?" McFarland asked.

"Captain, it wouldn't stand to reason for our government to destroy something that could be harmful to mankind."

McFarland ignored his sarcasm. "We brought the project home, and it's been on our shelves for the past thirty years."

"So why now?" Ed asked.

"Yes," David said. "Why don't we just destroy it?"

"Recent evidence from CIA briefings have suggested that at the end of the war, there was not just one sample of these organisms but two, and we only procured the one."

"Where is the other one?" Ed asked.

"We are not sure, maybe the Soviet Republic, Israel, Africa."

"Africa?" David asked.

"That's correct. Of course both of you know how unreliable intelligence information can be, but nevertheless it is our responsibility to find out if this organism exists somewhere else in the world. If so, could it be a threat to our country."

"So, what would you like us to do?" Ed asked.

"What I would like you to do is to study it, use it, test it, find out all you can about this organism and see if it could be a potential threat to our country."

"And all we know is that the organism is some type of virus?" David asked.

"That's correct. Can you do that?"

David and Ed looked at each other and nodded. "Sure."

"Good. I have taken the liberty of supplying your lab facilities with the materials you may need. Just let my secretary know of anything else you desire, and we will get it for you." McFarland stood. Both David and Ed stood at the same time and turned to leave. "Oh, one other thing, gentlemen." They both turned back toward Captain McFarland. "No one, I mean no one, is to know of your findings except me. "

"We understand," Ed said. They both then turned and left the office.

Once they had left, McFarland picked up the phone receiver. "Secure line." He then dialed the number.

Someone answered. "Yes?"

"Michael, McFarland here. Everything has been arranged."

"Good, I'll let Matthias know."

They both then hung up the receivers.

Elaine looked up from her reading out the motel window. *Night has fallen*, she thought to herself. *Where's Jim? He should have been back by now with the food.* She then returned to the diary and began reading once again.

———⟫◇⟨———

"What do you mean I have to come in?" Jim exclaimed. "Just charge the food to my credit card."

"So sorry, Mr. Crockett," the Chinese worker said. "But there seems to be a problem with the credit card."

Disgusted, Jim answered. "All right, I'll be right in." Jim pulled away from the drive thru window and parked the car on the side lot.

An arm crossed the shoulder of the Chinese worker. "Good job, Ho Chi Minh," Scarface said as he watched Jim park the car. "He's doing just what we want."

"Ho Chin," the worker corrected.

"What?" Scarface asked.

"My name is Ho Chin, not Ho Chi Minh."

"Whatever," Scarface exclaimed and pushed the worker to the side. He and Lenny walked out the back as Jim walked in the front. "Here, try this card," Jim stated as he handed Ho another card."

"Okay, sir," Ho answered, "just a few minutes."

Jim noticed the headlines of the *Salt Lake Tribune* lying next to the cash register. He picked the paper and read the headlines. *How can this be?* he thought. He became so engrossed with the article that he did not notice Lenny and Scarface near his car.

Eventually Ho came back with his card. "This one is good," he said. He then handed Jim his credit card and the food.

Jim turned and walked out the front door. *Elaine's not going to believe this*, Jim thought to himself as he tucked the newspaper inside his jacket. He opened the door and sat down in the driver's seat. Before he could shut the door, he felt someone grab his arm and rapidly pulled him out the vehicle. "Hey," Jim yelled. "What's going on?" Next Jim felt himself fly in the air over a nearby cement wall and land painfully on his back. Another individual jumped the wall and landed directly on top of him. Jim tried to get up, but couldn't. He looked up into person's face. "Indian," he yelled. "What are you doing?"

"Cover yourself," Indian screamed.

Scarface held the public phone receiver away from his ear. Suddenly Jim's car exploded, bursting into a mushroom cloud of smoke and flames. He then put the receiver back to his ear. "Did you hear that?"

"Crockett?" the voice asked.

"Yes, General."

"Good, now I want you two to lay low until we leave for Cancun."

"Yes, sir."

"And, Scarface, good job."

McFarland and Scarface hung up the receivers. Scarface climbed into the car. "Well?" Lenny asked.

"Back to the base." Lenny started the car and sped away.

Even behind the cement wall Jim and Indian felt dazed from the impact of the blast. Finally Indian arose to his feet. "Come on, Jim, we got to get out of here." Jim was still too dazed to stand. Indian lifted him on his shoulder and carried him to another waiting car. He put Jim in the passenger's side and entered the driver's side, started the car, and fled away. They hadn't driven four blocks when Indian pulled over to the side of the road to allow the police cars with sirens to pass going the opposite way.

"Indian, you saved my life. How did you..." He paused. "I mean, what are you doing here?"

"It was Scarface and Lenny. I was following them."

"The bomb?"

"They placed it under your car while you were in the restaurant."

"But why? I don't understand."

"Well whatever you are doing, it must be making someone very nervous." Indian changed lanes, heading back into Salt Lake City proper.

"I think you are right." He pulled out the newspaper from his coat. "Look at this story." Indian quickly glanced at the headlines. "Tooele Family of Three Die in House Fire." Indian turned his attention again back on the road. "Did you know them?"

"This is Ed Sorenson's family."

"Ed Sorenson?"

"Yes, he was David's laboratory partner at Dugway." Jim then told Indian what they had learned from their visits with Debbie and Mrs. Sorenson.

"You visited with Mrs. Sorenson yesterday?"

"And today the family is dead. Elaine will blame herself when she hears this." Jim thought for a moment. "It has to be McFarland."

"I agree. By the way, where's Elaine?"

"She's at the motel waiting. The exit is a ways further."

———❦———

From the journal of Ed Sorenson…
Dr. Smith and I worked with this virus sample for the next several months. We were able to identify it as a retrovirus. But this type of retrovirus was unfamiliar to us. Most of our experiments were performed on white mice.

"David, would you come look at this?"

David stopped what he was doing and walked across the lab to where Ed was located. "What is it?"

"Well I autopsied this mouse that we injected three weeks ago," Ed answered. "Look at the mouse's ovaries."

"They're black as coal."

"With all the female mice so far, the virus has focused on and destroyed their ovaries."

"How about the testicles?"

"No, the virus doesn't seem to affect them."

David looked at Ed. "What do you make of that?"

"I'm not sure."

Suddenly Elaine's reading was interrupted by a knock at the door. She put down the journal and looked through the peephole. She then unlatched and opened the door. "Jim, where have you been?"

"I ran into some problems. I was nearly killed."

"What happened?"

"The car blew up."

"How did the car blow up?"

"Car bomb," a voice explained from behind.

Elaine turned toward the voice. Recognizing Indian, she approached and hugged him. "Where did you come from?" Before he answered, Jim explained what had happened, and how Indian had saved his life. "Why would they want to kill us?" Elaine murmured. Indian and Jim were silent. "Anyway it's good to see you, Indian. I have so much to tell you two about this journal."

"Journal?" Indian asked.

"David's message," Elaine explained. "We figured it out."

"What does it mean?"

"Well we learned that Uintathere refers to an animal that used to live in Utah, and the music symbol referred to Jazz. The message he left us was the Utah Jazz."

"You mean the basketball team?"

"When we were talking with Mrs. Sorenson, she told us that David and her husband were huge fans of the Jazz. But every time the Jazz played badly, they would call them the 'Uintathere Jazz.'"

"So that was the message that David was trying to tell us," Indian repeated.

"Mrs. Sorenson gave us a key," Elaine explained. "It fit one of the lockers at the Utah Jazz arena."

Indian looked at Jim as if to say, "This is the family that died in the fire?" Jim nodded his head yes.

"We found Dr. Sorenson's journal in the locker," Elaine continued, "and wait until I tell you what I have read."

Jim sat down at the table. "Okay, what did you read?"

Elaine looked over at Jim. "Well?"

"Well what?"

"Jim, where's the food?"

"Food?"

"Yeah, you know the stuff you went out to get."

"Well I don't have it."

"You mean you didn't get it?"

"No, I got it."

"Then where is it?" Indian started to smile. He knew what was coming.

"Elaine, the food blew up."

"You blew up our food?"

"I didn't blow up the food, the food just happened to be in the car when the car blew up."

"Why didn't you get the food out first?"

"Because I didn't stop to think about that. They were blowing me up at the time."

Elaine shook her head. "You're right, I'm sorry. You know I get cranky when I'm hungry. You did stop and get some more food, didn't you?" Indian turned his head to hide his smile. Jim did not answer. "Don't tell me you didn't?"

"Well, in all the excitement I guess I forgot."

Elaine scowled at Jim. "Give me your keys." Indian handed Elaine the keys. "I'll do it myself." She stormed out of the motel room and slammed the door. Indian and Jim sat and looked at each other for a brief moment. Suddenly they both burst out laughing.

When they had settled down Jim asked, "So you think Jason and the girl are here at the base?"

"Then you heard about them already?"

"Yes, I talked with Mom earlier, and she told me."

"My guess would be army intelligence officers. I think they brought them here to Dugway."

"I still don't understand what the Sprudiths and the army would want with Jason."

"Maybe it isn't Jason," Indian said. "Maybe it's the girl."

"The girl? I don't understand."

"Well you remember that girl they found up on Yankee Fork?"

"Yes, the one that disappeared from the hospital."

"Well it was her mother who took her from the hospital and hid her in the Jordans' home."

"Yes, Mom told me about that."

"Well the Sprudiths were going to kill her, and her mother was trying to protect her daughter. Maybe, it has something to do with this girl's ovary."

"That's another thing, Indian, how does this black ovary thing fit in?"

"I don't know, but something happened yesterday just as I was about to leave to come here."

"What was that?"

"A letter came in the mail, from that Dr. Williams in Phoenix. It was a report to the Doc stating what he found out on those girls' slides and tissue."

"What did it say?"

"Well it had some terms which I didn't understand. But in his written opinion, there were two things that stuck in my mind. He said he found two viruses instead of one. He called both of them retroviruses."

"You mean he said these three girls were infected with two germs?"

"That's right. He went on to say that he thought one virus was a mutation of the other."

"What does that mean?"

"It means that one virus changed its makeup somehow, making two types of viruses rather than one."

"But how could that happen?"

Indian shrugged. "I don't know. He said one virus caused the ovaries to turn black. He went into some terms I didn't understand to explain what happens. But the other virus did not attack the ovaries. It attacked the immune system. He said the second retrovirus is the same virus that causes AIDS."

"The second virus is the AIDS virus?"

Indian nodded his head. "Yes, all three girls were HIV positive."

"I wish Doc was here to explain this to us. I am not understanding this very well."

"Me either, so I called this Dr. Williams yesterday to see if he could explain these findings to me, and Dr. Williams was murdered two days ago."

"Murdered?"

"Yes, the same day this letter report was sent."

Jim shook his head. He looked into Indian's eyes. "What have we stumbled into?"

"I don't know, but we need Doc to help us sort this out."

"I agree, but I still don't see how Jason fits into all of this."

"Well Jason was the first to find the girl hiding in the Jordan house, and didn't tell anyone. Three nights ago, the Sprudiths found out where she was and came to the house. Dr. Jordan was back east on a trip. The Sprudiths took Mrs. Jordan and one of her friends, but the children escaped.

"Why did they take Mrs. Jordan and her friend?"

"I don't know that either, unless it is like a challenge for us to come after them."

"With the Sprudiths being involved, do you think there is any chance Mrs. Jordan and the other lady are still alive?"

"Grandfather thinks so. He feels the Sprudiths would have killed them both immediately if they wanted them dead."

"Good point. So how did the children escape?"

"Well after they escaped from the Sprudiths, by accident Grandfather and I found them. We then took them to the ranch, actually to the High Meadow cabin. We felt they would be safe there."

"Safe from the Sprudiths, right?"

"Right, but we didn't figure on the army. While grandfather and I were up in the high country visiting with—" Indian interrupted himself.

Jim looked up. "Visiting who?"

Should I tell him about Nicole? Indian thought. *No, she said to tell no one.* Indian stood and approached the coffeemaker. He poured himself a cup. "Would you like one?" he asked.

"Yes, please. Visiting who?"

"I didn't mean visiting. I meant traveling up in the high country."

Indian's holding something back, Jim thought. *Something happened in the high country that he is not telling me.*

"While we were up there, the army came and took them. I think they brought them here to Dugway."

"So first they confiscated and cremated the two dead girls without an autopsy. Now they have taken Jason and the third girl to Dugway—why?"

Indian handed the hot coffee to Jim. "Maybe it has to do with these black ovaries, AIDS, and these retroviruses that Dr. Williams referred to."

"You think so?"

"Well Solomon, Ed Sorenson, his family, and now Dr. Williams were killed for something. I don't think it was coincidence. I think somebody's trying to hide something."

"What can we do?"

"We need to find the children."

"How do we do that?" Jim asked.

"I have a plan, but we will need Elaine's help."

"What about me?" Jim asked.

"I have my suspicions that McFarland thinks you are dead. Let's let him think so at least until he finds out there wasn't a body in the bomb blast wreckage."

"So when are you going to do this?"

"If Elaine agrees, tomorrow."

CHAPTER FORTY-ONE

JULIE'S SEDUCTION

Mary opened the door to the terrace. "Julie, she said we could leave on the next available plane, so why not enjoy ourselves. The rooms are elegant, the service is the best, and the food is absolutely fabulous."

Julie grimaced. "I know. I'm just a little homesick."

Mary looked around the terrace. "Look, we're just in time. They're opening the smorgasbord." Mary looked at Julie. "Are you coming?"

"You go ahead. I'll be along in a moment." She watched as Mary left. She then sat down at a nearby table.

"My lady, is the food not to your liking?" Julie turned. It was Mira.

"No, I'm just not that hungry this evening."

Mira stopped her duties. She could see the troubled looked on Mrs. Jordan's face. "Pardon me, but is something wrong?"

"I guess I miss home."

She placed a cup in front of Julie and filled it with fresh coffee. "Here, this will make you feel better."

"Thanks." She then took a sip. "The coffee is excellent."

"Thank you. Is this what you Americans call 'homesick'?"

Julie smiled. "Yes, it is." She looked at Mira. "How about you? Don't you ever get homesick?"

Mira smiled. "Sometimes."

"Then you have a husband, too?"

"Once, but we are not together anymore."

"I'm sorry to hear that." She motioned with her head. "What about the gardener over there? I've seen you talking with him on several occasions."

Mira looked where Julie was motioning. "You mean Matt?"

"Yes, is he like a boyfriend or something?" They watched him speak with others at a nearby table.

Mira sadly shook her head. *Mrs. Jordan, if you only knew the truth about Matt, you would avoid him,* she thought. Mira looked back at Mrs. Jordan. "No, Matt is not my boyfriend. He is my master."

Julie was surprised by Mira's answer. "Your master?"

Mira realized she had said too much. "I must go." She quickly turned and left.

"But wait—" Julie pleaded, but her words were unheeded. Mira had already walked away. *Mary's right,* Julie thought, *something's not right here at this place.* Julie could see Mary was still at the buffet table. She focused again on the gardener at a nearby table. *Why am I so physically drawn to this man?* she thought. *I've been attracted to other men, but never like this.* Suddenly Matt looked up and caught Julie's glance. He smiled. Julie looked away. *Damn, he caught me staring.* Julie stood from the table. *I've got to get out of here.* She left the terrace, and began walking the compound perimeter. She reflected on Mira's words. *He is her 'master.' Is Mira some kind of slave to him? There's more to this Matt guy than Mira is willing to tell.* The full moon was now rising in the eastern sky. Julie stopped to gaze.

"It's beautiful, isn't it?"

Julie turned. It was Matt following her. *I will not answer and just ignore him,* she thought. But the words just came. "Yes, it is."

Matt was now at her side. "People think the tropical full moon looks larger than normal."

"I wonder why?"

"The natives have this legend about the moon."

Julie looked at Matt. "What's that?"

"That the love between a man and woman draws the moon closer to them."

Julie chuckled. "That sounds more like a pickup line than a legend. You made that line up, didn't you?"

Matt smiled. "Yes, I did. How good is it?"

Julie smiled back. "It's pretty good." She turned her attention again to the moon. "Look, there are all these colors in the sky."

"Come over here, you can see the various colors much better." Matt led Julie farther down the perimeter pathway until there was an opening between the trees. "There, now look at them."

"So many different colors. What are they?"

"We call them the southern lights. When the moonlight passes through the river mist, it creates all these different colors."

"How does the mist get that high in the air?"

"From the river waterfalls."

"You have river waterfalls here?"

"You mean you haven't seen Rainbow Falls?"

"No, I didn't even know there was a falls."

"Oh, the falls are so beautiful. Listen, why don't you let me show them to you?"

Julie looked up into Matt's face, his sparkling eyes, and tender smile. She knew she should say no, but… "I would like that."

"Great, we'll plan to go in the morning."

Julie noticed how easy and comfortable it was for her to talk with him. "Tell me, what are the towers?"

Matt looked at the towers. "They are called the four towers of Eden. They were built many years ago right here in the heart of this rain forest." Julie listened as Matt explained the history of the four towers. As they walked together around the compound, every so often you would hear one or both laugh. They spoke freely about many things. Matt took hold of Julie's hand. She did not resist. Before they knew it, they had completely circled the compound perimeter.

Matt stopped. He took hold of Julie's other hand and turned her toward him. "Julie, that was nice. Thanks for letting me walk with you."

She gazed into his eyes. "Yes, it was, and you're welcome."

"Then tomorrow morning at seven?"

Julie smiled. "Tomorrow at seven." Julie noticed that his face was starting to draw nearer to hers. *I think he's going to kiss me*, Julie thought.

Now she noticed that her face was drawing near to his. "Matt, you know I'm married, don't you?"

"Yes, I do," he whispered, "but it's only a kiss."

Why can't I stop myself, Julie thought. It was then that her soft lips parted and met his. Slowly she slipped into his waiting arms and warm embrace. The kiss immediately became more passionate. *I know why*, Julie thought, *it's because I don't want to stop*. Passions began to stir inside her being.

"Yoo-hoo, Julie," a voice interrupted from the terrace. Startled Julie immediately jumped back and broke the embrace.

"Yes, Mary, I'm here." She then turned to Matt. "I've got to go."

"Remember right here tomorrow morning. I'll bring a picnic basket."

Julie smiled. "I'll remember." Julie then raced up the terrace steps where Mary was waiting.

"I've been looking all over for you," Mary scolded. "You were going to rub some lotion on my sunburn."

"I forgot. Let's go up to the room right now."

Julie and Mary walked toward the elevators. "You were with that Matt guy, weren't you?"

Julie looked at Mary. "Yes, I was." The elevator doors opened and they stepped inside.

"Julie, you're happily married. Why are you messing around with this guy?"

"Come on, it was just an innocent walk."

"An innocent walk, and was that an innocent kiss also?"

Oh, great, Julie thought, *Mary saw us kiss.*

Julie remained silent. Mary turned to face Julie full front. "Listen, this guy is no good."

"Come on, you're blowing this out of proportion."

"No, listen too me. I have a bad feeling about him. If you are not careful, I fear he will seduce you."

Julie's temper flared. "Now you're way out of line."

Mary defended his herself. "Am I?"

"Yes, you are. To think I would cheat on my husband." Julie opened the door to her room. "It's none of your business anyway, so back off." She slammed the door in Mary's face.

Mary heard someone chuckling behind her. She turned. It was Matthias. He had been listening to their conversation. Mary walked over to him and glared. "Ms. Cratch, your advice for Julie is too late."

"Too late?"

"Yes, too late. Just accept what's going to happen between the two of us, and that there is nothing you can do to stop it."

Mary studied his face for a brief moment. "Who are you really?"

"Who am I? You know me. I'm Matt, the gardener."

"Gardener my butt. I've seen the way the women here look at you."

"What do you mean?"

"What do you do, hypnotize them or something?"

Matt chuckled. "I wish that were true, but women have their own minds to do what they want."

"I'm not so sure. But one thing is certain—you better stay away from Mrs. Jordan. She's a happily married woman who doesn't need you to complicate her life."

"Look, Ms. Cratch, I resent what you're imply—"

"Resent all you want, jackass, but I know you are trying to seduce Julie." Mary then paused and looked Matthias over from head to toe. "What puzzles me is why?" Mary then turned and entered her room.

From behind an arm intertwined with Matthias's own. He turned around to see Tess. "She sure has you pegged."

Matt smiled. "She is of no consequence."

"Well?"

"Well what?"

"Matthias, in two days we leave for Cancun, remember?"

Matthias smiled and took Tess into his arms. "Tomorrow, my love, I only need tomorrow."

Tess chuckled. "Not according to Ms. Cratch."

"I'll specifically derive great pleasure in Ms. Cratch's departure to the fields."

"What about Mrs. Jordan?"

"Give me until tomorrow."

Tess reached up and wrapped her arms around Matthias's neck. She passionately kissed him and then broke the embrace. "And then?"

Matthias smiled. "No different than the others," he said reassuringly. "When I am through, she's off to the fields like the rest."

———◆———

Harrison rolled over and looked at the clock. *It's 2:30 in the morning.* He couldn't stop thinking about Julie. *Where and why would have they have taken her?* Frustrated, he arose from his bed. "Maybe a walk would clear my head," he murmured. He quickly dressed and left the house by his bedroom's sliding door leading to the porch. As he gazed at the full moon, he failed to notice the person hidden by the dark.

"You're up late."

Startled, Harrison turned. He recognized Cresta's voice. Now he could see her dark outline sitting on the porch. He came closer. "I couldn't sleep."

"Yeah, me either. Would you like to join me?"

"Sure." She motioned to the chair next to her. They were quiet for a brief moment.

She turned her attention back to the moon. "It's beautiful tonight."

"I had forgotten the beauty of the African moon."

"Tell me, do you ever miss Africa?"

"All the time. If I hadn't met Julie, I think I would have come back here."

Cresta reflected back to the time when she saw Harrison and Julie together in her daughter's room. "So how do you like Idaho?"

"Oh, I like it. You surprised me earlier when you said you had been there."

"The time I saw you and your wife, I was with my daughter."

"I wish I had known. I could have met her, and you my wife."

Cresta smiled. "That would have been nice." She paused for a moment and then spoke again. "What's Julie like?"

Harrison smiled. "She's a lot like you."

"Like me? How's that?"

"Well your both pretty, sexy, and—" he paused.

"Pretty and sexy," she interrupted. "Is that all you can see in women are our physical features?"

"And that too," he chuckled.

"'And that too' what?"

"Just what you did, you know, that quick independent fire you and Julie have for that which you feel is right and true."

She smiled. "I guess I fell into that one."

They were both silent for a brief moment. "So, are you involved with anyone?"

"Cerce," she said quietly.

"Oh," Harrison said quietly, remembering the earlier conversation. "I'm sorry, that was careless of me. I don't want to bring up any painful memories for you."

Cresta looked away. "That's all right."

The silence stretched between them again. "Why did you come home?" Harrison finally asked.

"Lone Wolf and I thought I would be safer here, and I heard father was sick."

"When Joseph said your father was sick, I wanted to see him, too. Plus I have some questions to ask him."

"What kind of questions?"

"About some black ovaries we found."

Cresta was startled by his last comment, "Black ovaries?"

"Yes, your daughter, Sondra, has black ovaries."

"But why ask my father about it?"

"Your father wrote an article about black ovaries back in the 1940s."

"I didn't know that. Have you talked to him yet?"

"Not yet. There just hasn't been a real good opportunity to do so."

"Well why not now?"

"Now?"

"I took him down to his clinic office about an hour ago. In fact it's about time for me to go get him. Do you want to come with me?"

Harrison nodded his head yes. "Sure." They left the porch and walked together across the compound yard to the nearby medical clinic. As they entered, they could see a dim light coming from one of the rooms. Cresta pushed the door open. "Father, I'm back."

Sullivan looked up. "Has it been an hour already?" He then noticed she was not alone. "Harrison, what are you doing up?"

"I couldn't sleep."

"Yes, me either. This damn pain makes it hard to rest."

"Do you need your pain pills?"

"No, I'll be all right. Please, both of you come in and sit down. I just made a fresh pot of coffee." He poured two cups of coffee and refilled his own. "Now what should we talk about?"

Harrison looked at Cresta. She nodded her head as if to say, "Go ahead."

"Stephen, I wanted to talk to you about this black ovary stuff."

"Yes, you mentioned that earlier. First tell me again, why you are so interested?"

Harrison told them about the three girls and how two were dead with their ovaries missing. He then told him that Sondra, his grand-daughter, had been saved. "What happened to the other two girls?" Sullivan asked.

"That's the unusual part. The army came and took them."

The army wanting the girls, Dr. Sullivan thought, *that's not unusual.*

"They also wanted Sondra and were upset when they couldn't find her. That's when I ordered a computer search with the CDC and found your article."

"I see, and you want to know what I know."

"Yes, sir."

He looked at his daughter. She knew what her father was thinking. "You don't want me to stay. You're worried that your past will bother me."

Dr. Sullivan bowed his head. "Some things that happened in my past are not pleasant. When I pass on from this life, I have always hoped that you would think good of me. If you stay and listen, you may not."

"Please let me stay. I want to know."

Stephen studied his daughter's face. A smile slowly came over his face. "Okay, then let's begin. When I graduated from medical school, World War II had already started. I was assigned to work at Auschwitz with Dr. Mengele, Joseph Mengele."

Cresta gasped. "The Angel of Death who did experiments on the Jews?"

Sullivan nodded. "Unfortunately he wasn't the only one that performed experiments on them."

Cresta looked at her father. "You mean you—" she paused.

"Yes, I did, before I knew better." Cresta was silent and looked down.

Harrison touched Cresta's arm. "Maybe you should leave."

"No, I'll be all right. Please go on."

"Are you sure?" Sullivan asked. She nodded her head yes. "Mengele informed me of many of his experiments. At first I didn't realize that we were doing these experiments on the prisoners. Maybe it was because he was so well respected, and I felt it an honor to work with him." He began to explain his first visit with Mengele.

"Dr. Krugar, you come with good recommendations from Berlin." He extended his hand.

Stephen took and shook it. "Thank you. It is a real honor for me to work with you, sir."

"Please come in and sit down." He turned toward the cabinet behind his desk. "Care for a drink?"

"No, thank you." Stephen watched Mengele pour himself a drink and sit down across from him.

"Let me try to explain what we do here." Mengele intertwined his fingers in a fist and rested his arms on his desk. "We are here to keep the prisoners healthy, and at the same time try to find out some things about various diseases. Would this interest you?"

"Absolutely."

"Good, because I have something that will rely on your surgical skills. I'm going to assign you to the Black Ovary Research Project."

"Black ovary?"

"Yes, we've been finding black ovaries among some of the women prisoners, and we don't know why. Would you be willing to help?"

"It would be my honor, sir."

"Good."

"And then he dismissed me from his office. That's how I first came in contact with Mengele and black ovaries."

"Father, did you ever find out what caused them?" Cresta asked.

How much should I tell them? Sullivan thought. "No, not then."

"Not then? Then you encountered black ovaries again?"

"Yes, again in the late 70s and early 80s here in Africa."

Cresta didn't understand. "Why, then? I mean, why was there a gap of thirty years?"

"I'm not sure, but this time I encountered something else that was unusual."

"What was that?" Harrison asked.

"I found out that all the females with black ovaries were HIV positive."

Harrison and Cresta were stunned by his comment. "You mean the HIV virus caused the ovaries to turn black?"

"I don't think so. It wasn't that all HIV positive women had black ovaries, but rather all women with black ovaries were HIV positive."

Harrison thought for a brief moment. "How do you explain that?"

Sullivan turned around and reached into a small refrigerator behind him. "With this." He then handed Cresta and Harrison two vials. "Immunization vials. Back in the early 80s when there were so many Africans coming down with AIDS, I did some research on various things to try isolate where this virus was coming from."

"And you found the virus in these vials?"

"Not all. I isolated the retrovirus only in those immunization vials that came from one pharmaceutical company."

"Which one?"

"Tierra Madre Pharmaceutical Company out of Mexico."

"Tierra Madre," Cresta said, "means Mother Earth."

"But how did their immunizations get here in Central Africa?"

"I researched this company. Mother Earth specializes in making and donating immunizations to third world countries."

"Stephen, let me get this straight. You reason that in the late 70s and the early 80s, this Mother Earth company donated immunization vials to various African countries which may have been contaminated with the retrovirus that causes AIDS?"

Sullivan nodded his head. "Yes, I am."

"But, Father, if that's true, it would mean the AIDS epidemic was started by man and not born naturally."

"I had hoped to live long enough to find out the truth, but I will not make it."

"What would you like us to do?"

"When I am gone, I want you to continue to investigate. The world needs to know the truth."

CHAPTER FORTY-TWO
THE SHOWER

Joseph turned off the ignition. The sun was barely clearing the eastern mountains. They were silent as they watched the wild animal herds grazing in the vast green valley. Dr. Sullivan spoke first. "You know, I going to miss this place."

Joseph turned to his father. "Maybe there's still something we can do, you know like one of those cancer centers that Dr. Jordan mentioned."

Sullivan grasped his chest as the sharp pain passed through. He shook his head. "No, there isn't time." Joseph's head dropped. He knew his father was dying. "Joseph, what is it?"

Joseph could not look at him. "I can't watch you die."

"Die! Son, I'm not going to die. I'm just leaving."

Joseph was confused. "I don't understand."

"Lone Wolf is taking me home to the place we lived as boys." Sullivan smiled at the confusion on his son's face. "Imagine living in a place where there is no war, hate, hunger, pain, or suffering."

"Is that what this place is like?"

"Yes, it is."

"And you won't die there either?"

"No, I won't."

Joseph thought for a moment. "Then you must go." He paused. "And I will go with you."

Dr. Sullivan smiled and shook his head no. "No, you can't. It's not your time."

Sullivan could see his son's disappointment. *What great faith Joseph has*, he thought. *He has believed every word I said without any doubt.*

Stephen reached into his pocket and pulled out a small leather pouch and handed it to Joseph. "Here, this is for you."

Joseph felt the leather covering. "It feels like a book."

"It is."

Joseph unzipped the leather covering and removed the book. He scanned the first few pages. "Father, I can't read this language."

"I know. I should have prepared you better."

"Prepared me for what?"

"For the Apocalypse."

Joseph was stunned by his answer. "You mean the end of the world."

Stephen nodded his head. "Lone Wolf and I came first to prepare the way. Now it is your destiny to help usher in the Apocalypse."

"But, I know nothing about the Apocalypse.

"With the instructions in this book, you will. And there is something else." Joseph looked up. "You must find and give this book to someone."

"Who?"

"Your older brother. He will know what to do with it."

Joseph was stunned by his father's words. "I have a brother?"

"Yes, you do."

"But you've never mentioned him before."

"I couldn't. After the war he and his mother had to be hidden. Their lives were in great danger."

Danger from what? Joseph thought.

Sullivan nodded to his side of the jeep. "Come, help me out. It is time to go." Joseph came around to the other side of the vehicle. He opened the door and helped his father out. "Ah, good, Lone Wolf is here."

Joseph looked around him but didn't see anyone. "Where?"

"Behind you."

Joseph turned to see him standing there. "Lone Wolf, I didn't see you come." He searched the area. "Where's your vehicle?"

"Son, he doesn't need a vehicle. He travels in a different way."

Lone Wolf watched Sullivan wince with pain. "Your time is drawing near."

He winced a second time with pain. "I know. I can feel it."

"Then we better leave soon."

"Wait, you're not leaving yet, are you?"

"I'm afraid we have to. Your father hasn't much time."

"But what about the others? Aren't you going to tell them good-bye?"

"It's best this way."

"You know they will have questions."

"Don't worry. I promise, you will not need to explain. Their hearts will comfort them and tell them what they have to do."

Joseph looked at his father and Lone Wolf. "Will I ever see you two again?"

They both smiled. "Many times. Our separation will only be for a little while."

"Joseph, you will be fighting a battle, and we will be fighting this battle with you, only from a different place." He extended his hand. "Good-bye, Joseph."

Joseph took his hand. "Good-bye, Lone Wolf."

Joseph turned to his father. Tears formed in his eyes. "I will miss you."

Sullivan's eyes moistened too. They threw their arms around each other. "I will miss you too." Sullivan broke their embrace. His hands grasped both of Joseph's shoulders. "Remember, I will always be with you." He stumbled as he turned. Lone Wolf caught and helped him walk some distance away. Joseph was now standing alone. "You know what I will miss the most?" Sullivan whispered."

Lone Wolf watched Sullivan staring at his son. "Yes, I know."

Sullivan looked at his old friend and smiled. "Are you ready?"

"Yes, I am ready."

Lone Wolf bent space. In an instant they were gone.

⋙◆⋘

Pepe looked around. "Disciple, there aren't any walls."

"Yes, I know." Disciple stripped off his clothes and turned on the shower.

"You mean you don't separate the men and women?"

"Don't worry, no one here even cares."

"But I care."

"Pepe, if you don't take a shower, then you'll have to sleep in another tent."

"Why?"

"Because you stink."

Doug watched as Disciple stepped naked into the community shower. Pepe and Doug then smelled each other. "Pepe, we really do stink."

"Sí, I know, but to shower with naked women?"

"So that's what's bothering you."

"Yes, that's what's bothering me. What if..." Pepe paused. "You know."

"What if what?" Doug asked.

Pepe nodded his head toward his lower body. "You know, what if it gets stimulated?" he whispered.

Disciple was listening to the conversation. "Come on, Pepe, just use your mind to control it."

"Control it? Disciple, you got to be kidding!"

"Well it works for me."

"That's because you're a two-thousand-year-old man. Yours probably doesn't work anymore, anyway." Doug attempted to hide his smile. "That mind thing crap just doesn't work for me."

"Why not?" Disciple asked.

"Because mine has a mind of its own, that's why."

Doug chuckled at the conversation. "Listen, Pepe, why don't you do what I am going to do."

"What's that, boss?"

"Just get into the shower, shower, and not look at anyone."

"Think it will work?"

"Well that's what I'm going to do."

Pepe took a deep breath and blew it out. "Okay, I'll try it."

Both Doug and Pepe undressed and turned on their showers. "Disciple, did you get a chance to look at the language on that microfilm sheet?"

"Yes, I did. The words are an ancient Hebrew dialect. That's why no one could read it."

"Hebrew? Boss, did Tina know Hebrew?"

"I doubt it."

"The message isn't Tina's," Disciple explained further. "It's a written message from Tina's husband named Gabriel to a man named Matthias."

"I've never heard of either one," Doug stated. Although Disciple knew both men very well, he dared not say anything further. "Did you find out what the message said?"

"Not yet, I need a little more time."

"Can we come in," a voice asked from behind.

Pepe looked over his shoulder to see Maggie naked being helped into the shower with two other naked women. "Ah, Maggie," Pepe exclaimed closing his eyes tight. "We're naked in here. Can't you come back later?"

"Oh, Pepe, you ain't got nothing I haven't seen before. Now you're not going to rape us, are you?" Maggie chuckled.

Pepe choked. "Maggie, that's not even funny. You know we're not that kind of people."

Maggie continued to chuckle. "Well that isn't how yesterday's newspaper described you."

"Come on," Pepe exclaimed. "You know that article is a bunch of crap. We wouldn't hurt anyone."

Maggie stopped and grabbed one of Pepe's large love handles. "I can't believe that?"

"Now cut that out. This is serious business."

"Oh, I'm only teasing."

"I know, but boss and I think we are in real trouble."

"What bothers me," Doug added, "is that the press can get away with printing those lies."

Disciple turned to Doug. "Back at the prison, didn't you say you saw Warden Parks come into the room, when we were escaping?"

"Yes, he did."

"I remember Warden Parks, when I was in there," Maggie said. "He was a real horse's butt. At least he won't bother you anymore."

"Why is that?" Pepe asked.

"Didn't you read this morning's paper? Warden Parks and two women prisoners named Ellen and Marge were found dead last night at the prison."

"Did it say what happened?" Doug asked.

"Only that they blame you and Pepe for their deaths," Maggie answered.

"But they were still alive. Just before I ducked under the water, I saw Warden Parks, Ellen, and Large Marge come through the secret passageway into the inner prison together."

"Well someone killed them," Maggie said.

"You two will need to stay down here for a while," Disciple informed. "It will be too risky for you to leave the city."

"For how long?" Doug asked.

"Two weeks. By then maybe we could slip out of the city."

Pepe noticed one of the naked ladies that accompanied Maggie staring at him. "Boss," Pepe whispered.

"What?"

"That woman there is looking at me."

"So don't look back."

Disciple could hear the two murmuring. "What's the matter?"

"Oh, Pepe thinks one of the women is staring at him."

"Just ignore her," Disciple suggested. He then handed Pepe a bar of soap. "If you lather up real good, soon you'll forget you're even naked."

Pepe lathered up his face with soap. *Two weeks*, Pepe thought. *I'll never make it down here two weeks.* Just then he felt a hand touch his shoulder. "Hey," he yelled. Startled, he backed away. He tried to peer through the soap on his face only to have it burn his eyes.

"Susan," Maggie exclaimed, "what are you doing over there with Pepe?"

Susan, Pepe thought, *over here with me?* He quickly washed the soap from his face. He opened his eyes to see Susan, the same young woman who had been staring at him.

"Disciple, there's this naked lady standing next to me."

Disciple looked over. "Yes, that's Susan."

"Well what does she want?"

"Maybe she wants to borrow your towel," Doug teased.

"Oh, real funny, boss."

Susan did not say anything initially, but kept staring at Pepe. Doug recognized her as the person that Disciple pointed out earlier, who heard voices and saw visions. In his medical mind he knew she was schizophrenic.

"May I shower next to you?" she finally asked Pepe. Stunned, Pepe tried to speak but the words wouldn't come.

Doug and Disciple smiled at each other. "Sure, Susan," Disciple finally replied for Pepe. "Please join us."

Pepe quickly turned his front away from her and began lathering his body again with soap. Every so often he would look over at Susan only to see her staring back at him. "Are you the one they call, Pepe?" she finally asked.

Pepe looked at her again and answered. "Yes, I am."

She again tried to touch his shoulder, but Pepe backed away quickly. "Susan," Disciple finally said. "Do you want Pepe for something?"

"I want to warn him."

"Warn me of what?"

"You must leave. They are coming to hurt you."

"Who's coming to hurt me?"

She did not answer. She turned off her shower, wrapped her towel around her, and returned to help Maggie. "Well, men," Maggie exclaimed, "thanks for the show."

"Anytime, Maggie," Disciple chuckled.

Pepe gave Disciple a frown. They watched as the three women left the shower area. "That Susan lady's crazy," Pepe said firmly. "She gives me the creeps."

"Crazy, maybe," Disciple agreed, "but don't downplay her visions."

"What do you mean?" Doug asked.

"Some of her visions have helped people. I'm going ahead to talk with her some more." They all three dressed quickly and reentered the arena. Disciple ran forward to catch up with Susan.

⟫◆⟪

Mary frowned in disgust. She paced the lobby and then returned to Mira. "What do you mean they left together?"

"They left early this morning for Rainbow Falls."

"Where's that?"

"It's about a two-mile walk from here."

"Why didn't you tell me they were leaving?"

"Because Matthias asked me not to awaken you."

"And you listened to that jackass? Dammit, Mira, I thought Tess told you to take care of Mrs. Jordan."

Mira defended herself. "She did."

"Then why didn't you go along with them?"

"Well I was going to go—"

"But the gardener told you to stay, right?" Mary interrupted.

"That's right. He said he wanted to be alone with Mrs. Jordan."

"You bet he wanted to be alone, so that swamp slime could nail my friend."

"Nail your friend?"

"You know, seduce her. Now tell me where in hell this place is."

"It's kind of hard to find."

"But you know where it is, right?"

"Well yes, but—"

"But nothing. I want you to take me there."

Mira shook her head no. "Please, Ms. Cratch, I can't do that."

"Why can't you?"

"Because I would be severely punished if I did."

"By a gardener? Come on, what can a gardener do to you, unless—" Mary interrupted herself. She paused for a few seconds. "Unless I am right, and that scumbucket isn't a gardener at all." She again turned back to Mira. "Please, take me to them. He'll destroy her and her marriage, and you know in your heart she doesn't deserve this."

Mira knew Mary was right. She knew Matthias would devastate Julie's life, the same way he had hers and countless others. She knew she could not let this happen. She came out from behind the counter. "Come, I'll show you the way."

CHAPTER FORTY-THREE
THE SEDUCTION

Motumbo parked the car in the compound. He rushed into the house. "Motumbo," Cresta called out, "where is everyone?"

Motumbo looked up quickly then turned away. He did not want her to see his red, swollen eyes. "Well I just took Mr. Goldberg to the airport. He's trying to catch an early flight back to the states." Keeping his head down, he quickly passed by Cresta and into the kitchen.

"But I was going with him. He thought he knew where Sondra was."

"I told him that, but he said someone else needs your help more than Sondra does."

"Who would need my help more than my own daughter?"

"He said that it was your destiny to help Dr. Jordan find his wife. He also said in your heart you already know this."

Cresta threw the magazine she had been reading across the room. "Damn him. That destiny crap is a bunch of bull." She then stood and began pacing. "Why would I care about Harrison's wife over my own daughter?" Motumbo cleared his throat and nodded his head in Harrison's direction. Cresta turned toward Harrison. "Did you hear?"

"Yes, I heard."

"Listen, I didn't mean it that way—"

"I know you didn't, and you're right. Your daughter should come first."

Motumbo noticed Harrison's stare as he came closer. He quickly ducked to hide his face.

"Motumbo, your eyes are all swollen."

Motumbo wiped the excessive tears. "Ah, these bloody allergies, they really get to me this time of year."

"You've never had allergies before," Cresta said. Now she came closer. "You've been crying, haven't you?" Motumbo looked away, and Cresta became alarmed. "It's my father, isn't it." Motumbo paused for a brief moment, then nodded his head yes. "Where is he?"

Motumbo turned to face her. He was initially silent. "He's gone."

Harrison approached Motumbo. "You mean Dr. Sullivan passed away?"

"No, I mean he left early this morning. He said he didn't want to be here when he died."

"Does Joseph know?" Cresta asked.

"Yes, he knows. He went with your father." Suddenly a vehicle pulled up in the compound. The three looked at each other. "It must be Joseph," Motumbo suggested. All three exited the house to the porch. They watched as Joseph climbed out of the vehicle and approached them. They waited for him to speak. He looked up and realized they were all staring at him. "What?" he asked.

"Master Joseph," Motumbo finally asked, "are you all right?"

"Sure."

"Well, can I get you anything?"

Joseph thought for a moment. "How about a sandwich? I'm kind of hungry."

Motumbo smiled. "Right away, sir." Motumbo excused himself and went back into the house.

"Kind of hungry? Joseph, is that all you can think of—food? What about our father?"

Joseph collapsed on the nearby lounge chair. "Boy am I tired. Father and I were up very early this morning." Cresta and Harrison sat down across from him.

"Well?"

"Well what?"

"Our father, is he all right?"

"Father's gone."

"Gone. You mean he's dead?"

"No, not dead. He's just kind of gone."

"How can he be 'kind of gone'?" Cresta asked impatiently.

"Because he is. Early this morning we were up on the ridge. I helped him out of the car." Motumbo brought Joseph a sandwich on a plate with a glass of milk.

"Here you are, Master Joseph."

"Oh, this looks good. Thanks." He picked up the sandwich and took a bite.

"Okay, you helped Father out of the car, and then what happened?"

"He and Lone Wolf disappeared."

"Disappeared?" Harrison asked. "You mean they walked or drove away."

"No. I mean Lone Wolf kind of waved his hand, and both he and father just disappeared into thin air."

Harrison was confused. "But, how can two men disappear into thin air?"

By bending space, Cresta thought. *Lone Wolf has taken Father to the mountain people.*

———⊱◈⊰———

"How much farther?"

"Not far now, it's just up ahead."

They walked in silence until Mary spoke. "Tell me, Mira, why does Matt have such a hold on you and the other women at the tower?"

"What do you mean?"

"I have noticed how you and all the others seem to indulge his every whim." Mira did not answer. "He's not really a gardener, is he?"

"No, he's not the gardener."

"What is he?"

"He's our Lord and Master."

"Lord and Master! What kind of talk is that?" Again Mira did not answer. Mary could tell she was hesitant. "Come on, what's really going on here? What is this guy trying to prove with Julie?"

Mira thought and then began to explain. "To him Julie Jordan is just a challenge. He cares nothing for the feelings of others. Once Matthias conquers her, like the rest of us, he will become her Lord and Master also."

Frustrated, Mary shook her head and threw her hands into the air. "This is so completely unbelievable. What's wrong with all you women? Why don't you stand up to this lowlife butthead?"

Mira attempted to explain. "Look, Ms. Cratch, you just don't understand. It's not that easy."

"What do you mean, it is not that easy. You act like you are his slaves."

"In a sense we are his slaves, but we are willing slaves, desiring to fulfill all his wants and desires."

Mary was disgusted. "This makes me sick. No man has the right to be Lord and Master over any woman."

"I know you're right, but in our hearts all of us want to be with him, forever."

Again Mary shook her head. "All I know is that if this turd touches Julie Jordan, I'm personally going to rip off his testicles."

Mira smiled.

⟫◆⟪

Harrison placed his bags near the door. "Did you get a ticket?" Cresta asked.

"No, I'm on standby."

"That may be awhile. Would you like a cup of coffee?"

"That sounds good."

Cresta poured a cup and handed it to him. "When is your tentative flight out?"

Harrison sat down at the kitchen table "Hopefully sometime this evening."

Cresta sat down across the table. "Listen, I'm sorry about what I said earlier about your wife."

"Forget it, we're both emotionally upset."

"Do you know this General McFarland guy that took the children?"

"No, I've never met him, but Mr. Goldberg told me some things about him last night. He thinks this McFarland may be responsible for his own daughter's death. Someone you definitely can't trust."

Cresta sat down across the table from him. "I can understand why the Sprudiths would want my daughter, but why would the army want her also?"

"Lone Wolf thinks it's for the same thing, this black ovary stuff, and this McFarland and the Sprudiths are somehow connected."

"What do you think?"

Harrison bit his lip. "I just don't know, but Lone Wolf's grandson is already looking for the children. Believe me, if anyone can find the children, he will."

Both took sips of their coffee. "So, what are you going to do first?"

"To be perfectly honest, I don't even know where to start." He looked at Cresta. "Motumbo said Mr. Goldberg returned to the states this morning. I thought you planned to go with him?"

"I was, but he left without me."

Harrison didn't understand. "That doesn't make sense. Why would he do that?"

"Something about my destiny was not to find my daughter."

"Well Mr. Goldberg is wrong. Your first priority is to find your daughter."

Cresta took another sip of her coffee. She then put her cup on the table. "No, I've thought about it, and I think Mr. Goldberg is right."

"You do?"

"Harrison, I think I'm supposed to go with you. I think I'm supposed to help you find your wife."

"No, it will make it easier for Micah and the Testantes to find you. Anyway, there's a good chance Julie may be dead."

Cresta subtly shook her head. "No, I know how the Testantes think. Lone Wolf is right. If Micah wanted Julie dead, he would have killed her instead of taking her."

"But why would they want her? She knows absolutely nothing."

"It is not the Sprudiths and her knowledge they want. Someone else wanted her."

"Who?

Cresta watched Harrison pace. *I can't tell him*, she thought, *it would break his heart.*

"You know, I don't even know where to begin to look for her."

"Matthias."

"What?"

"We begin with Matthias."

"You mean the same Matthias—"

"Yes, the same that took me away years ago. There's a good chance she is with him."

"But why would Matthias want her? I don't understand."

"Harrison, do you remember how you felt when Matthias came for me?"

"Yes, I remember." He looked away. *I thought my heart would break*, he thought.

"I was with them so long, I know how they think."

"Then you know a way to find Julie?" Harrison waited for an answer. She glanced at Harrison and then away. "What is it?"

Cresta shook her head. "No, it's too dangerous." He sat down across from her. She became uncomfortable with his silence. "My idea is dangerous. There's a very good chance we would lose our lives or be sold to the fields."

He stood up and sat down next to her. "You're right. You shouldn't go because you have a daughter. She needs you, but you could tell me how."

"You'd never make it. You wouldn't stand a chance and only a very little one with me along.

Harrison took her hand. "Don't you see, Cresta? I have to try."

—◦◦◦—

Matthias placed the picnic basket in his right hand and extended his left down to her. "Take my hand." Julie reached up and grasped it. He then was able to help her up the rocks to the plateau. "That should be the last one."

"I sure hope so. That's quite a walk."

Matthias smiled. "Believe me, it's worth the climb."

Julie expected him to let go of her hand, but he didn't. He led her to a grassy knoll overlooking a small lake well hidden by cliffs and trees. Julie looked over the valley. She watched as the water fell from the high cliffs into the lake. "This is beautiful."

Matthias pointed with his hand. "Can you see them?"

"See what?"

"The two rainbows. There's one on each side."

Julie stepped to her left for a better view. "Yes, I see them."

"But most people miss the third one." He placed his arm around Julie's shoulders. He pointed again to the base of the falls. "See it right there?" Julie was more conscious about his arm around her shoulders than the third rainbow. She couldn't understand why she didn't seem to mind.

"Yes, I see it too."

"Come," he said. He laid the blanket on the soft grass. There they sat laughing and talking for the next couple of hours. Matt looked at the noonday sun high in the sky. "It's so warm, let's go for a swim."

"Oh no, you go ahead."

Matt pulled off his T-shirt and looked at her. "Are you sure?"

"I don't have a bathing suit." Matt laughed out loud. "What so funny?"

"Well here in Eden we don't use bathing suits." She was stunned as she watched him undressed.

"But I'd be too embarrassed."

"Embarrassed? I bet you're beautiful naked." Julie smiled. "I hope you change your mind." Julie's passions once again stirred as she watched him turn and dive into the water.

Mira and Mary rounded the corner. Mira stopped. "There," she said.

Mary could see the two of them. Matt was in the water, and Julie was on the shore. "Why that son of a pig is swimming naked. We better get up there quick before something happens." Mary continued down the pathway toward the lake. She then turned back. "Aren't you coming?" Mira shook her head no. "Why?"

"Once Matthias learns I led you here, I will be sent to the fields."

"What in hell are these fields?" Mary asked. Mira did not answer. Mary turned back and approached Mira. She gently grabbed both shoulders and looked her in the eye. "Okay, then you stay here, and I'll go alone." Mira nodded her head yes. Mary now smiled. "One other thing."

"What's that?"

She put her arms around the girl, and pulled her close. "I know it took courage to bring me here." She then broke the embrace and looked back into her eyes. "Thanks." She turned and followed the trail alone. Mira hid herself behind some nearby bushes and watched.

Matt swam near the edge of the water. He stood up. The water was barely to his waist. "Come on, Julie, the water is great."

How Julie wanted to go to him. "Is it cold?"

"Just perfect—not too warm and not too cold." Matt still could feel her resistance, but he was experienced in these matters. "Listen, I'll turn my back while you undress. That way I will not see anything. Will that make you more comfortable?" He waited for an answer. "I promise, I won't look." Still there was no answer. "Julie, can you hear me?" Suddenly there was a splash in the water off to his right. Matt looked and smiled. "She did it." Her smooth swim stroke hardly broke the water. He dove in after, and followed her to the rocks near the waterfall.

"Hello, Mira," a voice spoke from behind.

Startled, Mira turned. She gasped. "My lady, what are you doing here?"

Tess knelt down next to Mira and watched the two swimming in the lake. "The same as you, following the man I love."

"What do you mean?"

"Don't your passions stir within you when you see him swim?" Tess asked. Mira did not answer, but Tess was right. "Don't you wish it was you down there with him instead of Julie Jordan?" Again Mira did not answer. Tess turned and looked into Mira's eyes. "You fear answering me, don't you? I already know you sleep with Matthias when I am gone."

"No, my lady, that is not—"

"Don't lie. Matthias has already told me the truth."

Mira looked at Tess, and then returned her gaze to Matt and Julie. "I'm sorry, but I have never been able to resist his advances."

Tess also looked back at the two swimming. "Because of the gift he was given, very few women can."

Mira was confused. "What gift?"

Tess did not explain what she meant. "Bringing Ms. Cratch here, you know you will be sent to the fields, don't you?" Mira nodded her head. "Then why betray your master?"

When Mira turned to face Tess, she noticed tears in Mira's eyes. "Matthias destroyed my hopes, my dreams, and my marriage to my one true love." Mira looked at Ms. Cratch walking up the hill. "Maybe if someone like Mary was there for me, I would not be here today."

Her servant's words touched Tess's heart, for she too had been torn from her marriage. Tess reflected on that day so many years ago.

"Please, Matthias, do not take her and the children."

Matthias stopped at the doorway. He shook his head. "My dear brother, you embarrass me. What kind of a man would beg like this? Don't you have any pride?"

Tess entered from the back room and heard the conservation. "Matthias, don't make this any harder. Just put the children on the camels, and I will be with you shortly."

Matthias wrapped his arms around her, only to taunt his brother, and kissed her passionately. He looked at his brother. "Even when we were children, I always got what I wanted." He then turned and left.

Tess turned to her husband. "Please, don't make this any harder."

"But, Egyptess, I don't understand."

She reached up and wiped the tear from his cheek. "Husband, how could you not know? Matthias and I have been lovers even before our marriage. I was with him every time he came to visit or when we visited him in Jerusalem."

Tess could see sadness fill her husband's countenance. "All this time?"

She nodded her head yes. Now the tears began to flow down Tess's cheeks also. "I have chosen another way of life. I don't want to live life your way." Tess now turned to leave.

"Egyptess," he called after her.

Tess turned back to him. She then enclosed her arms around him and held him tight. "John, I am so sorry. I will always love you." She then kissed him on the cheek, turned, and walked out of her previous life.

Mira's voice brought Tess back to the present. "Look, my lady, I fear she will not be able to resist his advances." Tess also knew this to be true.

Both their heads broke the surface of the water at the same time. They both laughed at the same time. "The water, this place, they're just beautiful."

Matt smiled. "And so are you."

Their laughter stopped. The looks on their faces became more serious. *He's going to seduce me*, Julie thought. He placed his arm around her waist. *How can I do this?* She moved into his open arms and pressed her body against his. She put her arms around his neck. *I can't stop myself.* His lips touched hers with gentle, soft kiss that grew more intense with time.

"Julie Jordan," a voice screamed from the shore. "What in the hell's name are you doing?" Their embrace abruptly ended. They both looked toward the shoreline. "You get your butt over here right now and put some clothes on."

"You fat pig!" Matthias raged. "What are you doing here?" Julie stared at Matthias. She was shocked by his words. She tried to pull away, but Matthias wouldn't let her go. "How did you find us anyway?" He then looked in the direction that Tess and Mira were hiding.

"Listen, if you don't let Julie go right now, I'll personally rip off your testicles—understand, hot shot?"

"You bitch," he raged. Julie was able to break away and swim to the shore. "You will pay for this."

Mary wrapped a towel around Julie when she reached the shore. "As if I am scared," Mary sarcastically replied. "Why don't you go play with yourself, you big spoiled jackass." Mary helped Julie with her clothes and they started back down the pathway.

Matthias's frustrated yell echoed off the canyon walls. Mira and Tess watched. "Well, Mira, was it worth it?"

Mira turned toward Tess and smiled. "Yes, my lady, better than I could have imagined." Tess returned the smile.

CHAPTER FORTY-FOUR

VISIT TO BASE

Indian knocked on the adjacent motel room door. "Elaine, are you ready?"

Jim stood behind. "Indian, I don't like this."

"Well I don't like it either."

Elaine opened the door. "Don't like what?"

"You seeing him. He's too dangerous."

Elaine encircled her arms around Jim's neck. "I know, but what choice do we have? We need to find the children."

Jim knew she was right. "Okay, but be careful."

Elaine gave him a quick kiss. "I will." She turned toward Indian. "Let's go."

Indian nodded his head and followed her out. He stopped short of the door and turned back. "Don't worry, I'll watch her close." Jim nodded his head in agreement. "We should be back in a few hours."

Indian then closed the door. Jim took a deep breath and blew it out. He walked over to the coffee maker and poured a cup, and then sat down at the table where he had left Dr. Sorenson's journal open. "Now where was I?" he murmured. "Dr. Sorenson was explaining their work on the virus."

We knew that the virus turned female ovaries black, but didn't understand the significance. We felt the black ovaries were black pigment deposited into the ovary because of scarring and bleeding. We did some experimenting with mutating this virus, but it didn't seem to make any difference with regard to clinical outcome. Only the original virus turned the ovary black. We felt McFarland knew more than what he was telling us. Our suspicions were confirmed one day when we were reporting to him.

"What do you mean you found nothing? My superiors want some results."

"Superiors?" Dr. Sorenson asked. "Captain, I thought this was a top secret endeavor only among the three of us."

"Well there are others," McFarland said.

"Who?" David asked.

"That's confidential."

David smiled at Captain McFarland's frustrations. "Well just like Ed said, we found nothing."

"But a previous report informed us that this virus did something to the female reproductive system."

"Previous report?" Sorenson asked. "You didn't tell us about any previous report."

David slipped forward on his chair. "You mean someone else has studied this virus earlier, and you didn't tell us?"

"What difference would that make?"

"It makes a world of difference in how to test this virus."

"Captain," Sorenson explained, "don't you understand that having this information would have saved us countless hours. It would have allowed us to formulate more specific tests. Why didn't you tell us?"

"I wasn't allowed."

"Wasn't allowed," David exclaimed. "What else have you withheld from us?"

McFarland became angry. "You are only told what you need to know. You are dismissed."

We could tell that McFarland was suspicious. He felt we were not telling him all we knew, and he was right. Why we didn't destroy the virus then, I don't know, but unfortunately we elected instead to shelf the Apocalypse project.

Jim looked at his watch. It had been an hour since Indian and Elaine left. He looked out the window at the coffee shop across the street. "I'm kind of hungry." He picked up his jacket, the journal, and left the motel room.

———⊰•⊱———

"I'm sorry, ma'am," the guard said. "Your ID card is not being recognized. I can't let you on the base."

"I've never had a problem before."

"Well someone has put a block on your pass."

"Do you know who?"

"Sorry, but I don't."

"Well, Corporal, can you call the general?"

"General McFarland?"

"Yes, General Arthur McFarland. He's the person I want to see."

"I don't know, that's not standard procedure."

"Listen, the general and I are old friends. Please, just contact his office for me. I will take the blame."

The guard looked at the cars behind her starting to back up. "Wait a minute, ma'am, and I'll contact his office."

"Thank you."

The guard dialed the number. "General McFarland's office."

"This is Corporal Harris at the gate."

"Yes, Corporal."

"I'm sorry to bother you, but I have an Elaine Smith, used to be Robbins, with a restricted pass who is insistent about seeing General McFarland. She says she is an old friend."

"Hold, and I will check." The secretary then summoned the general.

"Yes, Peggy."

"Sir, there is an Elaine Smith, used to be Robbins, who claims she is an old friend and would like to see you."

Elaine is here. This should be interesting, he thought. "Tell the gate to let her pass."

"Yes, General." Peggy again placed the telephone receiver to her ear. "Corporal, the general says to let her pass."

The guard hung up the phone. "Okay, ma'am, the general says you can pass."

"Thanks." The guard rail rose and Elaine drove forward. "We're in." Indian pushed the backseat forward and cautiously crawled out from the space. "What do we do now?"

Indian looked over the large main parking lot. He motioned with his finger. "Park over there by those bushes. They should hide me." Elaine pulled into an empty parking space right next to them. She turned the car off. "I know you detest this guy, but I need at least an hour."

"Yes, I know."

"And be careful. He's smart, cunning, and will suspect you of everything."

"Don't worry, I have done this many times."

"Elaine." She looked at Indian in the rearview mirror. "I would never ask if it weren't for the children."

Elaine placed her hand back behind the seat and grasped his. She gave it a squeeze. "You know, you and Jim are the only family I have now." She looked at him in the mirror. He nodded his head yes. She smiled and let go of his hand. "But only one hour." Elaine opened and closed the door. She walked up the steps into the administration building. "I can do this," she whispered to herself. "I can handle one hour with this jack of an ass." Indian too left the vehicle and entered the bushes.

<hr />

"I'll have the country special with coffee," Jim said.

"Very good, sir," the waitress replied.

Jim opened Sorenson's journal once again and began reading.

I attended a conference in Miami put on by Disease Control Center when I first met her. I was sitting alone at one of the conference tables when she introduced herself.

"Hello, I'm Dr. Tess Thompson from Dallas."

"Hi, I'm Dr. Ed Sorenson from Salt Lake City."

Dr. Thompson extended a greeting hand. "Well, Dr. Sorenson from Salt Lake City, it's nice to meet you."

Ed grasped her extended hand. "Dr. Thompson, it's nice to meet you too."

She motioned to the seat next to his. "Anyone sitting here?"

"No."

"Do you mind?"

Ed pulled out the chair for her. "Please, have a seat."

We became very well acquainted. She was a beautiful, attractive woman with such charm and poise. She stated she was clinical microbiology profes-sor at Baylor University specializing in virology. She was quite impressed to learn that I worked in the germ warfare department for army intelligence. I should have seen what she was doing, but I don't ever remember a beautiful woman wanting to discuss viruses with me. We both took vigorous notes of the conference. Finally a break came, and she leaned over to me.

"Whew, that's a lot of information."

"It sure was."

She motioned to Dr. Sorenson rubbing his hand. "What's wrong?"

"Ah, sometimes I get this writer's cramp."

"Here, I know what to do for that." She took his hand in hers. "There's this special massage that will take the ache and pain away. I learned it from this monk in Tibet."

Her hands were so soft as she gently rubbed his. "So, Dr. Thompson, you do a lot of traveling?"

"Oh, yes, I love to travel. Been all over the world. How about you?"

"Not much, but maybe someday."

"So, Ed—you don't mind if I call you Ed, do you?"

"No, of course not."

"So, Ed, are you married?"

"Yes, Dr. Thompson—"

"Call me Tess," she interrupted.

"Yes, Tess, two years."

"Me too, but a bit longer than you. He works for a pharmaceutical company. Any children?"

"No, no children."

"Me neither, but maybe someday." She released his hand. "Does that feel better?"

Ed moved his hand. "Yes, it does."

She smiled at him. "I knew it would." She then looked at her watch. "Listen, the conference will be over in two hours, would you like to have dinner with me tonight?"

Ed was hesitant. "Well I don't know."

"Listen I know this fabulous French restaurant where the food is excellent." Again Ed hesitated. "Please, I don't know anyone here, and I hate to eat alone."

"Well, I guess it would be all right."

Jim looked up from the journal. "What was that?"

"I just wanted to know if there would be anything else?" the waitress asked.

"No, that will be all, thanks."

She handed him the check slip. Jim ended his reading, paid the bill, and left the coffee shop to return to the motel.

———⊰◈⊱———

Elaine walked into the outer office. "May I help you?" the secretary asked.

"Hi, I'm Elaine Robbins-Smith. I'm here to see General McFarland."

Peggy picked up the telephone receiver and buzzed the general's office. "Yes?"

"An Elaine Robbins-Smith here to see you, sir."

"Have her wait for just a moment."

"Yes, sir." She returned the phone receiver. She motioned with her hand. "Won't you have a seat? The general will be with you in a moment."

Elaine then sat down. "Is Debbie off today?"

Peggy hesitated. "Debbie, do you know her?"

"Yes, we have been friends for years."

"I guess you haven't heard."

"Heard what?"

"I'm sorry to be the one to tell you, but Debbie was killed in a car accident two days ago."

The news stunned Elaine.

"Now, Reed, are both jets ready to leave?"

"Yes, General."

"Like always, I want one jet for myself and the other for the staff."

"Yes, sir."

"What time are we leaving?"

"At 1400 hours."

"Good, that will be all. I have a guest waiting."

"Yes, sir." Captain Reed saluted, turned, and left the office. As he was walking through the outer office, he saw her sitting there. "Elaine Robbins, is that you?"

Elaine hurried to regain her composure. "Lieutenant Reed," she answered. She noticed the captain bars on his uniform. "I'm sorry," Elaine corrected herself, "not Lieutenant, but rather Captain Reed. Very impressive, congratulations."

"Thanks."

McFarland came out of his inner office. "Captain Reed, don't you have some things to do?"

"Yes, sir. Elaine, will you excuse me?"

"Sure, Captain, it's good to see you again."

"And you too, ma'am." Captain Reed then turned and left immediately.

"Elaine, what a pleasant surprise. It's so good to see you." McFarland came forward and embraced her.

"Hello, Arthur, it's good to see you again, too."

Elaine broke the embrace. He put his arm around Elaine. "Please, come in." He led her into his inner office.

Captain Reed walked down the hall. "McFarland's a real jerk," he murmured aloud. "Wouldn't even let me talk with Elaine." He entered the men's room and turned on the faucet to wash his hands. Out of nowhere two hands grasped him and put him in a position where he could not move. He struggled but still could not break free. "There's only one person I know that could do this," Reed finally exclaimed. "Indian, is that you?" Indian chuckled and relaxed his hold and turned Reed toward him. "You old goat. You know how many years it's been?"

"Too many, my friend, but you look good." He touched the Captain bars. "And seem to be doing okay."

"Yes, I made Captain last year. Hey, you'll never guess who's in the general's office right now."

"Elaine Robbins?"

"How did you know—" Reed interrupted himself. "Oh, I get it— you two came here together, didn't you?" Indian nodded yes. "Well, where's Crockett?"

"Jim Crockett?"

"I know he's around here somewhere."

"Why do you say that?"

"I saw him and Elaine together a couple nights ago on one of the base monitors."

"Did McFarland see them too?"

"Yes, he did. He was standing right next to me. In fact I saw Elaine and Jim's files sitting on his desk."

"Was that today?"

"This morning. I also saw yours."

"Why would McFarland have my file pulled?"

"I think it's because your name came up with the Boise investigation of those girls."

"Oh, I see. Tell me, Fred, why did McFarland cremate those two girls' bodies?"

"How did you know that?"

"I have my sources."

"Well they're good sources, because that information is top secret."

"But why did he do that?"

"You know, he didn't even let our people do an autopsy. We brought them from Boise, and within a day he had their bodies destroyed, completely out of protocol. I suggested he shouldn't rush it, but he ignored me. Mark my words, we haven't seen the last of that local sheriff."

"You mean Sheriff Bates?"

"Yes, that's the one. You know him?"

"Yes, I do."

"The general has done some crazy things the last couple of years." Reed shook his head.

"What do you mean?"

He hesitated to answer but finally shrugged. "It's like he doesn't work for the army anymore, but for someone else."

"Maybe he does."

"I have thought about that. He never follows army protocol anymore."

"Has anyone reported him?"

Reed chuckled. "No, we are all too afraid."

"Listen, I need to ask you something else. Where's the boy and girl?"

He kept a straight face. "What boy and girl?"

"C'mon, you know." Indian leaned against the bathroom sink. "The boy and girl you brought from Boise."

"Indian, you are asking things that you shouldn't—"

"Why?" he asked sharply.

"I don't know why, but I know if I divulge certain information, it may not only end my career, but could end my life."

"The boy is my nephew. We fear he and the girl are in danger."

Reed absorbed this news, and his mouth thinned into a grim line. "Indian, the girl mentioned the Sprudiths. Are they back?"

"Yes, they are. I have already encountered them several times."

"But why?"

"I think it involves the children."

He came to a quick decision. Indian was a good man. And right now, he trusted his old friend more than he did the general. "Well McFarland flew the two kids out of the country yesterday. To Mexico."

"Why Mexico?"

"I don't know, except he has some powerful contacts in that country. In fact we are flying there later today for some secret conference. It's some annual conference he goes to every year. He takes the whole staff. One jet's for him, and another for the rest of the staff."

"Can you get Jim and me on one of those planes?"

"You got to be kidding. How could I do that?"

"Fred, if you don't, you know he may kill those kids."

Reed looked at Indian. He did not answer.

After sitting Elaine in front of his desk, McFarland passed to the other side to his private bar. "Elaine, can I fix you a drink?"

"Please, a bourbon." Her stomach was still churning from the news of Debbie's death. She knew she needed something quickly to settle her down.

McFarland could sense something. "Are you all right?"

"Just a little nervous."

"About what?"

"About seeing you." A smile came over Arthur's face. Elaine could not have said something more correct.

He handed her the prepared drink. "Here, this should help."

"Thanks."

Arthur sat down next to her in the other seat facing his desk. "I'm sorry about David. How are you holding up?"

"As well as can be expected."

"Yes, I remember when Jean died. Some days I didn't know if I could make it another day."

Yeah, right, Elaine thought sarcastically. She took another sip of her drink. Finally she was starting to feel its calming effect. "Arthur, I know it must have been hard on you too."

He nodded absently and then focused in on her face. "Listen, I'm going to Cancun later this afternoon for a week. Why don't you come with me? It'll be a good way to get your mind off of everything."

"Mexico? Oh, I don't know."

"I promise, I'll be on my best behavior."

Sure, she thought to herself, *I've heard that before.*

"No worries, you can just relax. I think it would be good for you."

"I really need to get back to LA to tie up some loose ends with my attorney."

"Why don't you give him a call and put it off for a week."

What are you doing Arthur, she thought. *Is it only sex that you want, or do you have some other motive in mind?* She did not know. "Whew, that alcohol is running right through me." She stood. "May I?"

Arthur smiled and pointed to the side door. "It's right through that door and across the hall."

"I'll be right back." She left the inner office side door to the hall. She looked both ways and then entered the bathroom. "Now what do I do," she murmured. "It's been an hour, maybe I should leave."

"I found them," a voice said from behind.

Elaine turned. "Indian, it's you. Where are they?"

"Reed told me that McFarland flew the children to Mexico yesterday."

"But why?"

"He didn't know, but the general is flying to Cancun this afternoon. Maybe that is where the children are. Listen, I already talked with Jim and he agrees. Reed is going to sneak us on that second plane with him."

"You're both are going?"

"Yes. I'll call Edith and you can stay at the ranch until we get back. You'll be safe there."

"Forget it. I'm not going to the ranch."

"Well then how about to Phoenix with the Arturo and Nancy?"

"You don't understand. I'm going to Mexico too."

"I don't know if you can. It was hard enough just to get Jim and me on the staff plane."

"No need to worry about that. I'll be riding on the first plane."

"First plane, how can you?"

"Arthur already invited me." Elaine smiled at Indian, opened the bathroom door, and left. She crossed the hall and back into McFarland's office. "Arthur, if that offer to Cancun is still open, I think I would like to go. I could use the rest."

He put her hands on her shoulders. "Great, I'm glad you changed your mind. It will be like old times."

"I'll need to call my attorney and make some other arrangements."

"Why don't you use my phone, and I'll make your travel arrangements with the secretary's phone." He showed Elaine the phone line and offered her his seat. "Just ask for a secure line, and then dial the call."

Arthur then left the room and closed the door. "Peggy, have them trace this call."

"Yes, sir."

Elaine picked up the receiver and called the operator. "I need a secure line."

"Thank you," the operator answered.

Soon a line was available. Elaine then placed her call. "Room 244."

"Hello."

"Jim?"

"Elaine, where are you, are you okay?"

Elaine paused trying to hold back the tears. "Jim, they killed Debbie."

"Oh no, what happened?"

"They say it was a car accident the same night we talked with her.

"The same night?"

"First the Sorenson family, and now Debbie. You know they all died because of us."

"Oh, Elaine, I'm so sorry."

Elaine's voice cracked as she spoke. "Jim, what do we do now?"

"McFarland has to be behind this. He probably knows everything and is just playing games with us. But one good thing is we know where the kids are."

"Yes, Indian told me. They're in Mexico."

"Reed was able to get Indian and me on the plane, so we will be going with them. We have too, you understand. We have to get Jason and the girl.

Elaine's composure returned. "I understand. That's why I'm going to Mexico with McFarland. He invited me."

"No, it's too dangerous."

"Listen, if I am with him, maybe I can help find those children."

"McFarland already knows too much about us. I will fear for your life."

"As long as McFarland can use my body, he won't hurt me."

Jim was stunned by her words. "Use your body—you mean you would sleep with him?"

"For the sake of the children, you know I would." Jim was silent. "Jim, what's wrong?" He remained quiet. "Why are you so worried? You know I have done this many times before, so what's the big deal?"

Jim finally spoke. "I don't know, I was kind of hoping that part of our lives was over. You know, maybe a fresh start for the both of us."

Elaine's heart was touched. She realized he still loved her.

"Sir, the call is not to LA, but rather to downtown Salt Lake."

"I thought so," McFarland answered. He then entered his inner office once again.

"Yes, that's correct. Tell him I'll be back in town in about seven to ten days." She then hung up the phone on Jim.

"Everything set?"

Elaine forced a smile. "Yes, I'm ready to go."

"Good, come with me, and I'll show you where to go."

Elaine followed Arthur out of his office.

Jim knew that the phone call had been interrupted. He replaced the phone receiver. He sat down, waiting for Indian's arrival.

CHAPTER FORTY-FIVE

TESS'S DECEIT

Doug could smell the barbecue pig and knew the meat would be ready shortly. He walked behind the crowd of people who sat in the arena center watching the actors. The children's laughter brought a smile to his face as they watched Pepe play the part of the wolf.

"Little pig, little pig, come on in," Pepe would say.

"It's not The Three Little Pigs," one of the children yelled. "It's Little Red Riding Hood." Then the audience would laugh.

Doug chuckled too at Pepe's mistakes. For the most part, however, his mind wandered. He remembered what Disciple had said earlier that day. "Listen, there has been a change of plans. We are leaving tonight."

"But I thought you said two more weeks."

"Susan said you two were in danger," Disciple explained.

"You're not believing those things she told Pepe, are you? This lady is mentally ill."

"Listen, I feel very uncomfortable about what she said. By us being here, maybe we are bringing danger to the others."

Doug could see truth to his reasoning. "Okay, what do you want us to do?"

"Can you and Pepe be ready tonight?"

"What time?"

"Well I need to make some arrangements above ground. Let's plan on midnight."

By now Doug, in deep thought, had strolled to the back of the arena. "Hello," a voice said, disrupting his thoughts.

Doug turned. The woman smiled at him. "It's you."

She smiled that he recognized her. "How is the gunshot wound? Any more bleeding?"

"No, none, thanks to you."

The woman again smiled. "Well for a while there, I didn't think it was going to stop. May I look at it?"

"Sure." Doug lay down on the nearby bench. The woman lifted up his shirt and gently removed his dressing.

"Ah, that's looking good." Being a doctor, he could have saved her the time and told her, but the touch of her hands was nice.

"You left before I could thank you."

"Well after reading about you in the paper this morning, it sure looks like you and your friend are in a lot of trouble."

"Yes, we know. I'm not sure what we are going to do about that, either." Doug paused for a moment.

Well I know what you're going to do, she thought. *You just don't know yet.*

"What is your name?"

"Tess, my name is Tess."

"Tess, I thank you. You saved mine and Pepe's lives."

"Pepe?"

"Yes, that's my friend. He's the one up there playing the wolf in the play."

"And your name?" Tess deceitfully asked.

"I'm Doug, Doug Hunter."

"Nice to meet you, Doug."

"Tess, it's nice to meet you too." Doug stared at Tess's face. Now he understood why he remembered calling her Nicole previously. Except for her dark hair, Tess looked just like Nicole.

"Well, the wound looks like it's going to heal fine." She finished readjusting his bandages. "May I?" she asked, motioning to a portion of the empty bench next to him.

"Please do." She sat down next to Doug and began watching the play. "We looked for you yesterday to thank you, but you were gone."

"I had to do some things up on top."

"Tess, is that short for something?"

"Actually it is. Short for Egyptess."

"Egyptess, that's a beautiful name."

"Thank you."

"Egyptess, isn't that a bible name?"

"Almost," she answered, "her name is spelled with a *u* while mine is with an *e*."

"As I remember, Egyptuss was the granddaughter of Noah, and the mother of Egypt's first pharaoh."

Tess looked Doug. "Very impressive. You know you Biblical and Egyptian history."

"No, not really. My friend Pepe used to be a priest. I guess some of his knowledge may have rubbed off."

"Can I ask you something personal?"

"Sure."

"Who is Nicole?"

Doug was surprised by her question. "Why do you ask?"

"When I was taking care of you the other night, you kept calling me Nicole."

"That's kind of odd."

"Why is that?"

"Because I was just sitting here thinking how much you look like her. Nicole is my wife."

"Your wife?"

"Actually, was my wife. She died about five years ago."

"I'm sorry to hear that."

"That's okay. How about you, Egyptess, are you married?"

"Egyptess," she spoke softly. "I haven't heard someone call me that in a long time."

"I'm sorry, I hope I didn't offend you."

"No, I'm not offended. It just caught me off guard. My husband use to call me Egyptess."

"Then you are married?"

"No, my husband and I separated a long time ago."

Now the crowd was clapping at the end of the play. "The food is ready," Maggie announced. "So everyone line up."

"Tess, are you hungry?"

"Starved."

Doug stood up and took Tess by the hand. "It would be a real honor for me if you would consent to have dinner with me."

Tess smiled. "I would love to." Hand and hand they lined up with the rest.

Being first in line, Pepe filled his plate to the brim and sat down at a table by himself. He had no sooner commenced than a woman's voice asked, "Pepe, is this seat taken?"

Pepe looked up into Susan's face. "No, would you like to join me?"

Susan sat down next to him. "Pepe, is this more comfortable than being naked together in the shower?" she teased.

Pepe looked up and smiled. "Well, it is for me."

"I'm sorry that we made you so uncomfortable. I guess we have all showered together for so long, we sometimes forget how strangers may feel."

"That's all right, you don't need to apologize." It was then that Pepe saw the woman who had led them to safety. "Susan, there's the woman that brought us here."

"Where?"

"The woman standing in line with Doc." He pointed. "Do you know her?"

Susan looked in the couple's direction. She studied the woman for a brief moment. "No, I don't."

Pepe watched the woman for a few moments. *Well I do*, he thought to himself, *but from where?*

Susan interrupted his thoughts. "The children really enjoyed you as the wolf in the play."

Pepe smiled. "If I could just remember the right fairy tale."

Susan laughed. "That's what made it so funny."

Tess and Doug sat down at a vacant table. "That's just it. We didn't do anything that was reported in the papers. Warden Parks and the two women were still alive when we left."

"Then, why do you think they are after you?"

"We don't know."

"The paper mentioned another woman, a Tina something—"

"Tina Michaels. She's the person I went to see in the first place."

"Maybe it has something to do with her?" Tess slyly suggested.

Doug looked at Tess. "What do you mean?"

"Well, maybe this Tina Michaels told you something?"

"Well if she did, I don't know what it was."

Good, Tess thought, *we're all worried for nothing. Matthias and Niac will be happy to know.*

"Except…" Doug paused.

Tess again looked at Doug. "Except what?"

"Well we found a message in the locket she gave me."

"You mean there was a message in her locket?"

"Well, yes and no. There was a message, but we can't read it."

"Why not?"

"The message is in Hebrew." Doug took the locket off his neck and handed it to her. She opened the locket and immediately recognized Gabriel's children. "Beautiful children." She handed the locket back to Doug.

"We found microfilm replacing one of her children's eyes in the picture."

"Did this Tina Michaels speak Hebrew?"

"I don't think so. We think it must have been written by her husband, Gabriel."

"Well, I studied some Hebrew in college."

"Maybe you could translate it for us."

Tess wiped her mouth with a napkin. "I won't make any guarantees, but I can try."

Doug unfolded the sheet of paper from his pocket and handed it to Tess. "My friend Disciple says the words come from an ancient form of Hebrew which makes it hard to translate."

Tess studied the document. She read it easily, for it was her own native dialect. "Your friend is right. It's an ancient form of Hebrew."

"Then you can read it?"

"I believe so." Tess took out a pen from her purse and began writing down the translation. "Doug you are right. This memo note is from a man named Gabriel to another man named Matthias."

"What does it say?"

Tess looked up from the translation. "I'm not sure I should tell you what it says, because it talks about your wife and your baby."

"Then it isn't good news."

Tess shook her head no. "No, not for you."

Doug turned away from Tess. "Then what Tina told me about them is true."

"What did she tell you?"

"That Nicole and the baby were killed." Tess's silence told Doug that it was true. He looked back at Tess. "What do the words say exactly?"

"It says: 'Matthias. Happy to report that Nicole Crockett has been infected with the virus, and her newborn baby is dead. Sincerely, Gabriel.'"

"Then Nicole was given the AIDS virus on purpose." He looked at Tess. "But why?" Tess knew the answer but did not speak. "What kind of people could do such a thing?"

Tess touched his shoulder. "There's a second part to this message."

"Second part?"

Tess took a moment to translate the second part and folded the paper. She then looked up at him. "I don't want to tell you the second part."

"It is worse?" Tess nodded her head yes. "Please, I have to know."

Tess was pleased with herself. It was what she had desired. She had trapped Doug in the position she desired from the beginning. "Okay, if that's what you want. The second part of the message says that Nicole deceived you."

"Deceived me? What do you mean?"

"I hate to tell you this, but the message says here that Nicole never had any love or feelings for you. The message says she was ordered to marry you, have your child, and then leave you. She only wanted your seed." Tess smiled inside. She could tell that Doug was devastated by the news. *I have done it,* she thought. *I have planted a seed of doubt in his mind. All I need to do now is nurture it.*

That's exactly how it happened, Doug thought. *Once Nicole was pregnant, she left.*

"Hey, Pepe, look at the dog," Susan exclaimed. Pepe looked up to see the animal wander into the arena from the entrance. "It looks like a German Shepherd."

Pepe became alarmed. "That's no German Shepherd, that's a wolf." He looked over at Doug, still sitting with the familiar woman. "Now I remember her, she's the wolf woman."

"Wolf woman?" Susan thought. Immediately she saw the images of her dream about Pepe and Doug. She too was alarmed, for she knew exactly what was going to happen to all of them. "Come, Pepe," she yelled. "Soon there will be many more. You need to go now."

"Pepe tried to pull away. "No, I need to warn my boss."

Susan pushed him toward the back of arena. "No, there isn't time. They will kill you."

Suddenly, as if out of thin air, more wolves appeared, this time with men and women half-dressed in animal skins. Now they caught Doug's attention. He stood. "What is this?" he murmured.

Tess watched as Micah and the other Sprudiths appeared. Maggie went out alone to greet the strangers. Doug became alarmed when he saw the Sprudiths pull their knives. "What is going on?" he exclaimed. Suddenly a knife slashed forward, and all watched as Maggie fell to the ground. Doug started toward her, when there was a blow to the back of his head. Doug fell to the ground, unconscious. Micah searched the crowd until he found Tess. Tess nodded with approval. She then bent space. Doug and Tess disappeared. Then the panic and slaughter began. Blood-curdling screams were heard everywhere.

CHAPTER FORTY-SIX
THE SLAUGHTER

The three reappeared in the arena. Tess looked at the accompanying Sprudith. She nodded to the body he was carrying. "Dr. Hunter?"

"Still out, my lady."

She pointed to a nearby flat concrete slab. "Place him over there." The Sprudith obeyed. Tess searched among the carnage until she located Micah and motioned him to come. Shortly he was at Tess's side. He noticed the man lying on the slab.

"Do you want him terminated too?" Micah asked.

Tess turned to the unconscious man. "No, I have other plans for him." Tess motioned to the book in Micah's hand. "What do you have there?"

"I found it in one of the tents. It's Dr. Krugar's diary."

Surprised, she took the book from him. "Dr. Krugar's diary."

"I thought it was destroyed."

"I thought so too." She looked at the unconscious man lying on the flat slab. "This Dr. Hunter probably had it."

Micah put out his hand to take it back. "I'll destroy it."

Tess pulled her hands away. "No, I will take care of it." She placed it in the pocket of her jacket. "Micah, what's your report?"

"We've moved the captives to the towers, as you commanded, and killed all the rest. Do you want us to burn and dispose of the bodies now?"

Tess thought for a moment. "No, not just yet. I have something for you to do." Micah followed her to where Doug was laying. She pointed at Doug's healing bullet wound. "Open it."

Micah did not understand. "My lady?"

"The gunshot wound, open it up. I want him bleeding when he awakens." Micah didn't question her further. He bent down and unsheathed his knife. He drove the knife deep into the wound site. Blood spurted as he removed his knife. He took pleasure as the body winced with each knife movement. "Tess, he is awaking."

"Take the wolves and other Sprudiths and bend space. I want him alone when he awakens."

"And you."

Tess smiled. "I'll wait until the right time." Micah again nodded. Now he began to understand what she was trying to do. He signaled the other Sprudiths, bent space, and left Tess alone with Doug.

Doug began to moan. "I must hide." She hurried behind a nearby boulder.

Doug's hand reached down and felt the pain at the side of his abdomen. It was wet and warm. He opened his eyes and looked at his hand. *My wound is open. I must be bleeding again*, he thought. He rolled to his side and looked around. The arena was quiet, and the lights were dim. Slowly he pushed himself to his knees, and then to his feet. He steadied himself with the nearby wall. Doug gasped, for now his eyes adjusted to the arena dimness. The scene was a nightmare. "Oh no," Doug whispered. He slowly moved forward. Dead bodies were scattered everywhere. Dazed, he walked among them looking for any signs of life. None were found. *Who did this?* he wondered. The last thing he remembered were wolves and the half-naked people dressed in animal skins attacking the people of Hope.

Tess watched from behind the boulder. "No, not yet," she whispered.

Again he looked at the bleeding. *I've got to stop this bleeding*, he thought. Already he was feeling faint. He took off his shirt and belt. He made a bandage compress out of his shirt and held it in place with the belt. *The smell*, he thought. *The room is already starting to smell.* He staggered to the area where his tent had been. He again looked around. "Pepe, Disciple, anyone," he yelled. His voice echoed back off the walls. There was no answer. He again looked at his bleeding wound. Now his shirt was blood soaked. *I'm not stopping the bleeding.* He staggered to wall and slid down its side. He smiled and closed his eyes. *I guess this is it*, he thought, *I'm not going to make it.* Suddenly someone touched his leg.

Doug opened his eyes. "Nicole," he whispered, "Nicole, is that you?"

"No, it's Tess."

Doug studied her face and smiled, "Oh, Tess, it's you." She touched his blood-soaked shirt. His eyes again became heavy. "Tess, what happened here?"

"Sh, stop talking," she instructed. "You're bleeding again."

Doug closed his eyes. She reached up and forced his eyes open. "Good, he's out." She wrapped her arms around him, bent space, and the two disappeared.

———⊰•◈•⊱———

Julie and Mary stared out the window at the three other distant towers. Julie shook her head. "How could I have done such a thing?"

Mary turned to her. "What do you mean?"

"Being unfaithful to Harrison like that."

"You weren't unfaithful."

"I was naked with the man."

"Julie, this guy's not a man, he's a jerk. All the time he was just setting you up."

"Yes, I can see that now, but why wasn't I stronger?"

"What do you mean?"

"Well other men have come on to me, and I have always been able to resist. But with Matt, it was like he had complete control over me."

Mira had entered the room and heard part of the conversation coming from the balcony. "Well we'll be flying out of here soon, and you will never have to worry about this guy again."

"There is no plane."

Julie and Mary turned. "Mira, what did you say?"

"There are no airports or airplanes. You two have been deceived."

"Deceived, by who?"

"Who else but that turd-for-brains, Matthias," Mary exclaimed. Mira did not answer.

"But if there are no planes, then how did we get here?" Julie asked.

"They have a special way they travel."

"Special way, what do you mean?"

"There isn't time," Mira warned. "Matthias and Tess are on their way up here now."

"We're already here," a voice spoke from behind. All three turned to see Matthias and Tess standing in the doorway. Mira walked toward them and tried to dismiss herself from the room. Tess put her hand out and stopped her. "Matthias wants you to stay. He has something to say to all of you."

Matthias ignored Mira and Mary and walked forward toward Julie. *He is so handsome*, she thought to herself. No matter how hard she tried to stop it, her yearning for Matt returned. He reached up his hand and gently brushed her cheek. She turned her head to avoid his stare. Matthias turned to face the other two. "Unless I command it, you three will never be free."

"Then you better command it," Mary exclaimed, "for we aren't—"

Matthias's backhand smashed across Mary's face, sending flying to the floor. "Silence, woman," Matthias yelled. "I tire of your idle threats." Julie and Mira rushed to her side. Her lip gaped open and her nose was bleeding. Matthias looked at Tess. "Take her to the dungeons." Tess nodded to the accompanying Sprudiths.

Mary quickly arose to her feet. "Yeah, I would like to see you try." She picked up a nearby lamp and stood ready to strike the first one to approach. The Sprudiths maintained their distance. One of them waved their arm and said some unfamiliar words. To Julie's amazement, Mary and two of the Sprudiths disappeared.

Matthias turned to Mira. He smiled. "I will miss you. We were so good together." He motioned to two more Sprudiths who took Mira by the arms. Without another word, and in the same fashion, they too disappeared.

Matthias now turned to Julie. "Am I leaving too?"

"No, my love, you are staying here."

"Did you send Mira to the dungeons too?"

"No, Mira is going to the fields. A life of prostitution. Mira will be sold as a prostitute somewhere in the world."

"But why?" Julie inquired.

"Because that is what we do. We supply the women, men, girls, boys, babies, or whatever the client wants for their own pleasure and gratification."

Mira's being sold into slavery, Julie thought. "How long will Mary be in the dungeons?"

"Depends. Maybe a day, a week, a year, maybe for the rest of her life. Her length of stay depends on you, Julie Jordan."

"What do you mean?"

Matthias smiled. "The quicker I get what I want, the sooner Ms. Cratch will be released."

Julie understood exactly what Matthias wanted. Matthias wanted her. "It will never happen," Julie finally answered.

"Suit yourself." He and Tess turned and left the room.

Julie sat down on her bed and covered her eyes. "Harrison, where are you?" she whispered.

Joseph pulled the vehicle to a stop. "Cresta, are you sure?"

"Yes, I'm sure."

"But this is a dangerous part of the city."

"I know, but that is why we are here. As I remember, the Testantes will check out this area tonight."

"If we live that long," Harrison whispered to Joseph.

Cresta handed two bottles of whiskey to Harrison. "Okay, let's go."

"Wait a minute," Joseph interrupted, "I want to go with you."

"Look, we've already been through this. You have to stay here with Motumbo."

"But I can help."

Harrison placed his hand on Joseph's shoulder. "This is way too dangerous. If I didn't need your sister's help, I wouldn't even let her go."

They all climbed out of the car. Joseph looked at their old, tattered clothes. He then looked into their faces. He rushed forward, hugged Harrison, and then let him go. "Be careful," he whispered.

"I will," Harrison answered. "Continue to call my home just in case."

Joseph nodded yes. He looked at his sister. "I may never see you again."

"Sure you will." She hugged him. "We'll be back together before you know it."

Joseph broke their embrace. "You just got home, and now you are leaving again."

"I know, but we need to find Harrison's wife, and then Sondra." Joseph reluctantly nodded in agreement. "Now go back to the compound and find out all you can about our new brother."

Joseph smiled. "Okay, I will." He opened the door and entered the car. He then waved and drove off. Cresta and Harrison watched until he was out of sight.

Harrison looked at Cresta. "Now what?"

"There isn't much time. Pour most of the whiskey on your clothes. We want them to think we are completely dead drunk." Harrison followed Cresta's example, and poured most of the bottle on his tattered clothes. "Now take one swallow so they can smell the alcohol on your breath." Again Harrison followed Cresta's lead.

"There between the two buildings, under the railroad tracks," Cresta instructed. Harrison followed. "This is one of their favorite places to look. Come sit next to me."

They both settled down next to each other. "That's it?" Harrison asked.

"That's it. Now we wait."

Both were quiet for a brief moment. Harrison interrupted the silence. "Can I ask you something about Sondra?"

"What about her?"

"Well I don't know how to ask this but—" Harrison hesitated and then finally asked. "Is Sondra really my daughter?" Cresta looked at Harrison. He could see the shocked look on her face. "Well, we were only together that one time," he rationalized.

"Meaning what, that it takes more than one time to get pregnant?"

"No, I didn't mean it that way. I just wanted to be sure."

"Look, you may not like it, but Sondra is your daughter."

"It's not like that at all. I'm very happy about it."

"Well it doesn't sound like it to me."

Harrison took a deep breath and attempted to explain. "Look, I just said it wrong." Cresta remained quiet. "When I found out that Julie couldn't get pregnant, I just accepted the fact we would never have any children. But when you told me that there was a daughter, it kind of opened another world for me."

Cresta was surprised by his comment. "You really feel that way?"

"Yes, I do."

Cresta shook her head. "It may have opened another world to you, but maybe not for long."

"What do you mean?"

"We may never see our daughter again."

Harrison looked around at the surrounding buildings. He did not see anyone. "Well we won't if something doesn't happen soon. By the way, how are they going to get us out of this city—by plane, boat, or what?

"Or what," Cresta answered. "The Testantes have a special way they travel."

"Special way?"

"Yes, in fact it is the only way we will be able to get to your wife."

"You mean there isn't any other way to get there?"

"Not that I know of. That's why we are here to deceive Testantes into taking us to the Four Towers of Eden."

"Four Towers of Eden?"

"That's where I think your wife is."

"But you also said she may be in the fields."

"That's true, but I hope not."

"Why?"

"The term 'fields' refers to human slavery."

"What do you mean?"

"The Testantes work for one of the largest and richest world organizations on earth. One of their duties is to find people for the fields. These people are then sold into slavery. Mostly prostitution involving women, men, and children."

"Are you saying Julie may have already been sold?"

Cresta shook her head. "I hope not. It depends on how long she can resist Matthias."

"Matthias, the same guy that took—"

"Hush, they're coming," Cresta interrupted. "Now act like you are dead drunk."

Harrison had his eyes slightly opened. Before his very eyes, six half-naked individuals seemed to appear out of thin air. One of them walked over to them. He touched their clothes and shook them to see if they would awaken. "Here are two," he yelled to the others. "I'll take them back."

Harrison watched what looked like a clear blanket cover and hid them from the outside world. He felt himself moving. Cresta's hand grasped and squeezed his, as if to say "here we go."

CHAPTER FORTY-SEVEN

THE AFTERMATH

Smoke filled Disciple's nostrils as he entered the surface entrance. He picked up his pace, running through the maze of walls and tunnels that led to Hope, the underground city. His fears heightened as the smoke thickened and now the heat of a fire warmed his skin. Susan's prophetic words filled his mind as he raced toward the arena opening where he abruptly stopped. "Oh no," he whispered. Disciple realized his worse fears. Initially he thought the burning piles were tents, but that familiar stench of burning bodies told him differently. Slowly he walked the periphery of the arena, looking for any sign of life. Although the makeshift ventilation system to the surface attempted to clear the smoke, the bodies continued to burn. He picked up a partially burnt severed hand. The end of the fourth finger was missing, the Sprudiths' famous calling card. He stood and stumbled his way to the arena center where he sat down. *I should have been here*, he thought. Soon a hand touched his shoulder. Startled, Disciple turned. Although black smoke and soot covered his face, he could see where tears had streamed down his cheeks. Disciple stood and put his arms around him and pulled him close. "Oh, Pepe, I thought you were dead."

Pepe broke the embrace and nodded to the burning bodies. "I'm so sorry, but there were too many. I couldn't stop them."

Disciple led him to a nearby bench. "Come and tell me what happened." They both sat down.

Pepe motioned toward the entrance. "We just started to eat when Susan noticed this dog come through that entrance. Well, at first she thought it was a dog. Then we realized it was a wolf."

"What happened next?"

"Susan was upset. She grabbed my arm and herded me to the back of the arena. She told me we had to hide. I asked her from what, but she just kept pushing me. She told me they were the ones from her dreams. Near the back of the arena I saw the Wolf Lady hit Doug on the back of the head, and he fell to the ground. I tried to pull away to help Doc, but I couldn't break Susan's strong grip. She said it was too late for him. As we ran, more wolves and Sprudiths appeared. Susan pushed on this one particular wall and the wall slowly moved until there was a small opening. She pushed me through the opening first. As soon as I passed through, I heard the screams. I turned and looked." Pepe bowed his head. His voice cracked. "I couldn't believe what I saw. The Sprudiths and their wolves slaughtered the people. I tried to get back out through the crack to help them, but Susan wouldn't let me. She pushed the wall closed until it sealed up tight. When I was able to get out it was too late." Both were quiet. Finally he looked at Disciple. "Susan saved my life."

"I know."

Pepe was confused. "But why didn't she save herself and come with me?"

"It was not her destiny, and she knew it."

"But if she had come, she would still be alive."

Both were quiet as they looked around the arena. Disciple finally spoke. "Pepe, many of our friends were murdered here tonight, but Susan and Dr. Hunter were not among them."

"But, I heard the screams, I saw the knives—they killed every-one."

"Not everyone. Only the very old and weak, the ones they con-sidered useless to them. Susan is young and beautiful. She is much too valuable to take her life. The Sprudiths will sell her and some of the others in the fields. Fields is a term for human slavery, such as prostitu-tion and sexual abuse."

Pepe thought for a moment. "So what you are saying is that Susan, the children of Hope, and others will be sold somewhere?"

Disciple nodded his head yes. "I'm afraid so. There are many mar-kets throughout the world."

Pepe was visibly disturbed. "But there must be something we can do."

Disciple thought for a brief moment. "Perhaps. What did you mean when you called someone the wolf lady?"

"You mean the one that hit Doug on the head?"

"Yes, that's the one."

"Well, she's the same person that brought Doc and I here to Hope in the first place."

"Are you sure she's the one?"

"Positive. After she hit Doc on the head, I turned away for just a split second. When I looked back, they were both gone like they vanished into thin air."

Disciple thought for a moment. "Why do you call her the wolf lady?"

"One night near our home in Idaho, I thought I saw this same woman with a pack of wolves. But you know this lady too."

"I do?"

"She's the same woman that kissed you at Whispering Pines Hospital."

"Egyptess, her name is Egyptess. Most people call her Tess for short. She is the caretaker of the wolves."

"Then you have known her a long time?"

Disciple nodded his head. "Yes, for a very long time. Disciple noticed a piece of paper in Pepe's hand. "What do you have there?"

Pepe looked at his hand. "Oh, I think it's the translation of the microfilm that boss had. I found it over there on the ground."

"You mean the microfilm that Doc wanted me to translate?"

"Yes, that's the one, but there's writing on it. I think someone else has already translated it."

Disciple reached out his hand. "Can I see it?"

"Sure." Pepe handed the paper to him.

Disciple looked at the copy of the microfilm and its translation. "I wonder who wrote this translation."

"I'm not for sure, but I think it was that Egyptess person. I saw her writing on something when her and boss were sitting together."

Well, Egyptess would know Hebrew, Disciple thought. "This memo was originally from a Gabriel to a man named Matthias," he said.

"I think Doug told me that Gabriel was name of Tina Michaels's husband."

"This Gabriel wrote this in an ancient form of Hebrew that very few people would be able to translate." Disciple looked at the copy of the microfilm, and then at the translation next to it. Disciple then read the first part of the message aloud:

"Matthias, happy to report that Nicole Crockett has been infected with the virus, and her newborn son is dead. Gabriel."

"I don't understand. Are they saying that Nicole was infected with AIDS on purpose?"

"I'm afraid so."

"But why would someone do that?" Disciple knew the reason why, but did not say. "And I can't believe they are saying that Jason is not their son."

Should I tell Pepe more? Disciple thought. *No, this is not the time.*

"Boss must have been devastated when she told him—" Pepe continued.

"Wait, the second part of the memo is translated all wrong."

"You mean Egyptess made a mistake?"

"No mistake, Egyptess knows the language too well. She lied to the Doc on purpose. I think Tess wants to deceive him. She wants Doc to think that Nicole didn't love or care for him, that she only married him to have his child."

"But that isn't true. I was there. I know that Nicole loved Doc."

"I know that too, but I think Tess wanted to plant a seed of doubt in his mind." Disciple thought for a minute. "Now I'm beginning to understand."

"Understand what?"

"Why she has taken Dr. Hunter with her."

"Why?"

"For revenge."

"But what has boss done to her?"

"It's not revenge against Hunter; it's revenge against Nicole."

"But that doesn't make sense. What do Tess and Nicole have in common?"

Disciple looked at him. "Pepe, Nicole and Tess are twin sisters."

Pepe was shocked by the news. "Sisters."

Disciple looked around the facility to see if there was anyone else present. "We need to leave this place."

"But shouldn't we take care of all the bodies?"

"There isn't time. The Sprudiths will be returning soon. They will clean up everything and not leave a trace."

"Then where should we go? What should we do?"

"Why don't you go back to your ranch. It will be safe there."

"But what about you? What are you going to do?"

"I'm going after the Doc and the others."

"Then I'm going with you."

Disciple looked into his friend's eyes. "Pepe, where I go will not be safe."

Pepe nodded his head in agreement. He remained silent in thought for a brief moment. Then he spoke. "Disciple, do you remember when I told you and Doug about Sister Margarita's death?"

"Yes, I remember."

"And you told me that God would forgive me?"

"Yes, I remember that too."

"I didn't tell you the complete truth."

"What do you mean?"

"You remember when I told you that Margarita told our superiors that we didn't have sexual relations? Well Margarita was right. We didn't have sexual relations."

"But, if you didn't have relations, why didn't her superiors believe her?"

Pepe was silent for a brief moment, and then he spoke. "Because they believed me."

"Believed you, but how could they believe you and not Margarita unless—" Disciple paused. Both he and Pepe remained silent. Disciple now could see tears forming in Pepe's eyes. "You lied to your superiors, didn't you?" He nodded his head yes. "You told your superiors that you two had sexual relations and you didn't?" Again he nodded his head. "But why?"

Pepe looked away as tears formed in his eyes. "She would have never left. She loved the church too much. Selfishly I wanted her for my own. I lied and deceived our superiors. I lost the one person I loved the most." Now he understood Pepe's guilt. Disciple was quiet. He contemplated what Pepe just told them. Pepe looked up at Disciple. "How can God forgive that?"

Disciple placed his arm over his shoulder. He remained quiet for a brief period longer, and then he spoke. "Pepe, I don't know if you can be forgiven, but I promise that no matter what happens, I will always be your friend."

Pepe smiled. "That's why I want to go with you."

"It will be dangerous, and you could be killed."

"Those people they took are my friends. If I die helping them, then I die. You just tell me what you want me to do."

Disciple smiled at Pepe. *What great courage he has. Now I understand why God chose him too.* He helped Pepe to his feet and placed his hand on his shoulder. "Come," he chuckled, "you're going to like the way we travel." Disciple waved his hand over the both of them, bent space, and they were gone.

CHAPTER FORTY-EIGHT

THE APOCALYPSE FILE

Reed handed Jim and Indian the white clothing. Jim held the suit up. "What's this?"

"Your uniforms."

"You mean we have to work?"

"Look, how else can I get you two on the plane?"

Indian unfolded his. "Fred, what are we anyway?"

"You're the cooks."

"Cooks?" Jim complained. "But we don't know how to cook."

Reed nodded his head. "I know that, so don't attempt to cook anything or you'll give yourselves away."

Indian chuckled. "You don't need to worry about that."

Reed pointed toward the kitchen area. "Keep yourself hidden. Even though McFarland is on the other plane, we can't take any chances of him seeing you."

Indian nodded his head. "We'll keep out of sight."

Reed turned to leave. "Fred, how long before takeoff?" Jim asked.

"About an hour. I'll be back later." He left and closed the door.

Indian tossed the uniform off to the side and sat down on the nearby bunk. "I think I'll try to get some sleep. It's going to be a long trip to Cancun. How about you?"

Jim picked up Ed Sorenson's diary. "You go ahead. I want to read some more." Indian settled down in one of the bunks while Jim made himself comfy in the other. He opened the diary and began to read.

Ed couldn't keep his eyes off of her. *She is so pretty*, he thought as they walked down the hotel hall toward her room. *Not only is she beau-*

tiful, but she is intelligent, sexy, and has such a keen sense of humor. I can't remember when I have had such a good time.

Tess interrupted his thoughts. She clasped both of his hands. "The dinner was excellent. In fact the whole evening marvelous."

"I'm glad you enjoyed it. I did too."

"Then why end it so soon? Why don't you come in for a night-cap?"

Ed was hesitant. "I don't know. Maybe I shouldn't."

"Oh, please. I have to show you this fabulous view from the balcony."

Ed smiled. "Okay, maybe for a few minutes."

"Good." Tess took Ed by the hand and led him into her room. Her suite was stunning. "Wow, look at this place."

Tess closed the door behind them. "You like it?"

Ed wandered about the room. "Do I? It is so elegant."

Tess tossed the room key on the nearby counter. "This is the penthouse suite. Why not go first class if the university is paying for it." She removed her earrings and placed them on the coffee table. "Make yourself at home while I change into something more comfortable."

Ed watched as Tess left and entered the bedroom. He removed his coat and tie and placed them on the back of a chair. He noticed the bar in the corner. "Tess, would you like me to fix you a drink?"

"Please, a scotch on the rocks."

Ed made two drinks and carried them toward the patio door. "Wonder what it is she wants me to see from the balcony?" He pushed open the sliding glass door and walked out onto the balcony. The full moon was just starting to crest the eastern ocean skyline. The view was breathtaking.

"This is what I wanted you to see." Ed turned to see Tess exiting from the other sliding door leading from the bedroom. She was still fastening her gown buttons. Ed did not reply. Tess caught him gazing at her revealing silk leisure gown. *It is working,* she thought. She took the drink from his hand and encircled her free arm with his. She led him to the balcony railing. He could feel Tess rubbing her breast against his arm. For a brief moment he closed his eyes.

What am I doing here? he thought.

"You know I love to watch the rising moon reflect off the ocean. It is so beautiful."

Ed's mind was preoccupied with other things. *Will I cheat on my wife?* Ed thought. He took another sip of his drink to try and calm his nerves.

Tess turned toward him. "The view is so romantic, don't you think?" Ed did not answer but continued to look straight ahead.

Tess turned Ed toward her. She took his drink and placed both drinks on the nearby patio table. Gently she encircled her arms around his neck. He did not respond. "Ed," she murmured softly, "don't you find me attractive?"

It was then that Ed looked down into her eyes. "Very much so."

"Then why don't you hold me?" He did not answer. She then took both of his arms and placed them around her waist. She moved the full length of her body next to his. Even though she knew that Ed's passions were starting to stir, he was still reluctant. She again looked into his eyes. "What's wrong?"

"You know I can't do this."

"Why not?"

"Because I'm married."

Tess smiled. "So am I." She reached up and gently kissed his lips. "Just stay with me tonight. No one will ever know." She reached up and kissed him again. This time she felt him kiss back. "Tomorrow, you will go back to Salt Lake," she continued between kisses, "and I will go back Dallas." She pulled back and looked into his eyes. "It will be our little secret." He smiled and nodded his head yes. She took his hand and led him through the sliding patio door into the bedroom.

Our meetings did not stop with that one night. We kept seeing each other off and on for the next year. We discussed my work quite often. It was nice to talk with someone who had the same interests. She asked many questions about the Apocalypse File, and I love to discuss it with her. It wasn't until our last meeting that I realized what I had done, and the fool I had been. We were again in Miami for another conference.

Ed opened the door. "Tess," he exclaimed. He reached out to embrace her, but she back away. "What's wrong?"

"Dr. Sorenson, I have someone with me."

Dr. Sorenson? Ed thought. *Why the formality?* Without further invitation a gentleman abruptly entered Ed's hotel room. Ed looked at her. "Who's this person?"

Tess followed the man and also entered the hotel room. Ed closed the door. "Dr. Sorenson, I would like to introduce you to my husband, Matthias."

Ed was shocked. He quickly attempted to regain his composure. Ed extended him his hand. "Sir, it is nice to meet—"

"Stop the charade," Matthias interrupted, "I know what's been going on between you and my wife."

Ed tried to remain calm. "Sir, I don't know what you—"

"Stop," Tess interrupted, "he knows."

Ed slowly turned from them. He did not know what to say. After a brief moment he turned back to Matthias. "Sir, I don't know what to say. I want you to know how sorry—"

"Cut the crap," Matthias again interrupted. "My wife has had many affairs. Do you really think I care about yours?"

Shocked by his answer, he looked at Tess. Tess glanced at Ed but then again looked away. He looked back at Matthias. "Then, sir, why are you here?"

"I'm here only because you have something I want."

Now Ed was confused. "Something you want?"

Matthias looked at Tess. She knew she was to continue. "My husband wants the Apocalypse File samples."

Ed was shocked, and he glared at Tess. "You told him? That information is top secret."

"Look, she didn't tell me anything. We've known all along about the samples."

"What do you mean you've known all along?" Again Ed looked at Tess. "Did you set me up?"

Matthias shook his head in amazement. "You poor boy. Do you really think that she has any feelings for you?" Matthias laughed out loud. "Don't you know that you are one of many?"

"Matthias, that's enough," Tess interrupted. Ed looked into Tess's eyes and immediately knew that Matthias spoke the truth. He tried to hide his hurt, but Tess saw and knew. "Ed, just give him the virus, and we'll be gone and out of your life."

Ed looked at Matthias. "Why do you want the virus?"

"That's none of your business."

"Then go to hell. I'll never give you the virus."

Matthias smiled. "Dr. Sorenson, do you value life?"

"What's that suppose to mean, is it a threat?"

"You bet it's a threat," Matthias answered. Ed chuckled and sat down on the sofa. Matthias was confused by Ed's actions. "What are laughing about?"

"Your threat. Threatening a man who in his heart betrayed his wife does not frighten me." He then looked at Tess. "You have taken all that I hold dear and true from me."

Again Tess looked away. *Why do I do this?* she asked herself.

Matthias chuckled. "You waste your sentiment, Dr. Sorenson. Tess's heart is pure black with no feelings. Your words have absolutely no effect on her."

"Then go ahead," Ed taunted. "Kill me. I do not fear death. I would even welcome it."

"You don't understand. Matthias cares nothing of your death. It's your wife."

"You mean to tell her of our affair?" Ed asked.

"Oh no, Dr. Sorenson," Matthias corrected. "We mean that if you do not give us the virus, we will kill your wife. Now do you understand?"

Ed turned and peered out the window at the waves below. *What do I do now?* he thought.

Within the week Ed had taken the virus sample from the lab and given it to Matthias and Tess. Little did they know, however, that it was the mutated virus and not the pure form.

Several months later David and Ed were discussing the virus as they were having coffee. Ed poured two cups and gave one to David. Both were quiet for a brief moment.

"David, I need to tell you something."

"What's that?"

"I think we may be in danger."

David was surprised by his comment. "What do you mean?"

"Danger from the Apocalypse File."

"But we haven't worked on that for several months."

"Yes, I know."

"Then what is it?"

Ed was quiet for a moment and then began. "A while back I became involved with another woman."

David closed his eyes and shook his head. "Oh…does Megan know?"

Ed shook his head. "No, I haven't told her."

"Is it someone here at the base?"

"No, I met her at a conference in Miami about a year ago."

"Are you still seeing her?"

"No, it ended a while back."

David thought for a moment. "You know, I don't believe in keeping secrets from wives, but would it do any good to tell Megan now?" Ed did not answer. "Maybe you ought to consider letting the past stay in the past."

"If it was only that simple."

"What do you mean?"

Ed then explained the extent of the affair and ended with Tess and Matthias's visit. He then discussed their demands. Now David became alarmed. "You didn't give the virus to them, did you?" Ed's silence answered his question. "Oh no, how could you?"

"I didn't have a choice. They threatened to kill my wife. She doesn't deserve to be punished for my mistake."

David thought for a minute. "What's going to happen now?"

"I'm not sure."

"Do you know anything more about this Tess and Matthias?"

"I know that Tess said she worked in the Microbiology Department at Baylor University, but when I tried to find her there, they had never heard of her."

"What about her husband?"

"She once told me her husband worked for a pharmaceutical company."

"Did she tell you the name?"

"No, not that I can remember." Ed reflected for a moment. "Wait a moment, Tess once had this notebook with a logo."

"Do you remember the logo?" David asked.

"I remember the name was in Spanish." David walked over to a set of books on the nearby self. For the next hour they spent their time going over the names of numerous Spanish pharmaceutical companies.

"Tierra Madre," David named.

"That's it, Tierra Madre."

"It means Mother Earth. It's the Mother Earth Pharmaceutical Company."

"Does it say anything about them?" Ed asked.

"Only that the company is privately owned and located in Cancun, Mexico."

"Why would a company in Mexico be interested in this virus?"

"I don't know," David answered. "It does say here that they are one of the major suppliers of vaccines throughout the world. I'm going to do some checking and see what else I can find out about them."

"David, there's one other thing."

"What's that?"

"The virus, I didn't give them the pure form."

David was shocked. "You gave them the mutated form?"

"Yes. We still have the pure form here in the laboratory."

"How could you? We don't even know what the mutated form of the virus will do."

"I know. I guess I was just hoping the mutated form would be safer than the pure form."

David again shook his head. "You know we should have destroyed both of them while we had the chance."

Ed thought for a moment. "We still can destroy the pure form."

David looked at Ed. "Let's do it. It can't bring any good to this world."

They both agreed. "There may be repercussions from this."

"I know," Ed answered, "but there will be no regrets."

About a year later there was a knock at the laboratory door. Ed had a visitor. He opened the door. "Tess, what are you doing here?"

"Hello, Ed, it's been awhile." Ed invited her into the room.

David cleared his throat, getting Ed's attention. "Oh, excuse me, Tess, this is Dr. David Smith, my associate. David, this is Tess Thompson, an old acquaintance of mine."

"Tess...where have I heard that name before?"

"She's the one I told you about," Ed explained. "You know, the supposed virologist from Baylor University."

"Oh now I remember. You're the one that seduced my friend for the Apocalypse virus?"

Tess looked at Ed. "You told him?"

"Yes, he told me," David interrupted and then smiled. "How's that virus working out for you, anyway?"

"Well we've had some problems."

"Problems, oh that really breaks us up," David continued sarcastically.

Tess ignored David's comments. "Ed, that's why I'm here. Matthias sent me to talk with you."

"Well your problems are our problems," David snickered.

Tess turned to David. "Why don't you just shut up. I'm not talking to you anyway."

"Well I'm talking to you, lady," David exclaimed. "Why don't you get the hell out of our laboratory."

"I will, just as soon as you give me the virus."

"You got the virus," Ed said. "I gave it to you personally."

"You know you gave us the mutated and not the pure form."

"Yes, we know," David answered.

"What do you mean, you know?"

"Yes, we've known all along. Ed gave you the mutated virus on purpose."

Tess looked at Ed. "You did that?" He nodded his head yes. "Don't you know we reproduced that virus and have infected many people with it?"

"You did what?" Ed exclaimed. Tess did not answer. She now realized she had said too much.

David could not believe his ears either. "Infected many," he yelled, "how could you do that when we don't even know what the mutated virus does?"

"Because we thought it was the pure form," Tess answered. "If you had done what we asked in the first place, none of this would have happened."

"None of what would have happened?" Ed asked. She did not reply. "Tess, what did the mutated virus do?"

"Suffice it to say, it did not do what we wanted it to do."

"You mean destroy ovaries?" David asked. David and Ed recognized the shocked look on Tess's face. *She didn't know we knew*, David thought.

"We did some testing ourselves. We know the pure virus destroys ovaries and turns them black. What we don't know is what the mutated virus does."

Tess chuckled. "You think you're pretty clever. Who would have ever thought you would mutate the virus."

I'll bet they used vaccines to spread the virus, David thought. *They probably contaminated the vaccines with the virus.*

"You didn't answer our question," Ed said. "What does the mutated virus do?"

Tess smiled. "If you two are so smart, then you figure it out." Neither said a word. "I thought so. Now if you would just give me the pure form, I will leave you two alone and be on my way."

"Cold chance in hell for that," David advised.

Tess glared at David. "Look, you jackass, I'm tire of playing games. You have no idea who you are even dealing with."

"Lady, we have no idea who we are dealing with, and we don't even care."

Tess waved her hand, and out of thin air four half-dressed men in animal skins appeared in the laboratory. "Now, smart ass, maybe you will care."

"Who the hell are these guys?" Ed asked. Tess didn't answer. She nodded her head and the four pulled their knives. They began to circle them.

They are Sprudiths, David thought. *What are they doing here? I haven't seen them since the war.*

"Tess," Ed said, "there's no need for violence."

"I agree. Just give me the pure form, and we'll leave."

"Look, lady," David exclaimed, "we can't."

Tess instructed the Sprudiths to attack. "No, wait," Ed interrupted. "David speaks the truth."

Tess put up her hand to stop the attack. "What do you mean?"

"The pure form was destroyed. We do not have any samples of it."

"Destroyed, how?"

David smiled. "We destroyed it."

She looked at Ed. "Is this true?"

"You know me not to lie." Tess knew that Ed was one of the most honest men she had ever met. She knew he could not lie. "It is true. The pure form of the virus was destroyed."

Tess thought for a moment. She then looked at the Sprudiths. She waved her hand and the four disappeared. "You do not know what you two have done. By this action you have sealed your fates."

"We're just happy to say we destroyed the last source of that virus."

"Last source?" Tess chuckled. "I didn't say it was the last source."

Ed and David looked at her. "What do you mean?" Ed asked.

"Too bad the destruction was in vain. Just so you know, there's still another source of the virus."

"Where?" David asked.

"No need for you two to fret about that. Your days on this earth are limited anyway." She then walked up to Ed. She smiled. "I'm especially going to miss those good times with you." She kissed him on the cheek, waved her hand, and disappeared, leaving David and Ed staring at each other.

CHAPTER FORTY—NINE
THE EXPLOSION

Micah stared at them between the iron bars. Sondra immediately recognized him. She leaned back behind Jason to hide herself. He looked at the other Sprudith guarding the door. "Open the cell!"

"Michael ordered no one is to see the children until Niac arrives," he informed.

Without warning Micah pinned the Sprudith with his knife blade at his throat. "Who is you master?" he whispered.

"You are," he gasped.

He then released him from his grasp. "Then do what I command and open this door." The other Sprudith bowed and immediately opened the cell door. Micah entered and closed the door. He looked at the guard. "Leave us." The guard hurried up the dungeon steps, leaving the three alone. Micah turned to the children. "Sondra, come here."

By way of habit Sondra immediately stood to obey. Jason put forth his hand and stopped her. She looked at him. Jason shook his head no. "Sondra, did you not hear me? I said come here." Now Jason stood and placed himself between Sondra and Micah. "Where is your mother?" Sondra did not answer, but shrank back even farther behind Jason.

"Look, wolfman," Jason pleaded, "just leave her alone. She doesn't know where her mother is."

Micah smiled. He approached Jason. "I wasn't speaking to you." Without warning Micah's fist smashed Jason's face and sent him to the floor. Micah turned back to Sondra. With each step Micah took, Sondra backed farther into the corner. Micah smiled. "Now, again, where is your mother?"

"I don't know," she answered.

Micah backhanded her across the face and sent her crashing into the nearby wall. Jason wiped the blood from his nose with his hand. He attempted to stand, but Micah's blow had zapped his energy.

Micah turned toward Jason. He pulled his knife from its sheath. "You two should have died days ago." He grabbed Jason by the hair and placed the knife blade to his throat.

"Micah, what are you doing?"

Micah looked up and recognized the hooded figure. "Niac, your own plans call for their deaths."

Niac shook his head. "Our plans have changed. Lucifer wants them alive."

Micah did not understand. "But why the change of plans?"

"Soon it will be made known to us, so put the knife away."

Micah obeyed the command and sheathed his knife. He relaxed his grip on Jason's hair and looked at Niac for further instructions. Niac helped the children to their feet. Jason tried to see his face, but it was well hidden in his hood. "Transfer them to my tower," Niac commanded.

Micah nodded his head and bent space. He, Sondra, and Jason disappeared.

———⋙◆⋘———

McFarland bit his lip. "Scarface, are you sure?"

"Positive, I saw them get on the second plane."

"But how did they get past security?" Lenny questioned.

McFarland shook his head. "They must have had help."

Scarface looked at McFarland. "I bet it was Reed. I remember them being good friends."

McFarland looked at his watch. He picked up the nearby phone and buzzed the pilot. "Cockpit," a voice answered.

"Captain, this is General McFarland. How much time before we land? Uh huh, and how far behind is the second plane? Okay, Captain, thanks." He hung up the phone. "We have less than an hour before landing, and the second plane is about an hour behind." He reached up to the overhanging compartment and pulled out a carrying case. He handed it to Scarface. "Do you remember how to use this?"

Scarface took the case labeled stinger missile. He smiled. "Yes, I remember well."

"Good, now this is what I want you two to do."

The three did not notice the sleeping quarter's door behind them open slightly. Elaine listened as McFarland gave his instructions.

———⟫◦⟪———

Indian placed the hamburger back on the cook's shelf. Jim looked up. "Now what?"

"He says now it's cooked too much."

"Not enough and now too much," Jim started to untie his apron strings. "I'm going to kick Fred's butt."

Indian put up his hands to stop him. "Relax, we'll be landing in less than two hours. Just try it again."

Jim frowned. He threw another fresh beef patty on the grill. He looked up at Indian. "This time I'm going to spit on it." Indian chuckled. Jim returned the smile. "I wonder how Elaine's doing."

"Elaine will be all right. She's the best at what she does."

Jim nodded his head. "Yes, I know."

"Then why the concern?"

"It's just that McFarland is such a dangerous person."

Jim's answer still didn't make sense. "She's been around worse."

"Yeah, I guess your right." Jim took the spatula and turned the burger.

Indian could tell that something was wrong. "Okay, what is it?"

"What?"

"I know you. I know something is bothering you."

Jim looked at Indian. He was quiet for a brief moment. "Well…" Jim paused. "Ah, forget it."

"No, come on, what is it?"

Jim reached into the package to get a hamburger bun. He placed in on the grill. He again looked up at Indian, who was patiently waiting. Jim finally spoke. "It was the last thing Elaine said to me before she hung up. When I told her that I was concerned about her safety, she said 'Jim, as long as McFarland can use my body, he won't hurt me.'"

Indian had a puzzled look on his face. He looked at Jim and shrugged his shoulders. "That's it?"

"Yeah, that's it."

"Jim, that's what Elaine does."

"I know that. I know she's the best at what she does, but…"

It was then that Indian finally realized what was bothering Jim. "You don't want Elaine to do this anymore, do you?"

Jim looked away. "I was hoping that part of our lives was over."

He still loves her, Indian thought. "I sorry, I should have stopped her."

"You, stop Elaine?" Jim chuckled.

Indian smiled. "Well, there could always be a first time."

Jim shook his head. "To think of Elaine and McFarland together just churns my stomach."

Indian placed his hand on his friend's shoulder. "We all have changed. So don't sell Elaine short. Just believe in her. She would want that."

Jim smiled. "Yes, you're right."

Reed stuck his head through the galley door. "Hey, what's taking so long? Where's my burger?"

"Freddie, it's coming," Indian reassured.

"Well make it snappy. I'm hungry. By the way, Elaine just invited me to dinner."

"What?" Jim asked.

He demonstrated the message in his hand. "It's true. She just sent me this message from her pilot to ours."

Jim snapped the message from his hand. "Let me see that." He read the message, and then gave it to Indian.

"Didn't I tell you?"

Indian nodded his head and looked up at him. "Seems you are right."

Reed smiled. "You know, you guys, I didn't even know she was interested in me."

Now Jim was becoming agitated. "Freddie, just get back to your seat."

"But what about my burger?" Jim faked throwing the extra spatula at him.

"Just get out of here before I kick your butt."

Reed put up his hands. "Okay," he exclaimed and closed the door.

Jim placed the fresh-cooked meat in the bun. He noticed Indian still studying the message. "What is it?"

Indian looked up at Jim. "Why the message?"

"What do you mean?"

"Why didn't she wait until we landed? I mean why send this message from pilot to pilot?"

Jim thought for a moment. "You know, you're right. It's not like her to do that."

"Maybe she's trying to tell us something?"

Jim extended out his hand. "Let me see the message again." Indian handed him the note. He then read the message aloud. "Captain Reed, will you have dinner with me at Mili's Restaurant tonight at 8:00 p.m. Cordially, Elaine." Jim shook his head. "Why invite Freddie?"

"Jim, I don't think this message is for Reed, I think it is for us."

Jim closed his eyes trying to remember. "Mili's Restaurant, why does that name sound so familiar?"

Reed stuck his head through the door again. "Hey, is my burger ready yet?"

Jim placed the burger on a plate and handed it to him. "Okay, Fred, here's your burger."

Reed peeled back the bun and looked at the meat. He looked up at Jim. "You didn't spit on this, did you?"

"Believe me, I wanted to." Fred then turned to leave. "Wait," Indian called. Reed turned back. "Are you familiar with this Mili's Restaurant?"

"Why, sure, don't you remember? Vietnam? Saigon?" He saw the confused look on Indian's face. Reed then looked at Jim. "Surely you remember Mili's Restaurant in Saigon?"

"I think I remember something about that. Wasn't that the restaurant where a plane crashed into it?"

"Right, it was big news for a time. It killed Mili and several others."

Jim looked at Reed. "But, why would Elaine want to have dinner at a restaurant that no longer exists?"

"Well I thought about that. All I can figure is that there must be another Mili's restaurant in Cancun."

Indian shook his head. "I don't think so. Something here isn't right. Fred, tell us about this airplane crash at Mili's."

Reed sat down in the nearby chair. He began placing pickles and ketchup on the bun. "Well as I remember, the restaurant was not far from the Saigon base airport. One of our military planes was preparing to land when it crashed into the restaurant."

"Did they ever find out why it crashed?" Jim asked.

Reed took a bite of his hamburger and mumbled. "Someone on the ground shot it down with a shoulder missile set up."

"Someone on the ground shot down the plane?" Indian asked.

"Yes, why?"

Indian and Jim looked at each other. You could tell they were thinking the same thing.

—⟫◦◦⟪—

Together they stood looking off the balcony. "Jason, where are we?"

Jason took the ice pack away from his swollen eye. He looked at the immense green located below. "I don't know. It looks like some kind of jungle."

"If it hadn't been for that hooded guy, Micah would have killed us."

"Yes, I know."

Sondra pointed with her finger off in the distance. "What about those buildings over there?"

"Those are the towers," a voice spoke from behind. They both turned to see the hooded man standing before them. "This place is called the Four Towers of Eden, and you are in one of the towers—my tower."

Jason walked forward bravely. He tried to see the stranger's face, but it was well hidden. "Sir, can you help us? We are hungry, and we want to go home."

The hooded man motioned with his hand to his right. "There is food there on the table." The man now looked down at the two. "About your home…this place is now your home."

"But we don't want to stay here," Sondra explained.

The man folded his arms in front of him. "Little lady, you may as well get use to it. You will never leave this place." He then turned, left the room, and locked the door behind him.

Lenny took down the binoculars. "There it is."

"Where?"

Lenny handed the binoculars to Scarface and pointed with his finger. "It's right there."

Scarface took the binoculars and watched the second plane's landing approach. "Good, they're right on time." He picked the hand-held radio. "General."

"Yes," the voice responded.

"We are in place and positioned perfectly."

"Good. No screw ups. It needs to look like an accident."

"Don't worry, General, it will."

Just then McFarland noticed Elaine returning from the airport restroom. "Scarface, radio silence, understand?"

"Understood." They both turned off their radios.

McFarland smiled at Elaine. "Only a few minutes more and the second plane will be here."

"Good."

"It's on its final approach. Once they land we'll be off to the hotel for rest and relaxation."

Elaine forced a smile. "And a hot bath. That's sounds good."

McFarland smiled. "Wait right here while I make sure the ground transportation is arranged."

Elaine sat down. She watched McFarland leave to talk with the airport personnel. She could see the second plane approaching the runway. "Why didn't Jim and Indian divert the plane?" she murmured. "Maybe they didn't get my message."

McFarland now returned to where Elaine was sitting. "Well we're all set. The ground transportation team is on its way."

"Good." She again turned her attention to the approaching airplane. McFarland could see concern on her face.

"Are you all right?"

"Sure, just tired."

Arthur nodded his head toward the end of the runway. "It won't be long now. The plane is touching down." Without any warning, there was a loud explosion that rocked the walls of the airport. Elaine closed her eyes and turned her head down. "Oh no," McFarland screamed, "what the hell happened?" He raced to the spectator windows and watched as the ball of fire ballooned high into the sky.

Elaine could not look. Airport personnel were racing everywhere. Sirens were now sounding from the airport vehicles. She closed her eyes tight, but could not stop the flow of tears down her cheeks. "They are dead," she whispered. "My two best friends are dead."

CHAPTER FIFTY
NIAC AND THE COUNCIL

The lights of the city shone through the spacious windows reflecting off the long glass conference table. Tess subtly attempted to visualize his bodily curse, but quickly looked away when he began to speak.

"Council of twelve, I welcome you here once again." He slowly slid his chair back from the table and stood. "As you are aware, the seventh seal will soon be opened, which makes our time very short. Our master will not permit failure." Niac's blighted facial mark remained hidden in the darkened shadows of his head cloak. He slowly walked the circumference of the conference room, detailing their master's grand plan. As he spoke, he purposefully stopped behind the chairs of the other eleven disciples. His deep voice pierced their hearts with words of fear. All attendees' cloaked heads remained bowed with eyes focused down. None dared to look directly at him.

He finished as he once again arrived at the head of the table and sat down. "Now, I want to hear each of your reports." One by one the members of the council spoke of their regional stewardships and activities. They discussed their ongoing influence in various world governments, financial markets, sports, and entertainment industries. When the last disciple finished, Niac leaned back in his chair. A faint smile parted his lips. "Lucifer will be pleased with your reports." The ease the disciples felt was short-lived. "Now before we conclude this meeting, there is one other item to discuss."

He leaned forward in his chair and placed his clasped hands on the table. Slowly he purposely looked at each of the disciples surrounding the table. Then he spoke. "Tell me about the heir." The room was quiet.

All were shocked by the question. Uneasiness filled the air. Niac pushed his chair back and again stood. He walked over to the spacious window overlooking the city. The background of the bright Cancun lights demonstrated his majestic figure. Not a word was said for at least one minute. The uneasiness continued to grow.

We haven't discussed this topic for years, Tess thought. *Why does Niac bring it up now?*

Niac slowly turned to face them. His deep bass voice thundered throughout the room. "I will ask you again—tell me about the heir."

Michael finally broke the silence. "Forgive me for my boldness, but why do you refer to the chosen one after so many years?"

"Because, I want to know of his status."

"But you know his status," Matthias added. "The heir is dead."

Niac glared at Matthias. "How do you know this?"

Matthias nodded across the table. "Years ago Gabriel reported his death to me, and I reported it to you."

Niac nodded his head. "Yes, I remember that report." Once again he circled the table and stopped behind Gabriel's chair. Everyone cringed when Niac placed his hands on his shoulders. "Gabriel, are you sure the heir is dead?"

Sweat beads appeared on Gabriel's forehead. "Yes, Niac, I personally killed the child at birth."

Without warning Niac pulled a knife from under his cloak and put it to Gabriel's neck. He lowered his cloaked head next Gabriel's. Everyone else was taken back. "Gabriel, you lie. Did you think you could fool Lucifer, the master of all lies?"

All in the room held their breath, knowing that Niac could cut Gabriel's neck in an instant, like he had done with others in the past. "Wait, Niac," a voice spoke softly. Niac turned to Tess. "May I speak?"

Niac did not lower the knife. "You may speak."

"None of us doubt our master's words, but we do not understand. I was there with Gabriel. I saw the dead baby's body. How can the heir still be alive?"

"Well he is." Niac slowly lowered the knife from Gabriel's neck and straightened himself. "But it's not Gabriel's fault." He turned toward the head of the table. "You both were deceived. The Jews switched babies at birth."

Gabriel shook his head and rubbed his neck. "I watched the child from birth until its death. How could they have switched the babies?"

"Lucifer says the Jews had help."

"Help," Tess questioned, "from who?"

Niac caught Tess's eye and smiled. "Someone you know, Tess. Someone we all know. The Jews had help from the Loved One, Disciple."

Tess looked away from Niac's gaze. "Dammit," Matthias exclaimed, "then our work is in jeopardy."

"Yes, it is, but not because of the chosen one."

"Then who?" Matthias asked.

Now Niac stared at Matthias and spoke. "You, Matthias."

"Me? That's absurd. I haven't done anything to put Lucifer's plan in jeopardy."

Niac shook his head. "Matthias, you're such a fool. You distributed a contaminated virus to certain countries, instead of the pure one, and now hundreds of thousands of people are infected with the AIDS virus, bringing unwanted attention to our work."

Tess now spoke in Matthias's defense. "But, he didn't know they mutated the virus."

Niac turned his attention to Tess. "You want to explain that excuse to Lucifer? You know he has no tolerance for mistakes."

Matthias was concerned. He knew there were times when Lucifer required people's lives for their mistakes. "Is my life required?"

"It was at first, but Lucifer changed his mind." Matthias took a deep breath and blew it out. Niac now chuckled. "Instead, he's taking back his gift from you."

"Taking the gift—but he can't do that." Both Michael and Gabriel looked at each other and smiled. There was no love loss between them and Matthias. "I betrayed and sacrificed my brother, James for that gift. I'll be damned if the master tries to take it back."

"Matthias, you abused the gift. Lucifer commanded you to send all women directly to the fields. Not only did you abuse your power over women, but you failed to keep Lucifer's command."

Matthias now stood. He was angry. "Lucifer has no right to do this. He has broken his covenant with me."

"Would you like to speak with him personally about the matter?" Matthias did not answer. "Then sit down, and the matter is settled."

Now Micah spoke. "Niac, just give me the command, and I will find and kill the chosen one."

"No, there has been a change of plans. The master no longer wants the heir killed."

"But what about the prophecies?" Michael reminded. "They foretell of our destruction by him. I say we find and kill him."

"And we will, Michael, but not just yet." Once again Niac arrived at the head of the table. "Remember, disciples, we no longer have the pure form of the virus. That means there is only one pure source of the virus left here in this world. We need a Levite to get the virus for us." Now all present understood why Lucifer wanted the heir alive. They needed the chosen one to open the Ark of the Covenant. They needed the eleventh vial.

"Can you tell us where to look for the heir?" Micah asked.

"No need to search. Thanks to McFarland, we already have the heir." Niac's comment startled McFarland. "Me?"

"The boy," Niac explained.

Then I was right, McFarland thought. *This Jason is the chosen one.*

Michael looked at Niac. "You mean the boy is the heir?"

Niac smiled. "Yes, Michael, the boy is the heir." All the disciples murmured with pleasure at his capture. "I see that all present are pleased with how well recent events evolved. Lucifer is too. But, before we close this meeting, there is one remaining question. Matthias, you are in charge of security, correct?"

"That's right."

"When we started our meeting earlier, there were twelve of us present. Maybe you can explain to us why there are now thirteen?"

Quickly Matthias scanned the room and counted the number of hooded people present. "Eleven, twelve, and thirteen, but how is that possible?"

Niac chuckled. "Only one person could have joined us without any of us noticing. Isn't that right, Disciple?"

Disciple, Tess thought, *could John be here?*

Eyes of the group moved up and down the table. Otherwise there wasn't any movement. Finally one individual at the end stood. He loosened his hood strings and let the hood fall from his head. "Very perceptive, Niac, or should I say Cain."

Niac again chuckled. "I should have sensed your presence. Tell us, what do you want?"

"Only a few minutes of your time. I have a message for you."

"Dammit," Matthias exclaimed, "our security has been breached. He has heard everything we said."

"It doesn't matter. We didn't say anything that he didn't already know." Niac sat down at the head of the table. "John, speak your piece, then be on your way."

Disciple turned to the council. "The message is not mine, but comes from the Heavens."

Micah stood and pulled his knife. "Niac, this is a waste. Give me the command, and I will kill this pig."

"Disciple is an apostle of Christ," Tess explained.

"Apostle or not, he still bleeds, doesn't he?" Without warning he drove the knife blade deep into Disciple's abdomen. A shock passed through Micah's body, sending him to the floor.

Disciple eased blade from his body. Micah stared at the bloodless blade. "No, Micah, I don't bleed."

"Micah, John cannot be killed," Tess explained. She reached down and grabbed one of Micah's arms. Another hand reached down to help Micah from the other side. She looked up. It was Disciple helping her. He smiled, but she looked away. Micah sat back down in his chair.

He extended his hand. "My knife, may I have my knife back?"

Disciple looked at the knife. "So this is one of the infamous Anasazi knives that are not of this world." He looked down at Micah. "How many lives has this knife blade taken?"

Micah smiled with pleasure. "Thousands, maybe even tens of thousands."

Disciple looked into Micah's eyes. "You speak as if you are proud."

"Proud that these deaths give honor to my master."

"What honor is there when you slaughter defenseless men, women, and children?"

"You should be the one that's honored," Niac reminded. "For if it wasn't for you falling asleep when Christ was in the Garden of Gethsemane, the Anasazi knives would have never entered this world."

"I guess we have Disciple to thank for this," Micah added.

Disciple ignored their remarks. "God wants you to stop the slaughter. This is the message."

Micah chuckled. "Well this is my answer. Tell your God to go to hell."

"Micah, if you don't stop the slaughter, then he who you fear will stop you."

"Who is that?" Matthias asked.

"Micah knows who."

"If you speak of Indian, he isn't a threat anymore," Tess said. "He and Crockett were killed."

Disciple then turned to Tess. "If they are dead, then why is there fear in his eyes?"

"This talk is senseless," Niac exclaimed. "McFarland, tell Disciple what happened to Indian."

McFarland looked at Disciple. "Indian and Crockett were killed in a plane explosion yesterday. I was there."

Disciple ignored McFarland's explanation. "Micah, you heard the warning."

"And what of the rest of us?" Matthias asked sarcastically. "Does your God have any warnings for the rest of us?"

Disciple turned to Matthias. "How many women's lives have you destroyed?"

Matthias nodded toward Tess. "Oh, like your wife, who has everything a woman could ever want. How does it feel to have your own brother steal your wife and children?"

"I feel sorry for you, Matthias. You have betrayed the Master, the life of our brother, James, and now you have to live with that guilt." All present knew what Disciple meant.

Matthias turned to Niac. "Cast him out of our midst, so we don't have to listen to this drivel."

Niac knew he didn't have the power to do that. He'd rather enjoyed the tongue lashing that Matthias received. Disciple again looked at the members of the twelve. "You have enslaved thousands of men, women, and children in the fields. Stop this slavery now or God's army will."

"Ah, husband, such the fool," Tess taunted. "Children, a Native American, a cowboy, and an ex-priest. You call that an army?"

Disciple looked at each one of them. "Your hearts betray your fear. True, there are few, but yet you all still fear them—why?"

"That's preposterous," Matthias scoffed. "We control the armies and governments of the world. We have billions of dollars at our disposal. Everything we command or desire is given to us. We have no fear whatsoever of your misfits."

"Michael, Gabriel," he asked, "is this your answer?" Their silence spoke to their father for them. "Egyptess," he spoke softly. She looked up into those searching eyes. She knew he looked for any glimmer of hope.

"Your family wants nothing to do with you, and you waste your time with the rest of us. We have chosen the master we will serve," Niac said.

Disciple shook his head. There was a solemn look on his face. "I am saddened for all of you," he finally said. He knew he had given the final warning. "Children of Lucifer, you desire a war, so a war you shall have—a war that has never been seen before. And when it is over, you will weep and regret the decision you have made this day." With his final pronouncement, Disciple raised his arms, bent space, and disappeared.

ABOUT THE AUTHOR

As a family practitioner, Dr. Glen Page encounters a variety of society's illnesses. The principal characters in *The Last Plague* face many of these same illnesses in body, mind, and soul. Although the book is set on a stage of biblical proportions, Dr. Page hopes readers will be able to identify with and learn from the struggles and triumphs of his characters.

He is currently working on the next book in the Apocalypse Series in southern Idaho, where he lives with his wife, Jane, and their nine children.